'The train ran on without a driver, on and on, like some mindless, unseeing beast . . .'

Emile Zola
The Beast Within

Translated by
Roger Whitehouse

PENGUIN BOOKS

PENGUIN BOOKS

UK | USA | Canada | Ireland | Australia
India | New Zealand | South Africa

Penguin Books is part of the Penguin Random House group of companies
whose addresses can be found at global.penguinrandomhouse.com.

First published in 1890
This translation first published in Penguin Classics 2007
Published as a Penguin Pocket Classic 2016
001

Translation and Notes copyright © Roger Whitehouse, 2007

Set in 10.36/12.8 pt Haarlemmer MT Pro
Typeset by Jouve (UK), Milton Keynes
Printed in Great Britain by Clays Ltd, St Ives plc

A CIP catalogue record for this book is available from the British Library

ISBN: 978-0-241-26173-6

www.greenpenguin.co.uk

Emile Zola

Born 1840, Paris, France
Died 1902, Paris, France

In 1868, Zola decided to embark on an ambitious series of books that would trace the effects of heredity and environment on a single family, the Rougon-Macquarts. *The Beast Within* (*La Bête humaine*), the seventeenth novel in the series, was first published in 1890.

Contents

Contents

1

Roubaud walked into the room and placed his one-pound loaf, his pâté and his bottle of white wine on the table. That morning, before going to work, Madame Victoire must have put an extra heap of slack on the fire in her stove; the place was like an oven! The assistant stationmaster pulled open a window and leaned out.

The room was in the Impasse d'Amsterdam, in the last house on the right, a tall building in which the Western Railway Company housed certain of its employees. The window was on the fifth floor near the end corner of the mansard roof and looked out over the railway station, a broad trough gouged out of the Quartier de l'Europe.[1] The horizon suddenly opened out in front of him. That afternoon, distances seemed even greater than usual, beneath a sweep of grey, mid-February sky, a tepid, misty grey, with the sun struggling to come through.

Directly opposite, the houses in the Rue de Rome appeared blurred and indistinct, almost insubstantial in the hazy sunlight. To the left stood the gaping entrances of the train sheds, their glass roofs grimy with smoke. The largest of them – the mainline station – an immense structure stretching back inside as far as the eye could see, was separated from the two smaller ones for the trains to Argenteuil, Versailles and the Paris circle line by the post-office buildings and the foot-warmer depot.[2] To the right, the massive star-shaped iron structure of the Pont de l'Europe[3] straddled the railway cutting, which then reappeared and continued for some distance further, towards the mouth of the Batignolles tunnel. Directly beneath the window at which he was standing, and filling the whole area in front of him, the three sets of double track that emerged from the bridge split up and fanned out in a seemingly infinite proliferation of railway lines, which eventually disappeared under the station roofs. The three pointsmen's cabins in front of the arches of the bridge each sported their own bare patch of garden. Amidst the profusion of carriages and locomotives that crowded the lines, a large red signal added a vivid splash of colour in the pale afternoon light.[4]

Roubaud remained standing at the window, absorbed in the scene below and comparing it to his own station back at Le Havre. Whenever he came to Paris and stopped at Madame Victoire's like this, it never failed to remind him of his job. A mainline train had just arrived from Mantes, and the platforms were a buzz of activity. He watched the comings and goings of the shunting locomo-
2 tive, a little six-coupled tank engine with diminutive wheels, as it began to disconnect the train. It went about its work with a will, detaching the carriages and reversing them into the adjacent sidings. Another locomotive, a powerful express engine with four large, voracious driving wheels, stood on a separate track, emitting a thick column of black smoke which rose slowly from its chimney into the still air. What most caught his attention, however, was the 3.25 train for Caen. It already had its full comple-ment of passengers but still awaited a locomotive. The engine stood on the other side of the Pont de l'Europe just out of sight; Roubaud could hear it asking for the road, with short, repeated blasts on its whistle, like some-one getting impatient. One of the linemen shouted the all-clear, and the driver responded with a further toot on the whistle in acknowledgement. There was a brief pause, the cylinder taps[5] were opened, a deafening gush of steam shot along the ground from underneath the locomotive, and it slowly began to back on to its train. A

huge white cloud came welling up from beneath the bridge, spreading outwards and swirling through the iron lattice-work like a flurry of snow. One part of the station disappeared behind a swathe of white, while the smoke from the express engine draped itself across the sky in a dense pall of black. From somewhere beyond the murk came the insistent calls of the shunters' horns, orders being shouted and the clatter of turntables.[6] Through a brief clearing in the smoke he caught a glimpse of a Versailles train and an Auteuil train passing each other in opposite directions on the far side of the station, one of them leaving and the other arriving.

Roubaud was about to walk away from the window when he heard someone calling his name. He leaned out to look. On the fourth-floor balcony below him stood a young man, some thirty years old, by the name of Henri Dauvergne. He worked for the railway company as a guard and lived there with his father, who was an assistant stationmaster at the mainline station, and his two sisters, Claire and Sophie, a pair of very attractive fair-haired girls aged eighteen and twenty. The two men brought in six thousand francs[7] between them, and with this the girls saw to the family's daily needs. It always seemed a wonderfully happy household; the elder sister was forever laughing and the younger one singing songs, accompanied by lively competition from a cage full of exotic birds.

'Monsieur Roubaud!' Henri called. 'What brings you to Paris? Oh, of course . . . I heard about your little brush with the Sub-Prefect!'[8]

Roubaud stood at the window and explained how he'd had to come down from Le Havre that morning by the 6.40 express. He'd been hauled over the coals by the senior traffic manager. He'd been told to come and see him in Paris immediately. He was lucky he hadn't been given the sack.

'Is Madame Roubaud with you?' Henri inquired.

Yes, she had wanted to come too in order to do some shopping. He was expecting her back at any minute. Madame Victoire always let them have the key to her room whenever they came to Paris. They liked to have a quiet meal there on their own, while she, bless her, went off to her job as a lavatory attendant. They'd had a quick sandwich at Mantes so that they could get everything done before they had lunch, but it was now gone three o'clock, and he was starving.

Henri was in a chatty mood and asked if they were staying overnight.

No, they weren't. They were returning to Le Havre that evening, on the 6.30 express. Some holiday! A lot of fuss and bother just to get a ticking off, and then it was back to the grind![9]

4   The two men exchanged knowing looks, but their voices were drowned by a loud burst of spirited piano playing. The sisters must have been at the piano together; their laughter could be heard above the sound of the music, and it had obviously excited the birds in their cage. Henri, not wanting to miss out on the fun, waved goodbye and went back into the room. Left alone, Roubaud stood for a minute or two looking down at the balcony, from which the sounds of youthful merriment continued to rise. When he looked up again, he saw that the locomotive had closed its cylinder taps and that the pointsman was sending it on to the Caen train. A few last wisps of steam evaporated into the great swirls of dark smoke that blackened the sky. Roubaud turned and walked back into the room.

The cuckoo clock now said twenty past three. Roubaud shook his hand at it in frustration. Where on earth had Séverine got to? She only had to walk into a shop and you couldn't get her out of it! In an effort to take his mind off the pangs of hunger that were churning away inside his stomach, he decided to lay the table. He knew the room well. It was a large room with two windows and it served as bedroom, dining room and kitchen all in one. All the furniture was in walnut – a bed with a red cotton quilt, a sideboard-cum-dresser, a round table and a Normandy wardrobe. He opened the sideboard and took out napkins, plates, knives and forks and two glasses. Everything was spotlessly clean. He enjoyed performing his little domestic chores, like a little girl laying the table for a dolls' tea-party, admiring the beautiful white tablecloth, thinking how very much in love with his wife he was and smiling to himself as he thought of her breezing into the room and laughing when she saw his handiwork. He placed the pâté on a plate and put the bottle of white wine beside it. Suddenly a puzzled expression came over his face; there was something missing. He thrust his hand into his pocket and pulled out two packages that he had forgotten – a small tin of sardines and a piece of Gruyère cheese. 5

A clock chimed half past three. Roubaud paced up and down the room, listening intently for the least sound on the staircase. There was nothing he could do but wait. As he passed in front of the mirror he stopped and looked at himself. He didn't look his age. He was approaching forty, but still had a good head of strikingly red, curly hair, with not a sign of grey. He sported a full, vigorous, shiny blond beard. He was of no more than average height but he looked very fit. He prided himself on his appearance – the shape of his head, his low forehead, his strong neck, his round face, his fresh colouring and the glint in his big, bright eyes. His eyebrows met in a bristly line across his forehead, lending his face a permanent frown, like a jealous lover. He had married a woman fifteen years younger than himself and he often looked in the mirror; he found it reassuring.

He heard footsteps on the stairs and ran to open the

door. But it was a woman who sold newspapers at the station, coming home next door. He walked back across the room. On the sideboard he noticed a box decorated with sea-shells. It was something he remembered, a present from Séverine to Madame Victoire, who had nursed her when she was a baby. It was a tiny little thing, but one glance had reminded him of how he came to marry her. It was now almost three years ago.

He had been born in Plassans,[10] in the south of France. His father was a carter. He had completed his military service and gained his sergeant's stripes and had then worked for several years as a porter at the station at Mantes. He had been promoted to head porter at Barentin, and it was there that he had made the acquaintance of the woman he fell in love with, when she came to catch the train on her way back from Doinville with Mademoiselle Berthe, the daughter of President Grandmorin.[11] Séverine Aubry came from a fairly humble background; she was the youngest daughter of a gardener on the Grandmorins' estate, who had died while in their employ. But the President, who was Séverine's godfather and guardian, simply doted on her. He arranged to have her looked after at the château, and she and his daughter became the closest of friends. He sent them both to the same boarding school in Rouen. Séverine had such a naturally genteel manner that for some time Roubaud resigned himself to worshipping her from afar, with the same sort of passion as a working-class person who has risen in the world might covet a fine piece of jewellery that he thought was worth a lot of money. Séverine was the only love of his life, and he would have been quite happy to marry her without a penny, just for the pleasure of knowing she was his. When he eventually plucked up courage to ask for her hand, he found himself better off than he could ever have dreamed. Not only did Séverine become his wife, with a dowry of

ten thousand francs, but the President, who by then had
retired and was a member of the board of directors of the
Western Railway Company, took Roubaud himself under
his wing. On the day after his marriage he had been promoted to assistant stationmaster at Le Havre. This was
due partly, no doubt, to the fact that he had a very respectable work record; he was reliable, punctual and honest,
not particularly intelligent perhaps, but very practical – all
very laudable qualities which might explain why his application had been so quickly approved and why he had made
such rapid progress. But Roubaud was inclined to think
that he owed his success entirely to his wife. He simply
worshipped her.

He opened the tin of sardines. His patience was beginning to wear thin. They had agreed to meet at three o'clock.
Where could she be? Surely she wasn't going to tell him it
took a whole day to buy a pair of boots and half a dozen **7**
blouses. As he walked back in front of the mirror, he
caught sight of himself again, his eyebrows bristling, his
face set in a harsh scowl. In Le Havre he never worried
about what she might be up to. But here in Paris he found
himself imagining her involved in all sorts of escapades,
secret assignations and deceptions. The blood rushed to
his head. He clenched his fists; they were hard and tough
from the days when he used to work in the shunting yard
pushing goods wagons around. Suddenly he had become
a brute beast, an animal unaware of its own strength. He
was so angry he could have beaten the life out of her.

Séverine popped her face round the door. The fresh air
had brought the colour to her cheeks, and she looked full
of the joys of spring.

'Here I am,' she said. 'You must have thought I'd got
lost.'

She was twenty-five years old, tall, slim and athletic.
She was quite slightly built, but she had a good figure. At

first glance she was not what you would call pretty; she had a long face and a rather large mouth, but beautiful shiny teeth. Yet she had an attractiveness all of her own – strangely appealing big blue eyes and thick dark hair.

Her husband made no answer; he stood looking at her with the uneasy, mistrustful expression which she knew only too well.

'I've run all the way,' she said. 'There wasn't a bus anywhere, and I didn't want to have to pay for a cab, so I ran. Feel me; I'm all hot.'

'Come off it,' he said impatiently, 'you can't possibly have been in the Bon Marché[12] all this time.'

Suddenly, like a child trying to get round her father, she flung her arms round his neck and placed her chubby little hand over his mouth.

'Naughty, naughty!' she said. 'Stop being so grumpy. You know I love you.'

How could he have doubted her? She seemed so honest, so open, so trustworthy. He took her in his arms and hugged her tightly. His suspicions invariably ended like this. Séverine yielded to his embrace; she liked it when he made a fuss of her. He smothered her with kisses, but she did not respond. This was something that had always vaguely disturbed him; she remained passive, like a big child. She loved him as a daughter might love her father, but never as his lover.

'There can't have been much left on the shelves by the time you'd finished,' said Roubaud.

'I'll tell you what I've bought,' said Séverine. 'But first, let's eat. I'm starving . . . Oh, I nearly forgot. I've bought you a little present . . . But you've got to say "please".'

She held her face up to his, laughing. Her right hand was hidden in her pocket, holding something she didn't want him to see.

'Come on,' she said, 'you have to say "please".'

Roubaud was laughing too; he loved it when she teased him like this.

'I give in,' he said. 'Please.'

She had bought him a knife, to replace one that he had lost; he had been moaning about it for a fortnight. He was delighted. It was a beauty! Brand new, with a lovely shiny blade and an ivory handle. He said he was going to use it straight away! Séverine was glad to see him so pleased and told him jokingly that he now had to pay her a penny, so that their friendship would not be severed.

'Come on,' she said, 'let's eat! No, please don't close the window, leave it open for a bit, I'm so hot.'

She had walked over to the window where he was standing. She rested her head on his shoulder and stood for a while looking down at the station, sprawled out beneath them. The smoke had cleared for a moment, and the copper disc of the sun was sinking into the mist behind the houses in the Rue de Rome. A shunting engine was bringing in the train for Mantes. It had already been assembled and was due to leave at four twenty-five. The engine pushed the carriages up the platform under the station roof and was uncoupled. From the circle-line station, away to their left, came the clunk of buffers, as last-minute extra carriages were attached to the trains. Standing on its own on one of the middle tracks, its driver and fireman black with coal dust after the journey, a heavy locomotive which had just brought in a stopping train was waiting for the road back to the Batignolles engine shed. It waited patiently, as if tired and out of breath, a trickle of steam leaking from one of its valves. A red signal dropped with a clatter, and the engine moved off.

'They certainly know how to enjoy themselves, those two Dauvergne girls!' said Roubaud, as he came away from the window. 'Just listen to them at that piano! I saw Henri a bit earlier. He asked to be remembered to you.'

'Come on, let's eat,' said Séverine.

She helped herself to the sardines and started to eat hungrily. That sandwich at Mantes seemed ages ago. Coming to Paris always seemed to go to her head. She loved walking around the streets and she was itching to tell him what she had bought at the Bon Marché. Every spring she would spend all the money she had saved during the winter in one fell swoop. She preferred to buy everything in one go, she said; it worked out cheaper and made it worth the train journey. She couldn't stop talking, hardly even pausing to swallow her food. Eventually, blushing, and looking a bit shamefaced, she told him how much she had spent . . . Over three hundred francs!

Roubaud was amazed.

'Good heavens!' he said. 'You must be the best-dressed stationmaster's wife in the country! You told me you were only going to get a few blouses and a pair of boots!'

10 'But darling, there were some real bargains! A silk scarf with the most beautiful stripes you've ever seen! And a gorgeous hat; a dream! Petticoats, ready-made, with embroidered trims round the edges! For next to nothing! I'd have had to pay twice the price in Le Havre. Anyway, I've arranged to have them sent on, so you'll see.'

Roubaud couldn't help laughing; she was so pretty, she seemed so happy, and she had such a pleading, apologetic look in her eyes. He loved these cosy little lunches, with just the two of them in a room all to themselves. It was so much nicer than going to a restaurant. Normally, Séverine drank only water. But today she was enjoying herself and drank a whole glass of white wine without giving it a thought. They finished the tin of sardines and started on the pâté. Roubaud used his new knife to serve it. It was perfect; it cut beautifully.

'So what about you?' she asked. 'Here's me chattering away, and you haven't told me how you've got on. What's happening about the Sub-Prefect?'

Roubaud told her about his meeting with the traffic manager. He'd been given a real dressing-down. He'd stood up for himself, of course, and told him what had really happened; how that stupid, toffee-nosed Sub-Prefect had insisted on taking his dog into a first-class compartment, even though there was a second-class carriage specially reserved for huntsmen and their hounds, and how they'd had an argument and ended up exchanging angry words. The manager said that he had been perfectly within his rights to insist on the regulations. The real problem was something he had said; something, in fact, that Roubaud admitted he had said: 'You lot won't be the masters for much longer!' People were saying that he was a republican. There had recently been a considerable amount of debate at the opening of the 1869 session of Parliament and fears about the forthcoming general elections[13] were making the government very edgy. He would certainly have been sent **11** to another station had it not been for President Grandmorin, who had spoken up for him. Even so, he'd had to sign a letter of apology. It was Grandmorin himself who advised sending a letter; he even had it ready prepared.

Séverine interrupted him:

'So it was just as well I wrote to him and we went to see him this morning before you got your telling off. I knew he'd sort things out.'

'He's obviously very fond of you,' said Roubaud. 'And he knows how to influence people. But what's the point of trying to do your job properly? All right, they give credit where credit is due; could show more initiative perhaps, conduct impeccable, does what he's told, very willing. What more could you ask? But if I hadn't been married to you, and if Grandmorin hadn't spoken up for me just because he happened to have a soft spot for you, I'd have been out on my ear. They'd have sent me to some godforsaken station in the middle of nowhere.'

Séverine had a steady, faraway look in her eyes.

'Oh yes,' she murmured, as if talking to herself, 'he certainly knows how to influence people.'

For a while neither of them spoke. Séverine had stopped eating and sat gazing into the distance, with big wide eyes. She must have been thinking back to her childhood in the château at Doinville, just outside Rouen.

She had never known her mother, and was just thirteen when her father, Aubry, the gardener, died; and it was round about then that the President, who had lost his wife several years earlier, had taken her under his wing. He brought her up along with his own daughter, Berthe. The two girls were placed under the tutelage of Grandmorin's sister, Madame Bonnehon, who had been married to a factory owner but who was, like Grandmorin, also widowed, and now owned the château. Berthe was two years older than Séverine and she had married six months after her. Her husband was a Monsieur de Lachesnaye, a judge in the Rouen law courts, a sour-faced, sickly looking little man. Grandmorin had remained President of the Rouen law courts, in his native Normandy, up until only a year ago, when he retired, after a long and distinguished career. He was born in 1804, was appointed as deputy public prosecutor at Digne after the 1830 revolution and went on to hold similar posts at Fontainebleau and in Paris. He rose to become chief public prosecutor at Troyes, advocate-general at Rennes and eventually the presiding judge at Rouen. His fortune ran into millions. He had been a local government councillor[14] since 1855. On the day that he retired, he was made a Commander of the Legion of Honour. To Séverine, he didn't seem to have changed for as long as she could remember him – stocky, well built, his hair cut short and prematurely white, a lustrous golden white, the legacy of the fine blond hair of his youth. He wore a neat, close-cut beard, but no moustache. He had an angular, square-shaped face, with steely blue eyes and a prominent nose, which made him look very stern. He had an abrupt manner that was intimidating.

Roubaud raised his voice. Twice he had to ask her, 'Séverine, what are you thinking about?'

She jumped. A small shiver ran through her, as if something had suddenly startled her.

'Oh, nothing in particular,' she answered.

'Why aren't you eating? Have you lost your appetite?'

'No,' she said, 'I'm fine.'

She drank the remaining wine from her glass and finished the slice of pâté on her plate. Then, much to their consternation, they realized there was no more bread! The one-pound loaf had all been eaten and there was none left for the cheese. There were shouts and laughter as they ransacked the room and eventually found a stale crust at the back of Madame Victoire's sideboard. Although the window had been left open, the room was still very stuffy. Séverine, sitting with her back to the stove, was getting hotter and hotter; the unexpected lunch and trying to talk and eat at the same time had brought the colour to her cheeks. Being together in Madame Victoire's room reminded Roubaud of Grandmorin again. She's another one who's got a lot to thank him for, he thought.

Madame Victoire had been violated when she was very young. She had lost her baby, nursed Séverine when her mother had died in childbirth, married a fireman in the railway company and had then tried to eke out a living in Paris by taking in a bit of dressmaking, while her husband squandered every penny they earned. Fortunately, quite by chance, she had happened to bump into her foster child, which enabled her to renew her old contact with the President; Madame Victoire was another whom Grandmorin had taken under his wing. It was he who had arranged her present job with the Department of Health as a lavatory attendant at the first-class ladies' toilets; and a very good job it was, too. The Company only paid her a hundred francs a year, but she received nearly fourteen hundred in tips. She was provided with free accommodation, the room that they were in now, and even had heating included. All in all, she was doing quite well for herself. Her husband, Pecqueux, was earning two thousand eight hundred francs, including bonuses, as a fireman, and Roubaud calculated that if he had actually brought the money home rather than spending it on binges in nearly every tavern along the line, they would have been making more than four thousand francs between them, which was twice as much as he was earning as an assistant stationmaster at Le Havre.[15]

'I don't suppose working in a public convenience is to every woman's taste,' said Roubaud. 'But a job's a job!'

14　　Their hunger had by now subsided, and they ate more slowly, cutting little slices of cheese to make the meal last longer. Their conversation, too, had become more relaxed.

'Oh yes,' said Roubaud, 'I forgot . . . Why didn't you accept Grandmorin's invitation to stay with him at Doinville?'

He was beginning to feel the pleasant effects of the meal and was thinking of their visit earlier that morning to the house in the Rue du Rocher, near the station. He was back in the President's large, plainly furnished study. Grandmorin was telling them that he proposed to go to Doinville the following day. Then, as if the thought had just occurred to him, he suggested he might travel with them that evening, on the 6.30 express. He could take his goddaughter on to his sister's; she had been saying she wanted to see her for ages. But Séverine had come up with all manner of excuses, which, she said, 'prevented' her.

'I couldn't see any problem about going to Doinville,' said Roubaud. 'You could have stayed there till Thursday.

I'd have managed all right on my own. It was silly. People like us can't afford to refuse invitations from people in his position; it's our only chance of getting on. He wasn't pleased; you could tell. I kept trying to get you to agree; and then you started tugging on my coat. So in the end I said the same as you, but I really didn't know why. Why didn't you want to go? Come on, tell me!'

Séverine looked away and shrugged her shoulders impatiently.

'I couldn't just leave you on your own,' she said.

'That's not the reason,' said Roubaud. 'In the three years we've been married, you've been to Doinville twice already, and stayed there a week. What was to stop you going there again?'

Séverine was becoming increasingly uneasy. She avoided looking him in the eyes.

'I didn't fancy it,' she said. 'You can't force me to do something I don't want to do.'

Roubaud opened his arms, as if to say that he wasn't forcing her to do anything. There was something she was keeping back, and he knew it.

'Come on,' he said, 'you're not telling the truth, are you? When you went last time, was Madame Bonnehon unpleasant to you?'

Not at all! Madame Bonnehon had always made her very welcome. What a lovely person she was – tall, well built, with beautiful blonde hair, and still remarkably good-looking, despite her fifty-five years. People said that since becoming a widow, and even while her husband was still alive, she'd had quite a few romances. Everybody at Doinville adored her. She made the château a place of sheer enchantment; and the whole of Rouen society used to come for visits, especially those in the legal profession. Many of Madame Bonnehon's gentlemen friends were lawyers.

'Were the Lachesnayes unkind to you? Come on, tell me.'

She had to admit that, since Berthe's marriage to Monsieur de Lachesnaye, their friendship had not been what it used to be. Poor Berthe! Her looks didn't improve. She was so plain, and she had a red nose! The good ladies of Rouen spoke very highly of her; she was a woman of distinction, they said. Being married to such an ugly, intractable, tight-fisted husband could so easily have rubbed off on her and made her as insufferable as him. But no, Berthe had been perfectly civil to her old friend, and Séverine wouldn't hear a word said against her.

'Well, then, it must be the President who's done something to upset you,' said Roubaud.

Séverine had been answering his questions quietly and calmly, but at this she suddenly flared up.

16 'Don't be stupid!' she said sharply.

Her voice had suddenly become more agitated, and she spoke more quickly. You hardly ever saw him. He hid himself away in a cottage, in the grounds of the château, with a gate that opened on to a deserted country lane. He came and went as he pleased. No one ever knew whether he was there or not. He didn't even tell his sister when he was coming. He took a carriage at Barentin, had himself driven to Doinville in the middle of the night, and then spent days on end shut up in his cottage without anyone knowing a thing about it ... He never bothered anybody!

'I only asked because you've often said that when you were a child he used to scare you stiff.'

'He didn't scare me stiff, as you put it. Why must you always make things sound worse than they are? He didn't laugh much, it's true ... He had a way of staring you in the face, with his great big eyes ... it made you look away. I've seen people so nervous they couldn't say a thing. Everyone was frightened of him because he was strict and very clever. But he never spoke unkindly to me. I always thought he had a soft spot for me . . .'

She had begun to speak more slowly, with a dreamy, faraway look in her eyes.

'I remember . . . when I was a little girl, the children used to play together in the grounds. If we saw him coming, we'd all run away and hide; even his daughter, Berthe. She was always frightened she'd done something wrong. It didn't worry me; I just stood where I was. He'd come up to me and I'd stand there, looking up at him, smiling, and he'd give me a pat on the cheek . . . Later on, when I was sixteen, whenever Berthe wanted to ask him a favour, it was always me she sent to speak to him. I'd go up to him, look him straight in the face and say what I'd come to say. I could feel his eyes looking right into me. I wasn't bothered, because I knew he'd say yes to everything I asked **17** for! . . . I can see it now . . . Doinville! When I close my eyes, it all comes back – every tree in the park, every corridor, every room in the house.'

She fell silent, and sat with her eyes closed. A quiver seemed to run over her hot, flushed face, as she remembered those days gone by, and things she dared not tell him. She remained lost in thought; a little tremor moved across her lips, pulling at the corner of her mouth.

'He's certainly been very good to you,' said Roubaud, lighting his pipe. 'He brought you up like a young lady, he made sure your little bit of money went straight into a savings account and he even added to it himself when we got married. Apparently, he's going to leave you something in his will.'

'Yes,' murmured Séverine, 'the house at La Croix-de-Maufras. They built the railway through the grounds. We used to go and spend a week there sometimes. I'm not really counting on it. I dare say the Lachesnayes have made sure he leaves me nothing. Anyway, I don't want anything. I don't want him to leave me a thing!'

This was said with such conviction that Roubaud was amazed. He took his pipe from his mouth and stared at her round-eyed.

'I can't make you out sometimes,' he said. 'Everybody knows the President's worth millions. What's wrong with him leaving something to his goddaughter? Who could take exception to that? We'd have it made!'

A thought occurred to him which made him laugh out loud.

'You're not frightened people might think you're his daughter, are you? You know what they say about Grandmorin. It doesn't bear repeating, some of it. He's certainly no saint! Apparently, even when his wife was alive he managed to have his way with all the maids. He's a randy old sod. He'll still jump into bed with the first woman that takes his fancy . . . Anyway, what the hell! Even if you are his daughter, who cares!'

Séverine leaped to her feet, red with anger, looking all about her with big blue, frightened eyes, her hair falling across her face in thick black strands.

'Me, his daughter! How dare you! I won't have you making jokes like that, do you hear! How could I be his daughter? Do I look like him? I've had enough of this; let's change the subject. I didn't want to go to Doinville because I didn't! And that's all there is to it! I want to go back to Le Havre with you.'

Roubaud nodded and raised his hands to try to calm her down. Why insist if it was going to make her so upset? He smiled. He had never seen her get so worked up. It must have been the wine, he thought. He decided he had better show her he was sorry. He picked up the knife, wiped it carefully and told her a second time how he'd never seen a knife like it. And to show her how razor-sharp it was he began to pare his fingernails with it.

'It's already a quarter past four,' said Séverine, standing in front of the cuckoo clock. 'I've still got some shopping to do . . . and we need to be thinking about our train.'

She had still not fully recovered from her outburst and, before tidying things away, she went back over to the window and leaned out. Roubaud put down the knife and his pipe, walked over to her, stood behind her and gently put his arms round her. He held her against him, his chin resting on her shoulder, his head touching hers. Neither of them moved. They just stood there looking.

Down below, the little shunting engines plied tirelessly back and forth like industrious housewives; but for a muffled rattle of wheels and the occasional toot on their whistles, you would hardly know they were there. One of them went by beneath their window and disappeared **19** under the Pont de l'Europe on its way to the marshalling yard with a string of carriages from a Trouville train. As it got beyond the bridge it passed another engine coming in light from the sheds as though out on its own for an afternoon stroll, its brass and metal-work gleaming, bright and eager to be on its way. It came to a halt and gave two short blasts on its whistle to ask for the road. The signalman immediately directed it towards its train, which stood ready assembled under the great roof of the mainline station – the 4.25 for Dieppe. A crowd of passengers milled around the train, looking for their places, barrows laden with luggage clattered along the platform, attendants went from carriage to carriage placing foot-warmers in every compartment. The engine and its tender backed on to the luggage van at the head of the train with a gentle clunk as it made contact. The shunting foreman tightened the screw-coupling. Out towards Batignolles, the sky had darkened. An ashen haze seemed to settle over the vast network of railway lines, hiding the distant buildings from view. In the fading light they could still see the constant coming and going of trains on the suburban and circle lines, and above the brooding mass of the great station roofs, threads of red-coloured smoke drifted like strips of torn paper into the darkening Paris sky.

'Don't,' she said. 'Leave me alone.'

Without saying a word he had slowly tightened his arms round her, roused by the warmth and closeness of her young body. Her scent excited him and, as she wriggled to free herself, he was filled with desire. He lifted her up and carried her away from the window, pushing it to with his elbows as he turned. He put his mouth to hers, kissing her insistently, and carried her towards the bed.

'No, not here,' she pleaded. 'Not in this room, please, it's not ours.'

Séverine was a bit tipsy; she was feeling the effects of the food and the wine and had still not recovered from her mad dash across Paris. The heat from the stove, the table left uncleared, the unexpected journey from Le Havre and a private dinner party all to themselves ... She felt her heart beat faster, and a thrill of excitement ran through her. She must take a grip on herself. She must not give in. She sat on the bed, pressing her back against the wooden headboard. He frightened her, but, without fully knowing why, she was determined to resist him.

'No,' she said. 'I don't want to.'

He took his hands from her – strong, dangerous hands. His face was flushed, and he was shaking. He could have murdered her.

'Don't be silly,' he said. 'Who's to know? We can easily put the bed straight again.'

At home in Le Havre when he was on night duty, she would normally be quite willing to go to bed with him in the afternoon after they'd had their lunch. She never seemed to get much pleasure from it herself, but she had been happy to comply, if it gave him pleasure. What frustrated him now was that he sensed something different in her, something he had never known before – she was burning, passionate, sensual. She looked at him steadily. The shadow of her dark, shiny hair fell over her clear blue eyes; her lips, full and red, seemed like an open wound in the rounded softness of her face. This was a woman who was strange to him. Why would she not give herself?

'Tell me why not. We've got time.'

An inexplicable anguish had taken hold of her. Her mind was torn. Nothing seemed certain any more, and she felt a stranger even to herself. She let out a cry of genuine pain, which made him desist.

'Please, please,' she begged. 'Leave me alone. I can't explain it. Just the thought of it makes me feel sick. It wouldn't be right.'

They had both collapsed on to the edge of the bed. He rubbed his hand across his face, as if trying to wipe away the red flush that burned his skin. Seeing that he was now more settled, she leaned towards him and gently gave him a big kiss on the cheek to prove that she still loved him. They sat there, saying nothing, trying to regain their composure. He had taken her left hand in his and was running his fingers over an old gold ring in the form of a snake with a little ruby for its head. She wore it on the same finger as her wedding ring. She had worn it there ever since he had known her.

'My little snake,' she said dreamily, thinking that he was looking at the ring and that she ought to speak to him. 'He gave me that for my sixteenth birthday at La Croix-de-Maufras.'

Roubaud looked up in surprise.

'Who did? The President?'

As her husband's eyes met hers, Séverine seemed to wake up with a start. She felt a chill run across her cheeks. She tried to answer him, but no words came. She remained speechless, as if paralysed.

'You always told me that ring came from your mother,' he said.

She might still have saved the situation. The word could be retrieved. It was a momentary aberration. All she had to do was make a joke of it; pretend it was a slip of the tongue. But obstinacy got the better of her. Reason seemed to desert her.

'Darling,' she said, 'I never told you it came from my mother.'

Roubaud stared at her. His face went pale.

'What do you mean, you never told me it came from your mother? You've told me twenty times or more! I've 22 no objection to the President giving you a ring; he's given you lots of things. But why hide it from me? Why tell lies about it and say it was from your mother?'

'Darling, I tell you I never said anything about it being from my mother; you must have imagined it.'

She knew it was stupid to persist. She was just making things worse for herself. He could read her like a book. If only she could start again, take back what she had just said. But it was too late. She felt as though she were dissolving in front of him. Written across her face was a tacit admission of guilt. The pallor had spread from her cheeks to her whole face, and a nervous twitch played in the corner of her lips. Roubaud was fearsome. His face had turned bright red, as if he were about to burst a blood vessel. He grabbed her by the wrists and thrust his face into hers, trying to read from the fear and panic in her eyes what it was she refused to tell him.

'Good God!' he muttered. 'I don't believe it!'

She was terrified. She knew he was going to hit her. She

ducked her head and covered her face with her arm. It was so paltry, so trifling, almost nothing – a little fib about her ring. She had completely forgotten about it. One careless word, and the cat was out of the bag! It had taken no more than a second! He flung her across the bed, punching her wildly with both fists. In three years of marriage he had never once laid a finger on her and now he was attacking her like a wild beast, blind, demented. His hands struck her again and again, big brawny hands – hands which once had hauled railway wagons.

'You bitch!' he yelled. 'You dirty bitch! You slept with him, didn't you! You slept with him! . . . Slept with him! . . . Slept with him!'

In his fury, each time he said it, he punched her harder and harder as if he were trying to pound the words into her body.

'You're just an old man's cast-off! You lousy bitch! You 23 slept with him! . . . Admit it . . . You slept with him!'

He was so beside himself with rage that he was choking. He could no longer speak; all that came from his mouth were incoherent gasps of breath. He became aware of her voice as she cringed beneath the assault. 'No!' she was shouting, 'I didn't sleep with him.' How could she possibly convince him? All she could do was deny it, or he would kill her. But hearing her continue to lie to him simply angered him all the more.

'Admit you slept with him,' he cried.

'No! No!' she wept.

He had seized hold of her again and had lifted her up from the bed to stop her rolling over on to the cover to hide her face. He forced her to look at him.

'Admit you slept with him.'

She managed to escape his grasp and get away from him. She ran for the door, but he was after her like a shot. He raised his fist to strike her again. He pushed her towards the table and landed her a single, savage blow that sent her reeling to the floor. He flung himself down beside her and grabbed her by the hair to pin her down. They lay on the floor, face to face, without moving. In the dreadful silence that ensued came the sounds of singing and laughter from the room below. The Dauvergne girls were playing the piano and obviously enjoying themselves. Fortunately it had drowned the noise of the fight. Claire was singing children's nursery rhymes and Sophie was accompanying her on the piano with great gusto.

'Admit you slept with him!'

She was too frightened to go on denying it. She said nothing.

'Admit it! Admit you slept with him, damn you, or I'll slit your throat!'

She knew he meant it; she could tell from the look in his eyes. As she fell down, she had noticed the knife. It was lying on the table, open. She had seen the glint of the blade and she thought he was trying to reach it. She no longer had the courage to face up to him. She was beyond caring – about herself or about anything. She just wanted to get it over and done with.

'All right then, it's true. I did. Now let me go.'

What happened next was dreadful. The admission, which he had been trying with such violence to force from her, left him feeling stunned. It was impossible, monstrous. He could conceive of nothing more disgusting. He seized her head and banged it against the leg of the table. She struggled to get away from him but he dragged her across the floor by her hair, scattering chairs all round the room. Every time she tried to stand up he struck her with his fist and sent her flying to the floor. His breath came in short, sharp bursts. His teeth were clenched; he was like a crazed animal, demented. They crashed against the table and nearly overturned the stove. There were smears of blood and strands of hair stuck to the corner of the side-board. They staggered back towards the bed, gasping for breath, dazed and sickened by the force of his onslaught. They were both exhausted, he from striking her and she from the beating he had inflicted. Séverine lay slumped on the floor. Roubaud crouched behind her, still holding her by the shoulders. The blood pounded in their ears. From below rose the sound of music and the girls' happy laughter.

Roubaud pulled Séverine from the floor and propped her against the side of the bed. He knelt in front of her, still holding her down. Then, when he was at last able to speak, came a barrage of questions. His desire to know the truth was insatiable. He was no longer beating her, but this was another form of torture.

'So you slept with him, you bitch! Say it! You slept with him! An old man like him! How old were you? Tell me! I bet you were no more than a girl. A little schoolgirl.'

She suddenly burst into tears and could not speak for crying.

'Tell me, damn you! I bet you weren't even ten when he started playing around with you. The dirty sod! That's why he had you brought up out there at Doinville. Just so he could have his way with you, the bastard! Tell me, damn you, or I'll start again!'

Tears were streaming down her face. She couldn't speak. He raised his hand and struck her again, making her head spin. Still she did not answer him. Three times he struck her, each time repeating the same question.

'How old were you, you bitch? Tell me! How old were you?'

She was too weak to resist. She felt as if the life were draining from her. He could have clawed her heart out with his clumsy, workman's fingers. And still the questions came. She told him everything, so overcome with shame and terror that she spoke in a barely audible whisper. Roubaud, inflamed with jealousy, grew angrier and angrier as each painful chapter in the story unfolded. He wanted to know everything. He made her repeatedly go back over what she had already said, down to the last detail, in order to make sure he had got all the facts. He knelt in front of her with his ear pressed to the poor girl's lips, listening in horror as the confession continued. All the time he held his fist raised above her, ready to strike her again at the least thing she refused to tell him.

Once again he heard the story of the years at Doinville – when she had first gone there as a child, and later when she was a young girl. Where had it happened? In the woods in the great park? In a corner of some dark passageway in the château? The President had obviously already had his eyes on her when he asked her to stay there after his gardener died and had her brought up with his own daughter. It must have started when the children used to run away in the middle of a game if they saw him coming, while she waited behind, with her pretty little face looking up at him and smiling, so that he could give her a pat on the cheek as he walked past. And later on, if she wasn't frightened to go and ask him favours and always managed to get what she wanted, perhaps it was because she knew she could twist him round her little finger, whilst he, who was so strict and formal with other people, fed her the same blandishments he used to seduce all his servants. It was revolting. An old lecher, getting her to give him kisses as if he were her grandfather, watching her grow out of childhood, placing his hand on her, getting bolder every time he touched her, not able to wait until she had grown up!

Roubaud was breathless.

'How old were you? Tell me! How old were you?'

'Sixteen and a half.'

'You're a liar!'

Why should she lie, for goodness' sake? She shrugged her shoulders. She was beyond caring and she was sick with fatigue.

'Where were you, the first time it happened?'

'At La Croix-de-Maufras.'

For a moment he said nothing. A sickly look crept into his eyes as he next began to speak.

'Tell me what he did to you.'

She remained silent. He raised his fist.

'You wouldn't believe me,' she said.

'Tell me even so,' he said. 'He couldn't manage it, could he?'

She nodded. He was right; he couldn't manage it.

Then came an endless stream of questions. He wanted to know everything, down to the very last detail. He used words that sank below the level of decency and he asked her things that broke the bounds of all modesty. She kept **27** her mouth tightly closed, answering him with a mere nod or shake of the head, thinking that perhaps it might make it easier for both of them once the story was out. But for him every new revelation intensified his suffering. If she had taken a lover and had a normal affair, the images that now came to torment him would have disturbed him less. But this was something unnatural; it curdled his mind and drove the poisoned blade of jealousy twisting and turning deep inside him. Life was no longer possible; the awful truth would be with him for ever.

A loud sob came from his throat: 'Good God! It can't be true! No! It's not possible! It can't be true!'

He shook her violently.

'Why did you marry me, you bitch? Why did you lie to me, damn you? There are women locked up in prison with less on their conscience than you! You hated me, didn't you? You never loved me, did you? Why did you marry me? Tell me!'

She waved a hand vaguely. How could she answer him? Just then she hardly knew anything.

She had been happy to marry him at the time and she had hoped it would enable her to get away from Grandmorin. There were all sorts of things that you didn't particularly want to do, but that you did all the same, because they seemed the most sensible at the time. No, she didn't love him. What she refrained from telling him, though, was that, had it not been for this business with Grandmorin, she would never have agreed to marry him at all.

'He wanted to fix you up with a husband, didn't he? And he found a right mug! He wanted to set things up so that he could carry on seeing you! And he has carried on seeing you, hasn't he? You've been there twice. That's what he wanted you for, wasn't it?'

Once again she nodded.

'And that's why he was inviting you again this time, wasn't it? You'd have gone on seeing him for ever, you dirty bitch! For ever and ever! I'll strangle you!'

His hands were already clenched and reaching out to grab her by the throat. At last she managed to find her voice.

'You're not being fair,' she said. 'I was the one who said I didn't want to go. It was you who kept on trying to make me – remember? I had to get annoyed with you to make you shut up. I've had enough of him. It's over. Couldn't you see? It's finished. I never want anything more to do with him! Never!'

He sensed she was telling the truth, but it gave him no comfort. What had taken place between this man and her could not be altered. It remained, like a dagger planted in his chest, a searing pain that would not go away. He was powerless to undo what had been done, and it was an agony to him. He had still not taken his hands from her. He put his face up to hers, peering into her eyes as if mesmerized, drawn like an insect to probe the truth of her confession from the blood that pulsed through the tiny blue veins. He spoke quietly, as someone in a dream, someone obsessed.

'At La Croix-de-Maufras! The red bedroom! I remember it. The window looks out on to the railway. The bed's directly opposite. That's where he . . . No wonder he says he's going to leave the place to you. You've earned it! He got a good bargain, putting your savings into the bank for you and giving you a dowry! A judge, worth millions! So respected! So learned! So high up! I'm not surprised he managed to turn a few heads! But what if it turned out he was your father?[16] Tell me that.'

With an almighty effort Séverine pulled herself to her feet and, despite the pitifully bruised and battered condition she was in, angrily pushed Roubaud away from her.

'Never!' she shouted angrily. 'Never say that! Beat me! **29** Kill me! Do what you like with me! But never say that; it's a lie!'

Roubaud still held on to her by one hand.

'You must know something about it,' he said. 'You're only getting so worked up because you think it might be true.'

She pulled her hand away from him and as she did so he felt the ring, the little snake with the ruby head that by now he had completely forgotten about. He tore it from her finger and in a renewed access of fury crushed it with his heel on the floor. He then walked up and down the room, saying nothing, stunned. Séverine collapsed on to the edge of the bed and sat watching him with big, frightened eyes. The terrible silence continued.

Roubaud's fury had not abated; there would be a brief lull, but each time it came flooding back stronger than ever, as if he were drunk – wave upon wave of anger sweeping through him, making his head reel and leaving him dazed. He was no longer himself. He lashed out wildly at the air around him and lurched blindly about the room, the plaything of the violent storm that assailed him. He was driven by a single overriding need; he must appease the beast that raged within him. It was a physical need, urgent and imperious, like a craving for revenge which racked his body and would allow him no respite until it was sated.

As he paced the length of the room he beat his fists against his head, crying desperately, 'What am I to do? What am I to do?'

He might have killed her there and then. But he hadn't, and now the moment had gone. His cowardice at not killing her tormented him even more, for cowardice it was, and he knew it. He still desired her, the bitch; and that was why he hadn't strangled her. But he couldn't keep her now. So what was he to do? Send her packing? Throw her out on to the street and tell her never to come back? He realized he couldn't do even that, and a new wave of revulsion swept over him, a feeling of awful sickness. What could he do? Was he simply to accept what she had told him, go back with her to Le Havre and carry on living the quiet life they'd had before, as if nothing had happened? It was impossible! He would rather he were dead! He would rather they were both dead! Why wait longer?

He was so overcome with the horror of it all that he was shouting louder and louder, like a man who had lost his senses, 'What am I to do?'

Séverine sat watching him from the bed, her eyes wide with amazement. To her he had never been anything more than a friend, but she had loved him with all the steady, affectionate love that a friend can give. Seeing him now so distraught, she found herself beginning to pity him. She might have forgiven him the abuse and even the beating; but it was the sheer ferocity of his reaction that she could not understand. It left her feeling bewildered. She was by nature a docile, passive person. She was still only a girl when she had submitted to the gratification of an old man's desire; later she had agreed to be married so that everything might be sorted out. She failed to understand how anyone could be so insanely jealous over little misdeeds that she now regretted with all her heart. There was not an ounce of vice in her; she had not known what it was to be sexually aroused. Despite all that had happened she had remained chaste, and retained some of the blissful naivety of a child. She now watched her husband pacing backwards and forwards and turning furiously about the room, as she might have watched a wolf, or some creature of a different species. What had got into him? She had never seen such anger in a man. What terrified her was the sense of an animal nature, something she had dimly perceived on previous occasions during the three years of their marriage, now unleashed, driven wild and ready to pounce. What could she say to him to prevent some awful catastrophe?

Each time he walked back across the room, he came to the foot of the bed and stood facing her. She waited for him as he came towards her. At last she plucked up her courage and spoke:

'Love, listen to me . . .'

But he didn't hear her. He kept pacing the room, like a wisp of straw blown about in a gale.

'What am I to do? What am I to do?'

Eventually she managed to seize his wrist and made him stand still for a moment.

'Listen to me, love,' she pleaded. 'I was the one who didn't want to go to Doinville. I would never have gone there again. Never! You're the one I love.'

She spoke softly, trying to calm his temper, drawing him towards her and raising her lips so that he might kiss her. He had fallen on to the bed beside her but he suddenly pushed her away, horrified.

'So now you want to make love, you bitch! A moment ago you didn't fancy it; you didn't want me. And now you do, just so you can say you've got me back again! You think I can't resist it, don't you! Just because I'm a man! I'd sooner burn in hell! I'd sooner burn in hell, I tell you, than make love to the likes of you!'

He shuddered. The thought of possessing her, the thought of their two bodies falling together on to the bed seared into his brain. From somewhere in the troubled darkness of his flesh, from deep down amidst the stirrings of his wounded desire, there came the sudden, irresistible urge to kill.

'I must kill him,' he said. 'I can't sleep with you again, until I've killed him, do you hear? I must kill him! Kill him! Kill him!'

His voice became louder and louder. He stood up, saying it again and again. He felt himself grown in stature; it was as if, by simply repeating the words to himself, he had regained his composure and strengthened his resolve. Without a word he walked slowly over to the table and looked down at the knife, its blade open, shining. He picked it up mechanically, closed it and put it into his pocket. He stood there, his hands hanging loosely at his sides, a faraway look in his eyes, lost in thought. It would not be easy. Two deep lines furrowed his brow as he pondered the difficulties that lay ahead. To help himself think more clearly, he walked over to the window, opened it and stood with his face to the cool evening air. His wife had got up from the bed and had come to stand behind him. A new fear had taken hold of her. She did not dare speak to him and she waited, looking out at the broad sweep of sky and trying to guess what desperate schemes were taking shape inside his head.

As night began to fall, the distant houses stood out as dark silhouettes; a purplish mist settled over the huge expanse of the railway station below them. The deep cutting that led out towards Batignolles lay sunk beneath swirling clouds of ash which drifted up between the girders of the Pont de l'Europe. From the sky above Paris a last pale glimmer of daylight fell on to the glass roofs of the great train sheds. Inside the station all was shrouded in dark. Along the platforms, little points of light pierced the gloom as the gas lamps were lit. A beam of light shone from the headlamp of the train for Dieppe, crammed with passengers, all its doors closed, waiting for the traffic manager to give the right-away. There was a problem in getting the train off on time; the starting signal still showed red. The train had to be held in the station while a small locomotive came to clear some carriages that had accidentally come adrift in a shunting operation. In the gathering darkness, an endless stream of trains picked its way through the intricate network of lines between rows of carriages that stood waiting in the sidings. A train left for Argenteuil, followed by another for Saint-Germain. A train arrived from Cherbourg – a very long train. Signals were continually changing, engines blew their whistles, shunters sounded their horns; everywhere you looked there were lights – red lights, green lights, amber lights, white lights – a scene of utter confusion in the lurid glow of the departing day. It seemed that the trains were all going to collide with each other, but they found their way through, sometimes running close together side by side and then going their separate ways, all with the same smooth, snake-like movement, before they disappeared from view in the gathering darkness. The train for Dieppe was finally given the all-clear; it blew its whistle and began to move out of the station. A few spots of rain had begun to fall; it was going to be a wet night.

Roubaud turned away from the window. There was a dark, determined look in his eyes. It was as if the approaching night had forced its way inside him. He had decided; his plan was made. The light was fading fast; he looked at the cuckoo clock to see the time.

'Twenty past five,' he said aloud.

He was amazed. One hour! Even less than that! So much had happened! It seemed as though they had been in that room, locked in mortal combat, for weeks.

'Twenty past five,' he repeated. 'We still have time.'

Séverine did not dare ask him what he was going to do. She watched him anxiously as he felt inside the cupboard, eventually taking out a sheet of writing paper, a small bottle of ink and a pen.

'You're going to write a letter,' he said.

'Who to?' she asked.

'To him,' he replied. 'Come and sit down.'

She instinctively backed away from the chair, even though she still wasn't sure what he wanted her to do. But he pulled her forwards and sat her down at the table with such force that she dared not move.

'Write this,' he said. ' "Take the 6.30 express this evening and make sure you're not seen until we get to Rouen." '

She had the pen in her hand, but her hand was shaking. A wave of fear ran through her at the premonition of unknown horrors that these few simple words evoked. She raised her eyes from the table and looked at him, imploringly.

'What are you going to do?' she said. 'Tell me, love! I beg you!'

'Write!' he said. 'Write!'

His voice was harsh, inexorable. He looked her straight in the eyes, calmly and quietly, but so purposefully that she felt crushed, reduced to nothing.

'You'll see what I'm going to do,' he said. 'You'll see because you're going to do it with me. It's something we can share. Something that will keep us together. Something no one can ever take away from us.'

He terrified her. She drew back.

'No,' she said. 'I want to know. I'm not writing anything until I know.'

Without saying a word, he took hold of her hand, a child's hand, small, fragile; he gripped it as if in a vice, with a grip of iron, until she felt her hand was about to break. A violent pain ran through her as if his very will were boring its way into her flesh. She let out a cry. Something seemed to snap inside her; she had surrendered herself to him. This passive, sweet-natured, innocent woman could do nothing but obey. The instrument of love had become the instrument of death.

'Write!' he said. 'Write!'

She wrote. Her hand hurt terribly, and she could hardly direct the pen.

'Good,' he said, when he had the letter in his hands. 'It's just right. I'm going out for a bit. You can tidy up here while I'm gone and get our things ready. I'll be back for you later.'

He was now perfectly calm. He stood in front of the mirror and straightened his tie. Then he put on his hat and left. She heard him turn the door key twice and take it from the lock. It was getting darker and darker. She remained seated at the table, listening to the sounds from outside. From the room next door, where the woman from the newspaper kiosk lived, there came a continuous, low whining – a dog, no doubt, that she had forgotten to let out. In the room downstairs, the piano had stopped playing. All that could now be heard was the cheerful clatter of saucepans and dinner plates; the two young housewives were busy in their kitchen, Claire preparing a mutton stew and Sophie getting a salad ready. Séverine sat there exhausted, listening to their happy laughter, her heart aching, as the darkness gathered around her.

At a quarter past six sharp, the locomotive for the Le Havre express emerged from beneath the Pont de l'Europe, backed on to its train and was coupled up. Because of the unusual amount of traffic there was not room to bring the train in under the covered roof of the mainline station, and it was waiting under the open sky alongside the platform, which extended like a narrow jetty out into the inky blackness of the night. A line of gas lamps ran along it like a string of little smoky stars. It had just stopped raining, and there was a cold, damp chill in the air. A mist had gathered. Through it, across the vast, open space beyond, could be seen the little pale lights of the houses in the Rue de Rome. There was a sombre grandeur about it all. Everything was still wet from the rain; here and there a red light pierced the night like a splash of blood; dark shapes loomed out of the mist – locomotives, freight wagons and rows of empty carriages waiting in the sidings. From the depths of this lake of darkness there emerged sounds – giant gasps of breath like someone dying of a fever, sudden sharp whistles like the screams of women being violated, the dismal wailing of horns and the rumble of traffic in the nearby streets. Someone was shouting orders to attach another carriage to the train. The locomotive waiting at the head of the express released a great jet of steam from its safety valve, which rose high into the night sky and dispersed as tiny flecks of cloud drifting like white tears across the funereal blackness that draped the heavens.

At twenty past six Roubaud and Séverine appeared on the platform. Séverine had just taken the key back to Madame Victoire on her way past the lavatories next to the waiting rooms. Roubaud was pushing her forward like the typical husband in a hurry whose wife has kept him waiting, he brusque and impatient with his hat pushed back, she holding her hat-veil tightly to her face and walking more hesitantly, as if about to faint with weariness. A stream of passengers was making its way up the platform. The couple joined the crowd and walked along the train looking for an empty first-class compartment. All around them people were hurriedly trying to get things ready for the train to leave; porters were wheeling barrows of luggage up to the luggage van at the front; one of the inspectors was trying to find a compartment for a large family; the assistant traffic manager was checking the couplings, shining his signal lamp down between the carriages to make sure that they were all in place and the screws properly tightened.[17] Roubaud eventually found an empty compartment and was about to help Séverine get into it when he was spotted by the stationmaster, Monsieur Vandorpe, who happened to be walking past with his assistant for **37** the mainline section, Monsieur Dauvergne, both of them with their hands behind their backs, watching the preparations for attaching the extra carriage to the train. They exchanged greetings and felt obliged to stop and chat.

The two men were keen to know about Roubaud's brush with the Sub-Prefect. He assured them that everything had been sorted out and that the matter was now closed. They told him that there had been an accident at Le Havre that morning; it had come through on the telegraph. Apparently one of the locomotives that worked the 6.30 express on Thursdays and Saturdays, a locomotive named *La Lison*, had broken a coupling-rod just as it was coming into the station. It was being repaired, but the engine driver, Jacques Lantier, who came from the same part of the world as Roubaud, and his fireman, Pecqueux, Madame Victoire's husband, would both be stuck in Le Havre for the next two days. Séverine stood waiting by the open door of the compartment while her husband

affected a show of high spirits, laughing and joking with
his two colleagues. Suddenly the train moved backwards
several metres with a violent jolt, as the engine reversed
the leading carriages on to the one that was being added,
carriage number 293. It had a coupé compartment[18] that
had been individually reserved. Dauvergne's son, Henri,
who was travelling on the train as one of the guards, had
recognized Séverine through her veil and had quickly
pulled her to one side to stop her being hit by the open
door. He smiled and offered a polite apology. He told her
that the private compartment was for one of the directors
of the railway company, who had ordered it only half an
hour before the train was due to leave. For no apparent
reason she gave a nervous little laugh. Henri dashed off to
see to the train, delighted to have met Séverine; more than
once he had thought what a lovely woman she would be to
38 have as a mistress.

The station clock said six twenty-seven. Three more
minutes! Suddenly Roubaud, who had been keeping a careful eye on the waiting-room doors all the time he had been
chatting with the stationmaster, turned on his heels and
went to rejoin his wife. But the carriage had moved, and
their compartment was now a few steps further down the
platform. Roubaud turned round, pushed his wife forward
and, taking her by the wrist, helped her to climb into the
train. Powerless to resist, Séverine kept looking anxiously
over her shoulder; there was something happening, and
she wanted to know what it was. It was a passenger, arriving at the last minute and carrying only a travelling rug.
He was wearing a heavy, blue overcoat with the collar
turned up, and his hat pulled down over his eyes. All that
could be seen of his face, in the flickering light of the gas
lamps, was a few wisps of white beard. Monsieur Vandorpe and Monsieur Dauvergne, despite the latecomer's
all too obvious wish not to be seen, had moved forward to

greet him. They followed him as he walked along the train. He only acknowledged them when they had passed three carriages and arrived in front of the reserved compartment. He opened the door and quickly got in. Séverine had recognized him and was shaking uncontrollably. She collapsed on to the carriage seat. Roubaud seized her by the arm, tightening his grip in a final triumphant gesture of possession. He now knew that the deed would be done.

In one minute the station clock would sound the half hour. A newsvendor was valiantly trying to persuade people to buy his last remaining copies of the evening paper; a few passengers still stood on the platform, finishing their cigarettes. All of a sudden everyone got into the train. Two inspectors walked along it from each end, closing the doors with a bang. Roubaud, thinking he had chosen a compartment that was empty, discovered to his annoyance that one of the window-seats was occupied by 39 a person dressed in black, who sat there and neither moved nor spoke; he assumed it was a woman in mourning. To make matters worse, the carriage door was suddenly flung open again, and two more passengers were bundled into the compartment, a fat man and his equally fat wife, who collapsed on to the seat, breathless. Roubaud swore to himself angrily. The train was ready to leave. A fine drizzle had begun to fall. Trains continued to thread their way through the rain-swept night; all that could be seen were moving rows of lights from the carriage windows. Green lights shone through the gloom; here and there a lineman's lamp bobbed and curtsied close to the ground. All else was darkness, a vast impenetrable darkness, save for the two train sheds of the mainline station, illumined by the pallid glow from the gas lamps. Darkness engulfed everything; sounds faded to nothing. Suddenly the air was rent by a great gush of steam from the locomotive, as the cylinder taps were opened. White clouds swirled up into the sky, unfolding like the shroud of some ghastly apparition, and shot through with dark streaks of smoke. Once again, a cloud of soot drifted across the Paris sky, reddened by the fiery glow from the engine below.

The assistant traffic controller raised his lamp to tell the driver he could ask for the road. There were two blasts on the whistle. The red light in front of the signalman's cabin changed to white. The guard stood by the door of the luggage van waiting for the all clear. He then signalled to the driver, who gave one long blast on the whistle and opened the regulator. The train began to move; it was on its way, very slowly at first but gradually gathering speed. It ran under the Pont de l'Europe and plunged into the Batignolles tunnel. All that could be seen was the red triangle, formed by the three tail lamps, like drops of blood from an open wound, still visible as the train disappeared into the chill blackness of the night. Nothing could now stop it. It sped on its way and was gone.

The house at La Croix-de-Maufras[1] stands in a large garden, which is cut in two by the railway line. It is set at an angle and so close to the track that it shakes whenever a train goes by.

Once seen, it stays imprinted on the memory for ever. Everyone notices it as the train speeds past, but no one knows its history – why it remains locked up, why it stands abandoned, like a ship in distress, its grey shutters closed and slowly turning green from the gales that blow in from the west. It is a desolate place, and the house seems to add to its desolation, standing on its own, cut off from all human habitation.

The only other dwelling near by is the level-crossing keeper's cottage, standing where the road turns a bend and crosses the railway on its way to Doinville five kilometres away. It is a single-storey building, its walls full of cracks, its roof tiles eaten away by moss, and crouching like a destitute beggar in the garden that surrounds it. The garden, used for growing vegetables, is enclosed by a thick hedge and contains a large well, as tall as the house itself. The level-crossing is situated half-way between the two stations of Malaunay and Barentin, exactly four kilometres from each of them. It is very rarely used; the gate is old and falling apart and is only ever opened for wagons coming down from the quarries at Bécourt, half a league away in the forest. One cannot imagine a place more remote, more cut off from civilization. It is separated from Malaunay by a long tunnel, and the only way to Barentin is along an overgrown footpath that follows the railway line. Visitors are few and far between.

On this particular evening, sultry and overcast, a traveller, who had just got off a train from Le Havre at Barentin, was striding along the path to La Croix-de-Maufras as night was beginning to fall. The countryside at this point is a succession of hills and valleys, like waves at sea. The railway crosses them by a series of cuttings and embankments, but on either side of the line, the continual rise and fall of the terrain makes travelling by road extremely difficult; as a result this terribly lonely place feels even lonelier still. The colourless fields stand bare and neglected; the hilltops are covered with clumps of trees, and streams overhung with willow run down the narrow valleys. Outcrops of bare chalk lie strewn across the landscape, and the hills stretch away into the distance, sterile, and as silent and empty as the grave.[2] The traveller, a strong, athletic-looking young man, quickened his step as though he wanted to escape the gloomy approach of night in so desolate a place.

In the gate-keeper's garden a girl stood drawing water at the well. She was eighteen years old, tall, fair-haired and strongly built; she had a large mouth, big green eyes, a low forehead and a thick head of hair. She was not a pretty girl; she had strong, broad hips and the muscular arms of a man. As soon as she spotted the traveller walking along the path, she put down her bucket and ran over to the gate in the hedge.

'Why, it's Jacques!' she cried.

He looked up. He was just twenty-six. Like her, he was tall; a dark, handsome young man with a round face and regular features, but with a rather pronounced jaw. He had thick, curly hair and a big, curly moustache, so black that by contrast his face seemed quite pale. He might have been taken for a gentleman, looking at his delicate complexion and his carefully shaven cheeks. His hands, however, bore the tell-tale signs of his job – small, delicate hands, but stained yellow with grease, which came from driving a locomotive.

'Hello, Flore,' he said simply.

Suddenly, the lustre had gone from his big dark eyes. A red mist swam before them; they had become pale and strangely disturbed. His eyelids flickered. He looked away. He had suddenly become embarrassed and ill at ease. His whole body had instinctively recoiled from her.

She stood in front of him without moving, looking straight at him. She had noticed before how he tried to hide the sudden, involuntary shudder that ran through him whenever he came close to a woman. She found it very strange, and it saddened her. Jacques asked her if her mother was indoors, although he knew perfectly well that she was ill and unable to leave the house. In an attempt to cover her embarrassment, she simply nodded and stepped aside, so that he could enter without touching her. She **43** returned to the well, not deigning to speak, her head held high in a show of unconcern.

Jacques walked quickly across the little garden and went into the house. The first room he entered was the large kitchen, where the family lived and had their meals. In the middle of the room, Aunt Phasie,[3] as he had called her since he was a child, sat on her own by the table on a wicker chair with an old shawl wrapped round her legs. She was a cousin of his father, a Lantier.[4] She had stood as godmother to him, and when he was six she had taken him in to live with her, his mother and father having disappeared and run off to Paris. Jacques remained at Plassans and later attended classes at the local Technical College. He had always been especially grateful to Aunt Phasie. If he had managed to get on in life, he said, it was entirely thanks to her. He had spent two years with the Paris–Orléans company,[5] before becoming a top-link driver for the Western Railway, which was when he discovered that his godmother was remarried, to a level-crossing keeper by the name of Misard, and was now living in the middle of nowhere at La Croix-de-Maufras, along with her two daughters by her first marriage. Although she was barely forty-five, Aunt Phasie, once such a fine-looking woman, tall and strong, now looked sixty. She had grown pitifully thin, there was no colour in her face and she shook continuously.

She was overjoyed to see him.

'Jacques,' she cried. 'My own, dear Jacques! What a lovely surprise!'

He kissed her on both cheeks and told her that he had just been given two days' unexpected holiday; the engine that he drove, *La Lison*,[6] had broken a coupling-rod as the train was coming into Le Havre that morning. It was going to take at least twenty-four hours to repair, and he wouldn't
44 be able to start work again until the following evening, when he was due to drive the 6.40 express. He had thought it would be nice to come and see her. He was able to stay the night, as the train back didn't leave Barentin until seven twenty-six the next morning. He held her poor, shrunken hands in his and told her how worried he had been by her last letter.

'Yes, dear,' she said. 'I'm not well. I'm not well at all. How good of you to realize I wanted to see you! I know how busy you must be and I didn't dare ask you to come. But here you are! I'm frightened, Jacques. I'm really frightened.'

She paused and looked anxiously out of the window. In the fading light they could see her husband, Misard, standing inside a section box[7] on the other side of the railway track, one of those little wooden cabins situated every four or five kilometres along the line and connected by telegraph to make sure it is safe to receive the next train. When his wife, and later Flore, had been given the job of looking after the level-crossing, he had been appointed as section operator.

She shuddered and lowered her voice, as if she thought he might hear her.

'Jacques,' she whispered, 'he's trying to poison me!'

Jacques started in surprise. He turned towards the window. As he did so, the lustre once again went from his eyes; once again they became misty, pale and strangely disturbed.

'Oh, Aunt Phasie, how can you think that?' he murmured. 'He looks so frail and harmless.'

A train for Le Havre had just gone by, and Misard had emerged from his cabin to close the section behind it. Jacques watched him as he pulled back the lever and set the signal at red. He was a puny little man, with very little hair and a small straggly beard that was going grey; his face looked pinched and starved. He spoke very little, kept himself to himself, never lost his temper and was obsequiously polite to his superiors. He had gone back into his cabin to record the time of the train in his time-keeping book and to push the two buttons on the transmitter, one to pass the train on to the next section along the line and the other to open the line to the section which the train had just left.

'You don't know him,' Aunt Phasie continued. 'He's putting something horrible in my food; I swear he is. I used to know how to stand up for myself. At one time, I could have made mincemeat of him, and now it's him, that weakling, that scrap of nothing, that's making mincemeat of me!'

She poured out all her fears and hidden resentment, delighted at last to have someone she could confide in. Whatever had possessed her to get married again to a pathetic creature like him, with not a penny to his name and stingy as they come, and she five years older, with two daughters already, one six years old and one eight? It was ten years now since she had tied the knot, and not a minute had gone by when she didn't regret it. Her life was a misery, stuck up there in the north, where it was perpetually cold, miles from anywhere, chilled to the bone, bored stiff, with no one to talk to, and not a neighbour within walking distance.

Misard had been a plate-layer when she first met him, but now all he earned was a meagre twelve hundred francs as a section operator. She used to be paid fifty francs for looking after the level-crossing when she first got the job, but Flore had taken that over now. That was how it was and that was how it was going to remain. It was hopeless. All she knew for certain was that she was going to spend the rest of her days and die in this godforsaken hole, with not a living soul to comfort her. What she didn't tell him 46 about were the good times she had had, the occasions, before she became ill, when her husband was away working as a plate-layer and she had stayed at home on her own with her daughters, to look after the level-crossing. In those days her good looks were known to everyone who worked on the railway from Rouen to Le Havre, and all the permanent way inspectors made a point of calling at the level-crossing to see her. She even had men competing for her attention – two foremen plate-layers from different gangs who kept coming back to inspect the crossing, to make sure that everything was in proper working order. Her husband didn't seem to bother; he was always very pleasant to anyone who called, made himself scarce and came and went without noticing a thing. But these excitements were a thing of the past. All she did now was sit on her own for weeks and months on end, feeling herself getting weaker and weaker by the hour.

'He's after me,' she said. 'And he'll finish me off, even if he is only a midget.'

Suddenly a bell rang. She looked through the window with the same anxious look as before. It was the next section box down the line sending on a train for Paris; the needle on the section indicator in front of the window showed the direction in which it was travelling. Misard stopped the bell, came out of his cabin and gave two blasts on his horn to warn of the approaching train. Thereupon, Flore walked over to the gate, closed it and assumed her position, raising the flag in its leather holster high in the air. The train, an express, was hidden from view by a bend in the line, but it could be heard getting louder and louder as it came rumbling towards them. It went past like a clap of thunder, making the house shake, almost blowing it away in a mighty rush of wind. As soon as it had gone, Flore went back to her vegetables. Misard closed the up line after the train, and walked over to open the down line again, by changing the signal from red. A further ring on the bell and the movement of the other needle on his section indicator told him that the train which had gone by five minutes earlier had now cleared the next section. He returned to his cabin, telegraphed the two other section boxes, noted down the time of the train and waited. It was the same routine day in day out, all day long, never moving from his cabin, eating his meals there, not even bothering to read a newspaper, and apparently with never so much as a thought passing through his empty head.

Jacques, who used to pull his godmother's leg about the many inspectors whose hearts she had broken, couldn't help smiling.

'Perhaps he's jealous,' he said.

Phasie shrugged her shoulders as if she felt sorry for him, but she couldn't prevent a mischievous little twinkle suddenly appearing in her poor, lifeless eyes.

'Him, jealous!' she said. 'He doesn't know the meaning

of the word! So long as he wasn't out of pocket, he couldn't care a fig what I got up to.'

Again she started to shake.

'That side of things never bothered him,' she said. 'All he cares about is money. What's really upset him is that I won't give him the thousand francs that Father left me last year. It's brought bad luck, just like he said it would. It's made me ill. I've been ill ever since. Ever since then.'

Jacques sensed what she was trying to tell him, but assumed it was her illness that made her entertain such dark thoughts. He attempted to reassure her. But she kept shaking her head and would not be persuaded otherwise. Eventually Jacques said, 'Look, there's a simple answer. If you want him to stop bothering you, give him the money.'

With an extraordinary effort she dragged herself to her feet, suddenly transformed, exclaiming furiously:

'Give him my money! Never! I'd rather die! I've hidden it! No one will ever find it! Never! Not even if they turn the house upside down! I tell you, he's been looking everywhere, hoping to lay his greedy hands on it! I've heard him in the night, tapping on the walls. Well, he can go on looking for all he's worth. It makes me laugh to see him poking around all over the house. We shall see who dies first, him or me! I'm careful now. I don't eat a thing if he's been anywhere near it. Even if I was the first to die, he still wouldn't get the money. I'd rather see it buried.'

She fell back on to her chair, exhausted. The sound of Misard's horn came in through the window. He was standing at the door of his cabin, setting the signal for a train to Le Havre. Despite her determination not to give in to him over the legacy, she was secretly frightened of him, and her fear was growing, just as a giant fears the bite of a tiny insect. The rumble of the approaching train could be heard in the distance, a stopping train that had left Paris at twelve forty-five that afternoon. They heard it emerge from the tunnel, the bark of its exhaust getting suddenly louder as it ran out into the open country. It came thundering past them, its wheels pounding on the track, its long string of carriages whisked along behind it like an unstoppable hurricane.

Jacques watched as the line of little square windows rushed by, each with the shape of a passenger outlined in it. In an attempt to take Phasie's mind off her gloomy thoughts, he said jokingly, 'Aunt, you grumble about never seeing anyone from one week to the next, but look at all those people!'

At first she didn't understand him.

'What people?' she asked him, puzzled. 'Oh, you mean the people in the train! A fat lot of good they are! I don't know them from Adam, and you can't stop and have a chat with them!'

Jacques laughed.

'But, Aunt Phasie, you know me,' he said, 'and I go past nearly every day.'

'Oh, I know you,' she answered. 'And I know the time of your train. I look out for you, driving the engine. But you go so fast! Yesterday you gave me a little wave, like this, but I didn't even have time to wave back! That's no way of getting to know people.'

The thought of all the people that went rushing past on the trains, backwards and forwards, day after day, while she sat there on her own in the silence of her room, left her wondering. She looked out at the railway line. It was almost dark. When she was fit and well and could move about, standing at the crossing, holding her flag, she never thought about things like this. But now, having to spend days on end tied to her chair, with nothing else to think about but how to cope with her husband's murderous schemes, she found all manner of vague, half-formed notions floating around inside her head. It

was strange: here was she, living in a wilderness, miles from anywhere, with no one to talk to, when day and night an endless stream of men and women came rushing past her front door in trains that came and went like thunder, nearly shaking the house down, and vanishing as quickly as they had come. It wasn't just French people either; there were people from everywhere, foreigners, people from the other side of the world. No one was content to stay at home these days; all the peoples of the world, so it was said, would soon be one big family. Such was progress! All men would be brothers, moving as one towards the Promised Land! She tried to put a figure on them, working out a rough estimate of passengers per carriage, but there were so many that she lost count. There were one or two faces she thought she recognized – a gentleman with a white beard, an Englishman perhaps, who made the same jour-
50 ney to Paris every week, and a little lady with brown hair who travelled regularly on Wednesdays and Saturdays. But they came and went in a flash; she could never be sure she had actually seen them. The faces were an indistinct blur, all merging into each other and all ending up looking alike. The stream flowed on, leaving nothing behind. What saddened her most was the thought that all these people, rushing constantly past her window, flaunting their wealth and finery and always in a hurry to be somewhere else, were totally unaware that she was there and that her life was at risk. Even if one night her husband finished her off, the trains would still pass by each other a few feet from her corpse without anyone even suspecting that a murder had been committed in this isolated house.

Phasie sat gazing at the window. It was impossible to explain to Jacques precisely what she was thinking. She hardly understood it herself. Then, as if her thoughts had suddenly crystallized, she said, 'It's a fine invention; there's no denying it. It gets people about quickly, it broadens the mind . . . But a beast will always be a beast. You can go on inventing better machines till the cows come home. It won't change a thing. In the end we're at the mercy of beasts.'

Jacques nodded his agreement. For the last minute or two he had been watching Flore, who was opening the crossing-gate for a wagon from the quarry carrying two huge blocks of stone. The road was only ever used by wagons from the quarries at Brécourt, so at night the gate was kept locked, and it was very seldom that Flore was disturbed. Jacques watched her as she chatted with the short, dark-skinned man who drove the wagon.

'Is Cabuche ill?' he asked Phasie. 'That's his cousin Louis driving the horses, isn't it? Poor old Cabuche! Do you see much of him these days?'

She raised her hands without answering and let out a long sigh. The previous autumn something terrible had happened, and it had done nothing to improve her health. Her younger daughter, Louisette, who was working as a maid for Madame Bonnehon at Doinville, had run away in the middle of the night. She had been badly knocked about and was scared out of her wits. She ran for help to her sweetheart Cabuche, in his shack in the forest, but when she got there she died. There were rumours that she had been maltreated by Grandmorin, but nobody dared say anything publicly. Aunt Phasie knew what had happened, but she couldn't bring herself to repeat it.[8] All she eventually said was: 'No, Cabuche doesn't come here any more. He keeps himself to himself. Poor Louisette! She was so pretty, so innocent. She was a dear! She really loved me! She would have looked after me! Flore does her best, of course; I can't complain. But there's something crazy about her; she's got a will of her own. She disappears for hours on end. Sometimes I hardly dare speak to her. And she has such tantrums! It's sad. Very sad.'

Jacques was watching the quarry wagon as it moved over

the crossing. The wheels had become stuck between the tracks. The driver was cracking his whip, and Flore was shouting at the top of her voice, trying to urge on the horses.

'Goodness me,' said Jacques, 'I hope a train doesn't come; there'd be a nasty accident!'

'Oh, you needn't worry,' said Aunt Phasie. 'Flore may be a bit weird sometimes, but she knows how to do her job. She keeps her eyes open. We haven't had an accident for five years, thank God. Before we came here, there was a man who was cut in two. All we've had is a cow that nearly caused a derailment. Poor thing; they found its body here, and its head down there, by the tunnel. No, you can sleep easy when Flore's around.'

The wagon had got across and they could hear the wheels bumping in the ruts as it lumbered off down the
52 road.

'Tell me, Jacques,' said Aunt Phasie, when the wagon had disappeared, 'are you feeling all right these days?'

She had an obsessive interest in people's health: not only her own, but everyone else's too.

'Do you remember those funny turns you used to have when you were at home?' she continued. 'The doctor couldn't work them out.'

A worried look crept into his eyes.

'I feel fine,' he said.

'Are you sure you're telling me the truth?' she said. 'Have they stopped? You used to get a splitting headache behind your ears, and sudden temperatures, and bouts of depression. You'd go and hide yourself away, like a frightened animal.'

Jacques was becoming more and more disturbed. He interrupted her.

'Listen, Aunt,' he said tersely, 'I'm fine. There's nothing wrong with me. Nothing at all!'

'I'm glad to hear it,' she said. 'Anyway, if you were ill it wouldn't make me any better, would it? Besides, you should be well at your age! Ah, good health, what could be better? It really was kind of you to come and see me when you could have gone and enjoyed yourself somewhere else. You can have some supper and you can sleep upstairs in the attic, in the room next to Flore's.'

Once again she was interrupted by the sound of Misard's horn. It was now dark outside, and as they looked through the window they could dimly make out the shape of her husband talking to someone else. It had just struck six, and he was handing over to the night man who was replacing him. At last he was relieved of duty, after a twelve-hour stint cooped up in his cabin, sitting on a little stool in front of a table underneath the instrument panel, with a stove that got so hot that for most of the time he had to leave the door wide open.

'Here he comes; he's finished work,' murmured Aunt Phasie, all her fears returning. The train that had just been signalled was approaching, a long, heavy train, getting louder and louder. Aunt Phasie was so weak that Jacques had to lean forward so that she could hear him. It upset him to see the pitiful state she was in; he wished there was something he could do to comfort her.

'Listen,' he said, 'if he really is up to something, it might make him think twice if he knew that he had me to reckon with. Why not let me look after your money for you?'

Once again she protested vehemently.

'That thousand francs is mine!' she insisted. 'I wouldn't give it to you any more than I'd give it to him! I tell you I'd sooner die.'

Just then the train went past, like a violent storm sweeping all before it. The house shook, buffeted by a great gust of wind. The train was heading for Le Havre and it was packed; there was to be a grand celebration on the

following day, Sunday, for the launching of a new ship. Even though it was moving so fast, through the lighted carriage windows they caught sight of compartments crammed with passengers, rows of heads all in a line, tightly packed together, each with its own face on it. They rushed by, one after another, and disappeared. So many people! The same crowd endlessly streaming past their window, with the wheels of the carriages drumming in their ears, locomotives blowing their whistles, telegraphs buzzing and bells ringing! The railway was like a giant creature, a colossus that lay sprawled across the country, its head in Paris, its backbone stretching the length of the main line, its arms and legs spreading out sideways along the branch lines and its hands and feet at Le Havre and at other towns it found its way to. On and on it went, soulless, triumphant, striding towards the future, straight as a die,
54 wilfully disregarding whatever shreds of humanity survived on either side of it, hidden from view yet still clinging to their own hardy inner life,[9] their ceaseless round of passion and crime.

It was Flore who came in first. She lit the lamp, a small paraffin lamp without a shade, and then laid the table. She said nothing. She hardly looked at Jacques, who stood with his back to her at the window. She had left some cabbage soup on the stove to keep it hot and was beginning to serve it when Misard walked in. He didn't seem in the least surprised to find Jacques there. Perhaps he had seen him arrive, but he didn't ask him what brought him there and he appeared totally indifferent towards him; he gave him a quick handshake, a cursory greeting and that was all. It was left to Jacques to explain, a second time, how his engine had broken a coupling-rod and how he thought he might come and say hello to his godmother and spend the night there. Misard slowly nodded his head as he listened, as much as to say that that was all right by him. Everyone sat down to eat. They ate slowly, and for a while no one spoke. Phasie, who since the morning hadn't taken her eyes off the pot of soup that had been simmering on the stove, accepted a bowlful. But when her husband got up from the table to give her her iron water from a jug in which some nails had been left to soak, which Flore had forgotten to do, she refused to take it. Misard, unobtrusive, frail and with a nasty little cough, didn't seem to notice the anxious way she watched his every movement. When she asked for some salt, as there wasn't any on the table, he told her that she shouldn't put so much salt on her food and that that was what was making her ill. He got up again to fetch some and brought her a little pinch on a spoon. She took it without hesitation, declaring that salt was a great purifier. They talked about the exceptionally mild weather they had been having for the last few days, and about a derailment at Maromme. Jacques was coming to 55 the conclusion that his godmother must be having waking nightmares; he really couldn't see anything odd about this dreamy-eyed, mild-mannered little man. They sat talking for more than an hour. Twice the night man had sounded his horn, and Flore had left the room for a moment or two. The trains went by, shaking the glasses on the table, but nobody seemed to notice.

When the horn sounded a third time, Flore, who had just cleared everything away, went out, leaving her mother and the two men sitting at the table with a bottle of apple brandy. The three of them sat there for another half hour. Then Misard, who for the last few minutes had been looking intently into one of the corners of the room, picked up his cap and with a simple 'goodnight' walked out. He went poaching in the streams near by, where there were superb eels, and he never went to bed before he had been to check his ground-lines.

Once he had gone, Phasie looked at Jacques.

'What do you make of that?' she said. 'Did you see the way he was looking into that corner? He was thinking I might have hidden my money behind the butter pot. I know him. You mark my words! Tonight he'll move it to see if it's there.'

She had broken out into a sweat and was shaking from head to toe.

'See, it's happening again! He's drugged my food. I've got a bitter taste in my mouth as if I'd swallowed a lot of old pennies. But I swear I haven't taken anything from him. It's enough to make you throw yourself in the river! I can't take any more tonight. I'd better get to bed. I'll say goodbye to you now. If you're leaving at seven twenty-six it'll be too early for me. Come and see me again, won't you? Let's hope I'm still here.'

Jacques had to help her into the bedroom, where she lay down and went to sleep, exhausted. Left alone, he wondered whether he too shouldn't go up to the attic and get some sleep. But it was still only ten to eight. Sleep could come later; he decided he would take a walk outside. The little paraffin lamp was left burning on the table, and the empty house slept quietly, shaken from time to time by the thunder of a passing train.

Once outside, Jacques was surprised to discover how soft the night air felt. Perhaps there was more rain on the way. A milky white cloud had spread itself across the entire sky, and the full moon, hidden behind it out of sight, filled the heavens with a reddish glow. He could see the countryside clearly; the nearby fields, the hills and the trees stood out black in the uniformly pale light of the moon, no brighter than a night-light. He wandered round the little vegetable garden and then thought he would go for a walk towards Doinville, as the road was less steep in that direction. He was about to set off when he caught sight of the house standing on its own on the other side of the railway track. He opened the wicket gate beside the level-crossing, the main gate being already shut for the night, and crossed the railway line. The house was one he recognized; he had looked at it from the lurching footplate of his locomotive every time he drove the train past. For some reason it haunted him; he had a vague notion that it was somehow connected with his own life. He had the same feelings each time – initially a kind of fear that it might no longer be there, and then a strange uneasiness when he discovered that it still was. Never had he seen either the doors or the windows open. The only thing he had managed to find out about it was that it belonged to President Grandmorin. He was seized by an irresistible desire to take a closer look, to see what he might discover.

For some time he stood in the road, facing the railings. He then took a few paces back and stood on tiptoe to try to get a better view. Where the railway cut through the garden, it had left only a narrow strip of ground with a wall round it in front of the steps to the main door. At the back of the house, however, there was a larger piece of ground, surrounded by a simple hedge. The whole place had a dismal, forsaken appearance, standing there abandoned, in the misty red glow from the night sky. He felt a shiver run through him and he was about to turn away when he noticed a gap in the hedge. Telling himself that he had nothing to fear, he stepped through. He felt his heart beating. Suddenly, as he came round a small, tumbledown greenhouse, he saw a shadowy figure crouching by the door. He stopped quickly.

'What are you doing here?' he exclaimed with astonishment.

It was Flore.

'You can see what I'm doing,' she said, trying to make her voice sound calm, for his appearance had taken her by surprise. 'I'm helping myself to this twine. It's all been left here to rot; it's no use to anyone. I use it in the garden, so I come and take what I want.'

She had a big pair of scissors in her hand and was sitting on the ground, untangling lengths of twine and cutting it when it got caught in a knot.

'Doesn't the owner come here any more?' asked Jacques. She laughed.

'The President's hardly likely to show his face round here,' she said, 'after what happened to Louisette! So I'm taking his twine.'

Jacques was silent for a while, recalling the sad tale of Louisette's death. He frowned.

'Do you believe what Louisette said?' he asked. 'That Grandmorin tried to rape her, and she got hurt when it turned nasty?'

Flore suddenly became angry.

58   'Louisette never lied,' she protested. 'Nor Cabuche either! Cabuche is my friend.'

'I bet he's your lover, too,' said Jacques.

'You'd be scraping the barrel if you had him as a lover,' she said. 'He's my friend. I haven't got any lovers and I don't want any.'

She raised her head defiantly. Her thick blonde hair fell down over her face. Her lithe, muscular body exuded a sense of wild, wilful independence. She had acquired something of a reputation locally. There were stories of her pulling a farm wagon single-handed from the path of an oncoming train and stopping a runaway goods wagon as it careered out of control down the Barentin incline towards an approaching express. These astonishing feats of strength made her much sought after by the young men in the neighbourhood, all the more so because they thought at first she would be an easy catch, always wandering off into the fields as soon as she had finished work and finding some hidden spot where she could just lie on the ground gazing quietly into the sky undisturbed. But the first who were rash enough to approach her never wished to repeat the experience. She used to spend hours bathing in a nearby stream, naked. A group of lads, the same age as her, got together to go to watch her. Without even bothering to get dressed, she had grabbed hold of one of them and knocked him nearly senseless. No one tried to spy on her again. There was an even stranger story about her treatment of a signalman at the junction for Dieppe at the other end of the tunnel, a man called Ozil, a perfectly ordinary sort of chap, about thirty years old, whom she seemed to fancy, or so it was said. One night, thinking she wanted to make love, he had put his hands on her, and she had nearly beaten him to death with a stick. She held men in utter contempt, like an Amazon. Most people took this as proof that she was a bit wrong in the head.

Jacques listened with amusement to her protestations that she had no time for lovers.

'What about Ozil?' he asked. 'Is the wedding off? I heard you used to run through the tunnel every day to see him.'

She shrugged her shoulders.

'Wedding, my foot!' she said. 'I run through the tunnel because I like it! Two and a half kilometres in the dark! If you didn't watch out you'd get cut to pieces by a train! You should hear the noise they make inside! Ozil was starting to get on my nerves. He's not the man for me.'

'Are you looking for somebody else, then?' Jacques ventured.

She hesitated.

'No,' she said. 'Certainly not.'

She started to laugh. She had become suddenly embarrassed and started untying a particularly awkward knot.

'What about you?' she asked without looking up, as if absorbed in her task, 'Have you got a girlfriend?'

Jacques became more serious. He looked away, staring unsteadily into the night.

'No,' he said tersely.

'So it's true what they say, then,' she continued. 'That you can't stand women. Come on, Jacques, I've known you long enough; you haven't got a kind word to say for us. What have we done to upset you?'

He made no answer. She pondered a moment, put down the knot that she was trying to untie and looked at him.

'Is it true that the only thing you're in love with is your locomotive?' she asked him. 'Everybody makes jokes about it. They say you're always polishing it and making it look shiny. They say it's the only thing you really care about. I'm only telling you, Jacques, because I'm your friend.'

He looked at her as she sat in front of him, in the pale, misty light from the moon. He remembered when she was
60 a little girl, boisterous and headstrong even then, flinging her arms round his neck the minute he came home and clinging to him in childish glee. Later they had gone their separate ways. Each time he met her again he noticed how much she had grown. Yet she would still fling her arms round him as before and gaze at him lovingly with her big bright eyes. Jacques found it more and more embarrassing. And now, she was a fully grown woman, handsome, desirable. She had loved him, he imagined, from the earliest days of her childhood. His heart began to beat quickly. He suddenly felt that he was the one she had been waiting for. The blood rushed to his head; he felt that it would burst. In the confusion that came over him, his first impulse was to flee. Desire had always driven him mad. He saw red.

'Sit beside me, Jacques,' she said.

He remained standing where he was, not knowing what to do. Suddenly his legs felt very tired. Then, yielding to the insistent call of his desire, he dropped to the ground beside her on the pile of twine. He could not speak; his throat was dry. Flore, normally so distant, so taciturn, chatted away ten to the dozen, till her head was in a whirl.

'Mother made a mistake marrying Misard,' she said. 'It'll do her no good . . . I couldn't care less . . . I've got enough on my plate. Whenever I try to help she tells me to mind my own business . . . So she can sort it out herself. I keep out of the house. I think about all the things I'm going to do. I saw you go past on your train this morning. I was sitting over there in those bushes, but you never look. I'll tell you what I'm going to do. Not now. Another day perhaps . . . when we're best friends.'

She had dropped her scissors. Still without speaking, Jacques took her two hands in his. She thrilled to his touch. But the minute he raised her hands to his burning lips, she recoiled from him in horror, like an untouched virgin. In an instant she was again the Amazon, the despiser of men, defiant, hostile, spurning his advance.

'Leave me alone,' she said. 'I don't want to. Let's just sit quietly . . . That's all you men ever think of! You wouldn't believe what Louisette told me the day she died at Cabuche's! Not that it was anything I didn't know already. I've seen the President up to his dirty tricks with girls. He used to bring them here. There's one that nobody knows about. He married her off.'

Jacques was no longer listening to her; her words fell on deaf ears. He seized her in a violent embrace and fastened his lips to hers. She gave a small cry, a moan, so deep, so tender, so clearly betraying the long-concealed love she bore him. Yet still she fought against him, blindly, instinctively refusing to yield. She desired him, yet she resisted him. She needed him to conquer her. They did not speak. They remained locked together, breast to breast, each trying desperately to overpower the other. It appeared briefly that she might be the stronger. He was beginning to weaken, and she had almost managed to pin him down beneath her when he grabbed her by the throat. He tore open her bodice, exposing her breasts, hard and swollen from the struggle, milky white in the pale light of the moon. She fell to the ground on her back and surrendered herself to him, defeated.

But he did not take her. He drew back, gasping for breath, looking at her. He seemed to be possessed; some wild impulse made him look around him for a weapon, a stone, anything that he might use to kill her. His eyes fell upon the scissors glinting in the moonlight among the pieces of twine that she had been cutting. He grabbed them and was on the point of plunging them into her body between the two rose-tipped white breasts when a chill ran through him and his mind suddenly became clear. He threw the scissors to the ground and fled from her, horrified. Flore lay with her eyes closed, thinking that he had rejected her because she had resisted him.

62

Jacques ran off into the night. He followed a path which led up a hill and then back down into a narrow dell, running as fast as he could. His feet sent stones clattering noisily down the path in front of him. He swerved off to the left into the bushes and then went right again, coming out on to a bare hilltop. He rushed down the slope and collided with the railway fence at the bottom. A train was approaching, snorting and belching out sparks; at first he didn't realize what it was and he was terrified. Then he remembered. Ah, yes, he thought, all those people, the never-ending stream; and here was he, alone, in torment! He got to his feet and started running again, up a hill and down the other side. Whichever way he went, he found himself back at the railway line, sometimes deep in a cutting that opened up before him like a bottomless chasm, sometimes high on an embankment that shut out the horizon like an enormous barricade. The deserted countryside with its endless succession of hills was like a maze with no way out; he was lost in a dreary wasteland of barren fields, from which his distracted mind could find no escape. He had been walking for what seemed like ages over one hill after another when he noticed in front of him a round opening: the black mouth of the tunnel. A train was disappearing into it with a great roaring and hissing of steam, making the ground shake behind it as it vanished into the bowels of the earth.

His legs would carry him no further. He collapsed beside the railway line and wept convulsively, sprawled on his stomach, his face buried in the grass. He could not believe it. The terrible affliction, which he had thought was cured, had returned. He had wanted to kill her. He had wanted to kill this girl. Kill a woman! Kill a woman! The words had sounded in his ears since his early adolescence with the maddening, feverish insistence of unsated desire. Whereas other boys coming to puberty dreamed of pos- 63 sessing a woman, the only thing that had excited him was the thought of killing one. It was pointless trying to deceive himself. As soon as he had seen her naked, he had taken the scissors to plant them into her flesh, into the warm, white flesh of her breast, not simply because she had resisted him, but because he had wanted to do it. Indeed, he had wanted to do it so badly that, had he not clung with both hands to the tufts of grass beneath him, he might even then have run back and slit her throat. Good God! To think that it was Flore! The little girl he had watched growing up! That wild, unruly little girl! To think it was only now that he had discovered how much she loved him! He clenched his fists and dug his fingers into the earth, sobbing uncontrollably, choking with despair.

Eventually he managed to calm himself. If only he could understand why this should be. What was so different about him, compared with others? Even when he was a boy, in Plassans, he had often asked himself the same question. His mother, Gervaise, it is true, had had him when she was very young, at fifteen and a half. What is more, he was her second child; she was barely fourteen years old when she had given birth to her first, Claude. But neither of his two brothers, Claude or Étienne, who had been born later, seemed to suffer any ill effects from having a mother who was so young and a father who, like her, was little more than a child, the handsome young Lantier, the ne'er-do-well who was to cause Gervaise so much unhappiness. Perhaps his brothers had had problems they weren't prepared to admit to, the elder especially, who wore himself out trying to become a painter. It had become an obsession with him; people said he was besotted with his own genius. It couldn't really be called a normal family. So many of them had some flaw, and he often thought he must have inherited this family flaw himself.[10] Not that his health was poor; it was the anxiety and the shame he felt about his attacks that had made him lose weight when he was younger. But there were times when his mind seemed to be suddenly tipped off balance, when he felt as if there were breaches or holes in him, through which his identity evaporated, and he was surrounded by a thick fog that prevented him from seeing things clearly. At such times his body took on a life of its own; he became the slave of the beast within. And yet he did not drink, not even a tiny sip of brandy, knowing full well that the least drop of alcohol sent him crazy. He had become convinced that he was paying the penalty for all the drinkers who had gone before him, fathers and grandfathers, whole generations of drunkards, whose tainted blood he had inherited. It was a poison slowly eating away inside him, unleashing savage instincts, like a wolf lurking in the depths of the forest waiting to kill.

Such were the thoughts that ran through his mind. He raised himself on to one elbow and gazed into the dark mouth of the tunnel. A new wave of sobbing shook his frame, and he sank down again, rolling his head from side to side on the ground and crying out in anguish. That little girl! He had wanted to kill her! The thought kept returning, sharp and incisive, as if the scissors were piercing his own flesh. He could find no solace to dispel his tormented fears; he had wanted to kill her, and would kill her still if she were there now with her blouse ripped open and her breasts laid bare. He recalled the first time this malady had struck. He was barely sixteen. He was out playing with a girl, the daughter of one of his relatives, two years younger than him. She had fallen down, showing her legs, and he had tried to molest her. The following year, he remembered, he had sharpened a knife so as to stab another girl in the neck, a fair-haired girl who used to walk past his house every morning. She had a pink, fleshy neck, with a little brown birthmark underneath one ear; he had 65 decided that that was where the knife would go in. There had been others, many others, a nightmare succession of women who, by the mere fact of being near him, had made him suddenly want to kill them – women he had brushed past in the street, women he simply happened to find himself next to. He remembered once sitting beside a young newlywed at the theatre. She had a very loud laugh, and he had had to rush out in the middle of the performance to prevent himself from attacking her. None of these women were known to him personally, so what could he possibly have against them? Each time it happened it came as a flash of blind rage, an insatiable desire to exact revenge for offences done to him in the distant past, offences which no longer found room in his conscious memory. Could it really come from so far back, from the accumulated ill that women had inflicted upon the entire race of men? Was this the swollen legacy of a grudge that had passed from man to man since the first infidelity in the dark recesses of some primeval cave?[11] When the frenzy came upon him, his one desire was to attack, to conquer and to dominate a woman. It was a perverse wish to sling her over his back, dead, as if she were his own personal trophy, his alone and his for ever. He felt that his head would burst. He had no answer to all these questions. He knew nothing. His brain was numb. There seemed no way out for him. He was a man driven to acts beyond his control, and whose cause was beyond his understanding.

Another train came past, its headlamps ablaze, and plunged into the tunnel; from within its dark interior came a rumble like thunder that echoed and re-echoed before finally dying away. Almost as if he feared that this anonymous crowd rushing past absorbed in their own affairs might have heard him, Jacques sat up, choked back his tears and tried to look as if nothing had happened. How often in the past, after one of his fits, had the slightest sound made him start, guiltily, like someone caught in the act! The only times he felt relaxed, happy and at ease with the world were when he was driving his locomotive. When he was being hurtled along at full speed, with his ears ringing from the din of the wheels, with his hand on the regulator and his eyes fixed on the line ahead watching out for signals, his mind was at rest, and he filled his lungs with the fresh, clean air that whistled past him. This was why he loved his locomotive as he did; it was like a mistress, soothing him and bringing him only happiness. When he left the Technical College, he had chosen to be an engine driver, despite being highly intelligent, because it allowed him to be on his own, and it took his mind off other things; this was his one ambition. He had become a top-link driver within four years, which earned him 2,800 francs. He also received bonuses for firing and greasing the locomotive, which brought his earnings to over 4,000 francs. He had no wish to earn more. Most of his fellow drivers, in the class-two and class-three grades,[12] fitters taken on as apprentices and trained by the company, married an ordinary sort of woman doing a menial job somewhere behind the scenes, the sort of woman you might see occasionally when, for instance, she came to deliver a passenger's lunch basket just before a train was due to leave. The more ambitious of his colleagues, especially those who had been to college, preferred to wait until they had become shed foremen before getting married, in the hope that they might be able to find someone a bit better, a woman with class! But Jacques kept away from women altogether. He wasn't interested in them. He knew he could never marry. The only future for him lay in driving his locomotive, alone, for mile upon mile, endlessly. Small wonder that his superiors held him up as an example to all the others; he didn't drink and he didn't chase women. In fact his excesses of good conduct had become something of a joke amongst his more boisterous companions. The only thing they found a little disturbing was when he was in one of his gloomy moods, not speaking, walking round with a vacant expression on his face and looking washed out. He rented a little room in the Rue Cardinet which looked out on to the Batignolles engine shed, where his locomotive was stationed. Every minute of his free time, hour after hour, he remembered, he had spent in this room, like a monk immured in his cell, lying on his stomach, attempting to drown his wayward desires in sleep!

Jacques tried to drag himself to his feet. What was he doing sitting outside on the grass on a cold misty night in the middle of winter? The countryside lay in darkness. The only light came from the sky. A fine mist was spread across it like a vast dome of frosted glass, suffused by a pale yellow glow from the moon which lay hidden from view behind it. The black horizon lay stretched out as silent and still as a corpse. It must be nearly nine o'clock, he thought to himself. The best thing to do would be to go back to the house and get some sleep. As if in a daze, he saw himself opening the door, climbing the stairs to the attic and lying down on the straw next to Flore's bedroom with only a wooden dividing wall between them. She would be there. He would hear her breathing. He even knew that she always slept with the door open and that nothing could prevent him from walking into her room. Once more he began to shake violently. He saw her lying there undressed, her body spread out, warm from sleep, defenceless. Weeping uncontrollably, he fell back to the ground. He had wanted to kill her! He had wanted to kill her! He was gasping for breath. He shuddered at the thought that within minutes from now, if he went back to 68 the house, he would go and kill her in her bed. Not having a weapon wouldn't prevent him. Try as he might to bury his head in his hands and make it all go away, he knew that the male within him, no matter how hard he resisted, would push open the door and strangle her in her bed, goaded by its born instinct to rape, by its overwhelming need to avenge the wrong inflicted on it since the world began. No, he must not go back to the house. He must stay out there tramping the fields! He leaped to his feet and began to run.

For half an hour he chased frantically through the darkened countryside, fleeing before the horrors in his mind, like the quarry pursued by a snarling pack of hounds. He ran up hills and down steep-sided ravines, never stopping. He waded two streams which crossed his path, waist-deep in water. His way was barred by a clump of trees. How would he get through? His one thought was to keep moving forward in a straight line, on and on, to escape from himself, to escape from the beast, from the creature that dwelled within him. But to no avail; the creature ran as fast as he did; he carried it with him wherever he went. For the last seven months he had thought he had got rid of it; things had begun to return to normal. But now it was about to start again; his life would once more become a constant battle with himself, lest the beast should leap out at the first woman who happened to come near him. Fortunately, the vast stillness of the countryside, the great emptiness that surrounded him brought some solace to his troubled thoughts; he found himself imagining a life as silent and empty as this desolate landscape, through which he might walk for ever, without meeting a soul. He must have come round in a big circle without realizing it, scrambling about in the dense undergrowth above the tunnel; he now found himself back beside the railway line, on the other side of the track. He stepped back, frightened that someone might walk by and see him. He took a path **69** that led round a small hill, but lost his way. Eventually he found himself back beside the railway fence at the entrance to the tunnel, directly opposite the field in which he had lain sobbing not long before. He could go no further and remained there, unable to move. Suddenly, from within the bowels of the earth, he heard the rumble of an approaching train, faintly at first but getting louder and louder every second. It was the express for Le Havre. It had left Paris at six thirty and it passed here at nine twenty-five. It was the train that Jacques himself drove every other day.

He saw the black mouth of the tunnel light up, like the open door of a blazing furnace. The train shot out of the tunnel with a deafening roar, the dazzling beam from the big round eye of the headlamp cutting through the landscape and lighting up the rails ahead like twin strips of flame. The locomotive came and went like a flash of lightning, followed by a long string of carriages, a procession of little square windows, brightly lit, and compartments full of passengers, all rushing past at such speed that it was impossible to be sure afterwards what the eye had actually seen. Even so, for one split-second through the brilliantly lit windows of a reserved compartment, Jacques distinctly saw a man holding another man down on the carriage seat and thrusting a knife into his throat. There was also another dark shape, possibly a third person, possibly some bags that had fallen off the luggage rack, pinning the struggling victim down by his legs. The train shot past him and was already disappearing in the direction of La Croix-de-Maufras. All that could be seen in the darkness was the red triangle formed by its three tail lamps.

Jacques remained fixed to the spot, gazing at the train as the noise faded into the dead stillness of the countryside. Had his eyes deceived him? Now the train had gone, he couldn't be sure. The image had come and gone in a flash; he couldn't believe he had really seen it. He couldn't recall a single detail of the appearance of the two people involved in the scene. The dark shape was probably a travelling rug that had fallen over the victim's body, but at first what he thought he had seen was a face, a delicate face with a fair complexion and long, thick hair. It was all so confused and fleeting, like something seen in a dream. For a brief moment the face came back to him; then it vanished completely. He must have imagined it. The whole thing left him feeling numb; it seemed so incredible. He concluded that his mind must be playing tricks on him after the awful shock he had just had.

Jacques walked on aimlessly for nearly another hour, trying to make sense of the confused thoughts that turned in his mind. Although he was exhausted, he was beginning to feel more composed; he felt very cold inside, and his panic had left him. Without intending to, he ended up walking back towards La Croix-de-Maufras. He found himself outside the gate-keeper's cottage, but decided that, rather than go inside, he would sleep in the little lean-to shed, built on to one of the end walls. Then he noticed a slit of light under the door. Without thinking, he pushed it open. As he stood in the doorway a strange sight greeted his eyes.

Misard was in the corner of the room. He had moved the butter pot to one side and he was on all fours, with a lighted lamp beside him on the floor. He was tapping the wall with his knuckles, looking for something. The sound of the door opening made him sit up, but otherwise he didn't appear in the least concerned.

'I was looking for some matches,' he said simply. 'I dropped them here somewhere.'

He put the butter pot back in its place.

'I came to get my lamp,' he added, 'because I saw someone lying on the track when I was coming back just now. **71** I think he must be dead.'

When Jacques first opened the door, his immediate thought was that he had caught Misard in the act of hunting for Aunt Phasie's hidden money, and the doubts he had had about his aunt's suspicions had immediately changed to certainty. However, Misard's announcement that he had discovered a body came as such a shock that the other private drama being played out in this isolated little cottage was driven straight from his mind, ousted by the recollection of the scene in the carriage, the fleeting glimpse of a man cutting someone's throat.

'A man on the track,' he said, turning pale. 'Where?'

Misard had been about to explain that he was on his way back with two eels that he had found caught on his ground-lines and that he wanted to get home as quickly as possible to hide them. But why bother telling all this to Jacques?

'It's up there,' he said, gesticulating vaguely. 'Five

hundred metres perhaps ... You need a light to see properly.'

Just then Jacques heard a noise from upstairs. He was so on edge that it made him jump out of his skin.

'Don't worry,' said Misard. 'It's only Flore.'

Jacques heard the sound of bare feet walking over the tiled floor. She must have been waiting for him to come back. The door had been left ajar, and she had come to listen.

'I'll come with you,' said Jacques. 'Are you sure he's dead?'

'That's what it looked like to me,' Misard replied. 'We'll soon find out. We'll take the lamp.'

'What do you think happened to him?' said Jacques. 'Was it an accident?'

'Probably,' said Misard. 'Some chap who's got himself run over, or maybe someone who's jumped out of a train.'

Jacques shuddered.

'Come on!' he said. 'Hurry up.'

Never had Jacques felt driven by such an all-consuming need to know what had happened. Once outside, Misard, totally unperturbed, walked along the track, swinging his lamp, which cast a little pool of light on the railway lines. Jacques ran on ahead, irritated that Misard would walk no faster. It was like a physical urge, the sort of burning desire that compels lovers to quicken their step as the hour of their appointed assignation draws near. He dreaded what he might find, yet he ran towards it, straining every muscle in his body. When he reached the spot, nearly tripping over a dark shape that lay in a heap beside the down line, he stopped short, rooted to the ground, and a shiver ran from the tips of his toes to the nape of his neck. He could see nothing clearly, and such was his frustration that he began to swear at his companion, who was still dawdling along some thirty paces behind.

'For God's sake,' he yelled, 'hurry up! If he's still alive we might be able to save him!'

Misard came ambling towards him, still in no great hurry. He held up the lamp so that he could see the body.

'He's had it,' he said.

The man, whoever it was, had probably fallen from a carriage. He had landed on his stomach, face down, no more than fifty centimetres from the track. All that could be seen of his head was a mass of white hair. His legs were spread apart. His right arm lay on the ground as though it had been torn off, whilst his left arm was pinned under his chest. He was very well dressed, wearing a large blue overcoat, a pair of stylish boots and an expensive shirt. The body bore no signs of having been run over, but his neck had bled profusely, and there were bloodstains on his shirt collar.

'He wasn't short of a penny or two,' said Misard calmly, **73** after a cursory examination of the body. 'Looks as if someone had it in for him!'

He turned towards Jacques, who was standing there open-mouthed.

'Don't touch anything,' he said. 'It's against the law. You stay here and keep an eye on him. I'll run down to Barentin and tell the stationmaster.'

He raised his lamp to look at the kilometre post.

'Good,' he said. 'Number 153, exactly!'

He placed the lamp on the ground next to the body and sauntered off down the line.

Jacques was left on his own. He stood looking at the lifeless body slumped on the ground in front of him. He could still not see it clearly; the light from the lamp was too dim. His thoughts were racing inside his head; the excitement that had made him rush headlong to the spot and the horrible fascination that now held him fixed there had resulted in the sudden, acute realization, sensed in every fibre of his body, that the man he had seen in the train, the man who was holding a knife, had dared to do the deed! He had followed his desire to its end! He had killed! If only he were not a coward! If only he could satisfy his desire! If only he could kill! For ten years he had been tortured by the desire to kill. His mind was in turmoil; he despised himself and he admired the man who had committed this murder. Above all, he felt the need to look at the body in front of him, an insatiable desire to feast his eyes on this tattered shred of human life, on the broken puppet, the limp rag that, before the knife had struck, had been a living creature. What he had merely dreamed of that man had actually done, and there was the body in front of him. If he killed, the body would be like that, there, on the ground. His heart was beating fit to burst. At the sight of this tragic corpse his craving to kill grew 74 more intense, like lust that is denied gratification. He took a step nearer, like a nervous child trying to overcome its fear. Yes! He would do it! When the time came, he would do it!

There was a sudden rumble of wheels behind him, and he leaped to one side. A train was approaching; he had been so lost in thought that he hadn't even heard it. He would have been run over; it was only the heat from the engine and the loud hiss of steam that had brought him to his senses. The train roared past him, throwing out fiery clouds of smoke. Yet more people! All on their way to Le Havre for the celebrations the following day! A child pressed its nose to one of the windows, peering out at the dark countryside. He saw faces, men's faces. A young woman lowered one of the windows and threw out a piece of paper, smeared with butter and sugar. The train with its happy crowd of revellers was already a good way off, unaware that its wheels had passed within an inch of the corpse that lay beside the track. There it was, face down, in the dim light of the lamp. Not a sound disturbed the eerie stillness of the night.

Jacques was suddenly seized by a desire to see the wound while there was no one else there. The only thing that held him back was the thought that if he moved the head it might be noticed. He had reckoned that Misard and the stationmaster wouldn't be back for another three-quarters of an hour. The minutes slipped by. Jacques thought of Misard; how pathetic he was, how slow and unbothered! But he too had the courage to kill, and to kill as coolly as you please, with poison! It must be easy to kill, then! Everybody did it! He took another step nearer. The thought of seeing the wound made his flesh tingle, as if he had been stung. He wanted to see how it had been done and where the blood had run! He wanted to see the red hole! If he replaced the head carefully, no one would know. But something else held him back – a fear that he refused to admit **75** to, the fear of blood itself. It had always been the same; whatever he had wanted to do, desire had been accompanied by fear. He still had another quarter of an hour before the others returned. He was about to touch the body when a sound beside him made him jump back.

It was Flore. She had come to look at the body, too. Accidents had always fascinated her. The minute she heard that an animal had been knocked down or that someone had been run over by a train she would come running to see. She had got dressed again to come to inspect the corpse. She took one look and, without hesitation, she bent down, raised the lamp with one hand and with the other took hold of the head and turned it over.

'Watch what you're doing,' mumbled Jacques. 'You're not supposed to touch it.'

Flore merely shrugged her shoulders. They could now see the face in the yellow lamplight. It was the face of an old man. He had a large nose, hair that had once been

blond and big blue staring eyes. Under his chin there was
a terrible, gaping wound, a deep gash cut into his neck, a
jagged furrow as if the knife had been sunk in deep and
twisted. The right side of his chest was drenched in blood.
On the left lapel of his overcoat he wore the rosette of a
Commander of the Legion of Honour; it looked like a stray
clot of blood that had fallen there.

Flore uttered a little cry of surprise.

'It's the President!' she said.

Jacques leaned forward closer to see, brushing his hair
against hers. He gasped for breath as he gorged his eyes
on the sight in front of him.

'The President . . . the President . . .' he kept repeating,
mystified.

'Yes,' said Flore. 'It's the President . . . old Grandmorin.'

She continued to examine the face, now deathly white,
its mouth twisted into a horrible grimace, its eyes staring
in terror. Rigor mortis had begun to set in, and its features
were already becoming stiff. Flore let the head drop; it fell
back to the ground, and the wound closed up again.

'That's the end of your fun and games!' she muttered
under her breath. 'This is the result of one of his affairs;
I'll bet you anything. Ah! Poor Louisette! . . . The swine!
He's got what he deserved!'

There was a long silence. Flore put the lamp back on the
ground and waited, casting occasional glances at Jacques,
who stood on the other side of the body, unable to move,
dazed and totally overwhelmed by what he had just seen.
It must have been almost eleven o'clock. After the embarrassing scene earlier that evening, she was reluctant to be
the first to speak. Suddenly they heard voices; it was her
father on his way back with the stationmaster. She didn't
want them to see her there, so, plucking up her courage,
she said, 'Are you coming back to sleep?'

The question took Jacques by surprise and for a moment

he appeared torn. He searched desperately for some excuse.

'No,' he said.

There was no reaction from Flore, but from the way her arms hung limp at her side Jacques could tell that she was disappointed. As if she were trying to make amends for having refused him earlier, she began to plead with him, asking him again, 'Will you not come back to the house? Will I never see you again?'

'No!' said Jacques. 'No! No! No!'

The approaching voices were now very near. Without attempting to shake his hand, for Jacques seemed to be trying deliberately to keep the corpse between them, without even saying cheerio as she always used to do when they had been friends as children, Flore walked away and vanished into the night. Jacques heard the sharp intake of her breath, as though she were fighting back tears.

A moment later the stationmaster arrived with Misard and two other railwaymen. He too checked the identity of the body. Yes, it was certainly President Grandmorin. He recognized him because he used to see him getting off the train at Barentin every time he came to visit his sister at Doinville. He said that the body could be left where it had fallen. He covered it with a coat, which one of the men had brought with him. The stationmaster had sent one of his assistants on the eleven o'clock train from Barentin to report the news to the Public Prosecutor at Rouen, but there was little chance that he would be able to get there before five or six in the morning because he would also have to bring the examining magistrate, the clerk of the court and a doctor. The stationmaster arranged with his men to guard the body; they would take turns throughout the night so that someone was there all the time, keeping watch with the lamp.

Jacques thought that he might sleep in one of the station

buildings at Barentin; his train wasn't due to leave for Le Havre until seven twenty.[13] But he couldn't bring himself to leave; he stood there for a long time, unable to tear himself away, mesmerized. The thought of the examining magistrate coming to inspect the scene disturbed him, almost as if he considered himself to be an accomplice to the murder. Should he say what he had seen as the express went by? He decided at first that he would; after all, he had nothing to fear. Besides it was his duty to speak; of that there was no question. But then he wondered whether it was worth it. There was nothing he could tell them for certain, not a single thing about the murderer that he could swear to. It would be silly to get himself involved; it would be a waste of time, he would find it stressful, and it would do nobody any good. He decided he would say nothing. Eventually he walked away, turning round twice 78 to look at the black shape of the body humped on the ground in the yellow circle of lamplight. The sky was still overcast, and a distinct chill had fallen over the empty hillsides and the desolate countryside. Several trains had gone by, and another was approaching, a very long train, heading towards Paris. As they all passed each other, speeding towards their destinations somewhere far away, in the future, these powerful, inexorable machines had, without realizing it, passed within inches of the half-severed head of a man whom another man had murdered.

3

On the following day, a Sunday, early in the morning, the bells in Le Havre had just struck five when Roubaud came down to the station to begin his day's work. It was still dark, but the wind blowing in from the sea had freshened and was dispersing the mists that covered the hilltops from Sainte-Adresse to the old castle at Tourneville; out to the west, over the open sea, there was a clear patch of sky in which the last stars still twinkled. Under the platform roof the gas lamps burned palely in the chill, damp air of early morning. The first train, for Montivilliers, was already in the station, being coupled together by a gang of shunters under the direction of the night foreman. The waiting **79** rooms had not yet been opened, and the platforms were deserted as the station sluggishly began to come back to life.

As Roubaud was leaving his apartment in the upper part of the station above the waiting rooms, whom should he meet but Madame Lebleu, the cashier's wife, standing in the central corridor that gave access to the employees' lodgings. For weeks now Madame Lebleu had been getting up in the middle of the night to snoop on Mademoiselle Guichon, who worked in the office and whom she suspected of having an affair with the stationmaster, Monsieur Dabadie. Not that she had ever seen anything; there was not the slightest bit of evidence, nothing at all. That morning she was just about to dodge back into her room, when Roubaud opened his door. In the three seconds or so that it took Roubaud to open and close it again, she was surprised to catch sight of his wife, the delectable Séverine, standing in the dining room, already fully dressed, with her hair done and her shoes on. Usually she lazed about in bed till nine in the morning. Madame Lebleu had immediately woken her husband up to impart this extraordinary piece of news. The evening before, they had both stayed up waiting for the Paris express to arrive at five past eleven, itching to find out what had happened about Roubaud's clash with the Sub-Prefect. But there was nothing they could glean from just looking at them; they had seemed their usual selves. They had stayed up till midnight, straining their ears, but to no avail; there was not a sound from their neighbours. They must have gone to bed straight away and fallen into a deep sleep. The trip to Paris had obviously not gone well. Why else would Séverine have got up so early? Lebleu asked how Séverine appeared, and his wife tried to describe her; she seemed stiff and pale, her big blue eyes looked very bright under her dark hair, and she was standing completely still, like someone who was still asleep. No doubt they would find out all about it later on in the day.

When he got down to the station, Roubaud went to find his colleague Moulin, who had been on night duty. Moulin walked along the platform with him, passing the time of day and bringing him up to date with what had been happening while he had been away. A gang of prowlers had been caught trying to break into the left-luggage office, three shunters had been disciplined for misconduct, and a coupling had just broken while they were making up the train for Montivilliers. Roubaud listened calmly and quietly. Moulin thought he looked a little pale; no doubt he was still tired – he had rings under his eyes. Moulin obviously had nothing more to tell him, but Roubaud continued to look at him inquiringly, as if expecting to hear something else. But that was it. Roubaud lowered his head and looked at the ground.

The two men had now reached the far end of the

platform awning. On the right was a carriage shed which housed the carriages in service that had arrived the day before and would be used to make up the trains for the following day. As Roubaud looked up, his eye was caught by a first-class carriage with a coupé compartment. He could read the number in the flickering light of an adjacent gas lamp; it was number 293.

'Ah, that reminds me . . .' said Moulin suddenly.

A flush of colour ran across Roubaud's pale features. He gave a start.

'That reminds me,' Moulin continued. 'That carriage mustn't leave the station, so make sure it's not put on the 6.40 express this morning.'

Roubaud paused a moment.

'Oh, why not?' he asked, trying to make his voice sound natural.

'Because someone's reserved a coupé for the express **81** this evening,' Moulin answered. 'We don't know whether there'll be another coming in today, so we'd better hang on to this one.'

Roubaud continued to gaze at the carriage.

'I suppose so,' he answered. His mind was on other things.

'It's a disgrace how those buggers do the cleaning,' he exclaimed angrily. 'That carriage doesn't look as if it's been touched for a week!'

'I know,' said Moulin. 'When a train gets in after eleven, the last thing they want to do is start getting the mops and dusters out! You're lucky if they even bother to check that the train's empty! The other day they left someone fast asleep on the seat, and he didn't wake up till the next morning!'

Moulin stifled a yawn and said he was off to bed. He was about to leave when he suddenly remembered something.

'By the way,' he said, 'what happened about your brush with the Sub-Prefect? Did you get it sorted out?'

'Yes,' said Roubaud. 'It all went well. Everything's fine.'

'Glad to hear it!' said Moulin. 'Don't forget, the 293 must stay here.'

Left alone, Roubaud sauntered back towards the Montivilliers train, which now stood ready to leave. The waiting-room doors had been opened, and passengers were beginning to make their way on to the platform – a few men, off for a day's hunting with their dogs, and the odd shopkeeper and his family taking advantage of the Sunday off. It was very quiet, really. Once the first train of the day had left, Roubaud had no time to waste. His first task was to see that the 5.45 stopping train to Rouen and Paris was assembled. At this early hour there were not many staff on duty, and the assistant stationmaster had a lot to attend to. He supervised the shunting of the carriages, each of them hauled from the carriage shed by a gang of men, manoeuvred on to the turntable and pushed back into the station. He then dashed down to the booking hall to issue tickets and register luggage. He had to settle an argument between a group of soldiers and one of the station staff. Icy winds blew in every direction, and passengers stood around on the platform, shivering. His eyes were still heavy with sleep, and all these people, milling around impatiently in the dark, began to annoy him. For half an hour Roubaud was here, there and everywhere; he didn't have a minute to think about himself. Once the stopping train had pulled out of the station and the platform was cleared, he ran down to the signalman's box to make sure that everything was all right there. Another train was due in, the through train from Paris, and it was running late. He came back to the station to make sure that everyone got off the train safely and waited until the passengers had handed in their tickets and piled into the hotel conveyances, which in those days came to wait inside the station itself, separated from the trains by nothing more than a makeshift fence. Only then, when the station was again quiet and deserted, did he have a minute to breathe.

The clocks chimed six. Roubaud wandered out to the end of the platform, beyond the station roof. Standing outside in the open air, he raised his head and looked up at the sky, breathing deeply. Dawn was finally breaking. The wind coming in from the sea had blown away the lingering mist. A beautiful clear morning heralded a fine day. He looked northwards, towards the hills of Ingouville. In the distance he could see the trees in the cemetery standing out purple against the whitening sky. To the south and west a few remaining flecks of thin white cloud hung over the sea, drifting slowly across the sky like a fleet of ships. To the east, with the approaching sunrise, a fiery glow began to spread across the great open space over the mouth of the Seine. For a moment Roubaud forgot that he was on duty and removed his silver-braided cap to cool his brow in the pure morning air. He looked out over the station yard. It was all so familiar. With its profusion of long, low buildings – the unloading bays on the left, then the engine shed, and over to the right the goods depot – it was like a separate little town. It seemed to soothe his nerves and brought his mind back to the unchanging, humdrum routine of the day's work that lay ahead. Over the wall along the Rue Charles-Lafitte, he could see the smoke rising from the factory chimneys and the huge stacks of coal in the coal-yards beside the Vauban dock. Sounds of activity could be heard from the other docks – goods-trains blowing their whistles, the hum of the city coming to life. With these sounds came the smell of the sea, carried to him on the wind. Roubaud thought of the celebrations for the launch of the new ship, of the crowds that would come thronging to see it.

As he walked back under the station roof, he noticed the men assembling carriages for the 6.40 express. He thought they were trying to attach the 293. The calming effect of the fresh morning air vanished in an instant. In a sudden access of blind rage he screamed, 'Not that one, damn you! You were told to leave it where it is! That carriage isn't going out till tonight!'

The foreman endeavoured to explain that they were only moving it forward in order to get at another carriage behind. But Roubaud was so angry that he couldn't hear what he was saying.

'You stupid buggers,' he yelled. 'You were told not to touch it!'

Eventually he realized what the foreman was trying to tell him. But he was still furious, and launched into a diatribe on the poor design of the station. There wasn't even room to turn a carriage round! The station, it was true, was one of the first on the line to have been built and it 84 was now totally inadequate. It was unworthy of a fine city like Le Havre. The carriage sheds were old-fashioned and made of wood, the station roof was constructed of wood and zinc, with tiny panes of glass, and the station buildings were dull and dreary, with cracks everywhere.[1]

'This place is a disgrace!' he fulminated. 'I don't know why the Company hasn't knocked the whole bloody lot down!'

The men stared at him in amazement. They had never heard him lose his temper like this; normally when he had to discipline someone, he remained properly spoken. Roubaud noticed their reaction and stopped himself quickly. He stood there, stiff and silent, watching them as they went about their work. Lines of annoyance puckered his forehead; his round, flushed face and vigorous red beard were frozen in a supreme effort of will.

Having regained his composure, Roubaud turned his attention to the express, carefully checking every detail. Some of the couplings seemed loose, and he insisted that someone come and tighten them, while he watched to see that it was done properly. A mother, with her two daughters, a friend of his wife's, asked if he would find them a 'Ladies Only' compartment. Only when he had again checked that everything was in order did he blow his whistle for the train to leave. He stood for some time, looking after it as it moved out of the station, watching it intently like someone who knows that a moment's absentmindedness may cost human lives. As soon as it had gone, he had to walk across the line to see in a train from Rouen, which was just arriving. One of the mail-sorters on the train was a friend of Roubaud's, and he always enjoyed having a chat with him. For Roubaud it was a quarter-of-an-hour's break in a busy morning, a moment when nothing needed doing urgently and he could take a breather. That morning as usual he rolled a cigarette, and the two men exchanged pleasantries. It was now quite light. The gas lamps under the station roof had just been extinguished. The roof was so poorly glazed that the station remained in shadow, but the stretch of sky visible beyond it was already ablaze with radiant sunlight. A rosy hue adorned the distant horizon, each detail of which stood out sharply in the clear air of a fine winter's morning.

Usually at eight o'clock, Monsieur Dabadie, the stationmaster, came down to his office, and his assistant went to report to him. Monsieur Dabadie was a handsome man with strikingly dark hair. He was always smartly dressed and had the self-assured demeanour of a successful businessman, with little time for anything but the next contract to be signed. He took little interest in the running of the passenger station, concentrating instead on the dock traffic and the enormous transhipments of cargo that passed through the goods yard. He was in constant touch with major companies in Le Havre and all over the world. This morning he was late. Twice already Roubaud had looked round the door of his office and found no one there. The mail lay unopened on his desk. Roubaud had noticed a telegram among the letters and had not been able to walk away, involuntarily turning back, as if drawn by a magnet, to look at the table again.

Eventually, at ten past eight, Monsieur Dabadie arrived. Roubaud sat down and waited, saying nothing, allowing him time to open the telegram. The stationmaster, however, seemed to be in no hurry and sat chatting amicably with his assistant. He had a high opinion of Roubaud.

'I assume everything went well in Paris,' he said.

'Yes, sir, thank you,' said Roubaud.

Monsieur Dabadie had opened the telegram, but instead of reading it he continued to look at Roubaud. Roubaud's voice had become very quiet, and he was desperately trying to control a nervous twitch in the corner of his mouth.

86 'We are most pleased that you will be staying with us,' said Monsieur Dabadie.

'I'm very pleased to be staying too,' Roubaud answered.

Monsieur Dabadie turned his attention to the telegram. Roubaud watched him as he read it. He felt beads of perspiration breaking out on his face. He was expecting some sort of reaction, but nothing happened. The stationmaster quietly finished reading the telegram and tossed it on to his desk. It must have been about some minor administrative matter. Monsieur Dabadie proceeded to open the rest of his mail while Roubaud, in the usual way, delivered his report for that morning and the previous night. Today, however, he found himself having to stop and think, in order to remember what his colleague had told him about prowlers trying to break into the left-luggage office. Roubaud finished his report, and the stationmaster indicated with a wave of his hand that he could go back to his work. He was on the point of leaving when two of the yard foremen came in, one from the docks and the other from the goods yard. They had come, like Roubaud, to make their reports, and brought with them another telegram, which had just been handed to them on the platform.

'You needn't wait,' said Monsieur Dabadie to Roubaud, noticing that he was still hovering near the door.

But Roubaud couldn't bring himself to leave and stayed watching with big, round eyes. It was only when the little slip of paper had been tossed on to the table with the same lack of concern as the previous one that he turned and went. For a while he wandered about on the platform. His mind was in a whirl; he felt dazed. The station clock now registered eight thirty-five; there were no more scheduled departures until the 9.50 stopping train. Usually he used the hour's breathing space to do an inspection tour of the station, but this morning he drifted from place to place without knowing where his legs were taking him. Looking up, he found himself once more in front of carriage num- **87** ber 293. He turned on his heels and walked away towards the engine shed, even though there was nothing there that required his attention. The sun had now risen above the horizon, filling the air with a gold-coloured haze. But the fine weather was of no concern to Roubaud; he quickened his step and tried to appear busy, in an effort to put the awful suspense from his mind.

A voice behind him caused him to stop and turn: 'Monsieur Roubaud! Good morning! Did you see my wife when you were in Paris?'

It was Pecqueux, the fireman, a tall chap, forty-three years old, very thin, with strong bony arms, his face scorched by fire and smoke from his engine. He had grey eyes, a low forehead, a large mouth and a prominent chin. He always seemed to be grinning, like someone who was permanently tipsy.

'Oh, it's you!' said Roubaud, taken by surprise. 'I'd for-gotten. They told me in Paris about the engine being repaired. Back on duty tonight, I suppose? A day off! You lucky devil!'

'I am indeed!' answered Pecqueux. He was still slightly drunk after a binge the night before.

Pecqueux had been born in a village just outside Rouen and had joined the Company while still a lad, as a fitter's mate. By the time he was thirty, he had had enough of working in the repair shop and started training as a fireman, hoping eventually to become a driver. He then married Victoire, who came from the same village as him. The years went by. Pecqueux had still not become a driver. In fact he never did; he was too disorganized and he always looked a mess. All he seemed interested in was getting drunk and chasing after women. He'd have been given the sack twenty times over had not President Grandmorin put in a good word for him. But he was a very likeable chap and good at his job, which made up for his other failings and led people to turn a blind eye to them. When he was drunk, however, he was a liability; he became an animal, capable of anything.

'Did you see my wife?' he asked again, grinning from ear to ear.

'We certainly did,' answered Roubaud. 'We even had lunch in your room. You have a good wife there, Pecqueux. You should try to see more of her.'

Pecqueux seemed to find this hilarious.

'Try to see more of her!' he chortled. 'Come off it, it's her as wants me to see more of other women!'

What he said was true. Victoire was two years older than him. She had grown fat and had lost interest in sex. She secretly put five-franc coins in his pocket so that he could procure his delights elsewhere; it had never bothered her that he cavorted with other women and preferred to spend half his life in brothels. But things had now settled into a more regular routine. Pecqueux had two women, one at each end of the line – his wife in Paris, when he needed to spend a night there, and another woman in Le Havre, when he had a few hours to kill between trains. Victoire was careful with her money and lived frugally. She was fully aware of what her husband got up to, yet still looked after him like a mother. She often said that she would hate him to feel embarrassed when he was with his other woman; she even got his underwear ready for him whenever he went to Le Havre. She couldn't bear to think she might be accused of not looking after 'their man'.

'I still think you're not being very nice to her,' continued Roubaud. 'My wife adores Victoire; she was her foster-mother. She thinks you're being unkind.'

Roubaud was about to say more when he saw a tall, thin woman emerge from the little hut by which they were standing. It was Philomène Sauvagnat, the shed foreman's sister. Philomène was the other woman that Pecqueux had **89** been seeing in Le Havre for the past year. The two of them must have been in the hut chatting when Pecqueux had come out and called to Roubaud. Philomène still looked young, despite the fact that she was thirty-two; she was tall, bony and flat-chested, and her skin bore the unmistakable signs of a life of profligacy. Her head seemed to lunge forward, with big blazing eyes, like a racehorse straining at the leash. It was said that she drank. All the men at the station had at one time or another called to pay her their respects in the house near the engine shed, which she shared with her brother and which she allowed to get into the most dreadful state of neglect. Her brother came from the Auvergne. He was one of those men who always got his own way – very strict on discipline and highly thought of by his employers. But his sister was an embarrassment to him. At one point he had even been threatened with the sack. It was only thanks to him that the Company kept Philomène on; he himself let her live in the house out of family loyalty. Even so, whenever he caught her there with a man, he would beat her black and blue and leave her lying on the floor half dead. But Philomène and Pecqueux were just right for each other; he was someone she could get on with – a rough, happy-go-lucky chap who didn't take life too seriously. Pecqueux went round joking about it, telling everyone he'd never need another woman in his life. He'd traded in his fat wife for a thin one! But Séverine, who was strongly attached to Victoire, found it very insulting and had told Philomène in no uncertain terms what she thought of her. She now avoided her as much as possible. She wouldn't even say hello to her.

'I'll see you later, Pecqueux,' Philomène called out rudely. 'I'm not hanging around here, listening to Monsieur Roubaud giving you a lecture from his missus!'

But Pecqueux seemed to find it all very amusing.

90   'Hang on,' he said. 'He's only joking.'

'I promised I'd take a couple of eggs round to Madame Lebleu,' she said. 'I'll see you later!'

She had mentioned Madame Lebleu quite deliberately, knowing the secret rivalry that existed between the cashier's wife and Séverine, and wanting to annoy Séverine by making it appear that she was well in with Madame Lebleu. Even so, when she heard Pecqueux ask Roubaud about his tussle with the Sub-Prefect, her ears pricked up and she stayed to listen.

'I hear it's been sorted out,' said Pecqueux. 'You must be very pleased, Monsieur Roubaud.'

'Very pleased,' answered Roubaud.

Pecqueux gave him a knowing wink.

'You didn't need to worry though, did you?' he said. 'When you've got the big guns on your side, eh! You know who I mean . . . My wife's got a lot to thank him for too.'

Roubaud couldn't bear to listen to these allusions to Grandmorin and quickly interrupted.

'So you're not leaving till tonight?' he said.

'That's right,' Pecqueux answered. 'The engine's nearly ready. They've just finished adjusting the coupling-rod. I'm still waiting for my driver; he went away for the day. You know him, don't you? Jacques Lantier. He comes from your neck of the woods.'

Roubaud made no answer; he was lost in thought – miles away. He came to with a start: 'Who did you say? Jacques Lantier? Yes, I know Lantier. Only to say hello to, mind you. I didn't know him in Plassans. He was younger than me. The first time I met him was here, in Le Havre. He did a little job for my wife last autumn; he took something over to two cousins of hers in Dieppe. He's a good driver, they tell me.'

Roubaud was saying whatever came into his head. He suddenly walked away.

'Cheerio, Pecqueux,' he said. 'There's something I need to see to.'

When Roubaud had gone, Philomène decided to leave too, walking away with long, loping strides. Pecqueux remained standing where he was, his hands in his pockets, delighted at having nothing to do on such a fine morning. Suddenly, much to his surprise, Roubaud reappeared round the side of the hut. Whatever it was he'd needed to see to had not taken him very long. What had he come to spy on, Pecqueux wondered.

It was almost nine o'clock as Roubaud made his way back under the platform roof. He walked to the far end of the platform, stopped outside the parcels office, looked all around him without apparently finding what he was looking for, then walked smartly back in the same direction that he had just come, quickly casting his eye over each of the station offices as he passed in front of them. At this time of day the station was quiet and deserted. The only person about was Roubaud himself. This inactivity was making him more and more edgy, like someone dreading a catastrophe who ends up wishing it would just happen. He was losing his grip on himself. He couldn't stand still. He kept looking at the clock. Nine o'clock. Five past nine. Normally it was ten o'clock, after the 9.50 train had left, when Roubaud went up to his apartment for some lunch. He thought of Séverine. She must have been there waiting anxiously like him. He could wait no longer. He turned and mounted the stairs.

At precisely the same moment as Roubaud walked into the corridor, Madame Lebleu opened her door to Philomène, who had just called on her neighbour, with her hair all over the place, bringing her two eggs. The two women remained standing at the doorway, and Roubaud had to enter his room watched intently by both of them. He had his key ready and was very quick. Even so, in the instant that the door opened and closed, they saw Séverine sitting on a chair in the dining room, her hands resting on the table, her face as white as a sheet, motionless. Madame Lebleu pulled Philomène into her room and shut the door. She told her that she had seen Séverine looking exactly the same earlier that morning. They must be in trouble over that business with the Sub-Prefect. No, it had been sorted out, Philomène said. She had called round to bring her the news. Philomène then told Madame Lebleu what she had just heard Roubaud saying himself. They both launched into endless speculations on what might have happened. Every time they met, it was the same – a never-ending stream of idle gossip.

'They've been given a telling-off, you mark my words, my dear. They're in deep trouble, you see if I'm not right!'

'Let's hope we'll soon see the back of them, then . . .'

The increasingly venomous rivalry between the Lebleus and the Roubauds sprang from a simple question of accommodation. The first floor of the station building above the waiting rooms was used as lodgings for the staff. The floor was divided into two by a central corridor, like the corridor in a hotel, painted cream, with lights in the ceiling, and brown doors facing each other on either side. The apartments on the right of the corridor had windows looking out over the station forecourt, which was surrounded by old elm trees, with a wonderful view of the Ingouville hills in the distance. The apartments on the left of the corridor had low, arched windows looking directly on to the station roof, which rose steeply in front of them, blotting out the horizon with its zinc cladding and panes of dirty glass. The apartments on the right were a delight to live in, looking out on to the constant bustle of the station yard, the green trees and the open countryside beyond. The apartments on the left were a misery, with scarcely enough light to see by and the sky hemmed in as if by prison walls. At the front lived the stationmaster, the other 93 assistant stationmaster, Moulin, and the Lebleus. At the rear lived the Roubauds and Mademoiselle Guichon, the office secretary. There were also three rooms which were kept empty for visiting inspectors. It had always been Company policy to provide the two assistant stationmasters with apartments next door to each other. How the Lebleus came to occupy an apartment at the front was due to an act of generosity on the part of a previous assistant stationmaster, Roubaud's predecessor. He was a widower with no children and thought it would be a nice gesture to offer his apartment to Madame Lebleu. But the Roubauds felt that the apartment should have reverted to them. It wasn't right that they should be forced to live at the rear when they were entitled to live at the front. As long as the two families had managed to avoid arguments, Séverine had remained polite to her neighbour, who was twenty years older than her and not in the best of health, so fat in fact that she was constantly short of breath. The trouble began when they lost their temper with each other, as a result of Philomène's malicious scandal-mongering.

'When they went down to Paris,' she had said to Madame Lebleu, 'I bet they tried to get you kicked out of your flat. I've been told they wrote a long letter about it to the Managing Director.'

Madame Lebleu was incensed.

'It's outrageous!' she said. 'I reckon they're trying to get that office girl on their side too; she's hardly spoken to me for a fortnight. And she's another one! I'm keeping an eye on her . . .'

She lowered her voice to a whisper and told Philomène how she was certain that Mademoiselle Guichon went into the stationmaster's room every night. Their two doors were opposite each other. Monsieur Dabadie was a widower and had a grown-up daughter of his own who for most of the time was away at school. It was Monsieur Dabadie who had appointed this thirty-year-old blonde with her quiet ways and her slim figure, although already past her best, gliding smoothly about the office like a snake. She was supposed to have been some sort of schoolteacher. Madame Lebleu had never actually caught her out; she moved about so quietly and she seemed able to disappear through chinks in the wall. On her own she was no danger, but if she was sleeping with the stationmaster her influence could be crucial. The only way Madame Lebleu could have a hold over her was by discovering her secret.

'Oh, I'll find out in the end,' she continued. 'They're not going to walk all over me! Here we are and here we stay! All the best people are on our side, aren't they, my dear?'

Indeed, this dispute over the two apartments had aroused the interest of nearly everyone in the station; for the people living along the corridor especially it was a major talking point. The only person who remained unconcerned was the other assistant stationmaster,

Moulin. He was happy living at the front with his timid, little wife, a frail creature whom no one ever saw and who provided him with a child once every twenty months.

'Anyway,' said Philomène finally, 'even if they are in trouble it won't be the end of them; they know people who can pull strings. So just you watch out!'

She was still holding her two eggs, newly laid that morning by her own chickens. She gave them to Madame Lebleu, who thanked her profusely.

'Oh, you're so kind,' she said. 'I really don't deserve it. You must come and see me more often. You know how my husband never leaves the office, and I get so bored, stuck here on my own because of my poor legs. Whatever shall I do if those wicked people steal my nice view from me?'

As she opened the door to see her out, she put her finger to her lips.

'Sh!' she whispered. 'Let's listen!'

The two women stood in the corridor for a full five minutes, not making a move and holding their breath. They leaned forwards, listening at the door of Roubaud's dining room. But they couldn't hear a thing; it was as quiet as the grave. Not wanting to be caught eavesdropping, they eventually went their separate ways, bidding each other a final farewell with a silent nod of the head. Philomène walked off along the corridor on tiptoe, and Madame Lebleu went back into her room, closing the door so quietly that the latch made no sound as she slipped it into place.

By twenty past nine, Roubaud was back down on the station platform, supervising the assembly of the 9.50 stopping train. Although he was doing his best to appear calm, he was waving his hands about, moving restlessly from one foot to another and constantly looking round to make sure that the platform was clear. There was nothing happening. His hands were shaking.

Suddenly, as he turned his head to inspect the platform yet again, he heard someone calling his name. It was one of the telegraph operators, running towards him, breathless: 'Monsieur Roubaud, have you seen the stationmaster or the safety officer?[2] I've got two telegrams for them; I've been trying to find them for the last ten minutes.'

Roubaud turned round. His body had gone stiff; not a muscle in his face moved. His eyes caught sight of the two telegrams that the operator clutched in his hand. From the note of panic in the young man's voice, he knew that this was what he had been waiting for. The moment of crisis had arrived.

'I saw Monsieur Dabadie going that way, a short while ago,' he said calmly.

Never had he felt so cool and collected, so lucid, so ready to defend himself, so confident.

96   'Look!' he said. 'Here comes Monsieur Dabadie, now!'

The stationmaster was on his way back from the goods depot. He quickly ran his eyes over the telegram.

'I don't believe it,' he said. 'There's been a murder! This is a telegram from the inspector at Rouen.'

'What?' said Roubaud. 'Who's been murdered? One of our staff?'

'No,' said the stationmaster. 'It was a passenger, travelling in a coupé . . . the body was thrown out of the train at the end of the Malaunay tunnel, by the 153 kilometre post. It seems that it was one of our Company directors . . . President Grandmorin.'

Roubaud knew that he must express some surprise.

'President Grandmorin!' he exclaimed. 'My poor wife will be devastated!'

The comment sounded so unforced and heartfelt that Monsieur Dabadie paused a moment and looked at him.

'Of course,' he said, 'you knew him, didn't you? He was a very kind man, wasn't he?'

Then, turning his attention to the second telegram, addressed to the safety officer, he continued:

'I imagine this will be from the examining magistrate; I dare say there will be forms to fill in … It's only twenty-five past nine … I don't suppose Monsieur Cauche is here yet, is he! Get someone to run over to the Café du Commerce on the Cours Napoléon; that's where he'll be. Tell him we need him here now!'

Monsieur Cauche arrived on the scene five minutes later, having been dragged from the café by one of the porters. He was a retired army officer and regarded his job as an extension of his retirement. He never turned up before ten o'clock; he would take a five-minute stroll round the station and then head straight for the café. He was in the middle of a game of piquet[3] when the amazing news was brought to him. It took him a moment or two to register just how serious it was; normally he was asked to deal with **97** more mundane matters. The telegram was indeed from the examining magistrate at Rouen. The fact that it had arrived twelve hours after the body had been discovered was because the magistrate had first telegraphed the stationmaster in Paris to ascertain what travelling arrangements the passenger had made. Only when he had verified the number of the train and the carriage had he issued the authorization for the safety officer to inspect the coupé compartment in carriage number 293, if it was still at Le Havre. Straight away Monsieur Cauche's bad temper at having been disturbed for something he imagined was of no importance evaporated, and he assumed an air of great authority, appropriate to the extreme gravity of the situation.

'Oh, my goodness me!' he said, suddenly realizing that he might already have lost his chance to inspect the carriage. 'It won't be here; it will have left this morning.'

Roubaud, seemingly undisturbed, told him not to worry.

'Begging your pardon,' he said, 'it hasn't left. It's still here. There was a coupé reserved for tonight. It's in the carriage shed.'

Roubaud led the way, the safety officer and the station-master following him. The news must have spread. The men in the yard had stopped what they were doing and had wandered quietly over behind them. All along the platform, office doors opened, and people came out to look, eventually walking across in ones and twos to where they stood. Before long there was quite a gathering.

As they reached the carriage Monsieur Dabadie commented: 'The train was inspected by the cleaners last night; surely, if there had been anything unusual, they would have mentioned it in their report.'

'We shall see,' said Monsieur Cauche.

He opened the door and climbed into the coupé. No **98** sooner was he inside than they heard him let out a series of oaths and exclamations.

'Bloody hell!' he yelled, barely able to control himself. 'It looks as if someone has bled a pig in here!'

A murmur of horror ran through the crowd; people craned their necks to see. Monsieur Dabadie was the first to step forward, standing on the carriage step to look inside. Roubaud stood behind him, straining his neck to make it appear that he was as curious as everyone else.

Nothing had been disturbed inside the coupé; the windows remained closed, and everything was in its proper place. But a foul smell issued from the open door, and there was a dark patch of congealed blood on one of the seat-cushions. The blood had formed a pool so broad and deep that a stream had trickled on to the floor carpet, like water from a spring. It had fallen in splashes all over the seat covers; there was blood everywhere. It was sickening.

Monsieur Dabadie was furious.

'Who were the men responsible for cleaning this

carriage last night?' he shouted. 'I want them here, immediately!'

They were in fact already there. They shuffled forward, muttering excuses . . . they hadn't been able to see properly in the dark, they'd felt in all the compartments, they swore they hadn't noticed a smell the night before.

Monsieur Cauche remained inside the carriage, scribbling notes for his report. He called down to Roubaud. Roubaud was a friend of his; the two men often took a stroll along the platform and had a smoke together when there was not much to do.

'Monsieur Roubaud,' he called, 'would you come up and give me a hand, please?'

Roubaud stepped over the bloodstain on the carpet, careful not to tread on it.

'Have a look under the other cushion,' said Monsieur Cauche. 'Something might have slipped down behind it.' **99**

Roubaud lifted the cushion, feeling carefully with his hands and quickly looking underneath it. There was nothing there. But he noticed a mark on the upholstery on the back of the seat. He pointed it out to Monsieur Cauche; perhaps it was a bloodstained fingerprint.[4] They both inspected it carefully and finally agreed that it was just another splash of blood. The crowd of onlookers, sensing that a crime had been committed, had edged closer to watch the investigation. They were all pushing forward behind the stationmaster, who, being a sensitive sort of man and easily upset, had refrained from entering the compartment and was still standing on the carriage step.

A thought suddenly occurred to him.

'Monsieur Roubaud,' he said, 'weren't you on the train last night? You came back on the express, didn't you? You might be able to give us some information.'

'Why yes!' exclaimed Monsieur Cauche. 'Was there anything you noticed?'

For a moment or two Roubaud made no reply; he was stooping to look at the carpet. He quickly straightened himself and, in his usual rather gruff voice, answered:

'Yes there was. I'll tell you what I can . . . My wife was with me too, by the way. In fact, if this has to go in your report, I would like her to be present too, to make sure her account matches mine.'

Monsieur Cauche said that this seemed a very reasonable request. Pecqueux, who had just arrived on the scene, offered to go and look for her and hurried off immediately. There was nothing to do but wait. Philomène, who had arrived at the same time as Pecqueux, was not at all pleased to see him so eager to offer his assistance, but, catching sight of Madame Lebleu hurrying towards them as fast as her poor swollen legs would carry her, she ran over to give her a helping hand. The two women raised their hands to 100 the heavens and uttered cries of amazement, thrilled by the discovery of such a heinous crime. Although nothing about the murder was yet known, various accounts of what had happened were already circulating amongst the crowd, accompanied by looks of horror and much arm waving. Above the general murmur of voices, Philomène herself could be heard declaring on her honour, although it was she who had just invented it, that Madame Roubaud had seen the murderer. At that moment Madame Roubaud herself appeared, accompanied by Pecqueux. Everyone became silent.

'Look at her!' hissed Madame Lebleu. 'I ask you! Just because she's married to an assistant stationmaster, she thinks she's a queen! She was like that first thing this morning; I saw her in her room – hair done and all dolled up! Anyone would think she was going out visiting!'

Séverine walked down the platform, careful not to hurry; it was a long platform, and all eyes were on her as she moved towards them. She managed to stay calm, discreetly applying her handkerchief to her eyes to show how upset she was at just learning who it was that had been murdered. She wore a black woollen dress and looked very elegant, as if in mourning for the man who had been her life-long guardian. Her thick black hair shone radiantly in the morning sunlight; despite the cold, she hadn't stopped to put on a hat. Her sorrowful blue eyes were brimming with tears. It was all very touching.

'I'm not surprised she's upset,' whispered Philomène. 'Now they haven't got his lordship to look after them, they're done for!'

Séverine made her way through the crowd towards the open door of the coupé. Monsieur Cauche and Roubaud climbed out of the carriage, and Roubaud immediately began to tell him what he knew.

'We went to see Monsieur Grandmorin yesterday morning, as soon as we got to Paris, didn't we, my dear? It was about a quarter past eleven, wasn't it?'

He looked her straight in the eyes and she said quietly, 'Yes, a quarter past eleven.'

She suddenly caught sight of the carriage seat covered in blood. A shudder ran through her, and she began to sob bitterly. The stationmaster, feeling sorry for her, quickly interposed.

'Madame,' he said, 'we fully understand how deeply distressing this must be for you. If you find it too much, perhaps . . .'

'It will only take a minute or two,' Monsieur Cauche interrupted. 'And then we'll get someone to accompany Madame back to her apartment.'

Roubaud promptly resumed what he was saying: 'We talked about various things, and then Monsieur Grandmorin suddenly said that he was planning to go to Doinville the next day to visit his sister. I can see him now, sitting at his desk. I was standing here, and my wife was standing there . . . Yes, he said he intended to leave the next day. Is that not so, my dear?'

'Yes, the next day.'

Monsieur Cauche, who was jotting down notes with his pencil, looked up.

'The next day?' he queried. 'But surely he left the same evening!'

'Quite so,' said Roubaud. 'He knew that we were leaving in the evening, and at one point he suggested he might travel with us on the express. He thought my wife might like to go to Doinville with him and spend a few days there with his sister, as she has done before. But my wife had too much to do here in Le Havre, so she declined the invitation. That's right, isn't it, my dear? You declined the invitation.'

'Yes, I declined the invitation.'

102   'He was very nice about it,' continued Roubaud. 'And that seemed to be the end of the matter. We then talked about some business of mine, and he showed us out. Is that not so, my dear?'

'Yes, he showed us out.'

'We left in the evening. Just before we got into the train I had a chat with Monsieur Vandorpe, the stationmaster. I didn't notice anything unusual. I was rather irritated because I thought we had a compartment to ourselves, but I hadn't noticed a woman who was sitting in one of the window seats. Then two more people got in at the last minute, a married couple. That irritated me even more. Everything seemed perfectly normal all the way to Rouen. I didn't see anything. At Rouen we got out to stretch our legs. You can imagine our surprise when we saw Monsieur Grandmorin standing by the door of a coupé, three or four carriages down from our own. "Why, Monsieur Grandmorin!" I said. "So you left this evening after all! We didn't expect to be travelling with you." He explained that he had received a telegram . . . The guard blew his whistle, and we jumped back into our compartment. It was empty, by the way. Much to our relief, the other passengers had got off at Rouen! So there you are! That's about it, isn't it, my dear?'

'Yes,' Séverine whispered, 'that's about it.'

This seemingly unremarkable tale of events made a deep impression on the crowd of bystanders. Everyone listened spellbound, expecting to pick up some clue to the murder. The safety officer replaced his pencil in his pocket. He was as puzzled as everyone else.

'Are you quite sure there was no one else in the coupé with Monsieur Grandmorin?' he asked.

'Quite sure,' Roubaud replied.

A shudder ran through the crowd. Something inexplicable had happened and it was very frightening; everyone sensed a shiver run down their spine. If the passenger had been **103** alone in the compartment at Rouen, who could have killed him and thrown him out of the carriage ten miles further on, before the train had stopped at another station?

In the general hush, Philomène could be heard making her usual scathing comments.

'Very peculiar, if you ask me!' she was saying.

Sensing that her remarks were directed at him, Roubaud looked at her and nodded, as if to say that he found it peculiar too. He noticed Pecqueux and Madame Lebleu standing next to her, both of them nodding their agreement. The eyes of everyone were turned towards him; they were all waiting for something more, some detail that he might have forgotten, which would shed light on the mystery. They were not accusing him, but they all eyed him with such intense curiosity that he detected the first faint glimmerings of disbelief, the sort of vague suspicion that needs only one tiny detail to make it a certainty.

'Extraordinary!' murmured Monsieur Cauche.

'Quite extraordinary!' added Monsieur Dabadie.

Roubaud decided he must say something.

'One thing I'm certain of,' he said, 'is that the train was travelling at its normal speed. It runs non-stop from Rouen to Barentin, and I didn't notice anything unusual . . . I only know because we were on our own in the compartment and I had opened the window to smoke a cigarette. I could see outside and I could hear the sound of the train. I even spotted Monsieur Bessière on the platform at Barentin; he took over from me as stationmaster there. I called him over, and we had a few words together; he stood on the step and shook hands with me. Is that not so, my dear? Anyway, you can ask him; Monsieur Bessière will tell you himself.'

Séverine did not move. She stood there, looking pale and grief-stricken. Once again she confirmed what her husband had just said: 'Yes, Monsieur Bessière will tell you himself.'

For a moment all doubts were dispelled; the Roubauds had got back into their own compartment at Rouen and a friend had stood on the carriage-step and said hello to them at Barentin. The suspicious looks that Roubaud thought he had seen in the crowd had vanished. But everyone was becoming more and more confused; the mystery had deepened.

'Are you absolutely sure that no one could have got into the coupé after you had left Monsieur Grandmorin?' the safety officer asked.

Roubaud had clearly not foreseen this question, and for the first time he appeared flummoxed; presumably he had no ready-made answer. He looked at his wife and hesitated.

'It is most unlikely,' he said. 'The doors were being closed and the guard was blowing his whistle. We only just had time to get back into our carriage. Besides, the coupé was reserved; I assume no one was allowed into it . . .'

He noticed his wife looking at him hard, her big blue eyes open wide. He decided it would be better to sound less positive.

'But I don't really know,' he continued. 'Yes, perhaps someone could have got in . . . There was such a crush on the platform . . .'

As he spoke his voice became more assured; a new and better version of the story was taking shape in his mind.

'Yes, there was such a crowd on the platform,' he continued. 'All going to Le Havre for the celebrations, I suppose. There were second-class passengers and even third-class passengers trying to get into our compartment . . . And of course the station is not very well lit; you can't see a thing. The train was about to leave, and everyone was pushing and shouting; it was a mad scramble . . . Yes, I dare say it was possible for someone to force his way into the coupé at the last minute, someone who couldn't find a seat and thought no one would notice in all the confusion.'

He paused a moment.

'Yes, that's what must have happened, mustn't it, my dear?'

Séverine looked exhausted; she held her handkerchief to her face to hide the bruising round her eyes.

'Yes,' she said. 'That's what happened, I'm sure it did.'

The mystery seemed to be solved. The safety officer and the stationmaster looked at each other in agreement without saying a word. The crowd had begun to grow restless; everyone sensed that the questioning was now over, and they were all itching to go off and talk about it. Theories abounded, and everyone had their own version of events. For a while the usual business of the station had been suspended as everyone had left their work and come over to find out about the murder. It came as quite a surprise when

105

the 9.38 train pulled in alongside the platform. Everyone scurried back to their jobs; the carriage doors opened, and streams of passengers poured from the train. The more curious dallied behind, standing in a group round the safety officer, who, determined to do his job thoroughly, had gone to take a final look at the bloodstained coupé. Pecqueux, standing between Madame Lebleu and Philomène, caught sight of his driver, Jacques Lantier, who had just got off the train and stood looking at the little group of people at the far end of the platform. He waved to him frantically, but Jacques remained where he was. Eventually he decided to come over to them, walking very slowly.

'What's happened?' he asked Pecqueux.

He knew perfectly well what had happened and listened with only half an ear to the news of the murder and the different explanations of how it had been done. He felt
106 surprised and strangely disturbed to find himself suddenly plunged into a murder inquiry and standing in front of the same coupé he had seen only the night before, rushing at full speed through the night. He craned his neck and looked at the patch of dried blood on the cushion. Straight away he was back at the scene of the murder; he saw the body lying beside the track with its throat slit open. As he turned his eyes away he caught sight of Roubaud and Séverine; Pecqueux was still explaining what had happened and how the Roubauds had come to be involved, catching the same train from Paris as the victim, and being the last people to speak to him on the platform at Rouen. Jacques had met Roubaud; they sometimes stopped to have a chat when he was in charge of the express. He had occasionally seen his wife too, at a distance, but had deliberately kept clear of her, as he did of other women, knowing the fearful effect they had on him. But as he looked at Séverine, tearful and so dreadfully pale, with such a frightened look in her big, gentle, blue eyes, and her hair falling thick

and dark around her face, he found her very appealing. He could not take his eyes off her. He became lost in thought; how was it, he wondered, that he and the Roubauds came to be standing there together beside this carriage, the scene of a crime, they having returned from Paris the night before, and he just that minute arriving from Barentin?

'Yes, yes, I know!' he suddenly exclaimed, interrupting Pecqueux. 'I was there myself, last night, just outside the tunnel, as the train went past, and I thought I saw something.'

Everyone gasped in astonishment and they all crowded round him. No one was more astonished than Jacques himself; he was shaking, utterly taken aback and confused by what he had just said. Why had he spoken when he had solemnly sworn to himself that he would say nothing? He had so many reasons to remain silent! Yet the words had come unbidden from his lips as he was looking at Séverine. Séverine suddenly took her handkerchief from her face **107** and stared at Jacques, her big, tearful eyes opening wider and wider.

The safety officer walked quickly over to Jacques.

'What?' he said. 'What did you see?'

Jacques told him what he had seen – the brightly lit coupé hurtling through the night, the shapes of two men, one on his back, the other holding a knife. Séverine could not take her eyes from him as he spoke. Roubaud stood beside his wife, gazing intently at Jacques and listening to every word.

'Would you recognize the murderer?' inquired the safety officer.

'No, I don't think I would,' said Jacques.

'Was he wearing a coat or working clothes?'

'I couldn't tell. The train must have been doing eighty kilometres an hour!'

Séverine glanced involuntarily at Roubaud; he needed to say something.

'Quite!' he intervened. 'You'd need good eyesight to see anything at that speed.'

'Even so,' Monsieur Cauche concluded, 'it's a vital piece of evidence. The examining magistrate will help you to clarify your statements. Monsieur Lantier and Monsieur Roubaud, may I take your full names, please, so that you can be called as witnesses?'

And that was that. The little group of bystanders drifted away, and the station returned to its normal business. Roubaud had to dash off to see to the 9.50 stopping train, which was already half full of passengers. He shook hands with Jacques, more firmly than usual. Madame Lebleu, Pecqueux and Philomène walked away whispering to each other, leaving Jacques alone with Séverine. He felt obliged to accompany her back along the platform to the staff stairway; he could think of nothing to say but felt drawn **108** towards her, as if a common bond had just been established between them.

It was going to be a fine day. The sun had risen in the clear blue sky and driven away the morning mists. A breeze blew in from the sea over the incoming tide, bringing with it a whiff of fresh, salt sea air. As Jacques said goodbye to Séverine, he once again found himself captivated by her big blue eyes, looking at him, as before, so gently, so frightened, so appealing.

Someone blew a whistle. It was Roubaud, giving the right-away. The engine driver sounded a long whistle in reply. The 9.50 moved out of the station, gathered speed and vanished into the distance in a golden cloud of sunshine.

It was the second week in March. Monsieur Denizet, the examining magistrate,[1] had recalled a number of key witnesses in the Grandmorin case to his office in the Rouen law courts.

For three weeks now, the murder had been on everyone's lips. In Rouen, people found it unbelievable. In Paris there was talk of nothing else. The opposition newspapers[2] were quick to seize on it as ammunition in their hard-fought campaign against the government. Political discussion was dominated by the approaching general elections, and the atmosphere was very tense. There had recently been a number of stormy debates in Parliament, one in which there had been violent objections to ratifying the powers of two deputies who held official positions in the Emperor's personal entourage,[3] and another involving a fierce attack on the financial administration of the Prefect of the Seine[4] and a call for the election of a municipal council. The Grandmorin affair had come at just the right moment to fuel this unrest. The most amazing stories were circulating. Every morning the newspapers were full of speculation that was very damaging to the government. They claimed that the victim of the murder, a regular visitor at the Tuileries Palace,[5] a former magistrate, a Grand Commander of the Legion of Honour, a man worth millions, had been addicted to the worst kinds of debauchery. On top of this, because the investigation had so far got nowhere, they also accused the police and the judiciary of complacency and joked about the mythical murderer who was still at large. The fact that there was more than a grain of truth in these allegations made them all the more difficult to refute.

109

Monsieur Denizet was well aware of the great responsibility he carried on his shoulders, but he was also very excited by the affair. He was a man of ambition and had eagerly awaited an opportunity like this that would allow him to demonstrate the singular qualities of intelligence and energy on which he prided himself. He was the son of a prosperous cattle farmer in Normandy. He had studied law at Caen, entering the profession relatively late in life. As a result of his peasant upbringing and his father's untimely bankruptcy, promotion had been slow. He had been deputy prosecutor at Bernay, Dieppe and Le Havre, but had had to wait a further ten years before being appointed as public prosecutor at Pont-Audemer. He was then transferred, as deputy prosecutor, to Rouen, and had served as examining magistrate there for the last eighteen months. Now, however, he was over fifty. He had no private income, and his meagre salary hardly sufficed to cover his most immediate needs, so he had had to continue to work as a poorly paid magistrate in order to earn a living – the sort of job which none but the mediocre would happily resign themselves to, and which anyone worth their salt would suffer only as an irksome prelude to something more lucrative. Monsieur Denizet was actually very intelligent and extremely sharp-witted, an honourable man, who took pleasure in doing the job he did and rather relished the authority vested in him, as he sat in judgement with absolute power to acquit or to condemn. The one thing that tempered his passion for justice was his longing for promotion. There was nothing he desired more than to receive a decoration and to be transferred to Paris, which was why, after the first day of the hearings, when he had insisted that his sole concern was to establish the truth, he now proceeded more circumspectly, alert to the many hazards that might spell the end of his career.

A friend of his, it should be said, had advised caution the moment the inquiry began, urging him to speak with someone at the Ministry of Justice[6] in Paris. Denizet had gone to Paris and had had a long conversation with the Secretary-General, Monsieur Camy-Lamotte, a person of considerable influence, responsible for all legal appointments and in close touch with the Tuileries. Monsieur Camy-Lamotte was a man of distinctive appearance. Like Denizet, he had started his career as a deputy prosecutor, but thanks to family connections and the influence of his wife, he had become a Member of Parliament and had been awarded the title of Grand Officer of the Legion of Honour. The Grandmorin affair had landed on his desk because the Rouen prosecutor, unwilling to take on a sordid affair involving a former colleague who had been murdered, had taken the precaution of referring the matter to the Minister of Justice. He in turn had passed it on to his Secretary-General. By a strange coincidence, Monsieur Camy-Lamotte and President Grandmorin had been students together. Camy-Lamotte was a few years younger than Grandmorin, but had remained one of his closest friends. There was little that he didn't know about him, including his insatiable sexual appetite. He assured Denizet that the tragic death of his friend had been a great sadness to him and impressed upon him how passionately he desired to see the guilty party brought to justice. At the same time he made it clear that the Tuileries regretted the current spate of exaggerated rumour and suggested to Denizet, without of course wishing to appear presumptuous, that what was needed above all in this investigation was tact. In short, Denizet was led to understand that he should not try to rush things through too quickly and that he should take no decision without prior consultation. He returned to Rouen convinced that the Secretary-General had set up a separate inquiry into the affair. The truth needed to be ascertained in order, if necessary, to conceal it.

The days went by. Monsieur Denizet, although doing his best to remain patient, was becoming increasingly irritated by the jokes in the press. The detective in him was itching to get the investigation under way. Like a hound with its nose to the wind, he wanted to track down the villain and have the honour of being the first to solve the mystery, even if he was subsequently told to abandon his endeavours. He waited expectantly for a letter from the ministry, for a word of advice or some indication to proceed. But none came. So he had decided to resume his investigation. He had already made a number of arrests but had not had sufficient evidence to take matters further. Now, however, as he read through the details of President Grandmorin's will, he recalled something he had vaguely suspected at the very
112 beginning of his inquiries – the possibility that the murder had been committed by the Roubauds. The will was a quagmire of strange bequests, but among them was one stipulating that Séverine should inherit a house at La Croix-de-Maufras. Instantly a motive for the murder, which he had hitherto sought in vain, suggested itself; the Roubauds, knowing the contents of the will, could have murdered their benefactor in order to get their hands on the property as soon as possible. The thought had played on his mind increasingly ever since Monsieur Camy-Lamotte had mentioned Madame Roubaud as someone he had met some time ago at the President's château, when she was a girl. But the whole thing seemed implausible, and from both a practical and a moral point of view the case was fraught with difficulties. The more he tried to pursue this line of investigation, the more he came up against things that simply did not fit into the classic pattern of a murder inquiry. It didn't make sense; there was no underlying motive, no prime cause that made it all fall into place.

There was, of course, another line of inquiry which he had not yet discounted, namely the possibility, suggested by Roubaud himself, that, in the rush for seats just before the train left Rouen, someone had managed to get into the coupé – the mythical killer that the police had failed to track down and whom the opposition newspapers were constantly joking about. His initial inquiry had sought to identify the appearance of this individual, at Rouen where he had boarded the train, and at Barentin where he must have got out, but nothing definite had emerged; some witnesses insisted that no one could possibly have forced their way into the reserved coupé, and others had given the most contradictory accounts. It was beginning to appear that this line of inquiry too would lead nowhere. But then, as he was questioning Misard, the crossing keeper, Denizet quite by chance came to hear of the tragic story of Cabuche and Louisette, the girl who had been assaulted by the President, who had run away to her lover's cottage and who had apparently died there. For Denizet this had come as a flash of light in the dark; he could now establish a clear-cut case against the murderer. All the necessary ingredients were there – death threats made against the victim by Cabuche, a previous record of violence, and an unconvincing alibi that could not be proved. The day before, in a sudden moment of inspiration, Denizet had had Cabuche secretly arrested in his shack in the woods. A pair of bloodstained trousers had been found there. Denizet was careful not to let himself get too carried away with the new idea that was beginning to take shape in his mind, and he had certainly not abandoned his Roubaud hypothesis, but he was none the less delighted to think that he alone had been canny enough to put his finger on the real killer. It was in order to establish firm evidence for his suspicions that he had that morning recalled a number of witnesses who had already given evidence on the day following the crime.

The entrance to the magistrate's office was from the Rue Jeanne d'Arc. It was in an old building which had seen better days, tacked incongruously on to one side of what had once been the palace of the Dukes of Normandy and now served as the law courts. It was a large, gloomy room on the ground floor, with so little natural light that in winter a lamp had to be lit as early as three o'clock in the afternoon. The walls were hung with faded green wallpaper, and the furniture consisted simply of two armchairs, four other chairs, the magistrate's desk and a smaller desk for the clerk. On the mantelpiece above the empty fireplace stood two bronze urns on either side of a black marble clock. Behind the magistrate's desk was a door leading to a second room, which was used to accommodate anyone he wished to retain for further questioning. The main door opened directly on to a wide corridor lined with benches, where the witnesses sat while waiting their turn to be called.

The Roubauds had arrived as early as half past one, even though their appointment was not until two o'clock. They had come directly from Le Havre, stopping only to snatch some lunch in a little restaurant in the Grande-Rue. They were both dressed in black, he in a frock-coat and she in a long, elegant silk dress, and both displayed the air of subdued solemnity that betokens the loss of a close relative. Séverine had sat down to wait on one of the benches, saying nothing and not moving. Roubaud paced slowly up and down in front of her with his hands behind his back. Each time he walked past her, their eyes met, and, although they did not speak, their anxiety drifted like a dark shadow across their faces. They had been delighted to receive the legacy of La Croix-de-Maufras, but it had also revived their fears. The President's family, and his daughter in particular, had been incensed by the large number of strange bequests contained in the will, amounting to virtually half of the entire estate, and they were now talking of contesting it. Madame de Lachesnaye, prompted by her husband, had been especially critical of her former friend Séverine, about whom she harboured the most serious misgivings. Added to this was the thought that the investigation might reveal some piece of incriminating evidence. Initially, the possibility had never occurred to him, but for Roubaud it had now become a constant nagging fear. There was the letter that he had made his wife write to Grandmorin to persuade him to take the 6.30 express from Paris. If Grandmorin hadn't destroyed it, it would eventually be found, and the handwriting might be recognized. Fortunately, the days had gone by, and nothing had happened; the letter must have been torn up. None the less, the new summons to appear before the examining magistrate had brought the Roubauds out into a cold sweat, even though the ostensible reason for their presence was as beneficiaries of the 115 will and as witnesses in the eventual trial.

A clock struck two. The next person to arrive was Jacques Lantier. He had come from Paris. Immediately, Roubaud went up to him, extending his hand in a gesture of friendly greeting.

'So you've been roped in too!' he said. 'What a wretched business this is! Will there be no end to it? It seems to be dragging on for ever!'

Jacques caught sight of Séverine, sitting motionless on the bench in front of him, and stopped short. During the last three weeks, on the days when Lantier had been driving the train to Le Havre, Roubaud had gone out of his way to be friendly to him. On one occasion he had even insisted that he come and have lunch. In the presence of a young woman like Séverine, Jacques had immediately felt the stirrings of his old malady and a growing sense of panic. Was this yet another woman he would be driven to desire? He had only to glimpse the circle of lighter skin above the opening of her dress, and his heart had begun to beat, his hands had begun to tingle. He had resolved that in future he must keep away from her.

'What are people saying about this in Paris?' continued Roubaud. 'Nothing new, I suppose. No one knows anything, of course. No one ever will. Come and say hello to my wife.'

He took him by the arm. Jacques had no alternative; he went up to Séverine and greeted her, while she sat there, feeling embarrassed and smiling at him like a frightened child. Jacques endeavoured to make polite conversation. Roubaud and Séverine looked at him intently, not taking their eyes off him for a minute, as if they were trying to read beyond his thoughts and probe those corners of the mind that he himself preferred to ignore. Why was he so distant? Why did he seem to want to avoid them? Were there things that he remembered? Had they all been summoned together, in order to bring them face to face?[7] Lantier was the one witness they dreaded. They wished they could make him their friend so that he wouldn't have the heart to testify against them.

Tormented by thoughts such as these, Roubaud brought the conversation back to the investigation.

'So you've no idea why we've been summoned again?' he asked. 'Is there some new evidence?'

Jacques shrugged his shoulders.

'There's talk of an arrest,' he said. 'That's what I heard at the station just now, when I arrived.'

The Roubauds were simultaneously amazed, curious and very disturbed. An arrest! No one had said anything to them about an arrest. Had the arrest already been made or had it yet to happen? They plied him with questions. But he could tell them nothing more.

Just then Séverine heard footsteps coming along the corridor.

'It's Berthe and her husband,' she whispered.

It was indeed Monsieur and Madame Lachesnaye. They walked stiffly past the Roubauds, Madame Lachesnaye not even deigning to look at her old school friend, and were immediately shown into the examining magistrate's office by an usher.

'Well,' said Roubaud. 'We shall have to be patient. This will take at least two hours. Come and sit down.'

Roubaud had seated himself on Séverine's left and beckoned to Jacques to take the other seat beside her. For a moment he hesitated. But Séverine looked at him so sweetly and timidly that he overcame his qualms and came to sit next to her. She seemed so fragile, sitting there between them, so gentle and submissive. As they waited, Jacques felt the warmth from her body gradually relaxing him.

Inside Monsieur Denizet's office the questioning was about to begin. The inquiry had already amassed a substantial dossier of information filling several files of documents, all bound in blue folders. The investigation had sought to trace the victim's movements from the moment he left Paris. Monsieur Vandorpe, the stationmaster, had testified that the 6.30 express had left on time, that carriage number 293 had been attached to the train at the last minute, that he had chatted briefly with Roubaud, who had got into his compartment shortly before President Grandmorin arrived at the station, that the latter had been safely conducted to his coupé and that there was definitely no one else in the compartment. The guard, Henri Dauvergne, had been questioned about what happened at Rouen during the train's ten-minute stop there. He was unable to offer any clear statement. He had seen Monsieur and Madame Roubaud chatting on the platform outside the coupé and was fairly sure that they had returned to their own compartment and that one of the inspectors had closed the carriage door behind them. He couldn't be absolutely sure because there were so many people milling about on the platform, and the station was poorly lit. As to whether some person or other – namely the mystery killer, whom the police had so far failed to find – could have jumped into the coupé as the train was leaving the station, he said he thought it highly unlikely albeit not impossible, as similar occurrences had to his knowledge happened twice before. Other station employees at Rouen had been asked the same questions, but far from shedding any light on the matter, they had merely succeeded in confusing things further, by making statements that completely contradicted each other. One fact that appeared to be established beyond doubt was that Roubaud, standing on the inside of a carriage, shook hands with the stationmaster at Barentin, who was standing on the carriage footboard. The stationmaster in question, Monsieur Bessière, had formally testified that this was the case. He also added that his colleague had been alone in the compartment with his wife, who was lying on one of the seats apparently fast asleep. The inquiry had been extended further – to the other passengers who had travelled from Paris in the same compartment as the Roubauds. The fat lady and her fat spouse, who had arrived late and got into the train at the last minute, turned out to be a perfectly respectable couple who lived at Petit-Couronne;[8] they stated that they had both gone straight to sleep and hadn't seen a thing. As for the woman dressed in black sitting silently in the corner of the compartment, she had vanished into thin air like a ghost; it had proved absolutely impossible to trace her. All sorts of other people had been asked to give evidence, in an attempt to identify passengers who had left the train that evening at Barentin, since that was where the murderer must have alighted. All the tickets had been checked and all the passengers were accounted for except one – a tall man with a blue handkerchief tied across his face. Some said he was wearing an overcoat and others said he was wearing working clothes. On this one man alone, who had disappeared like someone in a dream, the dossier contained three hundred and ten separate statements, all of them so vague that each was contradicted by another.

To make things yet more complicated, the dossier contained a number of legal documents. There was the official report drawn up by the clerk of the court, who had accompanied the public prosecutor and the examining magistrate to the scene of the crime, a voluminous description of the exact point on the railway line at which the body had been found, including the position it was lying in, the clothes it was wearing, and the items found in the pockets, whereby the identity of the victim had been established. Then there was the report of the doctor, who had likewise visited the **119** scene, a long description in highly technical language of the wound to the victim's throat, a single deep incision made with some sort of cutting implement, presumably a knife. There were other reports and documents concerning the removal of the body to the hospital in Rouen, and the length of time it had been kept there before its unexpectedly swift decomposition had obliged the authorities to return it to the family. Out of this huge mountain of paperwork, however, there emerged only two or three points of any real significance. Firstly, among the contents of Grandmorin's pockets, they had found neither his watch nor a little wallet, which should have contained ten one-thousand-franc notes, money which the President owed his sister, Madame Bonnehon, and which she was expecting. This might have suggested robbery as the motive for the killing, had not a ring with a large inset diamond been left on the victim's finger, which prompted a string of other hypotheses. Unfortunately, the numbers of the banknotes were not known. There was, however, information about the watch; it was a large pocket-watch with a winder, the case was engraved with the President's two initials intertwined, and inside was the maker's number – 2516. Finally, the murder weapon, the knife used by the killer, had been the object of extensive searches along the railway line, in the adjoining undergrowth and anywhere else it might possibly have been thrown, but without success. The murderer must have hidden the knife in the same place as the banknotes and the watch. The only thing that had been found, one hundred metres down the line from the station at Barentin, was the victim's travelling rug, which had been thrown from the train to prevent it being used as evidence. The rug was included amongst the exhibits.

As Monsieur and Madame Lachesnaye walked into the magistrate's office, Monsieur Denizet was standing in front of his desk rereading a transcript of one of the earlier interviews, which his clerk had just found for him in the file. The magistrate was a man of short stature, quite well built, clean-shaven and with hair that was prematurely grey. His heavy jowls, square jaw and broad nose bore the waxed fixity of a mask, an impression further accentuated by his drooping eyelids, which half covered his big, bright eyes. The store of wisdom and expertise on which he prided himself found expression in his mouth; it was the mouth of an actor who has been trained to perform feelings on a public stage, a mouth that was never still, except at times when he wished to make a particularly subtle distinction, when it became compressed into a thin line. Subtlety was often his failing; he examined things too closely, and liked to complicate something that was perfectly plain and simple, out of a sense of professionalism, casting himself as an arbiter of public morality, gifted with foresight and very sharp-witted. However, he was certainly no fool.

As Madame Lachesnaye walked in, he immediately turned on the charm; he was well versed in the social niceties and made it his duty to attend gatherings of the elite in Rouen and places near by.

'Please take a seat, madame,' he said, proffering a chair.

Madame Lachesnaye moved forward. She was dressed in mourning, a young woman with fair hair, looking unwell, but also rather surly and unattractive. To Monsieur Lachesnaye, who also had fair hair and who also looked unwell, Monsieur Denizet extended only token politeness; he was even rather brusque. Lachesnaye had been appointed as judge in the Court of Appeal when he was only thirty-six and had even received a decoration, thanks to the influence of both his father-in-law and his father, who had also been a magistrate and had served on a number of important joint committees. To Denizet, Lachesnaye was the prime example of a lawyer who had got where he was as a result of favouritism and money, one of those undeserving individuals who had obtained a position and was assured of rapid advancement through family connections and an inherited fortune, whereas he, lacking both wealth and connections, was reduced to constantly begging favours in an endless, uphill struggle for promotion. So he derived great satisfaction from having Lachesnaye there in front of him in his office, aware of his authority, of the absolute power he exercised over the freedom of others, and knowing that, if such were his whim, he had only to pronounce a word for a witness to stand accused and be immediately arrested.

'Madame,' he continued, 'please forgive me for having to inflict this tragic affair upon you yet again; I realize how distressing it must be for you. I am sure that you are as keen as we ourselves to have the matter resolved and to see the guilty party brought to justice.'

He nodded to the clerk, a tall, sallow-looking youth with a lean face. The interview began.

No sooner had Monsieur Denizet begun to put his questions to Madame Lachesnaye, however, than her husband, who by then had sat down, as it was quite plain that no one was going to invite him to do so, insisted on answering on her behalf. He made it very obvious how bitterly he resented his father-in-law's will. It was beyond belief! There were so many bequests, and all of them so generous that they amounted to almost half the estate, an estate worth three million, seven hundred thousand francs! Nearly all these bequests were to people nobody knew, mainly to women of inferior status. There was even one bequest to a girl who sold violets on a doorstep in the Rue du Rocher. It was outrageous. As soon as the investigation was over, he intended to have this invidious will declared null and void.

Monsieur Lachesnaye went on at great length, airing his grievances through clenched teeth and revealing himself for what he was – a fool, a petty-minded provincial, driven by pure greed. Monsieur Denizet sat looking at him with his big, bright eyes, his eyelids half closed, and his lips drawn tightly together in an expression of jealous contempt for this nonentity who was not content with his two millions and whom, thanks to his acquired fortune, he would one day see clad in purple as a High Court judge.

'That, I think, would be ill advised, monsieur,' said Denizet, when Lachesnaye had at last finished. 'The will could only be overturned if the total bequests amounted to more than half of the estate, which is not the case.'

Then, turning towards his clerk, he said:

'I hope you are not writing all this down, Laurent.'

The clerk gave him a quick smile, as much as to say that he knew what was expected of him.

'Surely,' continued Monsieur Lachesnaye even more

acrimoniously, 'you don't expect me to stand by and see La Croix-de-Maufras go to this Roubaud couple! A gift like that to the daughter of one of his servants! Why, for goodness' sake? What right does she have to it? Besides, if it's proved that they had a hand in the crime . . .'

Monsieur Denizet quickly returned to the subject of his investigation.

'Do you think they were involved?' he asked.

'Good heavens!' Lachesnaye exclaimed. 'If they knew what was in the will, they had an obvious interest in our poor father's death . . . What's more, they were the last people to speak to him . . . It all seems very suspicious.'

The magistrate was becoming irritated; he had allowed himself to be side-tracked from his new line of inquiry. He turned towards Berthe.

'Tell me, madame,' he said, 'do you consider that your former school friend would be capable of such a crime?'

Madame Lachesnaye glanced at her husband before answering. They had been married for only a few months, and the marriage had done nothing to improve the unpleasant, acerbic nature of either of them. They each grew nastier by the day. Lachesnaye had so turned his wife against Séverine that, in order to get the house back, she would have been quite prepared to see her arrested there and then.

'All I will say, monsieur,' she eventually replied, 'is that the person you refer to had some rather disagreeable tendencies as a child.'

'Am I to understand that she misbehaved when she was at Doinville?'

'That she misbehaved! Certainly not, monsieur! Misbehaviour was something my father would never have allowed!'

This was the voice of prudish, middle-class respectability, incensed at the mere thought of anything untoward.

Madame Lachesnaye prided herself on being a paragon of virtue, respected throughout Rouen and welcomed at every door.

'Even so,' she continued, 'some people have a certain ingrained wantonness and ease of manners . . . Suffice it to say, monsieur, that a number of things which I would never have thought possible now seem to me to be beyond doubt.'

Monsieur Denizet was again beginning to grow irritated. This was not the line of inquiry he had intended to pursue. The fact that Monsieur and Madame Lachesnaye continued to insist on raising these issues seemed to be a challenge to his authority, a questioning of his intelligence.

'Come, come!' he exclaimed. 'Let us be reasonable. People like the Roubauds do not kill someone like your father simply to get their hands on an inheritance. If this had been the case there would have been other signs, some indication that they were anxious to have the property made over to them. No, the motive is insufficient. There would have to have been some other reason; but there isn't one, and what you are saying doesn't provide one either. Besides, you have only to consider the facts of the case to see that from a practical point of view it is impossible. No one saw the Roubauds get into the coupé, and one witness assures us that they returned to their own compartment. They were certainly in their own compartment when the train arrived at Barentin. So we would need to assume that they managed to get from their carriage to the President's, three carriages further down the train, and back again, in a matter of minutes, while the train was travelling at full speed.[9] Is this likely? I have interviewed a number of engine drivers and guards, who all tell me that one would need to be well practised to have the strength and the nerve to perform such an operation. Madame Roubaud would certainly not have been up to it, which means that the husband would have had to risk it on his own. In order to do what? To kill a benefactor who had just got them out of a serious mess? No, it simply does not make sense. We need to look elsewhere – for a man who boarded the train at Rouen, who got out at the next stop and who had recently threatened to kill the victim . . .'

This was the new line of inquiry that had aroused his interest, and he was about to expand when the usher's head appeared round the door. Before he had a chance to speak, however, a gloved hand pushed the door wide open and in walked a fair-haired lady, very elegantly attired in mourning. She was in her fifties but still strikingly good-looking, with the distinctive charm and opulent grace of a goddess in an antique painting.

'Here I am at last, my dear judge. Do forgive me for being late. The roads are impassable! The three leagues from Doinville to Rouen seemed like six today.'

Monsieur Denizet courteously rose to his feet.

'I trust you have been keeping well since I saw you last Sunday, madame.'

'Yes, very well indeed . . . Tell me, my dear judge, have you recovered from the shock my coachman gave you? He said that he nearly overturned the carriage as he was driving you back, about two kilometres from the château.'

'A mere bump in the road, madame! I had forgotten all about it . . . Please, do take a seat. As I said to Madame de Lachesnaye a moment ago, I must apologize for distressing you yet again over this appalling business.'

'Heavens above! It has to be done . . . Good afternoon, Berthe. Good afternoon, Lachesnaye!'

The new arrival was Madame Bonnehon, the murdered man's sister. She kissed her niece and shook hands with the husband. She had been a widow since she was thirty. Her husband had owned a factory and had left her a large

125

fortune, although she was already very wealthy in her own right, having inherited the Doinville estate when the family property had been divided between her and her brother. She had led a very happy life there and had had numerous love affairs, so it was said, but she had always been so open and forthright in her dealings with other people that she continued to be regarded with great respect in the higher circles of Rouen society. Her lovers had all been men in the legal profession, to whom she was drawn by a mixture of chance encounter and natural inclination. For twenty-five years she had held receptions at the château for members of the judiciary. Important people from the law courts were driven out to Doinville and back again to Rouen in what seemed a never-ending round of parties and celebrations. Even now she had not lost her taste for such things, and it was said that she had a maternal attach-

126 ment to a young barrister who was the son of a judge at the Court of Appeal, Monsieur Chaumettes; she was seeking to obtain promotion for the son and showered invitations and attention upon the father. She was also still very close to an old friend from earlier days who was likewise a judge at the Court of Appeal, a certain Monsieur Desbazeilles, a bachelor and something of a celebrity in literary circles; his finely wrought sonnets were frequently quoted. For years she had kept a room at Doinville at his permanent disposal. He was now over sixty and was still regularly invited to dine, as a friend of long standing, although latterly his rheumatism allowed him to indulge in little more than nostalgia. So Madame Bonnehon continued to reign like a queen, as gracious as ever despite the threat of advancing years, and no one dreamed of trying to usurp her position. The first time she sensed she might have a rival had been during the previous winter, when she was invited to a reception by Madame Leboucq, the wife of yet another Appeal Court judge, a tall dark-haired

woman of thirty-four and very good-looking, whose house had become a centre of attraction for people at Court. This lent a certain wistfulness to her usually cheery disposition.

'If I may, madame,' continued Monsieur Denizet, 'I would like to ask you a few questions.'

He had finished questioning the Lachesnayes but had not yet asked them to leave. His office, usually so cold and uninviting, was beginning to feel more like a cosy drawing room. The clerk, with an air of resignation, once again prepared himself to take down the notes.

'One of our witnesses has mentioned a telegram which your brother allegedly received, asking him to come to Doinville urgently. We have found no trace of this telegram. Had you by any chance written to him yourself, madame?'

Madame Bonnehon, remaining perfectly relaxed, smiled 127 pleasantly and began to answer the magistrate, as if she were merely engaging in a friendly chat.

'No,' she said, 'I hadn't written to my brother. I was expecting him and I knew that he intended to come, but no date had been arranged. He usually just turned up without warning, nearly always by the night train. He stayed in a cottage in the grounds with a private lane leading to it, so we didn't even hear him arrive. He would hire a carriage at Barentin, and no one saw anything of him till the following day, sometimes quite late on. It was like having a neighbour who had moved away and who came back for the occasional flying visit. The reason I was expecting him this time was that he had promised to bring me ten thousand francs, which was money he owed me from a business transaction. I know for certain that he had the ten thousand francs in his possession, which is why I've always thought that the reason he was killed was purely and simply to steal his money.'

The magistrate remained silent for a moment or two. Then, looking her straight in the eyes, he said:

'What is your opinion of Madame Roubaud and her husband?'

Madame Bonnehon protested vehemently.

'My dear Monsieur Denizet,' she exclaimed, 'can we please not waste our time discussing the Roubauds! They are a perfectly decent couple! Séverine was a lovely girl, very quiet and well behaved, and extremely pretty what's more, which is no bad thing. In my opinion, since you insist on hearing it again, both she and her husband are quite incapable of a criminal act.'

Monsieur Denizet nodded approvingly. He looked triumphantly at Madame Lachesnaye, who, feeling wounded to the quick by this last remark from Madame Bonnehon, could not refrain from intervening.

128 'Dearest Aunt,' she said, 'I think you are very easily pleased.'

Madame Bonnehon contented herself by replying in her usual, plain-spoken manner.

'I think you have said enough, Berthe; we must agree to differ. Séverine was a very happy child, always laughing, and what harm is there in that, for goodness' sake? I know exactly what you and your husband think of her, but it's only money that makes you so upset about your father leaving her the house at La Croix-de-Maufras. He left it to Séverine because he was very fond of her . . . he brought her up and provided her with a dowry. Why shouldn't he include her in his will? Good heavens, he thought of her as if she were his own daughter! Money is not everything, my dear Berthe!'

For Madame Bonnehon, of course, having always been a person of considerable means, money was of little concern. Indeed, being the attractive and much-admired woman she was, she liked to think that the only things worth living for were love and beauty.

'It was Roubaud who mentioned the telegram,' observed Monsieur de Lachesnaye curtly. 'If there was no telegram, the President wouldn't have told him he'd received one. Why did Roubaud lie?'

'It is quite possible,' exclaimed Monsieur Denizet heatedly, 'that the President himself invented the telegram as a way of explaining his sudden departure to the Roubauds. According to them, he had said he wouldn't be leaving till the next day; when he then found himself on the same train as them, he needed to invent some excuse in order to hide the real reason for his journey, which, incidentally, no one knows . . . This is of no importance. It is leading us nowhere.'

There was another silence. When the magistrate resumed, he spoke more calmly and chose his words carefully: 'Madame, I now come to a particularly delicate issue; I trust that you will forgive the nature of my questions. No one respects the memory of your brother more than I . . . However, there were rumours, were there not, that he entertained a number of mistresses.'

Madame Bonnehon smiled, appearing not in the least disturbed by the question.

'Really, my dear sir, at his age!' she replied. 'My brother lost his wife in the early years of his marriage, and I have never presumed to find fault with the way he chose to enjoy himself. He lived his own life, and it was not my business to interfere. All I know is that he lived in a manner that befitted his position and that he remained a perfect gentleman to the last.'

Berthe, overcome with embarrassment at this discussion of her father's mistresses, lowered her eyes; her husband, equally embarrassed, walked over to the window and turned his back.

'Please forgive me for harping on this,' continued Monsieur Denizet, 'but was there not a story concerning a young chambermaid at Doinville?'

'Ah, yes, Louisette . . . Louisette, monsieur, was a thoroughly nasty piece of work. She was only fourteen and she was having an affair with a known criminal. People tried to blame her death on my brother. It was disgraceful. Allow me to tell you what happened.'

What she said was no doubt said in all sincerity, but she was well aware of the President's private life, and his tragic death had come as no surprise; she felt she needed to uphold the family's good name. As far as the unfortunate business with Louisette was concerned, even if she secretly admitted to herself that her brother was quite capable of taking a fancy to her, she was equally convinced that Louisette, even at her tender age, was totally depraved.

'Picture to yourself a young girl,' she said, 'sweet and gentle, lovely yellow hair, rosy cheeks, a little angel, butter wouldn't melt in her mouth, innocent as the day she was 130 born, never committed a sin in her life! Well, she was not yet fourteen and she was having an affair with a brute of a man, a quarry worker who had just spent five years in prison for killing someone in a public bar. He lived like some wild creature, on the edge of the Bécourt forest, in a shack made out of tree-trunks and mud that he had taken over from his father, who had died of shame. He scraped a living by digging rubble out of one of the abandoned quarries, which once, I believe, provided half the stones for building the city of Rouen. Louisette used to go and stay with this monster in his den; he lived there on his own because everyone was so frightened of him that they avoided him like the plague. The pair would often be seen wandering through the woods, holding hands, such a dainty little girl with an overgrown brute like him. What more can I say? It was scandalous, unbelievable! Obviously I only came to hear of all this afterwards. I had taken Louisette on almost out of charity, as an act of kindness. I knew that her family, the Misards, were poor, but what they didn't tell me was that they had beaten the child black and blue and still not managed to stop her running off to stay with Cabuche the minute she could get out of the house . . . And then the accident happened. When my brother came to Doinville he didn't bring his own servants with him. Louisette and another woman used to go over to his cottage to do the housework for him. One morning Louisette went on her own and disappeared. If you ask me, she had been intending to run away for some time. Her lover was probably waiting for her and took her away with him. The worst of it was that five days later we heard she was dead. People said that my brother had attempted to rape her in the most vicious way and that she had run to Cabuche, terrified, and died of brain fever.[10] What really happened no one knows; there are so many different stories that it's difficult to say. That she died of a fever is true; a doctor certified as much. My own opinion is that she did something foolish – slept out of doors at night or wandered around in the marshes . . . Surely, my dear sir, you don't imagine that my brother maltreated her. It's a horrible thought. It's impossible!'

Monsieur Denizet had listened attentively to this account, remaining impassive throughout. Before finally completing what she had to say, Madame Bonnehon became somewhat embarrassed. Eventually, taking her courage in both hands, she declared, 'I cannot deny that my brother may have been a little playful with her! He liked young people, despite seeming to be so strict. Perhaps he kissed her.'

Monsieur and Madame Lachesnaye appeared scandalized at the suggestion.

'Really, Aunt!' Berthe exclaimed.

Madame Bonnehon shrugged her shoulders; what was the point of lying to the law?

'Yes, he may have kissed her. Perhaps he tickled her.

What's the harm in that? The reason I'm telling you this is because the story didn't just come from Cabuche. Louisette was telling lies. She deliberately exaggerated things, so that her lover would look after her, I suppose. Anyway, Cabuche, being the unthinking fool he is, ended up genuinely believing that his mistress had been killed. It sent him crazy; he went round all the bars announcing that if ever he laid hands on Grandmorin he'd bleed him to death like a pig!'

The magistrate, who had thus far remained silent, instantly became keenly interested.

'Are you sure that is what he said?' he asked, interrupting Madame Bonnehon. 'Do you have witnesses to prove it?'

'My dear sir, there are no end of witnesses. This has been a very sorry business and it has been extremely trying. It was fortunate that my brother's position placed him above suspicion.'

Madame Bonnehon had realized the new turn that Monsieur Denizet's inquiry was taking, and it rather worried her. She preferred not to involve herself further by asking more questions. Monsieur Denizet stood up, saying that he did not wish to impose on the family's good will any longer at such a distressing time, and asked the clerk to read out copies of their statements for the witnesses to sign. The statements were very precisely worded, stripped of anything extraneous or compromising. Madame Bonnehon, pen in hand, cast a glance of grateful acknowledgement at the pale, lean-faced Laurent, whom up until then she had barely noticed.

As the magistrate accompanied her to the door with her nephew and niece, Madame Bonnehon took his hands in hers.

'I hope we shall meet again very soon,' she said. 'You know that you are always most welcome at Doinville.

Thank you; you are amongst the last of my faithful friends.'

She gave him a rather wistful smile, as her niece walked stiffly out of the room in front of her with a mere nod of the head.

Left alone, Monsieur Denizet had a moment to gather his thoughts. He stood reflecting on what he had just heard. It was all becoming clear. There had certainly been violence on the part of Grandmorin; his reputation was known. This made the magistrate's findings somewhat delicate; he reminded himself he must be extra careful, and wait until the advice he was expecting from the ministry had arrived. None the less, he was very pleased with himself. What was more, the murderer was already in custody.

He returned to his desk and rang for the usher.

'Please call Monsieur Jacques Lantier.'

The Roubauds were still sitting on the bench in the corridor, their faces devoid of expression, as if they had grown tired of waiting and had dropped off to sleep. Now and then their features were disturbed by an involuntary twitch of anxiety. The usher's voice, summoning Jacques, seemed to wake them up with a start. They watched him intently as he disappeared into the magistrate's office. They then settled themselves back to resume their wait, pale and silent as before.

The murder had been preying on Jacques's mind for the last three weeks, making him feel very uneasy, as if this investigation might somehow go against him. There was no reason why it should; he had nothing to reproach himself with, not even the fact that he had said nothing on the night of the murder. Yet, as he entered the magistrate's office, he felt a distinct shiver of guilt run through him, as if he were the one on trial and were about to be incriminated. He answered the magistrate's questions cautiously, choosing his words carefully for fear of saying too much. That night, he too had come close to being a murderer, and he was afraid it might show in his eyes. He hated having to appear in a court of law; he found it irritating, and he wished people would stop pestering him with matters that didn't concern him.

On this occasion, however, Monsieur Denizet's sole purpose was to ascertain the appearance of the murderer. Jacques, being the only witness who had actually seen him, was the one person who might provide exact information. But he could add nothing to his original statement. What he saw, he repeated, had lasted less than a second; it had come and gone so quickly that all it left in his mind was a general impression, a blur. What he had seen was a man slitting another man's throat. That was all he could say. For half an hour the magistrate doggedly tried to elicit something more precise, repeating his questions time and time again, in every manner conceivable. Was he tall? Was he short? Did he have a beard? Was his hair long or short? What sort of clothes was he wearing? Was he a professional person or was he working class? Jacques became more and more confused and could give only vague answers.

'Let me ask you one final question,' Monsieur Denizet said suddenly, looking him straight in the eye. 'If you saw the murderer, would you recognize him?'

Jacques felt a wave of anxiety run through him; it was as if Monsieur Denizet could see inside his mind. His eyelids fluttered; he seemed to be speaking his thoughts aloud.

'Would I recognize him?' he murmured. 'Yes . . . perhaps I would.'

But immediately the strange fear that he might unwittingly have been an accomplice to the crime made him draw back and evade the question.

'No, I don't think so,' he said. 'I couldn't be certain. You must remember that the train was travelling at eighty kilometres an hour!'

The magistrate threw up his hands in despair. He was about to ask Jacques to wait in the adjoining room for further questioning, when he suddenly changed his mind.

'Please wait here a moment,' he said. 'Take a seat.'

He once again rang for the usher.

'Please show in Monsieur and Madame Roubaud,' he said.

As soon as they walked through the door and saw Jacques, a look of anxiety shot across their faces. Had he said anything? Had he been asked to wait in order to bring them together face to face? In the presence of Jacques, their confidence vanished, and they sounded very unsure of themselves as they began to answer the magistrate's questions. Monsieur Denizet, however, simply ran through their earlier statement. The Roubauds merely had to repeat what **135** they had said before, almost word for word. The magistrate listened with his head lowered, not even looking at them.

Suddenly he turned towards Séverine.

'Madame,' he said, 'you told the safety officer at Le Havre, whose report I have here, that you were sure a man got into the coupé at Rouen just as the train was leaving the station.'

The question took Séverine by surprise. Why had he mentioned that? Was it a trap? Did he want to see whether what she said now would contradict what she had said before? She looked quickly at her husband. Roubaud felt he must say something.

'Monsieur,' he said, 'I don't think that my wife was quite as definite as that.'

'Forgive me, Monsieur Roubaud,' continued the magistrate, 'but when you admitted that this was a possibility, your wife said: "That's what happened, I'm sure it did."'

What I would like to know, madame, is whether you had any particular reason for saying that.'

Séverine was beginning to feel very worried. She was convinced that if she wasn't careful he would lead her from one question to another and force her to admit what had happened. On the other hand she couldn't just stand there and say nothing.

'No, monsieur,' she said. 'There was no particular reason. I must have said it because that was the only thing that seemed possible; how else can it have happened?'

'So you didn't actually see the man, and you can tell us nothing about him.'

'Absolutely nothing, monsieur.'

For a moment it seemed as if Monsieur Denizet was about to abandon this line of inquiry, but the minute he began to question Roubaud he returned to it.

136 'Tell me, monsieur,' he asked, 'how is it that you didn't see this man, if he really did get into the carriage, since it appears from your statement that you were still talking to the victim when the whistle blew for the train to leave?'

The persistence of the magistrate's questions was beginning to disturb Roubaud. He couldn't make up his mind which line to take; should he abandon the story of this other man or should he stick to it? If they had evidence against him, the theory of the unknown killer was scarcely plausible and could even make matters worse for him. He decided he must play for time and answered the magistrate with long, rambling explanations that shed no light on the matter at all.

'It is most unfortunate,' continued Monsieur Denizet, 'that your memory should be so vague, because your evidence could help us to clear the names of certain people who remain under suspicion.'

This last comment appeared to be addressed so directly to Roubaud himself that he felt it imperative to establish his innocence. He was about to be accused; he could hesitate no longer.

'It makes me feel guilty,' he said. 'I find it difficult to speak about it. Perhaps that is normal. I hope you will understand . . . Yes, I think I did see him, but . . .'

The magistrate clasped his hands together in a gesture of triumph, convinced that Roubaud's sudden willingness to talk was due entirely to his own inquisitorial skills. He assured him that he knew from long experience the peculiar difficulty some witnesses had in admitting what they knew. He prided himself on being able to coax information from even the most reluctant.

'Tell me then,' he continued, 'what did he look like? Was he short? Tall? About your own height perhaps?'

'Oh, no! Much taller ... At least that was my impression . . . just an impression, you understand. I'm fairly sure someone pushed past me, as I was running back to our carriage.' **137**

'Just a moment,' said Monsieur Denizet.

He turned towards Jacques.

'The man you saw holding a knife,' he asked him, 'was he taller than Monsieur Roubaud?'

Jacques was beginning to grow restive, thinking he might miss the five o'clock train. He raised his eyes and looked at Roubaud. It was as if he were looking at him for the first time. He was surprised at how short and how well built he was. But he had a quite distinctive face. It was a face he had seen somewhere else, or possibly dreamed of.

'No,' he murmured, 'he wasn't taller. He was about the same height.'

Roubaud protested vehemently.

'No,' he insisted, 'he was much taller than me; by a head at least.'

Jacques stared at him wide-eyed. A look of growing realization spread across his face. Roubaud began to fidget uneasily on his seat, as if trying to escape from his own likeness. His wife sat motionless, scrutinizing Jacques's face as he attempted to recall what he had seen. Initially, he had clearly been struck by certain similarities between Roubaud and the murderer. He had now become suddenly convinced that Roubaud was indeed the murderer, as some people had said. He sat there as if stunned, completely taken aback by the force of this new realization. What would he do next? He did not know himself. If he spoke, the two of them were done for. Roubaud's eyes met those of Jacques, and the two exchanged a look which went to the very depths of their souls. There was a silence.

'So you fail to agree,' resumed Monsieur Denizet. 'If you, Monsieur Lantier, thought he was shorter, it was probably because he was leaning forwards, struggling with his victim.'

138   Monsieur Denizet was studying the two men carefully. It had not been his intention to use the confrontation in this way, but some professional instinct told him that at that moment the truth was very close at hand. Even his conviction that the murderer was Cabuche was for a moment shaken. Could the Lachesnayes have been right? However unlikely it seemed, could the murderers have been this decent, hard-working stationmaster and his lovely young wife?

'Did the man have a full beard, like you?' he asked Roubaud.

Roubaud somehow managed to answer with a perfectly steady voice: 'A full beard? No. I don't think he had a beard at all.'

Jacques realized that he was going to be asked the same question. What should he say? He could have sworn that the man did have a beard. This couple were no concern of his; why not tell the truth? But as he turned his eyes away from Roubaud he saw his wife looking at him, with a look of such intense supplication, such utter surrender, that he was overcome. He felt the pernicious stirrings of his old passion. Was he in love with her? Was this the one woman he might love with a love that was true, untainted by the monstrous desire to kill? At that moment, thanks to some bizarre side-effect of his malady, his memory seemed to grow hazy; he no longer saw Roubaud as the man who had committed the murder. The picture became blurred; he was unsure of what he had seen. He knew that whatever he said now he would come to regret.

Monsieur Denizet was still waiting for an answer.

'Did the man have a full beard like Monsieur Roubaud?'

'Monsieur, I really cannot say,' Jacques replied in all honesty. 'The train was travelling so quickly. I don't know what I saw. I can't swear to anything.'

But Monsieur Denizet was insistent; he wanted to rule **139** out any suspicion attaching to Roubaud. He plied both Roubaud and Jacques with further questions. From Roubaud he succeeded in extracting a full description of the murderer – tall, well built, no beard, and dressed in working clothes – the exact opposite of himself. From Jacques he obtained only non-committal grunts, the effect of which was to substantiate Roubaud's description. The magistrate was now feeling more confident again in his previous line of inquiry; he was on the right track, and the description of the murderer that Roubaud had just provided was so accurate that his surmise was rapidly becoming a certainty. The Roubauds had been wrongfully suspected of the crime, but thanks to their overwhelming testimony, the real criminal would now be sent to the guillotine.

When they had signed their statements, the magistrate directed Jacques and the Roubauds into the adjoining room.

'Would you please wait in here,' he said. 'I shall require you again presently.'

He immediately ordered the prisoner to be brought in. He was so pleased with himself that he even ventured a smile at his clerk.

'Laurent,' he said, 'we've got him!'

The door opened and two constables appeared, escorting a tall young man of twenty-five or thirty. At a sign from the magistrate they withdrew, leaving Cabuche standing in front of him, with no idea why he was there, and bristling with animosity, like an animal caught in a trap. He had powerful shoulders and huge fists, fair hair and remarkably white skin. Apart from a few wisps of light brown hair around his chin, he had no beard. His coarse features and low forehead suggested that he was a violent man of limited intelligence, a man governed by the impulse

140 of the moment; but his broad mouth and rather flat nose reminded one of a faithful dog, and betokened a person who needed to be looked after and cared for. He had been unceremoniously arrested in his hovel in the early hours of the morning and dragged out of the forest. He could make no sense of the accusations that were being made against him, and this had infuriated him. Standing before the magistrate, flustered, his clothes torn, Cabuche had the look of a man who had already been found guilty, the shifty, devious look which a spell in prison leaves on even the most innocent. Night was beginning to fall and the room had grown dark, so dark that Cabuche was hidden in shadow. Suddenly the usher came in carrying a big lamp with a large round globe. The glare fell full on Cabuche's face. He stood there motionless, exposed.

Monsieur Denizet sat looking at him intently with his big, bright eyes and drooping eyelids, saying nothing. Silence was the first weapon in his armoury, the first test of his power, before he unleashed the devilish onslaught of tricks, traps and moral blackmail that was to come. This man was guilty, and any ploy that would determine his guilt was permissible. The only right left to him was the right to admit his crime.

The questioning began; at first very slowly.

'Do you know what crime you stand accused of?'

'No one's told me, but I've got a pretty good idea,' growled Cabuche, his voice choking with impotent rage. 'There's been enough talk about it.'

'Did you know Monsieur Grandmorin?'

'Only too well,' Cabuche replied.

'A girl called Louisette, your mistress, worked as a chambermaid for Madame Bonnehon.'

Cabuche was seized with a fit of rage; he was so angry he saw red.

'Whoever says that is a bloody liar,' he shouted. 'Louisette wasn't my mistress.'

141

The magistrate was surprised at the violence of his reaction. He decided to try a different approach.

'You are a violent man,' he said. 'You were sentenced to five years in prison for killing someone in a fight.'

Cabuche lowered his head. The prison sentence was something he was profoundly ashamed of.

'He hit me first,' he muttered. 'Anyway, I only did four years. I got a year's remission.'

'So,' continued Monsieur Denizet, 'you maintain that Louisette was not your mistress?'

Once again Cabuche clenched his fists. Then, in a low, faltering voice he said, 'Listen, when I came out of prison she was a little girl, not even fourteen. No one wanted to know me; they'd have chucked stones at me if they could. She came to see me in the forest. That's where we met. She used to talk to me. She was nice to me. So we got to be friends. We went for walks, holding hands. It was nice. It was really nice. She was a growing girl, I know. I couldn't stop thinking about her. I can't deny it. I loved her. She loved me too. Perhaps we'd have ended up being . . . what you said. But they took her away from me and sent her to work for that woman at Doinville. Then one night I came back from the quarry and found her outside my house, out of her mind, exhausted, burning hot, with a sort of fever. She didn't dare go back to her parents. She'd come to me . . . to die! I should've gone and slit his throat there and then, the swine!'

The magistrate pursed his lips; he was surprised at the note of sincerity in Cabuche's voice. He would have to play this close to his chest; it was going to be more difficult than he had anticipated.

'Yes, yes,' he said, 'we know the dreadful story that you and this girl cooked up between you. But you can take it from me that Monsieur Grandmorin was just not that sort of person; what you accuse him of is simply not possible.'

'What d'you mean . . . the story we cooked up?' stammered Cabuche, bewildered, wide-eyed, his hands shaking. 'It's them as is lying, and you're accusing us of being liars!'

'Yes, we most certainly do. Do not try and come the innocent . . . I've already spoken to Misard, the man who married your mistress's mother. I'll have him testify again in your presence if I need to, and you'll see what he thinks of your story. Be very careful what you say. We have witnesses and we know the full story. The best thing you can do is to tell the truth.'

This was the magistrate's usual method of trying to intimidate someone he was cross-examining, even when he knew nothing and had no witnesses.

'So . . . are you denying that you went around openly telling everyone that you were going to slit Monsieur Grandmorin's throat?'

'No, I don't deny it. That's what I said. And I meant it too. I couldn't wait to get my hands on the bugger!'

This answer took Monsieur Denizet completely by surprise. He had been expecting Cabuche to deny everything outright. Why was he admitting that he had made these threats? What game was he playing? He feared he was perhaps trying to move too quickly. He paused to reflect for a moment, then, looking Cabuche straight in the eye, he suddenly asked him:

'What did you do on the night of the fourteenth to the fifteenth of February?'

'I went to bed when it got dark, at about six o'clock . . . I wasn't feeling very well. In fact, my cousin Louis did me a favour and drove a load of stones to Doinville for me.'

'Yes, your cousin was seen driving the wagon over the railway line at the level-crossing. But when we questioned him, all he could tell us was that he had left you about midday and hadn't seen you since . . . Prove to me that you went to bed at six o'clock.'

'That's stupid,' retorted Cabuche. 'I can't prove it. I live on my own, in a house in the forest . . . That's where I was, I tell you, and that's all I can say.'

Monsieur Denizet decided that the moment had come to call Cabuche's bluff by presenting him with a statement of the facts as they were known. Assuming a totally impassive manner he described the sequence of events.

'I will tell you what you did on the evening of the fourteenth of February,' he said. 'At three in the afternoon you were at Barentin station, where you caught a train for Rouen. What the purpose of your journey was we have yet to ascertain. You had decided to travel back on the train from Paris, which arrives at Rouen at three minutes past nine. You were standing on the platform in the crowd, when you spotted Monsieur Grandmorin in his reserved compartment. I am quite prepared to admit that there was

143

no premeditation, and that the idea of committing a crime occurred to you on the spot . . . You took advantage of the congestion on the platform to get into his compartment. You waited until the train was in the tunnel at Malaunay, but you had miscalculated how fast it was travelling, and it was already leaving the tunnel when you committed the murder . . . You threw the body out of the carriage door and you got off the train at Barentin, having also disposed of the travelling rug . . . That is what you did.'

Monsieur Denizet had been scrutinizing the prisoner's face for the least flicker of assent, and was utterly dismayed when Cabuche, having at first listened to him very carefully, suddenly let out a great guffaw.

'What the hell are you talking about?' he yelled. 'If I'd done it I'd tell you!' Then, speaking more calmly, he said, 'I didn't do it, but I should've done. I wish to God I had!'

144   And that was all Monsieur Denizet could get out of him. He repeated his questions, tried time and again to put the same point in different ways, but all to no avail. Cabuche kept saying it wasn't him, shrugging his shoulders and claiming that the whole thing was ridiculous. When he had been arrested, they had searched his hovel. They had found no trace of the murder weapon, the ten banknotes or the watch, but they had found a pair of trousers with a few small bloodstains on them, a damning piece of evidence. Cabuche dismissed it scornfully as yet another piece of nonsense; he'd taken a rabbit from a snare and it had bled on his trousers! Things weren't going the way Monsieur Denizet wanted; he had started with a very clear idea of how the crime had been committed but in his determination to tie up every loose end he was complicating things and losing sight of the plain, simple truth. Cabuche was unintelligent and quite incapable of producing clever answers, but his repeated insistence that he had not committed the crime was something the magistrate had not

bargained for, and he found it disconcerting. Monsieur Denizet had persuaded himself that Cabuche was guilty, and each repeated denial annoyed him more and more, as if it were a deliberate indulgence in lawlessness and deceit. Somehow he would have to make him give in.

'So you deny it?' he said.

'Of course I deny it, because it wasn't me . . . If it had been me I'd be proud to own up to it.'

Monsieur Denizet suddenly rose to his feet and went over to the door of the adjoining room. He opened it and asked Jacques to come forward.

'Do you recognize this man?' he asked him.

'Of course,' answered Jacques, somewhat surprised at the question. 'I know him. I've seen him at the Misards.'

'No, no,' said Monsieur Denizet, 'do you recognize him as the man you saw in the train, the murderer?'

Immediately Jacques became more reticent. He didn't **145** recognize him. The man in the train seemed shorter; his hair was darker. He was on the point of saying so but decided he should err on the side of caution. He couldn't be sure.

'I don't know,' he said. 'I can't say . . . I assure you, monsieur, I really can't say.'

Without further ado, Monsieur Denizet called in Roubaud and his wife and asked them the same question: 'Do you recognize this man?'

Cabuche stood there smiling; he didn't seem a bit surprised to see the Roubauds. He nodded quickly at Séverine, whom he had known as a girl when she came to stay at La Croix-de-Maufras. Roubaud and Séverine, however, were quite taken aback to see Cabuche. They realized that this was the man who had been arrested, the man that Jacques had spoken of earlier. It was because of him that they had been called to answer further questions. Roubaud was astonished and appalled when he saw how closely Cabuche matched the description of the imaginary killer he had invented so as to be the opposite of himself. The likeness was purely fortuitous, but it came as such a shock that he was lost for words.

'Come, come,' said Monsieur Denizet, 'do you recognize him?'

'Really monsieur, I must repeat that it was only an impression . . . someone brushed past me . . . Obviously, this man is tall, like the one in the train; he is fair-haired, he has no beard . . .'

'Do you recognize him?'

Faced with such a direct question, Roubaud was torn both ways; it was an agonizing decision. Eventually the instinct of self-preservation won the day.

'I can't be absolutely sure, but he certainly looks like him; he looks very much like him.'

146   At this Cabuche began to shout and swear. He had had enough of all this nonsense. He hadn't done it and he wanted to go home. The blood rushed to his head, he thumped his fists on the desk and became so terribly agitated that Monsieur Denizet called for the constables, who came and led him away. This sudden display of violence, like a wild animal retaliating when attacked, was what the magistrate had been waiting for. He was now completely sure of himself and he showed it.

'Did you notice his eyes?' he said. 'I can always tell from the look in their eyes . . . The case is clear; we've got him!'

The Roubauds looked at each other without moving. It was all over. They were saved. The murderer was in the hands of the law. They were left feeling somewhat nonplussed and decidedly guilty about the part that they had just found themselves forced to play. At the same time they were overjoyed and quickly overcame their qualms. They smiled at Jacques and stood there, very relieved and eager to be out in the fresh air, waiting for the magistrate to give them all permission to leave. Just then the usher came in and handed Monsieur Denizet a letter.

Monsieur Denizet quickly returned to his desk and read the letter carefully, forgetting that the three witnesses were still waiting to go. The letter was from the ministry, containing the instructions he should have waited for before reopening his investigation. What was contained in the letter clearly took the edge off his moment of glory; his face gradually froze and resumed its fixed expression of seriousness. At one point he raised his head and glanced out of the corner of his eye at the Roubauds, as if something he had read had reminded him of them. The Roubauds' short-lived joy was immediately dispelled; all their fear returned, as they sensed once again that they had been found out. Why had he looked at them like that? Had someone in Paris discovered the tell-tale note that Séverine had written to Grandmorin, those three lines of handwriting that haunted them? Séverine knew Monsieur Camy-Lamotte; she had often seen him with the President at Doinville, and she knew that he had been put in charge of sorting out the dead man's papers. Roubaud was beginning to regret that he had not thought of sending his wife to Paris to make a few social calls on people who might be useful to them. She could at least have spoken to the Secretary-General and asked him to put in a good word for him, should the Railway Company become irritated by all the rumours and contemplate giving him the sack. They stood with their eyes fixed on the magistrate, sensing their anxiety increase as they saw his face darken. The letter had clearly disturbed him; his whole day's work had been undone.

At length, he dropped the letter on his desk and sat for a while, lost in thought, gazing at the Roubauds and at Jacques. Then, with a shrug of resignation and as if speaking to himself aloud, he said, 'Well, we shall see! We shall have to look at it all again . . . You may go.'

But as the three of them were leaving the room, Monsieur Denizet decided that there was one more thing he needed to know. Even though he had been specifically instructed to proceed no further without prior agreement, he felt he must clarify a crucial issue raised in the letter which seemed to invalidate his own theory of the murder.

'Please wait a moment,' he said to Jacques. 'I have one further question I would like to ask you.'

Outside in the corridor, the Roubauds stopped. The doors on to the street were open, but they could not bring themselves to leave. Something held them back; they needed to know what was happening inside the magistrate's office and they found it physically impossible to walk away until they had learned from Jacques what other question he was being asked. They walked frantically up and down the corridor until their legs ached. Eventually they came and sat down on the bench where they had waited so long already. They sat in silence, feeling sick with worry.

When Jacques reappeared, Roubaud stood up stiffly.

'We thought we would wait for you,' he said. 'We can go back to the station together. What did he ask you?'

Jacques looked away, embarrassed, as if he were trying to avoid Séverine's eyes, which were fixed on him.

'He's not sure about it any more,' he said at last. 'He's floundering. He just asked me if there weren't two people involved. When I was questioned at Le Havre, I mentioned a black shape holding down the victim's legs, and he asked me about that. He seems to think it was just the travelling rug. Anyway, he sent for the rug, and I had to tell him whether that was what I saw. I told him that it could have been.'

The Roubauds were shaking. The law was after them;

one word from Jacques and they were done for. There was no doubt he knew they had done it, and sooner or later he would talk. They left the law courts in silence, Séverine walking between the two men. When they were in the street, Roubaud said, 'By the way, my friend, Madame Roubaud has to spend a day in Paris on business. I'd appreciate it if you could help her find her way around; she may need someone to accompany her.'

5

At eleven fifteen, right on time, the signalman at the Pont
de l'Europe sounded the regulation two blasts on his horn
to announce the arrival of the express from Le Havre as
it emerged from the Batignolles tunnel. It came clattering
over the turntables and ran into the station with a short
toot on its whistle, a squealing of brakes, smoke pouring
from its chimney and dripping wet from the teeming rain
that had been falling steadily since it had left Rouen.

Even before the porters had unlatched the carriage doors,
one of them swung open, and Séverine jumped out on to
the platform without waiting for the train to stop. She had
150 been sitting at the rear of the train, and in order to get to
the engine she had to dash down the platform through the
sudden invasion of passengers who were climbing out of
the carriages laden with parcels and surrounded by children. Jacques stood on the footplate waiting to take the
engine back to the sheds, while Pecqueux cleaned the brass-
work with a rag.

'I'll see you in the Rue Cardinet at three o'clock,'
she said, standing on tiptoe. 'Is that all right? I need to
speak to your boss. I have a message for him from my
husband.'

Such was the scheme devised by Roubaud. Séverine was
to convey his thanks to the Batignolles shed foreman for
a favour he had done him. This would allow her to spend
time in the company of Jacques and would give her a
chance to strengthen their acquaintance and exercise her
charm on him.

Jacques, black with coal dust, soaked to the skin and
utterly exhausted after battling against wind and rain,

stared at her blankly and made no answer. He had been unable to refuse Roubaud as the train was leaving Le Havre, but the thought of finding himself alone with Séverine disturbed him, because he now knew that he desired her.

'Is that all right?' Séverine repeated, smiling and looking at him sweetly, attempting to overcome the surprise and the faint sense of disgust she felt at seeing him so filthy that she hardly recognized him. 'I'm counting on you.'

She placed her gloved hand on one of the iron handrails and attempted to lift herself on to the footplate. Pecqueux obligingly warned her to be careful.

'I wouldn't come up here,' he said, 'you'll get yourself dirty.'

Jacques had to give her an answer, but he sounded far from enthusiastic.

'All right,' he said, 'I'll see you in the Rue Cardinet . . . provided I don't get washed away in this bloody rain! Damned weather!'

She felt really quite sorry for him, seeing him in such a pitiful state.

'You poor thing!' she said, speaking to him as if he had been braving the elements just for her. 'There was I all warm and dry! I was thinking of you all the time. What a terrible storm! I can't tell you how frightened I was! I was so glad to think it was you bringing me here this morning and taking me back tonight on the express.'

These little confidences, well-meaning as they were, only served to make Jacques all the more uneasy. It came as a relief when a voice shouted: 'Right away! You can back her out!' He promptly gave a tug on the whistle, and Pecqueux motioned to Séverine to stand aside.

'I'll see you at three o'clock,' she called.

'All right,' he said, 'three o'clock.'

As the locomotive reversed out of the station, Séverine

151

left the platform, which was by now empty. She walked out on to the Rue d'Amsterdam and was about to open her umbrella when, to her relief, she saw that it had stopped raining. She walked down the street to the Place du Havre, stopped for a moment to deliberate on what she should do next and decided that it would be best to have some lunch. It was twenty-five past eleven. She went into a little restaurant at the corner of the Rue Saint-Lazare and ordered fried eggs and a chop. She ate slowly, ruminating on all that had happened over the last few weeks. She looked pale and drawn. There was no sign of her usual charming smile.

The day before, two days after the interview with the examining magistrate in Rouen, Roubaud, deeming further delay dangerous, had decided to send his wife to Paris to speak with Monsieur Camy-Lamotte, not at the ministry but at his private address in the Rue du Rocher, a large townhouse situated next door to that of Grand-morin. Séverine knew that he would be in at one o'clock,[1] so there was no rush. She sat preparing what she was going to say and trying to imagine how he might respond, in order to give herself more confidence. The day before, a further cause of anxiety had arisen which had made her journey to Paris even more urgent; they had heard through gossip at the station that Madame Lebleu and Philomène were telling everyone that the Company intended to dismiss Roubaud because it considered him a liability. Worse still, Monsieur Dabadie, when asked if it was true, had not denied it, which lent added weight to the rumour. It had become urgent that Séverine come to Paris as soon as possible to put their case and enlist the support of the Secretary-General, as they had done previously with the President. This was the ostensible reason for her trip, but behind it there lay something more compelling – a burning, insatiable desire to know if they had been found out, a desire so overpowering that it will drive a criminal to give himself up rather than continue in uncertainty. Ever since Jacques had told them that the prosecution now seemed to think that two people were involved in the murder, the Roubauds suspected that their crime had been discovered, and the uncertainty was driving them to distraction. They were wearing themselves out imagining one thing after another – perhaps they had found the letter, perhaps they had managed to work out their movements on the day of the crime. At any minute, they thought, someone would come with a search warrant or a warrant for their arrest. The strain was becoming unbearable; the least little things appeared threatening. They were beginning to think that it would be better to be found out rather than go on living in a state of continual panic; they would at least know where they stood, and their anxiety would be at an end.[2]

Séverine finished eating her chop. She had been deep **153** in thought and woke up with a start to find herself sitting in a restaurant. There was a bitter taste in her mouth. She couldn't swallow her food. She didn't even want any coffee. She had eaten slowly, but it was still barely a quarter past twelve when she left the restaurant. She had another three-quarters of an hour to kill! Usually, when she came to Paris, she loved being in the city and walking around the streets. But today she felt lost and frightened, wishing she had done what she had come to do, and that she could run away and hide. The pavement was by now almost dry. A warm breeze blew away the last of the clouds. She walked down the Rue Tronchet and arrived at the flower market on the Place de la Madeleine. It was a typical March flower market, with primroses and azaleas in full bloom, flaunting their colour in the pale light of a late-winter afternoon. For half an hour Séverine walked round the market, surrounded by this precocious flowering of spring, lost in her thoughts. Jacques was an enemy whom she must disarm.

She had spoken with Monsieur Camy-Lamotte, and everything had gone well. All she needed to do was persuade Jacques to remain silent. It would not be easy. She began to imagine all manner of romantic scenarios and discovered that, far from increasing her fatigue and anxiety, it had a pleasantly soothing effect. Suddenly she noticed the time, on a clock in one of the market stalls – ten past one! It brought her back to reality with a jolt. She had achieved nothing. She hurried off towards the Rue du Rocher.

Monsieur Camy-Lamotte's house stood at the corner of the Rue du Rocher and the Rue de Naples. In order to get to it, Séverine had to walk past Grandmorin's house, standing silent and empty, with its shutters closed. She glanced up at it and quickened her step. She remembered the last time she had come there. There it still stood, tall and sinister. A little further on, she stopped to look behind her, like someone pursued by an angry mob, and she caught sight of Monsieur Denizet, the examining magistrate from Rouen, walking on the opposite side of the street. His presence startled her. Had he seen her looking at Grandmorin's house? He seemed quite unconcerned. She allowed him to walk past her, following behind him in a state of trepidation. It came as an even greater shock when she saw him ring the doorbell of Monsieur Camy-Lamotte's house at the corner of the Rue de Naples.

She fell into a panic. How could she go and see him now? She rushed back down the street, turned into the Rue d'Edimbourg and came to the Pont de l'Europe. Only then did she feel able to pause for a moment. Not knowing where to go or what to do, she stood, motionless, leaning against the balustrade, looking down through the iron girders at the vast open space of the station below. Trains were continually coming and going; she watched them with fear in her eyes. She was convinced that the magistrate had gone to see Monsieur Camy-Lamotte in order to discuss the inquiry, and that at this very moment the two men were talking about her and deciding her fate. In a fit of despair, she felt she would rather throw herself there and then under a train than return to the Rue du Rocher. A train was emerging from under the roof of the mainline station; she watched it approach and pass beneath her, blowing a warm cloud of steam into her face. She knew that if she didn't muster the energy to put an end to their uncertainty, her trip would have been a foolish waste of time and she would return home in an unbearable agony of mind. She decided she would wait five minutes more in order to regain her nerve. She could hear locomotives whistling below her. She watched a little shunting engine moving a suburban train out of a siding. She looked up to her left, over the parcels delivery bay, and spotted the window of Madame Victoire's room, at the top of the house **155** in the Impasse d'Amsterdam, the window she had leaned out of with her husband before the terrible scene which had brought them to this desperate situation. It reminded her so forcibly of the danger she was in that she suddenly felt ready to face anything, if it would put an end to her misery. The sound of the shunters' horns reverberated in her ears. Trains rumbled interminably under the bridge beneath her. Clouds of thick smoke obscured the horizon as they rose into the clear Paris skies. She began to walk back to the Rue du Rocher, like a person intent on suicide, quickening her step for fear she might find no one in.

As she pulled the doorbell, a fresh wave of panic ran through her, but a manservant took her name, quickly ushered her into an anteroom and invited her to take a seat. The doors had been left slightly ajar, and through them she distinctly heard the sound of two voices engaged in heated conversation. There then came a long silence, during which all she was conscious of was a steady drumming in her temples. She concluded that the examining magistrate was still with Monsieur Camy-Lamotte, and that she would probably be kept waiting for a long time. It was more than she could bear. Suddenly, however, much to her surprise, the manservant summoned her, and she was conducted into the Secretary-General's study. She was sure that Denizet had not left; she sensed he was still there, hidden behind a door.

The Secretary-General's study was a large room with dark furniture, a thick carpet and heavy door-curtains. It felt very austere and enclosed. No sound reached it from outside. There was, however, a bronze vase containing a few pale roses, which suggested that behind this severe façade there lay a hidden gentility, a taste for the finer things in life. The master of the house stood waiting to receive her, dressed formally in a frock-coat and looking 156 as austere as his surroundings. He had a rather pinched face, filled out somewhat by his greying side-whiskers. He still had about him something of the stylish young beau he had been in his youth. He looked slim and distinguished, but one sensed a kindly nature beneath the cultivated stiffness of his official manner. The subdued light of the room made him appear very tall.

As she entered, Séverine was overwhelmed by the hot, enclosed atmosphere of the room, draped with curtains and wall-hangings. All she was aware of was Monsieur Camy-Lamotte watching her as she walked towards him. He did not invite her to sit down and made a point of not being the first to speak, leaving it to her to explain the reason for her visit. There was a long silence. Séverine was at a loss how to begin. Eventually, taking her courage in both hands, speaking calmly and choosing her words carefully, she said, 'Monsieur, please excuse my boldness in coming to seek your help. You will be aware of the irreparable loss I have suffered. I feel helpless. I ventured to think that you might assist us; that you might somehow be able to continue the protection that your friend, my guardian, afforded us . . . before his untimely death.'

Monsieur Camy-Lamotte had no alternative but to ask her to sit down. She had spoken eloquently, with no effusive display of humility or grief, but with an instinctive mastery of feminine artifice. He continued to say nothing. He sat down himself and waited for her to continue. Realizing that she was required to say more, Séverine began again.

'You may have forgotten, monsieur,' she said, 'but I had the honour of seeing you at Doinville. Ah, what happy times they were! But something terrible has happened, and you are the only one I can turn to. I beg you, monsieur, in the name of the dear friend we have lost, if you truly loved him, do not abandon me. Take his place beside me.'

Monsieur Camy-Lamotte had watched her carefully 157 as she spoke. She seemed so natural, so charming, as she sat there sadly pleading with him, that his suspicions were unsettled. He had suspected that the note he had found among Grandmorin's papers – two lines with no signature – had come from her, for he knew that the President had enjoyed her favours. When, a moment before, he was told that she had come to see him, his suspicions seemed to be confirmed. He had interrupted his discussion with the magistrate only in order to ascertain that these suspicions were correct. But how could he possibly think she was guilty, now that she sat there in front of him, so gentle and appealing?

He needed to get things clear in his mind. Maintaining his grave demeanour, he asked her, 'Perhaps you could explain, madame . . . I remember you at Doinville very well . . . there is nothing I would like more than to assist you, if it is within my power to do so.'

Séverine told him frankly how her husband was

threatened with dismissal. He had become the object of resentment among his colleagues, due partly to his own success and partly to the fact that he had received help from people in high places. Now that this help was no longer available, people were making even more determined efforts to get rid of him, and they seemed to think they would succeed. She named no names and was careful to remain discreet, despite the real danger that confronted them. It was only because she was convinced she needed to act quickly that she had decided to make the journey to Paris. Tomorrow might be too late; she needed help immediately. Her arguments were so well founded and persuasive that it seemed impossible to Monsieur Camy-Lamotte that there could be any other reason why she had gone to such trouble to come and see him.

He watched her intently as she spoke, observing the slightest tremor of her lips.

158

'Why should the Company wish to dismiss your husband?' he asked her suddenly. 'Surely he has done nothing seriously wrong.'

She too had been eyeing him carefully, looking for some flicker of response in the lines of his face, all the time wondering whether he had found the letter. His question had seemed a perfectly innocent one, yet the minute he asked it, she was convinced that the letter was there in the room, in a drawer somewhere. He had read it. He was setting a trap to see if she would dare mention the real reasons for her husband's dismissal. There was something too pointed about the way he had phrased the question. She felt as if his pale, weary eyes were reading her innermost thoughts.

Bravely she entered the fray.

'It is outrageous, monsieur,' she said. 'Just because of what was in that awful will, people are saying that we killed Monsieur Grandmorin. We proved that we were innocent, but such terrible accusations are not easily forgotten. I imagine the Company is afraid there might be some scandal.'

Once again Monsieur Camy-Lamotte was surprised and rather taken aback by the frankness of her response and the note of genuine anguish in her voice. What was more, having at first sight found her not particularly attractive, he was beginning to yield to the spell of her gently appealing blue eyes and her luxuriant black hair. He thought of his friend Grandmorin with a mixture of jealousy and admiration. How on earth had an old rake like him, ten years his senior, managed to attract creatures like this till the day he died, when he had already had to abandon such pleasures in order to preserve what little bit of energy he still had left? She was charming; quite delightful in fact. He sat looking at her, stiff and serious – a government minister with an awkward problem on his hands. A smile of wistful longing passed across his lips.

Séverine, emboldened by the effect she sensed she was having upon him, made the mistake of adding: 'We are not the sort of people who would kill for money. There would have to have been some other motive ... and there wasn't.'

Monsieur Camy-Lamotte looked at her and saw the corners of her mouth tremble. Yes, she was the murderer! He knew it instantly. Séverine too realized immediately that she had played into his hands; she could tell from the way he stopped smiling and pursed his lips awkwardly. She felt she was about to faint, as if all her energy were ebbing away. She managed to remain sitting upright. Monsieur Camy-Lamotte proceeded with his questions in the same unhurried manner as before, and the conversation continued. But each had already told the other all that they needed to know. The words they exchanged were immaterial. What they were really talking of were the two things that neither of them could mention – he had the letter, and she had written it. This was the message that passed between them, even as they sat there saying nothing.

'Madame,' the Secretary-General said eventually, 'I have no objection to interceding with the Company on your behalf if there is a genuine case to answer. As it happens, I am due to see the General Manager this evening on other business. I shall need a few details. Perhaps you would make a note of your husband's name, age and record of employment, and anything else that might help to clarify the situation.'

He pushed a little writing desk towards her, carefully averting his eyes so as not to appear intimidating. A shudder ran through her. He wanted a page of her handwriting in order to compare it with the letter. She desperately tried to think of an excuse, determined not to write. But then she asked herself what was the point, since he knew anyway? They could always get hold of a few lines of her writing. Without any sign of emotion, she steadied her nerves, picked up the pen and wrote down what he asked. Monsieur Camy-Lamotte, standing behind her, recognized the writing immediately, although it was more upright and less shaky than that of the letter. He couldn't help admiring her – a mere slip of a girl, but so brave-hearted! Now that she couldn't see him, he smiled again – the smile of a man inured by long experience to all but feminine charm. Justice was such a wearisome business! It really wasn't worth the trouble. His sole concern was the reputation of the government he served.

'Very well, madame,' he said, 'you may leave it with me. I will make inquiries and do what I can.'

'I am most grateful, monsieur,' she replied. 'May I count on you then to ensure that my husband is not dismissed?'

'I am afraid, madame, that it is not quite as simple as that,' he answered. 'I cannot promise anything. We must see what transpires. I need to give it some thought.'

Monsieur Camy-Lamotte was in something of a quandary, remaining undecided how to proceed with the Roubauds. Séverine, on the other hand, had but one thought in her mind. She knew that she was at his mercy. He had the power to save her or to destroy her. How would he decide?

'Monsieur,' she pleaded, 'think how terrible this is for us. Please do not send me away without your assurance that all will be well.'

'I am afraid I must, madame,' he said. 'There is nothing more I can do for the present. You must be patient.'

He led her towards the door. She stood there, distraught and confused, on the point of confessing everything, so desperate was she to know what his intentions were. In an attempt to gain a minute more and find some other way round him, she suddenly exclaimed:

'Oh, I almost forgot! I wanted to ask your advice about 161 this awful will which has caused us so much trouble . . . Do you think we should have declined the legacy?'

'The will quite clearly makes the property out to you,' Monsieur Camy-Lamotte answered circumspectly. 'It is a mark of appreciation and personal respect.'

She was still standing in the doorway. She made one last desperate plea.

'Monsieur, I beg you,' she said. 'I cannot leave without knowing. Please will you tell me if you can help us?'

Without thinking, she had seized his hand. Monsieur Camy-Lamotte withdrew it. She continued to gaze at him with her beautiful blue eyes, imploring him. He finally relented.

'Very well,' he said. 'Come back at five o'clock. Perhaps I will be able to tell you something then.'

Séverine left the house even more perturbed than when she had arrived. Monsieur Camy-Lamotte now knew what had happened. But her future was still uncertain. At any

minute she might find herself arrested. How could she sur-
vive until five o'clock? Suddenly she remembered Jacques.
She had forgotten all about him. If she were arrested, he was
another who might seal her fate. It was still not quite half
past two, but she hurried down the Rue du Rocher towards
the Rue Cardinet, as if there were not a minute to spare.

Left alone, Monsieur Camy-Lamotte remained standing in front of his desk. He was highly respected in
government circles, and in his capacity as Secretary-
General of the Ministry of Justice he was summoned to
the Tuileries Palace almost daily. He exercised as much
power as the Minister of Justice himself, and it was he who
was always entrusted with the more delicate matters. He
knew the concern and displeasure that the Grandmorin
affair was causing in high places. The opposition newspapers were still running a vociferous campaign, some
arguing that the police were so busy protecting politicians
that they didn't have time to arrest murderers,[3] others
delving into the President's private life and presenting him
as an acolyte of that notorious hive of profligacy, the
Court! As the elections drew nearer, the campaign was
having a disastrous effect. The Secretary-General had
been informed that the government wished to see the
affair closed as soon as possible, by whatever expedient
was necessary, and as the minister had delegated this delicate matter to him, he now had sole responsibility for
dealing with it. The decision would be his and his alone.
He therefore had to give it careful consideration. He knew
that if he made a mistake, he would be the one to pay for it.

Still deep in thought, he walked across the room and
opened the door to where Monsieur Denizet had been
waiting. Monsieur Denizet had been eavesdropping on
their conversation.

'Just as I said!' he exclaimed, as he re-entered the room.
'We were wrong to suspect the Roubauds. It is quite plain

that the only thing she was bothered about was preventing her husband being dismissed. She didn't say a single incriminating word.'

The Secretary-General made no answer. He stood looking at the magistrate as he continued to turn things over in his mind. He thought of all the men in law courts up and down the country whose future, by virtue of being in control of appointments, he held in his hands. It amazed him to think what worthy men they were despite their pitiful salaries, how intelligent they were despite the stultifying demands of their profession. Whether he was clever or not, the man standing in front of him, peering at him through half-closed eyes, was certainly very tenacious when he thought he had got hold of the truth.

'So,' he said, 'you still think that this Cabuche is the murderer?'

The question took Monsieur Denizet by surprise.

'Indeed I do!' he answered. 'The evidence is overwhelming. I've been through all of it with you and I can safely say that it's a classic case; there's not a single thing missing. I've done everything I can to ascertain whether he had an accomplice in the compartment, a woman as you gave me to understand. That seemed to tally with the statement of an engine driver, a man who caught a glimpse of the murder actually being committed. Of course, I questioned him thoroughly, but he was unable to confirm what he had originally said. He actually identified the travelling rug as being the black shape he had mentioned . . . Yes, I'm quite certain that Cabuche was the murderer. All the more so because, if we can't prove it was him, we can't prove it was anybody!'

The Secretary-General had been waiting to tell him about the written evidence that was in his possession, but now that he knew that Séverine was guilty, he was even less keen than before to establish the truth. Why upset the examining magistrate's mistaken conclusions if the true line of inquiry was going to lead to even more trouble. It all needed careful consideration.

'Well,' he continued with a weary smile, 'I dare say you're right. I only asked you to come and see me because there are a number of important matters we need to discuss. This is a very special case and it has now become a serious political issue, as I am sure you realize. We may therefore be obliged to consider what is in the government's best interests . . . Tell me honestly, do your inquiries lead you to believe that this girl, Cabuche's mistress, was raped?'

Monsieur Denizet was astute enough to realize where the question was leading; he pursed his lips and half closed his eyes.

'I think the President had certainly treated her badly,' he said, 'and that is bound to come out at the trial. What's more, she wasn't the only one. If the defence is entrusted 164 to an opposition lawyer, you can be sure that the President's name will be well and truly dragged through the mud; up in Rouen, stories of his amorous pursuits are in plentiful supply.'

This Denizet was no fool, especially when for a moment he put professional ethics to one side and stopped thinking of himself as some supreme being, all-knowing and all-powerful. He obviously understood perfectly well why he had been invited to see the Secretary-General in private rather than at the Ministry of Justice.

'In fact,' he concluded, seeing that Monsieur Camy-Lamotte didn't seem in the least surprised by what he had said, 'we are likely to end up with some pretty sordid business on our hands.'

Monsieur Camy-Lamotte merely nodded. He was trying to work out what would happen if, instead of Cabuche, it was the Roubauds who were put on trial. One thing was certain; Roubaud would tell everything – how his wife had also been violated when she was a young girl, the subsequent adultery, the jealous rage which had driven him to commit murder. Moreover, it would no longer be the trial of a domestic servant and a criminal who had already served time; Roubaud was respectably employed and he was married, to a very attractive woman. People would start asking all sorts of questions about middle-class morality and the sort of people that the railway companies chose to employ. What was more, with a man like President Grandmorin, you never knew what might come to light. How many other unforeseen scandals would they run into? No, the Roubauds might well be guilty, but to put them on trial would be a very messy affair. Monsieur Camy-Lamotte had decided; they must avoid proceeding against the Roubauds at all costs. If anyone was to be prosecuted, he tended to think it should be Cabuche, even though he was innocent.

'Your theory is very persuasive,' he finally said to Monsieur Denizet. 'There is a lot of circumstantial evidence against Cabuche, and he obviously felt he was justified in taking revenge . . . What a wretched business this is! I dread to think of the damage it's going to cause! . . . I know that the law must remain indifferent to the consequences of its findings, that it should rise above vested interest . . .'

He raised his hand dismissively, and his sentence was left unfinished. The magistrate too remained silent, glumly awaiting the instructions that he knew he was about to be given. If he was allowed to proceed with his own version of events, this singular product of his own intelligence, he was prepared to sacrifice justice to the needs of the government. The Secretary, however, although normally very adept at handling arrangements of this sort, was a little too hasty, coming quickly to the point, like someone used to being obeyed.

'In short,' he said, 'we want the case dismissed . . . I would like you to make the necessary arrangements.'

'I'm afraid, monsieur, that I can no longer do just as I please,' replied Denizet. 'It is a matter of professional conscience.'

Monsieur Camy-Lamotte smiled and immediately resumed his official manner.

'But of course!' he said, with a display of worldly-wise courtesy that barely disguised his contempt. 'It is your professional conscience that I am relying on. I leave you to take the decision which your conscience thinks best. I have every confidence that you will weigh the pros and cons fairly, that common sense will prevail and that the public interest will be well served . . . You will know better than I that it is sometimes more courageous to overlook a wrong if it enables us to avoid something even worse . . . We leave things to your better judgement and your sense of what is right and proper. We would not dream of imposing on your authority; the matter remains entirely within your jurisdiction, as indeed the law stipulates.' The magistrate relished the unlimited authority that was vested in him, especially when he was allowed to almost abuse it. He listened to everything that the Secretary-General said with a nod of satisfaction.

'Moreover,' continued Monsieur Camy-Lamotte, with an unctuousness that verged on the ironic, 'we know that we can depend on you. Your hard work over the last few years has not gone unnoticed, and I can assure you that, should a position ever become available in Paris, we would have no hesitation in calling upon your services.'

This last remark rather unsettled Denizet. What? If he did what he was being asked to do, was he still not going to get his cherished appointment in Paris?

Monsieur Camy-Lamotte had read his thoughts.

'The appointment has been decided,' he added quickly. 'It is merely a question of time . . . However, having already said more than I should, I am delighted to tell you that you have been nominated for the Legion of Honour on August the fifteenth.'

The magistrate thought for a moment. He would have preferred promotion, having calculated that it would mean a rise in salary of about one hundred and sixty-six francs a month. Compared with his present straitened circumstances, he would be able to live more comfortably, buy himself some new clothes, and his housekeeper Mélanie would be better fed and less cantankerous. But the Legion of Honour was not to be sniffed at. He had at least been given an assurance of promotion. Denizet was one of those lawyers who would never go far; he had been brought up to believe in the value of decent, hard-working dedication to duty. He would never have dreamed he could be bought. But here he was, yielding to temptation, prompted by nothing more than the rather flimsy prospect of advancement and the vague assurance **167** that the ministry would do what it could to help him. The law, after all, was a job like any other, and seeking promotion was a cross that had to be borne; one must learn to bow and scrape to those above one and be ready to do their every bidding.

'I am most honoured,' he murmured. 'Please convey my thanks to the minister.'

He had got up to leave, sensing that it would be embarrassing to continue the conversation further. His face was fixed and expressionless.

'Very well,' he said, 'I will continue my investigation bearing your concerns in mind. Obviously, if there is no absolute proof against Cabuche, it will be better to avoid risking the unnecessary scandal of a trial . . . he will be released, but will remain under surveillance.'

The Secretary-General politely accompanied him to the door.

'Monsieur Denizet,' he said, 'we place ourselves entirely

in your hands. We know that we can count on your infinite tact and your great integrity.'

When he was once again alone, Monsieur Camy-Lamotte, out of sheer curiosity, and knowing that the exercise was now pointless, compared the page that Séverine had written with the unsigned letter he had found amongst the President's papers. The writing was identical. He folded the letter and put it away carefully. Although he had made no mention of it to the examining magistrate, he still felt that such a vital piece of evidence was worth keeping. In his mind's eye he pictured Séverine, so frail yet so tough and determined. He shrugged his shoulders with a mixture of admiration and amusement. Ah, these women, he thought to himself, they certainly know how to get their own way!

Séverine reached the Rue Cardinet at twenty to three. She was early for her meeting with Jacques. This was where he lived, in a tiny room right at the top of a tall building, although he hardly ever went there except at night, to sleep. There were also two nights a week when he was away in Le Havre, having driven the evening express from Paris, only returning the next morning. On this occasion, however, being soaked and exhausted, he had gone to his room and gone straight to bed. Séverine might have waited indefinitely had Jacques not been woken up by a row in the next room – a woman screaming and being beaten by her husband. He looked out of his attic window and spotted Séverine on the pavement below. Feeling very disgruntled, he shaved and got dressed.

'There you are at last!' she cried, as he emerged on to the street. 'I thought I must have made a mistake. You did say to meet you at the corner of the Rue Saussure, didn't you?'

She didn't wait for him to reply.

'Is that where you live?' she said, looking up at the building.

He hadn't told her, but the reason he had arranged to meet her here was because the engine shed that he was supposed to be taking her to stood almost directly opposite. However, Séverine's question had rather embarrassed him; he thought that, in an effort to be friendly, she might ask him to show her his room, which was so barely furnished and so untidy that he was ashamed of it.

'I don't exactly live here,' he said, 'I just come here to roost. Come on, we'll have to hurry. I think the foreman might already have left.'

Indeed, when they reached the foreman's little house behind the engine shed inside the station precinct, he was not there. They walked from one end of the engine shed to the other and still could not find him. Everyone they spoke to told them that if they wanted to be sure of catching him, they should come back at four o'clock; he would be in the repair shops.

'All right,' said Séverine, 'we'll come back.'

When they were outside again and she found herself alone with Jacques, she asked him, 'If you're not doing anything, would you mind if I wait with you?'

He could hardly refuse. Besides, even though she made him feel strangely uneasy, he was beginning to find her company increasingly congenial. Every time she looked at him with her soft blue eyes, he felt the bad mood, which he had been quite determined to stay in for the rest of the day, gradually melting away. She looked so gentle, so timid . . . She must be very affectionate, he thought, like a faithful dog that you couldn't bear to hurt.

'Of course I won't leave you,' he said, speaking less sharply. 'But we have over an hour to kill. Would you like to go to a café?'

She smiled at him, delighted to hear him at last sounding a little more affable.

'Oh no,' she protested, 'I don't want to be indoors;

I would rather we went for a walk . . . in the open air . . . wherever you want.'

She gently slipped her arm into his. Now that he was no longer covered in dirt from driving the train, she found him quite handsome. He was wearing a suit, which made him look quite well-to-do, yet, despite his smart appearance, there was about him a sort of proud independence, a sense of being out in the open air, braving danger day by day. Never before had she noticed how good-looking he was – a round face with regular features, a very dark moustache and white skin. Only his eyes disturbed her. They were flecked with gold, but there was something shifty about them, and he held them constantly averted. Was he refusing to look at her because he didn't want to become too involved, because he wanted to remain free to do as he chose, perhaps even to denounce her? A shudder ran through her whenever she thought of the Secretary-General's study in the Rue du Rocher, where her fate was being decided. What would become of her? All she wanted was to feel that the man whose arm she was holding was hers, hers completely; she wanted to be able to raise her head towards him and see him look long and deeply into her eyes. Then she would know that he was hers. It was not that she was in love with him; the thought had not entered her head. She simply wanted to have him under her control, to know that she need no longer fear him.

For a few minutes they walked together without speaking, picking their way through the throng of passers-by, at times even having to step off the pavement and walk in the road amongst the traffic. Eventually they reached the Square des Batignolles. At this time of year it was almost deserted. The sky, washed clean by the morning's rain, was a beautiful clear blue, and the lilac trees were coming into bloom in the warm March sunshine.

'Can we get away from the street?' Séverine suggested. 'These crowds make me feel giddy.'

Jacques too wanted to find somewhere quieter. Without realizing it, he wanted to have her more to himself, to be away from all these people.

They were walking past the entrance to a little park.[4]

'What about here?' he said. 'Come on, let's go in.'

They walked slowly down the path along the edge of the lawn, beneath the bare trees. There were a few mothers taking their young children for a walk and people, obviously in a hurry, using the park as a short cut. They crossed the stream and walked up through the rock gardens. They turned to come back, not knowing quite what to do next. They wandered through a clump of pine trees, whose evergreen foliage shone dark green in the sunlight. There happened to be a bench there, in a quiet corner hidden from view. Without exchanging a word, they sat down, seemingly led to this spot by some mutual understanding.

'What a lovely day it is now,' she said, in an effort to break the silence.

'Yes,' he answered, 'the sun's come out again.'

But their minds were on other things. Jacques, who normally avoided the company of women, had been pondering the chain of events that had brought him and Séverine together. Here she was, sitting next to him, touching him, threatening to invade his life. How had it happened? Ever since the last interview with the examining magistrate at Rouen, he had absolutely no doubt that she had been an accomplice in the murder at La Croix-de-Maufras. But how had she come to do such a thing? What passion or motive had driven her? He had asked himself again and again, without ever finding any obvious answer. Eventually, he had worked out a possible explanation, based on a self-seeking and violent husband who sought to get his hands on the legacy as soon as possible, fearing the will might be changed to their disadvantage and perhaps thinking that his relationship with his wife might be strengthened by a shared act of murder. This was the only explanation that seemed to make any sense; it left many questions unanswered, and they intrigued him, but he hadn't attempted to pursue them further. He had also been in two minds whether it wasn't his duty to tell the law what he knew, and it was this that was uppermost in his mind as he sat beside her on the park bench, so close in fact that he could feel the warmth of her thigh against his.

'It's amazing to be able to sit outside like this in March,' he said. 'It's like summer.'

'Yes!' she replied. 'The minute the sun comes out you can feel it.'

Séverine, for her part, was thinking that Jacques would have to be unbelievably stupid not to realize that they were 172 guilty. It must have been so obvious how they had tried to win him over; even now, she knew that she was sitting too close to him. In the silences which punctuated their banal conversation, she tried to gauge his thoughts. Their eyes met briefly. She could tell that he was wondering whether the black shape he had seen in the train had indeed been her, pinning down the victim's legs with all her strength. What could she do, what could she say that would bind him to her irrevocably?

'It was very cold in Le Havre this morning,' she said.

'There was a lot of rain, too,' he replied.

Séverine had a sudden inspiration. She didn't stop to reflect or think about it; it came to her instinctively, from somewhere deep within her psyche. Had she stopped to give it thought, she would have said nothing; she simply felt that it was the right thing to do. She could win him over merely by talking to him.

She gently took his hand in hers and looked at him. They were hidden from passers-by in the nearby street by the green covering of trees. The only sound to be heard was the distant rumble of traffic, reaching them faintly in the sunlit solitude of the park. At the end of the path, a child was silently absorbed in shovelling sand into a little bucket with a spade. Without any change in her voice, but with a sudden intensity of feeling, she quietly asked him, 'Do you think I am guilty?'

He shuddered slightly and looked steadily into her eyes.

'Yes, I do,' he answered with the same quiet intensity in his voice as her.

She had kept his hand in hers and squeezed it more tightly. For a while she remained silent, sensing the two of them being drawn together in a rush of unspoken feeling.

'You are mistaken,' she said. 'I am not guilty.'

This was not so much an attempt to convince Jacques **173** as a plain assertion that in the eyes of the world she must surely be considered innocent. She hoped that by simply and steadfastly denying the truth she could make the truth go away.

'I am not guilty,' she repeated. 'Please don't continue to make me unhappy by thinking that I am.'

He looked into her eyes long and deeply, and her heart was gladdened.

She realized that what she had just done was to give herself to him. She had surrendered herself, and if later he claimed her, she would be unable to refuse. But there was now a bond between them, and it was indissoluble. She need no longer worry that he would denounce her; he was hers and she was his. She had confided in him and they were now united.

'Promise me you won't be unkind; tell me that you believe me.'

'Yes, I believe you,' he answered with a smile.

Why force her to go through all the painful details of this sordid affair? She would tell him about it in due course if she felt she needed to. He was deeply touched by the way she had sought to reassure herself, confiding in him whilst admitting nothing; it seemed a sign of great affection. She was so trusting, so vulnerable, with her soft periwinkle-blue eyes! She seemed to be pure womanhood, made for man, ready to submit herself to him in her search for happiness! Above all what pleased him, as they sat holding hands and looking into each other's eyes, was that she didn't cause him to feel the dreadful unease, the terrifying sickness that usually came over him in the presence of a woman when he thought of possessing her. With other women he had not even been able to touch them without wanting to sink his teeth into them to satisfy his abominable appetite for slaughter. Was this the woman he could love, and not
174 want to kill?

'Rest assured that I am your friend,' he whispered into her ear. 'You have nothing to fear from me. I will not pry into your affairs, I promise you. I will do as you wish. You may make use of me as you choose.'

His face was now so close to hers that he could feel the warmth of her breath on his lips. Only that morning, sitting close to a woman like this would have made him tremble with fear, lest one of his dreadful attacks should begin. What was happening to him? He felt perfectly calm and pleasantly weary, like someone recovering from an illness. Now that he knew she had committed murder, she seemed different, more impressive, someone special. Perhaps she wasn't merely an accomplice but had even done the deed herself. Jacques was convinced she had, although he had no proof. From that moment, as she sat there utterly oblivious of the fearful desire she aroused in him, she became as someone sacred to him, someone beyond the reach of mere reason.

They were both chatting happily away to each other like a couple who had just met and were beginning to fall in love.

'You should let me take your other hand so that I can warm it in mine,' he said.

'Not here,' she answered. 'Someone might see us.'

'Who's going to see us here?' he responded, 'We're alone . . . Anyway, what harm would it do? That's not how babies are made.'

'I should hope not too!' she exclaimed, laughing out loud.

She was delighted to know that he was now her friend. She didn't love him; of that she was sure. She may have offered herself to him, but she was already thinking of ways she might refuse him. He seemed a decent sort of chap, someone who wouldn't give her a lot of trouble; it was all working out very nicely.

175

'Good!' she said. 'We are friends. That's just a matter between you and me. No one else, not even my husband, need know about it. And now I think you should perhaps let go of my hand and stop staring at me. You'll wear your eyes out.'

But he continued to hold her hand, her delicate fingers entwined in his.

'I love you,' he whispered softly into her ear.

She pulled her hand away quickly and stood up. Jacques remained seated on the bench.

'Don't be silly!' she said. 'Behave yourself, there's somebody coming.'

A nursemaid was coming along the path towards them with a baby asleep in her arms. A young girl walked past, clearly in a hurry. The sun was beginning to sink, slipping beneath the horizon in a purplish haze; its rays gradually receded from the lawns and faded in a cloud of gold over the green tops of the pine trees. A sudden lull seemed to interrupt the continuous rumble of traffic. A nearby clock struck five.

'Goodness me!' exclaimed Séverine. 'It's five o'clock. I'm supposed to be seeing someone in the Rue du Rocher.'

Her joy quickly faded. Once again the agony of not knowing returned as she remembered that she was still not out of danger. She went very pale, and her lips trembled.

'What about the foreman you wanted to see at the engine shed?' said Jacques, standing up and offering her his arm.

'It can't be helped,' she said. 'I'll have to see him some other time. Look, Jacques, you don't need to stay with me; I can go on my own. What I have to do won't take me long. Thank you for looking after me. It really was very good of you.'

She shook his hand and rushed off.

'I'll see you on the train,' she called.

'I'll be there,' he shouted back.

She hurried away and disappeared between the trees in the square. Jacques wandered slowly back towards the Rue Cardinet.

Monsieur Camy-Lamotte had been having a long conversation with the General Manager of the Western Railway Company. He had originally been called there to discuss some other matter but had spent most of the time remonstrating with the Secretary-General about how much damage the Grandmorin affair was doing to the Company's reputation. There had been complaints in the newspapers about the lack of security for passengers who were travelling first class. In addition, the affair now implicated nearly every member of his staff, several of whom were actually suspected of being involved, not to mention this Roubaud character, who had more to answer for than most and who might be arrested at any moment. To make matters worse, there were all sorts of unpleasant rumours circulating about the President's private life and, because he had been on the board of directors, it reflected badly on the entire management. The end result was that a supposed crime by one insignificant assistant stationmaster, who no doubt had some sordid personal grudge to settle, was spreading upwards through the whole organization and upsetting the entire operational system of a major railway company, including its board of directors. In fact, the repercussions of the affair went even further. It affected the ministry and threatened the state. These were uncertain times, politically. They had reached a critical juncture in which the whole social structure was at risk; the least sign of infection could precipitate its collapse. Monsieur Camy-Lamotte realized this only too well, which was why, when the General Manager had announced that the Company had that morning decided to dismiss Roubaud, he had resolutely opposed the idea. No, he had insisted, that **177** could prove awkward. The press would be up in arms if it thought that we were trying to make Roubaud a political scapegoat. Everything could fall apart. God knew what other unsavoury revelations might come to light! The scandal had gone on too long. They needed to put an end to all the gossip as soon as possible. The General Manager was eventually persuaded and undertook to keep Roubaud on, even allowing him to remain at Le Havre. It would be made clear that there was no blame attached to anyone. The problem had been dealt with, and the inquiry would be shelved.

When Séverine once again found herself in Monsieur Camy-Lamotte's austerely furnished study, she was out of breath, and her heart was beating rapidly. The Secretary-General looked at her for a moment in silence, fascinated by the extraordinary effort she was making to appear calm. Yes, he thought to himself, she was most attractive, this shy little criminal with her bright blue eyes!

'Well, madame . . .' he began.

He paused in order to savour her anxiety for a second or two more. But she looked at him so earnestly, so beseechingly, so desperately anxious to know, that he took pity on her.

'Well, madame, I have spoken to the General Manager and have arranged for your husband to keep his job at Le Havre. Everything has been settled.'

She felt a wave of joy surge through her and she almost fainted. Her eyes filled with tears, and she was unable to speak. She stood there smiling.

'Everything has been settled,' Monsieur Camy-Lamotte repeated, deliberately emphasizing his words in order to make sure she understood exactly what he meant. 'You may return to Le Havre with your mind at rest.'

Séverine had understood his meaning perfectly; he was telling her that they would not be arrested, that they were pardoned. He wasn't simply talking about her husband keeping his job, he was telling her that the whole dreadful business was forgotten, dead and buried. With an instinctive gesture of gratitude, like a contented cat that rubs itself round its owner's legs, she put her face to his hands, kissed them and held them to her cheeks. He allowed his hands to rest in hers; he felt quite touched by such a charming and tender display of feeling.

'I don't need to remind you that you have both been very lucky,' he continued, attempting to resume an air of formality. 'You must ensure that in future you give us no further cause for complaint.'

'Of course, monsieur,' she replied.

He wanted her to know that he still held them both at his mercy and that the letter remained in his possession.

'Remember that everything is on file,' he emphasized. 'If either of you puts a foot wrong, the whole case can be reopened . . . In particular I suggest that you advise your husband to stop meddling in politics. If there were any further trouble on that front we would be quite ruthless. I know that he has had to be warned about it once before; I was told he had an unfortunate argument with the Sub-Prefect. It is also no secret that he has republican sympathies, which is appalling . . . Either he behaves himself or we get rid of him; it is as simple as that. Do I make myself clear?'

She was on her feet and eager to be outside, hardly able to contain the sheer joy that was almost choking her.

'Monsieur, we shall do as you say; we shall do as you please . . . No matter when, no matter where, you have only to say the word and I am yours.'

A weary smile played on his lips, a smile of faint contempt, the smile of a man who had drunk long and deep at the fount of human depravity.

'I shall not take advantage, madame,' he assured her. **179** 'That is not my way.'

He went over to the door and opened it for her. As she walked down the landing she turned twice to look at him, her face radiant with gratitude.

Outside in the Rue du Rocher, Séverine was beside herself with excitement. Realizing that she was walking up the street in the wrong direction, she walked back down it, crossed the road for no reason and was nearly run over. She needed to be on the move, to wave her arms about, to shout out loud. The reason why they had been let off was beginning to dawn on her.

'Why, of course,' she said to herself, 'it's they who are frightened. They're not going to give us any trouble; it's too risky. What a fool I've been to get so worked up about it! It's so obvious . . . This is my lucky day! I'm saved! It's all over! When I get back I'll give my husband the fright of his life. He won't dare open his mouth for weeks . . . I'm saved! Thank heavens! I'm saved!'

As she came out into the Rue Saint-Lazare she saw a clock in a jeweller's shop window which said twenty to six.

'There's plenty of time before the train leaves,' she said to herself. 'I'm going to buy myself a nice meal.'

Outside the station she chose the most expensive-looking restaurant. She installed herself at a table for one with a spotless white tablecloth in front of the plate glass window and sat watching the activity on the street outside. She ordered herself a choice meal of oysters, fillet of sole and roast wing of chicken. At least it made up for her dreadful lunch. She ate with relish. The *pain de gruau* was exquisite, and to finish she treated herself to a plate of *beignets soufflés.*[5] By the time she had drunk her coffee she had only a few minutes left to catch the train. She quickly made her way towards the station.

Upon leaving her, Jacques had returned to his room to 180 change into his working clothes and had then gone back to the engine shed. Normally he arrived there only half an hour before his locomotive was due to leave. He had come to rely on his fireman, Pecqueux, to get the engine ready, even though he was more often than not drunk. Today, however, perhaps because of the emotional state he was in, he felt he needed to check for himself that everything was in proper working order, particularly as on the way down from Le Havre he had sensed that the engine was not working as efficiently as it should have been.

Inside the vast engine shed, black with soot and lit by grimy windows high up in the roof, Jacques's locomotive, surrounded by other engines standing idle near by, was waiting near the entrance ready to leave. One of the shed firemen had just finished stoking the firebox; red-hot cinders dropped from beneath the engine into the ash-pit below. The engine was a four-coupled express locomotive of imposing yet delicate beauty. Its finely wrought driving wheels were linked by steel coupling-rods. It was a broad-chested, long-limbed, powerful machine,[6] yet possessed all the logic and mechanical certainty which constitutes the sovereign beauty of these creatures of shining steel. Precision coupled with strength! Along with the Western Railway Company's other locomotives, it carried both a number and a name, the name of one of the Company's stations, Lison, a town in the Cotentin. Jacques affectionately referred to his engine as *La Lison*, as if it were a woman, because he was so attached to it.

It was true: he had been driving this locomotive for four years and he had fallen in love with it. He had driven many other locomotives. Some were easy to handle and some were awkward, some worked hard and some were useless. He had come to realize that they all had their own individual characters and that many of them, as might be said of many women, left much to be desired. The fact that he loved *La Lison* was a sure sign that it possessed all the best qualities he could ever hope to find in a woman. It was gentle and responsive. Thanks to its excellent steaming capacity, it was easy to handle, steady and reliable. When it pulled out of a station so effortlessly, some said it was simply because its wheel tyres gave it a good grip on the rails or because the slide valves had been so finely adjusted. Similarly, they attributed the fact that it steamed so well on so little coal to the quality of the copper in the boiler tubes and the carefully calculated dimensions of the boiler. But Jacques knew that there was more to it than this, because other locomotives of identical construction, which had been assembled with just the same care and attention, displayed none of these qualities. It was something impossible to define, something special about the way it had been built, about the way the metal had been hammered into place or the fitter's hand had lined up the various parts: the locomotive had a personality, a life of its own.

So Jacques loved *La Lison*; she responded so willingly to his command. He felt grateful to her as a man might feel grateful to a mettlesome horse that always does as it is bidden. He loved it too because, as well as providing him with his regular wage, it also enabled him to earn a little extra money in fuel payments; in fact it steamed so well that it saved him a great deal on coal. Jacques had only one criticism, which was that it needed too much oiling. The cylinders especially consumed inordinate quantities of oil; they were insatiable. He had tried to reduce it, but the locomotive had quickly run short of breath; it needed oil, it was simply part of its character. Jacques had eventually decided that he would just have to put up with it, as one has to put up with the shortcomings of someone who is in other respects a paragon of virtue. He used to joke about it with his fireman, saying that *La Lison* was like a beautiful 182 woman; she needed to be kept well lubricated.

As the fire got hotter and *La Lison* began to build up pressure, Jacques walked around it examining every moving part and trying to find out why it had consumed more oil than usual that morning. He could find nothing wrong. The locomotive was clean and shiny, sparkling in fact, a clear indication that it was well looked after by its driver. He was always to be seen wiping it down and polishing it. When it had just arrived after a journey he made a point of rubbing it vigorously all over, as one rubs down a horse that is sweating after a long gallop; he found that it was easier to clean off stains and splashes when the engine was warm. He never drove it too hard, trying to maintain steady progress and not get behind time, which would have required sudden, extravagant bursts of speed. He had such a good relationship with his locomotive that never once in four years had he had to enter a fault on the shed register, where drivers listed items that needed repair. Poor drivers, because they were either lazy or drunk, were always complaining about their engines. Today, however, Jacques was seriously concerned about it using such huge amounts of oil. There was something else, too; he couldn't pin it down but he sensed it very strongly, something he had never felt before, a sort of anxiety or wariness, as if the locomotive couldn't be altogether trusted, and he needed to make sure that it wasn't going to let him down on the journey.

Pecqueux was nowhere to be seen. When he eventually turned up, his speech slurred after a meal with one of his mates, Jacques lost his temper. Normally the two men got on very well together, having worked side by side for many years, travelling from one end of the line to the other, flung together on the footplate, silently going about their work, united in a common task, braving the same dangers. Although he was more than ten years younger than Pecqueux, Jacques took a fatherly interest in his fireman, **183** making allowances for his failings and letting him take an hour's nap when he had had too much to drink. Pecqueux returned these favours with a dog-like devotion to his driver; he was a first-rate workman and despite his heavy drinking he was highly skilled at his job. What was more, he too was very attached to *La Lison*, which made for a good understanding between them. The two of them and the locomotive made a happy threesome, and there were hardly ever any arguments. So Pecqueux was taken aback to receive such a rough welcome and even more surprised to hear Jacques muttering doubts about the engine.

'What's the matter?' he asked. 'She goes like a dream.'

'No,' said Jacques, 'there's something not right.'

Even though everything appeared to be working as it should, he continued to shake his head. He tested the controls and checked that the safety-valve was working properly. He climbed up on to the running-plate and filled the cylinder lubricators. Pecqueux cleaned the dome, where there remained a few slight traces of rust. The sand boxes[7] were working normally. There should have been no cause for concern. The real trouble was that *La Lison* was no longer the only pull on Jacques's heart strings; another love had implanted itself – a slim, fragile little creature, whom he still saw sitting beside him on the park bench, pleading to be helped, so in need of love and protection. Never before, even when some unforeseen incident had made him lose time and he had driven the locomotive at speeds of eighty kilometres an hour, had it occurred to him that he might be putting his passengers at risk. But now, the mere thought of driving back to Le Havre with Séverine on the train worried him. Only that morning he had wanted nothing to do with her; she had irritated him. Now he was frightened there might be an accident; he imagined her wounded because of him, and dying in his arms. On him depended the safety of the woman he loved. *La Lison* had better behave herself if she was to stay in his good books.

It struck six. Jacques and Pecqueux climbed up on to the little steel connecting plate between the engine and tender. At a nod from his driver, Pecqueux opened the cylinder drain cocks, and a cloud of white steam filled the dark engine shed. As the driver eased open the regulator, *La Lison* moved out of the shed and whistled to be given the road. Almost immediately it was given the all-clear and ran into the Batignolles tunnel. At the Pont de l'Europe it had to wait; at the appointed time the signalman allowed it to back up to the 6.30 express, and two shunters ensured that it was firmly attached to the train.

The train was ready to leave; there were only five minutes left. Jacques leaned out, puzzled not to see Séverine amongst the crowd of passengers. He was sure she wouldn't get on the train without first coming to see him. Eventually she appeared; she was late and almost running.

She walked the whole length of the train, not stopping until she had reached the locomotive. Her face was flushed with excitement and she looked so happy.

She stood on tiptoe on her tiny feet, looking up at him and laughing.

'Don't worry,' she said. 'Here I am.'

Jacques too began to laugh, happy to see her there.

'Good,' he said, 'you made it.'

She raised herself higher so that she could speak to him more quietly.

'My dear friend,' she said, 'I'm so happy, so very happy. This has been my lucky day. I've got everything I could have wished for.'

He knew exactly what she meant and he was very pleased for her. As she ran back to get on the train she turned round and added as a joke: 'Hey! Make sure you don't run us off the rails!'

'Never fear!' he called back jovially. 'I'll be very careful.'

The carriage doors were already being slammed to, and Séverine only just had time to get on board. The guard waved his flag, Jacques gave a short blast on the whistle and opened the regulator. The train pulled out of the station. It was just as it had been on that tragic evening in February, the same time of day, the same hustle and bustle on the platform, the same sounds, the same smoke from the engine. But this time it was still daylight, a pleasant sunny evening, soft and gentle. Séverine opened the carriage window and looked out.

On the footplate, Jacques, warmly dressed in woollen trousers and smock,[8] and wearing a pair of goggles with felt eye protectors fastened at the back of his head beneath his cap, kept a careful eye on the road ahead. He stood on the right-hand side of the cab, leaning out of the window to get a better view, constantly shaken by the vibration of

185

the locomotive, which he hardly seemed to notice. He had his right hand on the reversing wheel,[9] like a pilot at the helm of his ship, gradually turning it by degrees in order to increase or decrease the speed of the train, while with his left hand he kept tugging at the whistle, for the way out of Paris is awkward to negotiate. He sounded the whistle at level-crossings, stations, tunnels and sharp curves. In the distance he saw a signal shining red in the fading light. He gave a long blast on the whistle to ask for the road, and the train thundered past. From time to time he glanced at the pressure gauge, turning the injector[10] on whenever the pressure reached ten kilogrammes. But his eyes quickly returned to the line ahead, looking out for anything that might hinder their progress, with such concentration that he saw nothing else and was not even aware of the wind that blew into his face like a gale. The pressure gauge dropped; Jacques lifted the ratchet on the firebox door and opened it. Pecqueux, from long familiarity, understood what had to be done. With his hammer he broke up coal from the tender and shovelled it evenly over the full width of the grate. They could feel the scorching heat from the fire burning their legs. Then, the firebox door was shut again, and the cold air returned.

It was getting dark, and Jacques needed to be even more vigilant. Rarely had he known *La Lison* respond so well. She was his to command, and he rode her as he willed, in total mastery. Not once did he relax his hold on her, treating her like a tamed animal that needs to be handled with caution. Behind him in the train, hurtling along at full speed, he pictured the delicate figure of Séverine, smiling happily and confidently entrusting herself to his care. The thought sent a slight shudder through him, and he gripped the reversing wheel more tightly. He peered intently into the gathering darkness, on the look-out for signals at red. Once past the junctions at Asnières and Colombes, he breathed more easily. Everything went well as far as Mantes; the line was dead level, and it was an easy run for the train. Beyond Mantes the engine had to be driven harder in order to climb a fairly steep incline for nearly half a league. Then, without any easing up, he ran her down through the Rolleboise tunnel, a gentle descent of two kilometres, which she covered in scarcely three minutes. There remained only one further tunnel – Roule, near Gaillon – before they reached Sotteville, a notorious station that needed to be approached with the utmost care, due to the great number of sidings, the continual shunting operations and the constant movement of trains. Every ounce of his energy was concentrated in his eyes, which were fixed on the track ahead, and his hand, which controlled the locomotive. *La Lison* rushed through Sotteville with her whistle shrieking, leaving behind her a long trail of smoke. She didn't stop until she reached Rouen. After **187** a brief rest, she set off again, more slowly, climbing the incline up to Malaunay.

The moon had risen, very clear, casting a pale light on the surrounding countryside; despite the speed at which the train was travelling, Jacques could make out small bushes growing beside the railway line and the individual stones used to surface the roads. As they came out of the tunnel at Malaunay, Jacques looked quickly to his right, having noticed a shadow cast across the line by a tall tree, and recognized in a tangle of undergrowth the lonely spot from which he had seen the murder. The countryside rushed past, wild and bare – a continual succession of hills and dark, tree-filled valleys, a desolate wasteland. At La Croix-de-Maufras, Jacques saw the house, standing at an angle to the railway line, with the moon motionless in the sky above it, its shutters, as always, closed, the whole place abandoned and forlorn, cheerless and forbidding. He didn't know why, but once again, and this time more than ever before, he felt his heart grow chill, as if the place boded him some misfortune.

Seconds later, another image assailed his eyes – Flore, leaning against the level-crossing gate next to the Misards' house. Nowadays, she was there every time he made this journey, waiting, looking out for him. She stood perfectly still, simply turning her head so that she could follow him for a moment or two longer as the train whisked him past her. All Jacques saw was a tall, dark shadow outlined against the night sky and a glimpse of golden hair shining in the pale light of the moon.

Jacques worked *La Lison* hard up the Motteville incline and then allowed her to coast along the level section through Bolbec before a final burst of speed over the three leagues between Saint-Romain and Harfleur, down the steepest gradient on the line, a stretch which locomotives charge over, like horses galloping madly for the stable when they sense they are near home. By the time the train reached Le Havre, Jacques was exhausted. Séverine got down from her carriage, but before going up to her apartment, she ran along the platform under the station roof, amidst all the smoke and noise of the train's arrival, went up to Jacques and said sweetly, 'Thank you, Jacques. See you tomorrow.'

6

A month went by. Calm had returned to the Roubauds'
apartment above the waiting rooms on the first floor of
the station building. For the Roubauds, for their neighbours along the corridor and for everyone employed at the
station, life had begun to return to its old monotonous
pattern, measured by the clock and the repetitive sameness
of the daily routine. It seemed that nothing violent or out
of the ordinary had ever happened.

The scandal and rumours surrounding the Grandmorin
affair were quietly being forgotten. The trial was to be
postponed indefinitely, because the law seemed incapable
of identifying the criminal. Cabuche had been detained   **189**
for a further fortnight, at which point Monsieur Denizet,
the examining magistrate, had dismissed the charge
against him on grounds of insufficient evidence. The murder became a subject of romanticized fantasy – centred on
a mysterious and elusive killer, a devotee of crime, in all
places at the same time, blamed for every murder that was
perpetrated, and who vanished in a puff of smoke the minute the police arrived on the scene. Occasional jokes about
the mythical assassin continued to appear in the opposition newspapers, all of which were now devoting their
energies to the forthcoming general elections. The general
state of political tension and the harsh measures being
taken by the local prefects provided them with a daily supply of other material to get their teeth into. They lost
interest in the Grandmorin affair. It had ceased to be a
matter of public concern. It was no longer even talked
about.

What finally restored calm to the Roubauds' household

was the fact that the legal complications, which the imple-
mentation of President Grandmorin's will had threatened
to raise, had been successfully ironed out. At the insistence
of Madame Bonnehon, the Lachesnayes had eventually
agreed not to contest the will. It risked reawakening the
scandal, and there was no guarantee that their objection
would be upheld. Consequently, the Roubauds had
received their legacy and for the last week had been the
owners of La Croix-de-Maufras. The house and garden
were valued at about forty thousand francs. They had
immediately decided to sell it. It was a place associated
with murder and debauchery and it haunted them like a
nightmare. They would never have dared sleep there for
fear of ghosts from the past. They had decided to sell it as
it stood, with the furniture intact, without having it
repaired and without even sweeping up the dust. Thinking
190 that it would fetch very little at a public auction, there
being few people likely to want a house in such an
out-of-the-way spot, they had decided to wait until someone showed any interest and had simply fixed a large notice
on the front of the house which could be read from the
passing trains. The announcement in large letters 'Abandoned House for Sale' merely emphasized the desolate
character of the place, with its shutters closed and the garden overrun by brambles. Roubaud wanted nothing to do
with the house; he refused to go near it. So, as certain
arrangements needed to be made, one afternoon, Séverine
went there herself. She left the keys with the Misards, with
instructions to show prospective buyers over the property,
should there be any. Anyone wanting to do so could have
moved in immediately; there was even linen in the
cupboards.

The Roubauds' worries were over. They lived each day
in quiet expectation of the next. Sooner or later the house
would be sold. They would invest the money, and their

difficulties would be at an end. In fact, they forgot all about it, happy to remain in the three rooms they were living in – the dining room, which opened directly on to the corridor, the large bedroom to the right and the tiny, airless kitchen to the left. Even the station roof, sloping up in front of their windows, blocking the view and hemming them in like a prison wall, instead of infuriating them as it used to do, seemed to have a calming effect and added to the sense of perfect repose, peace and tranquillity which enveloped them. At least they couldn't be seen by the neighbours and they didn't have nosey people constantly peering in at them. Their only cause for complaint, now that spring had come, was the stifling heat and the dazzling reflections that came off the cladding of the station roof when it was heated by the early-morning sun. After the dreadful trauma that for nearly two months had kept them in a state of constant trepidation, they were blissfully **191** happy to be free from care. They just wanted to stay where they were, to exist, without feeling afraid or worried sick. Never had Roubaud displayed such commitment and dedication to his job. During the weeks he was on day shift, he would be down on the platform by five in the morning, would not return for a meal until ten, would be back at work by eleven and would then continue without a break until five in the evening – a full eleven hours on duty. During the weeks he was on night shift, he would be on duty from five in the evening to five in the morning without even taking a break for a meal at home, snatching a bite to eat in his office. It was a demanding workload. Yet he shouldered it without complaint and seemed even to enjoy it. He overlooked nothing, insisting on inspecting and doing things himself, as if by working himself to a standstill he had found a way of forgetting, a way of once more living a normal, balanced existence. Séverine for her part found herself more often than not on her own, a widow one week in two, and during the other week only seeing her husband for lunch and dinner. She seemed to develop an obsession for housework. Previously she had sat about doing needlework; she hated housework and had left it to Madame Simon, an old lady who came in every day from nine till midday. But now that she felt happier to be at home and was sure that they would be staying there, she had an irresistible urge to do the cleaning and make things tidy. She would only sit down when everything had been seen to. Both she and her husband were sleeping well. On the rare occasions they had a chance to speak to each other, over meals, or on the nights they slept together, the murder was never mentioned. The whole thing seemed to be dead and buried.

For Séverine, life once more became very pleasant. She left the housework to Madame Simon and resumed her life of idleness, like a young lady of leisure whose sole purpose in life was to sit making delicate embroideries. Her present piece of handiwork was an embroidered bedspread, an endless undertaking that might have lasted her a lifetime. She rose quite late, happy to remain in bed on her own, lulled by the departure and arrival of trains which marked the passing hours as precisely as a clock. In the early days of her marriage, the noises from the station had disturbed her – engines blowing their whistles, turntables being slammed into position, rumblings and sudden vibrations like earthquakes that made her shake, along with all the furniture. But gradually she had grown accustomed to it; the station with all its noise and bustle had become a part of her life, and now she liked it. Its clamour and activity brought her a strange peace of mind. She would wander from one room to another until it was time for lunch, chatting with her cleaner and doing nothing. She would then spend the whole afternoon sitting in front of the dining-room window, her needlework more often than not lying untouched on her lap, happy to be left undisturbed. The weeks when her husband returned to bed in the early morning and lay snoring until evening were the weeks that Séverine looked forward to most, weeks when she could live as she used to do before she was married, with the bed to herself, and doing just as she pleased all day long. She hardly ever went out; all she saw of Le Havre was the smoke from the factories near by, great black clouds swirling up into the sky above the zinc-clad ridge of the station roof, which shut off the horizon a few metres in front of her. Beyond this immovable wall lay the town; she sensed its presence constantly. But her irritation at not being able to see it gradually softened. She had put five or six pots of wallflowers and verbena in the valley of the station roof[1] and she tended them with care; they provided her with a little garden and brought a touch of colour into her life of solitude. Sometimes she spoke of herself as a 193 recluse living in the depths of a wood. Whenever he had nothing else to do, Roubaud would climb out through the window on his own, walk along the valley to the end of the station roof, clamber up to the ridge and sit looking down at the Cours Napoléon. He would take out his pipe and sit smoking, high up in the sky, with the town spread out beneath him – the docks with their forest of tall masts and the wide open sea, pale green, stretching to the ends of the earth.

A similar sort of lethargy appeared to have affected the Roubauds' neighbours. The corridor on which they lived, which was normally buzzing with rumour and gossip, was now silent. When Philomène came to call on Madame Lebleu, they hardly raised their voices. Both women had been surprised by the way things had turned out and now, when they spoke of Roubaud, it was with a mixture of scorn and pity. It was quite obvious what madame had got up to in Paris in order to keep him in a job! Anyway,

Roubaud's name was mud, and nothing would ever convince them he was innocent. The cashier's wife was now confident that her neighbours were no longer in a position to take her apartment from her and she treated them with contempt, walking past them very stiffly and refusing to acknowledge them. In the end she even managed to alienate Philomène, who came to see her less and less, finding her too stuck up and irritating. Madame Lebleu, for want of anything better to do, still kept an eye open for any goings-on between Mademoiselle Guichon and the stationmaster, Monsieur Dabadie, not that she ever discovered anything. In the corridor the only sound to be heard was the shuffle of her felt slippers. One day followed another, and nothing stirred. A whole month went by. Peace reigned. After all the turmoil, everything seemed to sink into a deep slumber.

194   For the Roubauds, however, there was one thing that continued to disturb them and make them feel uneasy. It was a section of the parquet flooring in their dining room. Whenever they chanced to look at it all their old fears returned. It was to the left of the window, a piece of edging which they had lifted and then put back into place in order to hide the watch and the ten thousand francs that they had taken from Grandmorin's body, along with about three hundred francs in gold, in a purse. Roubaud had only taken them from Grandmorin's pockets to make it look like a robbery. He wasn't a thief and he would sooner starve, as he put it, than spend a single centime or sell the watch. It had belonged to a man who had defiled his wife and who had got his just deserts; it was tainted money, unclean ... No! It wasn't fit to be touched by a self-respecting man like himself. He had been willing to accept the legacy of La Croix-de-Maufras, and he now no longer gave it a thought. But what he couldn't come to terms with was the thought of going through

Grandmorin's pockets and taking his money after he had brutally murdered him; it played on his conscience and left him feeling shocked and frightened. Yet he had never got round to burning the money or going out one night and throwing the watch and the purse in the sea. He knew that this would be the wisest thing to do, but some obscure instinct prevented him. He had a subconscious respect for money; he could never have brought himself to simply get rid of such a large amount. At first, on the night of the murder, he had put it under his pillow, unable to think of anywhere safe enough to hide it. He spent the next few days racking his brains to think of hiding places. He tried one after another but kept changing them every day, frightened, at the least sound, that someone would present himself at his door with a search-warrant. Never had his ingenuity been so thoroughly tested. Eventually he ran out of ideas; his anxiety had worn him out. One day he couldn't 195 be bothered to look any further and had simply left the money and the watch under the floorboard, where he had hidden them the day before. Now he wouldn't disturb them for anything in the world; it was a place of death, of unspeakable horrors, a charnel house where ghosts lay in wait for him. He avoided walking on this particular strip of parquet; it gave him an unpleasant feeling and seemed to send a slight shock up his legs. In the afternoon, when Séverine sat in front of the window, she would draw her chair back so that it wasn't placed directly above the corpse that lay hidden beneath the floor. They didn't talk to each other about it and tried to convince themselves that they would get used to it. But, to their annoyance, they couldn't stop thinking about it; they sensed it there, under their feet, every minute of the day, refusing to go away. The unease it caused them was all the more surprising because they weren't at all bothered about the knife, the beautiful new knife which Séverine had bought her husband and which he had plunged into her lover's throat. It had simply been washed and left in the bottom of a drawer; Madame Simon sometimes used it to cut the bread.

The Roubauds' peaceful existence was further disturbed by another increasingly troublesome arrangement. At Roubaud's insistence, Jacques had regularly been joining them for meals. Being in charge of the Paris express meant that Jacques returned to Le Havre three times a week: on Monday from ten thirty-five in the morning to six twenty in the evening, and on Thursday and Saturday from five past eleven at night to six forty the following morning. He had first invited him on the Monday following Séverine's trip to Paris and he would not take no for an answer.

'Come on,' he said, 'you're not going to refuse a bite to eat with us, are you? You've been very good to my wife, and I owe you a favour in return.'

So Jacques had accepted his invitation to have lunch with them twice a month. It appeared that Roubaud had become embarrassed by the long silences between him and his wife whenever they ate together and he was relieved to have a guest to join them. He soon found plenty to talk about again and chatted and joked.

'Come as often as you like,' he said. 'It's no trouble at all.'

One Thursday evening, just as Jacques had finished cleaning himself and was about to return to his lodgings to get some sleep, he met Roubaud wandering around the engine shed. Although it was quite late, Roubaud, not wanting to return home alone, had asked Jacques to accompany him as far as the station and had then invited him back to his apartment. Séverine was still up, reading a book. They had a drink together and played cards until past midnight.

From then on, the Monday lunches and the little get-togethers on Thursday and Saturday evenings became a regular occurrence. If Jacques failed to turn up, Roubaud himself would go and find him and tell him off for forgetting to come. He grew more and more depressed and was only ever really happy when he was with his new friend. This fellow, who had at first so frightened him and whom, even now, he had good cause to loathe, as the witness and living reminder of all the terrible things he sought to forget, had on the contrary become indispensable to him, perhaps for the very reason that he knew the truth and had not talked. It remained a secret that they shared, a bond between them, a pact. Often Roubaud would give Jacques a knowing look and shake his hand with a sudden warmth of feeling that expressed far more than simple friendship.

None the less, the presence of Jacques helped the Roubauds to take their mind off things. Séverine, too, was always pleased to see him, greeting him with a little cry 197 of pleasure whenever he came through the door. She would drop whatever she was doing, her embroidery or her book, and talk and laugh, only too happy to escape the dull tedium in which she lived from day to day.

'It's so good of you to come!' she would say. 'I heard the express arrive and I was thinking about you.'

When he stayed for lunch, she always did him proud. She quickly got to know his likes and dislikes and would go out especially to buy new-laid eggs for him. She made him feel welcome, like a good housewife receiving a friend of the family, and for the time being at least, he had no reason to suppose that she was doing it out of any other motive than wanting to be pleasant and needing something to do.

'You'll come again on Monday, won't you?' she would say. 'There'll be some fresh cream!'

By the end of a month, however, by which time Jacques was a regular visitor, the rift between Roubaud and his wife had become more pronounced. Séverine more and more preferred to sleep on her own and contrived to share the bed with her husband as little as possible. Roubaud, who had been such a passionate, violent lover when they were first married, made no attempt to force her. His love-making had always lacked finesse; she had resigned herself to it as a dutiful wife, accepting that it had to be, but taking no pleasure in it. Since the crime, however, without knowing why, she found that it had become unbearable; it left her feeling exhausted and frightened. Once, when the candle was still alight, she had cried out; she had the distinct impression that the face peering down into hers, red and contorted, was the face of the murderer. Thereafter, it made her tremble every time; she had the horrible feeling that the murder was being re-enacted, as if he had thrown her on to her back and had a knife in his 198 hand. It was ridiculous, but it left her shaking with fear. Roubaud for his part gradually tired of insisting; her resistance robbed him of his pleasure. It seemed that their terrible crisis and the shedding of blood had produced in them the weariness and indifference that normally come with old age. On nights when they could not avoid sleeping in the same bed, they slept on opposite sides. Jacques undoubtedly helped to bring about this divorce. His presence drew them out of their self-obsession. He freed them from each other.

Roubaud felt no remorse. He had been frightened about what might happen to him before the case was shelved, and his main concern was about losing his job. But he still regretted nothing. Perhaps, if he had had to do it all over again, he would not have involved his wife; women tended to panic too easily, and if Séverine was drifting away from him, it was because he had placed too great a burden on her shoulders. Had he not dragged her into this terrifying and acrimonious partnership in crime, she would still have been his to command. But that was how things were and he just had to put up with it. He had to make a real effort these days to recall his feelings when Séverine had first confessed to him and he had decided that he must murder Grandmorin if he was to go on living. It had seemed to him then that if he hadn't killed him, life would have been impossible. But now, the flames of jealousy had died down, and there was no longer that unbearable, burning desire for revenge; a feeling of numbness had come over him, as if the blood he had spilt had somehow congealed the blood in his own veins. It was no longer obvious to him why the murder had seemed so necessary. He even began to wonder if it had been worth it. It wasn't that he regretted doing it; it was more a vague feeling of disappointment, a sense that people often do the most terrible things in order to achieve happiness, without becoming one bit happier than they were before. Although by nature a talkative man, he would **199** go for long periods without speaking; he sat thinking to himself and getting himself more and more confused, ending up even more depressed than before. Every day now, in order to avoid his wife's company after mealtimes, he would climb up on to the station roof and sit perched on the top, with the breeze from the open sea playing on his face, smoking pipe after pipe, in a world of his own, looking out over the town and watching the steamers disappearing over the horizon to the ocean beyond.

One evening Roubaud's old, fierce jealousy was rearoused. He had gone out to look for Jacques at the engine shed and was bringing him back home for a drink when he met Henri Dauvergne, the guard, coming down the stairs. Dauvergne appeared embarrassed and explained that he had just called in to see Madame Roubaud on an errand from his sisters. The truth was that he had had his eye on Séverine for some time and hoped to make an impression on her.

Roubaud opened the door and angrily confronted his wife:

'What's that Dauvergne character doing here again? You know I can't stand him!'

'Stop getting so upset, dear,' she answered, 'he came to pick up an embroidery pattern.'

'Embroidery pattern, my foot! Do you think I'm so stupid I don't know what he's after? You'd better watch your step!'

He advanced towards her, his fists clenched. Séverine stepped back from him, her face white. They had been quietly ignoring each other over the last few weeks, and this sudden outburst of temper amazed her. But his anger quickly subsided.

'It's true,' he said, turning to Jacques, 'there are jokers like him that come waltzing into your house and think your wife is going to throw herself into their arms while her husband is supposed to feel highly honoured and turn a blind eye! It makes my blood boil . . . I tell you, if I had a wife who did that, I wouldn't ask questions, I'd just strangle her . . . Just make sure that smart alec doesn't come here again, or I'll give him what for! It makes you sick, doesn't it?'

Jacques found the whole scene highly embarrassing and didn't know quite how to react. Was this display of anger for his benefit? Was it a husband's warning? His worries were dispelled when Roubaud continued with a laugh:

'Come on, you daft thing, I'm only joking. I know you wouldn't stand any nonsense from him. Go and get us some glasses! Let's all have a drink.'

He patted Jacques on the shoulder, and Séverine, having recovered from her shock, looked at them and smiled. They then had a drink and spent a very pleasant hour together.

And so it was that Roubaud helped and encouraged the

friendship between his wife and his companion, without appearing to realize what it might lead to. Roubaud's display of jealousy even prompted a greater intimacy between Jacques and Séverine, a secret sharing of affection and whispered confidences. When Jacques saw her again two days later, he told her how sorry he was that Roubaud had treated her so roughly, while she, with tears in her eyes and unable to hide her unhappiness from him, confessed what little joy her marriage had brought her. From then on, Séverine had someone in whom she could confide, a friend who sympathized. They came to understand each other through little signs and gestures. Every time he came, he would glance at her inquiringly, to know if Roubaud had done anything new to upset her. She would answer in the same manner, with a quick flutter of her eyelids. When Roubaud's back was turned, their hands would quickly meet. As they grew bolder, they allowed **201** their hands to remain together, seeking through little movements and tightenings of their fingers to share each other's thoughts. They rarely had the good fortune to be together for more than a minute on their own; Roubaud, ever more depressed, was always there, sitting at the table between them. They made no attempt to try to get away from him; it never occurred to them that they might arrange to meet elsewhere, in some quiet corner of the station building. For the time being, Roubaud's presence did not stand in the way of the growing friendship and the warm feeling that was developing between them; they were able to say all they needed to say with a mere look or a squeeze of the hand.

When Jacques first whispered into Séverine's ear that he would be waiting for her the following Thursday at midnight behind the engine shed, she was shocked, and snatched her hand away from him. It was her week of freedom; her husband was on night duty. But the thought of leaving the apartment and walking through the station in the dark to an assignation with another man scared her. Her mind was filled with doubts she had never experienced before, like an innocent young virgin, her heart all aflutter. At first she declined his offer. Jacques had to keep asking her for nearly a fortnight, before she finally relented, although the thought of this nocturnal rendezvous had made her heart burn with excitement. It was the beginning of June; the nights were very warm and barely cooled by the breeze from the sea. Jacques had already waited for her three times, hoping that she would come to meet him despite her refusal. This evening she had again said no. There was no moon, the sky was overcast and not a single star could be seen through the heavy pall of mist that filled the air. Standing in the shadows, Jacques at last saw her approaching, dressed in black, moving forward without a sound. It was so dark that she might have brushed past him without seeing him, but he caught her in his arms and kissed her. She gave a little cry of surprise. Then, with a laugh, she allowed her lips to remain upon his. Jacques suggested they might sit in one of the nearby sheds, but Séverine refused. They walked on, pressing themselves close to each other, talking in whispers. The engine shed yard occupied the entire area between the Rue Verte and the Rue François-Mazeline, each of which has a level-crossing over the railway line. The place was a vast piece of open ground, filled with sidings, storage tanks, water hydrants and buildings of every type and description – the two great sheds for the locomotives, the Sauvagnats' little house standing in its tiny vegetable garden, the ramshackle assortment of repair shops and the mess-room for the engine drivers and firemen. In such a tangle of deserted paths and alleyways it was easy for them to wander unseen, to disappear as if into the heart of a wood. For a whole hour they walked together, happy to be alone, exchanging the endearments that they had for so long stored in their hearts. She would not hear him talk of love; she had told him straight away that she could never be his, that she needed above all to regain her self-respect and that it would be wrong to sully a friendship as pure as theirs, a friendship of which she was so proud. He accompanied her as far as the Rue Verte, their lips met once more in a long kiss, and she returned home.

At just about the same time, Roubaud was beginning to nod off to sleep in the old leather armchair in the assistant stationmaster's office. Twenty times every night he would have to shake himself awake, get up and stretch his legs. Up until nine o'clock he had to supervise the arrival and departure of the night trains. He also had to see to the fish train, overseeing the shunting operations, checking the couplings and inspecting the delivery notices. Then, when the express from Paris had arrived and had been **203** backed on to a siding, he would sit in his office at a corner of the table and eat his lonely supper – a little cold meat from their evening meal between two slices of bread. The last arrival, a stopping train from Rouen, got in at half past midnight. The deserted platforms then fell silent, only a few gas lamps were left burning, and in the chill of nightfall the whole station fell asleep. The only other staff Roubaud had to help him were two foremen and four or five workmen, who were all snoring their heads off on the mess-room floor, while he, whose job it was to wake them up the minute they were needed, had to sleep with one ear cocked. To prevent weariness from overtaking him before it grew light, he would set his alarm clock for five, when he had to be on his feet to see in the first train from Paris. Sometimes, however, especially of late, he found sleep impossible and he would spend the night tossing and turning restlessly in his armchair. When this happened he would go out and do the rounds, or walk down to the

signalman in his cabin and have a chat. Eventually the stillness of the night and the great expanse of dark sky above
calmed his nerves. Following a scuffle with some intruders, he had been armed with a revolver, which he kept fully
loaded in his pocket. Often he would walk around until
dawn, stopping to take aim the minute he thought he saw
something moving in the darkness and then walking on
again, feeling vaguely disappointed that he hadn't had to
shoot. It came as a relief when the sky began to grow light
and the huge station emerged pale and ghostly from the
shadows. Now that day was breaking as early as three
o'clock, he would return to his office, sink into his armchair and sleep like a log, until his alarm clock woke him
up with a start.

Jacques and Séverine continued to meet every other
week on Thursdays and Saturdays. One night Séverine
204 happened to mention that her husband carried a revolver.
Although Roubaud never came out as far as the engine
shed, the thought of the revolver worried them. It added a
sense of danger to their nocturnal excursions and made
them seem all the more romantic. There was one place
they were particularly fond of, a little alleyway behind the
Sauvagnats' house which, because it ran between two rows
of huge coal stacks, made it look like the main street of
some strange city, lined with big, square palaces built of
black marble.[2] It was completely hidden from view, and at
the far end there was a little tool-shed with a pile of empty
sacks inside it, which would have provided them with
something soft to lie on. One Saturday, a sudden shower
of rain had driven them inside the shed to take shelter.
Séverine remained standing, offering him only her lips,
in kiss after kiss. She kissed him unashamedly, greedily,
holding her lips to his, seeking to tell him that she loved
him. When Jacques, inflamed with passion, attempted to
take her, she drew back with tears in her eyes, uttering the

same repeated plea – why did he wish to make her unhappy? Their love for each other seemed so beautiful; sex was so sordid. Although she had been defiled at the age of sixteen by a lecherous old man whose grizzly spectre still haunted her, and then, after her marriage, had been subjected to the brutal appetites of her husband, she had retained a childlike innocence and virginal purity, a charmingly naive sense of modesty. What so attracted her to Jacques was his gentleness and compliance; when his hands were tempted to stray, she simply enclosed them in hers, and he desisted. For the first time in her life she was in love. She did not give herself, for she knew that if she yielded to him now, as she had yielded to the two others, her love would be ruined. Unconsciously, she wanted this happiness to continue for ever; she longed to be young again, as she was before she had been abused, to be like a girl of fifteen, with a sweetheart she could kiss freely and in secret. Jacques for his part, except in moments when his passions were roused, was undemanding, happily savouring this voluptuous deferment of pleasure. Like her, he seemed to have rediscovered his youth and for the very first time in his life to be in love, something which until now had always filled him with horror. If he was docile, withdrawing his hands the moment she guided them away from her, it was because underlying his love for her there remained a vague fear, a nameless dread, that this love might unleash his old compulsion to kill. Séverine, who had committed murder herself, seemed the very embodiment of his worst dreams come true. But every day he grew more confident that he was cured; he had held her in his arms for hours on end, he had pressed his mouth to hers, drinking in her very soul, without awakening the savage urge to dominate and kill her. Yet he remained uncertain. It was good to wait, to allow love to unite them when the moment came, and their resistance had faded away in each other's arms. And so these joyful encounters continued. They seized every opportunity they could to meet, and walk together in the dark between the huge, black coal stacks that loomed out of the night around them.

One night in July, in order to reach Le Havre on time at five past eleven, Jacques had had to work *La Lison* hard. The stifling heat seemed to have made her lazy. A storm had been following the train all the way from Rouen, running alongside them on their left up the Seine valley, with great, blinding flashes of lightning. Jacques kept looking anxiously over his shoulder; he had arranged to meet Séverine that night and he was worried that if the storm broke it would prevent her from leaving her apartment. Having successfully reached Le Havre ahead of the storm, he was becoming impatient with the passengers, who seemed to be taking an inordinate amount of time getting off the train.

206

Roubaud was on night duty and was standing on the platform.

'You're in a hurry to get to bed,' he said, laughing. 'Sleep well!'

'Thanks!' Jacques replied.

Jacques backed the train on to a siding, gave a blast on the whistle and moved off towards the engine shed. The huge folding doors stood open, and *La Lison* disappeared inside. The shed was a sort of covered gallery some seventy metres long with two tracks running through it, capable of housing six locomotives. Inside, it was very dark, with four gas lamps that gave hardly any light and seemed to make it darker still, by casting long, flickering shadows. From time to time great flashes of lightning could be seen through the skylights and the windows high up on both walls, revealing, as if in the light of a huge fire, the cracks in the brickwork, the beams covered in soot and the general woebegone air of neglect and disrepair. Two other locomotives were already in the shed, cold and asleep.

Pecqueux immediately began to put the fire out, raking it vigorously and sending a shower of burning cinders into the ash-pit below.

'I'm starving,' he said. 'I'm going to get something to eat. Are you coming?'

Jacques made no answer. Although he was in a hurry, he didn't want to leave *La Lison* before the fire had been dropped and the boiler drained. It was a regular routine and, being a man who took his job seriously, he never departed from it. When he had time, he didn't leave until he had thoroughly inspected the locomotive and properly wiped it down, with the sort of care one might spend on grooming a favourite horse.

The water from the boiler gushed into the ash-pit. Only when his work was finished did Jacques answer 207 Pecqueux.

'Right,' he said, 'let's be off!'

He was interrupted by a violent clap of thunder. The windows were so clearly silhouetted against the fiery sky that you could have counted the broken panes of glass, and there were plenty of them. Along the left-hand side of the shed stood a row of vices used for repair work. A piece of sheet metal propped up against them resounded with a mighty clang, like a bell being struck. A great crack had appeared in the framework of the old roof.

'Bloody hell!' was all Pecqueux could say.

Jacques raised his hands in despair. There was nothing more they could do, especially as the rain was now pouring in torrents on to the shed. The storm threatened to smash the windows in the roof. There must have been broken panes of glass up there too because rain was falling on *La Lison* in great splashes. A howling gale blew in through the open doors, and it seemed as if the shell of the old building was about to be lifted off the ground.

Pecqueux had been getting the engine ready for its next shift.

'There we are,' he said. 'We'll be able to see things better tomorrow. That'll do for now.' Then, remembering that he still felt hungry, he said: 'Let's go and eat. It's raining too much to walk back to our rooms.'

The canteen adjoined the engine shed, whereas the house which the Company rented as a dormitory for drivers and firemen staying overnight in Le Havre was some distance away in the Rue François-Mazeline. In weather like this, they would have been soaked to the skin by the time they got there.

Jacques resigned himself to accompanying Pecqueux, who had picked up the driver's little lunch box, as if trying to save him the trouble of having to carry it. In fact, he knew that the box still contained two slices of cold veal, some bread and a bottle that had hardly been started, and it was the thought of this food that was making him feel hungry. The rain was heavier than ever. Yet another clap of thunder shook the building. The two men walked through the little door on the left of the shed, which led to the canteen. *La Lison* was already cooling down. They left her on her own in the dark, with the lightning flashing all around her and great splashes of rain water running down her back. Water trickled from a nearby tap which had not been properly turned off, forming a pool that ran down between her wheels into the ash-pit.

Before going into the canteen, Jacques wanted to clean himself up. One of the rooms was always provided with hot water and hand bowls. He fished a bar of soap out of his basket and washed his hands and face, which were black after the journey. He had taken the precaution of bringing a change of clothing with him, as all drivers are advised to do, so he had something clean to wear. In fact, when he arrived at Le Havre on a night that he was going to meet Séverine, he always changed into clean clothes in order to look his best. Pecqueux was already in the canteen, having only bothered to wash the end of his nose and his fingertips.

The canteen consisted simply of a little, bare room, painted yellow, with a stove for heating food on and a table that was fixed to the floor and had a zinc top which served as a tablecloth. The only other pieces of furniture in the room were two benches. The men had to bring their own food, which they ate off a sheet of paper with the end of a knife. The room was lit by one large window.

'What a downpour!' exclaimed Jacques, standing at the window.

Pecqueux had sat down on one of the benches at the table.

'Aren't you eating, then?' he asked.

'You carry on,' answered Jacques. 'I'm not hungry. Eat the rest of the bread and meat if you want it.'

Pecqueux didn't need to be asked twice. He attacked the veal and downed the rest of the bottle. These little windfalls often came his way because Jacques was such a small eater. Pecqueux had a dog-like devotion to his driver, and he liked him all the more for giving him his leftovers. After a pause, he spoke again, his mouth full: 'Who cares about the rain! We got here safely! If it goes on raining, mind you, I'll be going next door.'

He laughed. It was no secret between them. Pecqueux had had to tell Jacques about his affair with Philomène Sauvagnat so that he wouldn't wonder where he'd got to every time he went to see her. She lived in her brother's house on the ground floor next to the kitchen; he only had to tap on the shutters and she would open the window so that he could climb in. What could be easier! People said that all the engine men at Le Havre knew the routine. But now, it seemed, Pecqueux was all the company she needed.

'Bloody hell!' muttered Jacques under his breath, as, after a brief respite, the rain began to fall again more heavily than ever.

Pecqueux was brandishing the last piece of meat on the end of his knife. He laughed pleasantly.

'Had you got something planned for tonight?' he said. 'I tell you what, they can't accuse you and me of wearing the beds out in the Rue François-Mazeline, can they?'

Jacques turned quickly away from the window.

'What makes you say that?' he asked.

'Well,' said Pecqueux, 'ever since the spring, you've been like me. You're never in till two or three in the morning.'

He must know something, he thought. Perhaps he had seen them together. The dormitory had two beds in each
210 room, so that driver and fireman could sleep next to each other. The Company liked to encourage a sense of camaraderie between men whose work inevitably brought them so close together. So it was hardly surprising that Pecqueux had noticed his driver's sleeping habits becoming somewhat erratic, when previously they had been perfectly normal.

'I get headaches,' answered Jacques, saying the first thing that came to mind. 'It does me good to go for a walk at night.'

Pecqueux was quick to reassure him.

'I was only pulling your leg,' he said. 'You're free to do as you please . . . But don't forget, if ever you've got a problem, don't hesitate to say. That's what I'm there for; any time you want.'

Without a word more he took hold of Jacques's hand and squeezed it firmly, as a gesture of his unswerving loyalty. He screwed up the greasy piece of paper that the meat had been wrapped in, threw it away and put the empty bottle back in the food box, performing all these little chores like a dutiful manservant, trained to keep things looking neat and tidy. The rain continued to fall, although the thunder had stopped.

'Right,' said Pecqueux, 'I'm off. I'll leave you to your own devices.'

'It's still raining,' said Jacques, 'I'll go and stretch out on the camp bed.'

Next door to the engine shed there was a room with some mattresses and loose covers over them, where the men could take a rest without undressing if they were only in Le Havre for a few hours. He watched Pecqueux disappear into the rain in the direction of the Sauvagnats' house. As soon as he had gone, Jacques ventured out himself and ran across to the rest room. But he didn't go in. He stood at the entrance with the door wide open, overcome by the stifling heat inside. At the back of the room 211 an engine driver lay on his back, snoring, his mouth wide open.

He waited for a few more minutes. He could not put the meeting with Séverine out of his mind. His frustration at this infuriating storm was gradually giving way to a crazy desire to go to their rendezvous come what may. Even if he no longer expected to find Séverine waiting for him, he would still have the pleasure of being there himself. He felt as if his whole person were being drawn there. He went out into the storm, came to their usual meeting place and followed the dark alleyway between the coal stacks. He could not see in front of him because of the driving rain that cut into his face. He walked down the alleyway as far as the tool-shed, where once before he and Séverine had taken shelter. He thought he would feel less on his own in there.

Inside the shed it was pitch black. As he walked through the door, two arms lightly enfolded him, and he felt two lips being pressed warmly against his. It was Séverine.

'Good heavens!' said Jacques. 'You're here!'

'Yes,' she answered, 'I saw the storm coming. I ran here before it started to rain. Jacques, you've been so long.'

Her voice faded to a sigh. Never before had she abandoned herself to him like this. She lowered herself on to the empty sacks that lay heaped in the corner like a bed. Jacques fell to the ground beside her, held in her embrace. He felt his legs resting across hers. They could not see each other, but their breaths mingled. As if in a trance, they became lost to all sense of time and place. They kissed each other passionately, and their hearts seemed to beat as one.

'Darling,' he said, 'you waited for me . . .'

'Yes,' she answered, 'I waited for you. I waited and waited . . .'

Immediately, impulsively, Séverine held him tight. She drew him towards her and without a word compelled him to take her. How it happened she did not know. By the time he arrived she had resigned herself to not seeing him. Without stopping to consider or to think what she was doing, she had been carried away by the sheer, unexpected joy of holding him in her arms, by the sudden, irresistible need to be his. It had happened because it had to. The rain fell even more insistently on the shed roof. The ground shook, as the last train from Paris went whistling and clattering into the station.

When Jacques raised himself from her, he was puzzled to hear the sound of falling rain. Where was he? His hand brushed against the handle of a hammer, which he had felt on the floor near him as he lay down beside her. A surge of joy ran through him. Could it be true? He had possessed Séverine and had not taken the hammer to smash her skull. She was his, and there had been no bitter struggle, no instinctive desire to fling her across his back, dead, like some trophy won in battle. No longer did he feel the need

to avenge those ancient wrongs done from time imme-
morial, or sense the accumulated bitterness passed down
from man to man since the first infidelity in the dark
recesses of some primeval cave. Possessing Séverine was
like a magic spell. She had cured him. He saw her as someone different, someone who for all her weakness was
capable of violence, someone whose hands were steeped
in blood. It was this that had protected her, like a fearsome
coat of armour. She had overcome him. He had not dared
lay hands on her. When he once more took her in his arms,
it was with a feeling of deep indebtedness, and a desire to
surrender himself to her totally.

Séverine likewise abandoned herself to him, happy to
be released from the doubts which had beset her and which
now seemed so pointless. Why had she denied him for so
long? She should have yielded to him as she had promised
herself she would; it could bring her only pleasure and 213
delight. She knew now that this was what she had always
wanted, even when it had seemed so good to wait. She
needed to be loved body and soul, with a love that was
steadfast and true. What she had endured, the horrors she
had been drawn into, were too terrible for words. Life had
treated her cruelly, viciously, dragging her through the
mud and drawing her into crime. Her beautiful blue eyes,
so innocent and appealing beneath her tragic crown of
black hair, had a permanently frightened look about them.
In spite of everything, she had remained virgin.[3] And now
she had given herself for the first time, to a man she adored.
She wanted to lose herself in him. She wanted to be his
slave. She was his. He could make use of her as he wished.

'Take me, my darling,' she begged him. 'I am yours for
ever. I want only what you want.'

'No, my dearest,' he answered. 'It is for you to command.
I am here but to love and obey you.'

Hours went by. The rain had stopped falling long since.

A great silence hung over the station. All that could be heard was the distant murmur of the sea. They were still in each other's arms when a shot rang out. They sprang to their feet in alarm. Day was just beginning to break; a patch of pale light whitened the sky above the mouth of the Seine. What was that shot? They should not have stayed so long. It was madness. They had a sudden vision of Roubaud chasing after them with a revolver.

'Stay where you are,' said Jacques. 'I'll go and see what's happening.'

He cautiously advanced towards the door. Outside it was still dark. He could hear the sound of men running towards them. He recognized Roubaud's voice shouting to the night watchmen, telling them that there were three intruders and that he'd seen them stealing coal. For the past few weeks hardly a night had gone by without him having hallucinations about imaginary thieves. On this occasion something had suddenly alarmed him, and he had fired at random in the dark.

'Quick! We can't stay here,' whispered Jacques. 'They'll search the shed. You must go home.'

They flung themselves into each other's arms in a passionate embrace. Then Séverine ran quickly along the side of the engine shed, hidden by the high wall, while Jacques crept out quietly and hid himself amongst the coal stacks. They were only just in time, for, as Jacques had predicted, Roubaud did want to search the tool-shed. He was sure that that was where the intruders were. The watchmen's lamps swung to and fro. There were some angry exchanges, and then they all went back towards the station, annoyed at having wasted their time.

Jacques decided that the coast was clear and was just setting off back to his room in the Rue François-Mazeline when he almost collided with Pecqueux, who was hastily doing up his clothes and swearing furiously under his breath.

'What's up with you?' asked Jacques.

'Don't ask,' replied Pecqueux. 'Those bloody fools woke Sauvagnat up, and he heard me in bed with his sister. He came down in his nightshirt, and I had to get out through the window, quick. Listen! You can hear them.'

A woman was screaming and wailing. She was being beaten. A man's voice was yelling abuse at her.

'Did you hear that? He's giving her a real hiding! She's thirty-two years old, but if he catches her at it he thrashes her like a little girl! Ah well, too bad! I'm keeping out of it. He's her brother after all!'

'But I thought he didn't mind you going to see her,' said Jacques. 'I thought it was only when she was with other men that he got angry with her.'

'Who knows?' said Pecqueux. 'Sometimes he pretends not to see me. Other times, he beats her up. Listen to him now! The funny thing is that he still loves her. He'd give **215** up everything rather than be parted from her. But he expects good behaviour. Heavens above! She's getting the full treatment tonight!'

The screams subsided and were replaced by a series of long, pathetic moans. The two men walked away. Ten minutes later they were fast asleep side by side in their little bedroom with its yellow painted walls, its four chairs, a table and a metal wash-basin, which they shared.

During the following weeks, the nights when Jacques and Séverine met were nights of untold bliss. They did not always have a storm to protect them. On starry nights or when the moon was full, they felt uneasy and would look for pockets of shadow and little dark corners where they could happily hold each other close. All through August and September there were some wonderful nights, so mild that they would have lain asleep in each other's arms till daybreak, had they not been woken by sounds from the station as it began to stir and by locomotives letting off steam in the distance. Even in October, when it began to turn chilly, it did not bother them. Séverine came more warmly dressed, wrapped in a big coat, almost big enough for Jacques to squeeze into too. They would barricade themselves in the tool-shed, which they had found a way of locking from the inside with the help of an iron bar, and there they felt safe and snug. The fierce November gales might be blowing slates from the rooftops, but they felt not the slightest draught. Jacques, however, ever since the night he had first made love to her, had wanted to possess her in her own home, in her poky little apartment, where she seemed different, more desirable, a respectable married woman quietly going about her daily business. She had always refused, not so much because of her prying neighbours as from a lingering sense of propriety. She could not bring herself to sleep with him in her own marriage bed. One Monday, however, in broad daylight, when Jacques had come for lunch and Roubaud was late back, having had to see the stationmaster, he picked her up and carried her across to the bed for a joke. It was such a mad, foolhardy thing to do, and they were both beside themselves laughing. Needless to say, they very soon became carried away. After that she offered no further resistance and Jacques came to meet her in her apartment after midnight on Thursdays and Saturdays. It was terribly risky, and they hardly dared move in case the neighbours heard them, but this only redoubled their passion and added to their pleasure. Often they felt a desire to walk abroad in the dark, to escape like caged animals, into the icy stillness of a winter's night. Once they made love beneath the stars in the middle of a bitter December frost.

They had been living like this for four months, their love for each other growing stronger and stronger. To both of them love was something new. At heart they were still children, young innocents, amazed at falling in love for the first time, happy simply to be in each other's arms, each submitting to the other's will in a perpetual contest of self-sacrifice and surrender. Jacques was in no doubt that Séverine had cured him of the terrible malady he had inherited as a child; since he had possessed her the thought of murder no longer troubled him. Did physical possession satisfy the craving to kill? Was possession tantamount to killing? Who could fathom the shadowy mind of the beast within? He tried not to think about it. It was beyond him. The doorway to such horrors was best left unopened. Sometimes as he lay in her arms the thought of what she had done would suddenly come back to him. She had murdered; he had read it in her eyes as they sat together on the park bench in the Square des Batignolles. But he wanted to know no more. Séverine, on the other hand, seemed more and more anxious to tell him all that had happened. Sometimes, when she held him tight, he felt that she was 217 bursting and gasping to tell him her secret, that her only reason for wanting to give herself was to find relief from the thing that was choking her. A violent tremor would run through her body and cause her breast to heave; confused sighs broke from her lips, and her voice faded away as she reached her ecstasy. Was she trying to speak to him? Seized with panic, he would quickly press his lips to hers and silence her confession with a kiss. Why let this thing come between them? Who could tell how it might change their love for each other? He sensed danger; the thought of her recounting the gruesome details of her crime to him made him shudder. She no doubt guessed what he was thinking because she would lie beside him and run her hands over him gently, lovingly, wanting only to love him and to be loved in return. And then they would make love, madly, passionately, and lie fainting in each other's arms.

Since the summer, Roubaud had put on a lot of weight. Whereas Séverine seemed to be regaining the vivacity and

freshness of the twenty-year-old girl she was, he seemed
to be growing older and more sullen. As Séverine said, he
had changed a lot in four months. He was still on good
terms with Jacques, shaking his hand, inviting him back
to the flat and never happier than when he joined them for
a meal. But Jacques's company was no longer enough to
satisfy him. He would often go out as soon as he had finished eating, sometimes leaving Jacques alone with his
wife, on the pretext that it was stuffy indoors and that he
needed to get some fresh air. The truth was that he was
now in the habit of visiting a little café on the Cours
Napoléon, where he used to meet Monsieur Cauche, the
safety officer. He didn't drink much, bar the occasional tot
of rum, but he had developed a liking for cards. It was
becoming something of an obsession. It was only when
he had the cards in his hand and was absorbed in endless
218   rounds of piquet that he forgot his troubles and became
more cheerful. Monsieur Cauche, who was an inveterate
gambler, had insisted they play for money, and the stakes
had now risen to a hundred sous⁴ a game. This was a side
of himself that Roubaud had never been aware of. He
became completely carried away by the idea of winning a
fortune, by the mania for making money, which can so
take hold of a man that he will stake his job and his liveli-
hood on a throw of the dice. So far his work had not
suffered. He would go off to the café as soon as he was free,
and if he wasn't on duty he wouldn't get back home until
two or three in the morning. His wife didn't complain,
although she objected to him always coming back in a
worse mood than when he'd left, for he was extraordinarily
unlucky and ended up running into debt.

Then came the first quarrel. Although she had not yet
come to hate him, Séverine was finding Roubaud more
and more difficult to put up with. She felt as if he were a
weight bearing down on her whole life; but for the

constant burden of his presence, she would have been free and happy. She had no regrets about deceiving him. After all, it was his fault; hadn't he more or less forced her into it? As they gradually drifted apart, they each tried to overcome the disruption in their lives, seeking consolation or distraction in their own different ways. If he had his cards, she was entitled to have a lover. But what really annoyed her, what she simply could not come to terms with, was finding herself short of money as a result of his continual losses. Her housekeeping money was now being squandered at the café on the Cours Napoléon, and she sometimes couldn't see her way clear to paying the laundry bill. She had to do without all sorts of little comforts and items of clothing. That evening, they had quarrelled over a pair of shoes she needed to buy. Roubaud was about to leave and couldn't find a knife to cut himself a slice of bread. So he had taken a knife from the sideboard drawer. **219** It was the murder weapon. She looked him straight in the eyes as he refused to give her the fifteen francs she wanted for the shoes. He didn't have the money and he had no idea where he could find it. But she was insistent and asked him again. He refused a second time, becoming more and more exasperated. Suddenly, she pointed to the place under the floor, where the ghostly spoils still lay hidden. There was some money there, she said, and she wanted some of it. Roubaud turned pale; the knife fell with a clatter into the drawer. For a moment she thought he was going to hit her. He came towards her, muttering that the money down there could rot, that he'd sooner cut his hand off than take any of it. He clenched his fists and threatened to beat her if she tried to take the floorboard up or steal a single centime while he was out. He would never touch it! Never! It was dead and buried! Séverine, too, had turned pale. The thought of groping around under the floorboards made her feel faint. They might end up poor, they might be starving, but the money would stay where it was. They never mentioned it again, even when they were really hard up. But every time they chanced to walk on that part of the floor, the burning sensation in their feet got worse. They ended up always walking round it.

Other arguments followed, about La Croix-de-Maufras. Why hadn't the house been sold? Each accused the other of doing nothing to get things moving. Roubaud still refused to have anything to do with it, whilst Séverine, on the odd occasions she wrote to the Misards, received only vague information in reply; no one had shown any interest in it, the fruit trees had failed and the vegetables wouldn't grow because there was nobody to water them. In the weeks following the crisis, the Roubauds had lived blissfully free from care. But things were changing; it seemed that all their troubles were about to begin again. 220 The seeds of discontent – the hidden money, the secret lover – had begun to sprout, forcing them apart and setting them against each other. They grew to dislike each other more and more. Their life together was becoming a torment.

What was more, by a singular stroke of ill fortune, they began to have further trouble with their neighbours. A new spate of gossip and argument had broken out. Philomène had recently had a slanging match with Madame Lebleu, who accused her of selling her a chicken that had died of fowl pest. The real reason for their disagreement, however, was that Philomène had now developed a friendship with Séverine. One night, Pecqueux had seen Séverine in Jacques's arms. Because Pecqueux was Jacques's fireman, Philomène had overcome her earlier dislike of Séverine, having discovered that she was Jacques's mistress, and was doing her utmost to be pleasant towards her. She prided herself on being a friend of the most attractive and incontestably the most refined lady at the station and had turned against the cashier's wife, that old bag as she called her, whose sole aim in life was to make trouble. She blamed her for everything and went around telling everyone that the apartment overlooking the street belonged by rights to the Roubauds and that it was outrageous that it had not been returned to them. So things were not going well for Madame Lebleu. She also risked getting into serious trouble because of her constant spying on Mademoiselle Guichon in the hope of catching her with the stationmaster. She still hadn't succeeded but she had been foolish enough to get herself caught with her ear glued to their doors. Monsieur Dabadie, furious at this eavesdropping, had told Moulin, the other assistant stationmaster, that if Roubaud wished to reapply for the apartment, he would be happy to endorse his application. Moulin, who was normally not one for gossip, had repeated this to everyone on the corridor. Feelings had run very high, and at one point things had nearly come to blows.

Amidst all this growing unpleasantness, there was only one day that Séverine looked forward to – Friday. In her quietly determined way, she had invented an excuse for getting away. It was the first thing that came into her head; she had a pain in her knee and needed to see a specialist. So every Friday since October, she had been taking the 6.40 express in the morning, which was always driven by Jacques, and had spent the day with him in Paris, coming back in the evening on the 6.30. Initially she felt obliged to inform her husband how her knee was progressing; some days it felt better and some days it felt worse. But after a while, realizing that he wasn't even listening, she had simply given up mentioning it. Sometimes she looked at him and wondered whether he knew. How was it possible that someone so fiercely jealous, someone who had demanded bloody retribution and killed in a blind rage, could accept that she had taken a lover? She couldn't understand it. She thought he must be turning stupid.

It was a bitterly cold December night. Séverine had waited up very late for her husband to come home. The next day was Friday, and she had to be up before dawn to catch the train to Paris. She had got into the habit of getting everything ready beforehand, setting out her clothes so that she could dress the minute she got up. Eventually she went to bed, falling asleep at about one o'clock. Roubaud had still not returned. Already twice before, he had not arrived back until the small hours. He had become totally addicted to his passion for cards and seemed unable to drag himself away from the café, where a little back room had been set aside especially. It had become a veritable gambling den and large sums of money were being wagered at écarté.[5] Séverine was quite happy to have the bed to herself; with the bed covers tucked warmly around her, she fell into a deep sleep, dreaming about the delights of the day to come.

It was almost three in the morning when she was woken by a strange noise. She had no idea what it could have been, thought she must have been dreaming and went back to sleep. But then she heard heavy thuds and the sound of wood creaking, as if someone were trying to force open a door. Suddenly there was a loud thump and the sound of something snapping, which made her sit bolt upright in her bed. She was terrified and convinced that someone was trying to break in from the corridor outside. For a whole minute she sat not daring to move, straining her ears to listen. Eventually plucking up her courage, she got out of bed to investigate. She walked noiselessly across the room on her bare feet and quietly inched open the bedroom door. She was wearing only her nightdress; she was so cold that she had turned white and was shivering. The sight which now greeted her eyes in the dining room made her stand rooted to the ground in terror and amazement.

Roubaud was on the floor, lying on his stomach and leaning on his elbows. He had prised open the edge of the parquet floor with a chisel. He had placed a candle beside him, and its light cast a huge shadow on the ceiling. He was leaning over the hole, which ran like a black slit across the parquet floor, peering inside it. His eyes seemed to start from his head. The blood had run to his cheeks and turned them purple; his face was the face of a murderer. Wildly, he thrust his hand under the floorboard, but found nothing. He was shaking with fear and had to bring the candle nearer. There, down in the hole, he saw the purse, the banknotes and the watch.

Séverine let out a cry. Roubaud turned round, terrified. For a moment he didn't recognize her. He must have thought she was a ghost, standing there in her white night- **223** dress with big frightened eyes.

'What are you doing?' she asked.

He realized that it was Séverine but made no answer, merely grunting in reply. He looked at her. Her presence annoyed him; he wished she would go back to bed. What could he say? Seeing her standing in front of him, shivering, with nothing on, all he wanted to do was to hit her.

'So that's your game!' she continued. 'You refuse to buy me shoes and then you help yourself to his money, because you've lost at cards!'

Roubaud lost his temper. Was she still going to carry on ruining his life and stand in the way of his pleasures? He no longer desired her, and making love had become a torment. He was getting his enjoyment elsewhere and didn't need her any more. He reached down into the hole again and took out the purse containing the three gold hundred-franc coins. Having put the floorboard back in place with his heel, he came towards her.

'You're making my life a misery,' he hissed. 'I'll do what I like. Do I ask you what you get up to in Paris?'

With a furious shrug of the shoulders he went back to the café, leaving the candle burning on the floor.

Séverine picked it up and went back to bed, frozen to the marrow. She left the candle burning, unable to get back to sleep, her eyes wide open, counting the minutes until it was time to catch her train.

It was now perfectly clear to her that Roubaud had steadily deteriorated, as if the crime had seeped into him, eating him away and dissolving all links between them, and that he knew.

That Friday, passengers intending to catch the 6.40 express at Le Havre awoke with cries of dismay. Snow had been falling thick and fast since midnight, and the streets were ankle deep.

In the station, the train was ready to leave; seven carriages, three second class and four first, and *La Lison* steaming and ready to go. When Jacques and Pecqueux had arrived at the engine shed to inspect the locomotive at half past five, they couldn't believe how much snow had fallen. And the sky was still black, with more snow to come. They stood on the footplate listening for the whistle to proceed, looking out in front of them through the gap- **225** ing mouth of the train shed and watching the snowflakes falling swiftly and silently, streaking the darkness with a shimmer of white.

'I'm blowed if I can see the signal,' the driver muttered.

'We'll be lucky to get through!' said the fireman.

Roubaud was standing on the platform with his lamp, having arrived that minute to begin his shift. There were dark rings under his eyes, which kept closing from fatigue as he supervised the departure. Jacques asked him if he knew anything about the state of the line; he came over to him, shook his hand and said that he had received no report so far. At that moment Séverine came down the steps wrapped in a heavy overcoat. Roubaud led her to a first-class compartment and helped her to get in. He must have noticed the look of affection and anxiety that the two lovers exchanged. Yet it didn't occur to him to tell his wife that it was unwise to leave in weather like this and that she would do better to postpone her trip.

Other passengers were beginning to arrive, all muffled up and carrying luggage, jostling to get to the train in the terrible morning cold. With snow still clinging to their boots, they quickly shut the carriage doors and barricaded themselves in. The platform remained empty, dimly lit by the fitful glimmer of a few gas lamps; the headlamp on the locomotive, fixed to the base of the chimney, gleamed like a giant eye, casting its broad beam of light into the darkness.

Roubaud raised his lamp to give the signal for departure. The guard blew his whistle, and Jacques gave a whistle in reply. He opened the regulator and eased the reversing wheel forward. They were off. Roubaud stood for a minute quietly watching the train as it disappeared into the storm.

'Listen!' Jacques said to Pecqueux. 'I don't want any messing about today.'

He had noticed that, like Roubaud, his companion also seemed to be falling asleep on his feet; the result of a night on the tiles no doubt.

'Don't worry,' muttered Pecqueux. 'I'll be fine.'

As soon as the train emerged from the covered roof of the station, the two men were exposed to the snow. The wind was blowing from the east and it caught the locomotive head on, sending the snow in great swirls directly towards it. At first, standing behind the weather shield dressed in thick woollen clothes and with their eyes protected by goggles, Jacques and Pecqueux didn't find things too difficult. But the light from the headlamp blazing out into the night seemed to be swallowed up in dense clouds of whiteness. Instead of being lit up for two or three hundred metres ahead, the track seemed to come towards them out of a milky fog, with objects suddenly appearing only when they were very close to, as if from the depths of a dream. What most worried Jacques was the realization, as they passed the signal at the first section box, that, as he had feared, it would be impossible to see a signal at red from the regulation distance. So progress was extremely cautious. Yet he couldn't afford to go too slowly; there was already tremendous wind resistance, and it would be equally dangerous if the train fell too far behind schedule.

La Lison maintained a steady speed all the way to Harfleur. As yet, Jacques wasn't too worried about the depth of the snow; it was sixty centimetres deep at the most and the snowplough could easily clear a depth of one metre.[1] His principal concern was to keep the train running at speed. He knew that, as well as remaining sober and making sure his locomotive was kept in good condition, the mark of a good driver was to be able to keep his engine running smoothly and steadily while maintaining full pressure. In fact Jacques's one weakness was an obstinate unwillingness to bring his train to a stop. He sometimes even ignored signals, fully confident that he had *La Lison* under control. Occasionally he would get carried away and deliberately run over detonators.[2] He said it was like treading on someone's corns! It had twice earned him a week's suspension. On this occasion, however, he sensed that the situation was fraught with danger. The thought that his beloved Séverine was with him and that her life was in his hands increased his resolve to press on regardless down the iron highway that led to Paris, braving every obstacle that might confront him.

Jacques stood on the metal plate that linked the engine and tender, constantly jolted by the movement of the train and, despite the snow, leaning out to the right, trying to see ahead. Nothing was visible through the footplate window; it was streaked with water from the driving snow. Jacques stood looking into the icy blast, his face stung by a million sharp needles, lacerated by the cold, which cut into his skin like a razor. From time to time he drew back

227

to recover his breath, removed his goggles and wiped them and then returned to his lookout post in the teeth of the gale, peering intently into the darkness for signals at red. He was so absorbed in his task that he twice had the illusion of seeing a sudden shower of sparks scattered like spots of blood across the curtain of snow that floated in front of him.

Suddenly, in the darkness, Jacques sensed that his fireman was no longer there. In order to avoid dazzling the driver, there was only one light on the footplate – a small lamp which was used to check the water level in the boiler, but on the enamelled dial of the pressure gauge, which seemed to emit a light of its own, he could see the little blue needle quivering and falling rapidly. The fire was low, and his fireman lay sprawled out on the toolbox fast asleep.

228   'You bloody drunkard!' Jacques yelled, shaking him furiously.

Pecqueux got to his feet, muttering some unintelligible excuse. He could hardly stand. Through sheer force of habit he returned to his fire, breaking up lumps of coal with his hammer, spreading it evenly over the grate with his shovel and sweeping the footplate with his broom. With the firebox door open, a shaft of light from the fire stretched back over the train like the blazing tail of a comet, turning the snowflakes that fell through it into great drops of gold.

After Harfleur they began the stiff three-league climb to Saint-Romain, the steepest gradient on the line. Jacques needed to concentrate on his driving again, knowing that it would need a real effort to get up this incline, which was difficult enough even in fine weather. With his hand on the reversing wheel, he watched the telegraph poles go by, trying to calculate how quickly the train was moving. They were rapidly losing speed; *La Lison* was beginning to struggle, and he could feel the increasing resistance of the snow against the snowplough. He stretched out his foot and opened the firebox door again. Pecqueux, still half asleep, knew what he had to do and immediately started heaping extra coal on the fire in order to increase the pressure. The firebox door was by now red hot, sending a purplish glow about their legs, although neither of them felt its heat, as the surrounding air was so bitterly cold. At a nod from his driver, Pecqueux opened the damper[3] in the ash-pan, which increased the draught to the fire. The needle on the pressure gauge had quickly risen to ten atmospheres,[4] and *La Lison* was working flat out. At one point, Jacques noticed that the water level was falling and, although he knew it would reduce the pressure, he had to turn the injector on. Pressure was soon restored; the engine snorted and spat, like a horse being driven too hard, lunging and rearing so alarmingly that you might have imagined you could hear her bones cracking. Jacques was calling her all sorts of names, as if she were an old and ailing wife whom he no longer loved as he had done before.

'She'll never make it, the lazy thing!' he muttered through clenched teeth. Normally when he was driving, he didn't speak.

Pecqueux, who was still barely awake, looked at him in amazement. What had he suddenly got against *La Lison*? Wasn't this the good old engine they had both worked with for so long? She had always done everything that was asked of her, pulling away from stations so easily that it was a pleasure to drive her, and such a good steamer that she saved them a tenth of their coal between Paris and Le Havre! When a locomotive had a valve gear as good as hers, with perfect timing that reduced the expenditure of steam as if by magic, you could forgive her all sorts of other failings, as you would a crotchety wife, provided she was a good housekeeper and didn't spend too much money.

Admittedly, *La Lison* consumed too much oil. So what? You simply oiled her. That was all there was to it!

In fact it was oil that Jacques was complaining about at that very moment.

'She'll never make it unless we give her some oil,' he was saying.

Whereupon, he did something he had not done more than three times in his whole career; he took his oilcan and went to oil *La Lison* as she continued on her way. He climbed over the side of the cab on to the running plate and walked the length of the boiler. It was a very dangerous thing to do; his feet kept slipping on the narrow metal plate, which was wet from the snow. He couldn't see what he was doing, and the force of the wind threatened to blow him away like a wisp of straw. *La Lison* steamed forward into the night with Jacques clinging to her side, being jolted 230 and jarred as she ploughed her way through the immense covering of snow. He reached the buffer beam at the front of the locomotive and crouched over the lubricator of the right-hand cylinder, desperately trying to fill it, while clinging to the handrail with his other hand. Then, like an insect, he had to crawl round to the other side to oil the left-hand cylinder. When he got back to the footplate he was exhausted and as white as a sheet; he had come within a whisker of getting himself killed.

'The lousy bitch!' he muttered.

Pecqueux was amazed at the way Jacques had suddenly become so annoyed with *La Lison*. He couldn't help laughing and ventured his old joke: 'You should've let me do it. That's my speciality, oiling the ladies!'

By now he had woken up a little and was standing in his customary position, keeping a lookout on the left-hand side of the line. Normally his eyesight was very good, better in fact than his driver's. But the blizzard had wiped everything out. Jacques and Pecqueux both knew every kilometre of the line like the backs of their hands, but they could now scarcely recognize the places they were passing through; the track had disappeared beneath the snow, the hedges and even the houses seemed to have submerged. All that could be seen was a flat, unending plain, an undefined wilderness of white, through which *La Lison* seemed to be charging headlong, like a thing possessed. Never before had the two men experienced so intensely the ties of comradeship that united them, as when they stood together on the footplate of *La Lison* as she pursued her perilous course, feeling lonelier and more abandoned than if they had been locked away in a prison cell, and bearing the terrible, agonizing responsibility for all the lives that were being drawn along in the train behind them.

Pecqueux's joke had angered Jacques, but he simply smiled and contained his annoyance; this wasn't the time to quarrel. The snow was falling thicker than ever, and the horizon was closing in around them like a curtain. They were still climbing. Suddenly the fireman thought he saw a red signal in the distance. He shouted to his driver. But the signal had already disappeared. His eyes were 'playing tricks on him'; a not infrequent complaint of his. The driver had seen nothing, but the fireman's false alarm had disturbed him; his heart beat faster, he was beginning to lose confidence in himself. Beyond the whirling snowflakes he imagined he saw huge dark shapes, massive forms that loomed out of the night and moved towards them in front of the locomotive. Were they landslides that had piled up on the line? Was the train about to run into them? Seized with panic, he pulled frantically at the whistle; its long, mournful wail rose into the air above the noise of the storm. Much to his surprise, he had whistled at just the right moment, for the train was passing through Saint-Romain; he had thought it was two kilometres further on.

Once she had breasted the incline, *La Lison* began to run more easily, and Jacques could relax a little. From Saint-Romain to Bolbec the line was almost level, and there should be no further problems until they had crossed the plateau. Even so, during their three-minute stop at Beuzeville, Jacques called over to the stationmaster, whom he had spotted on the platform, to express his concern about the snow, which was getting deeper every minute. They would never make it to Rouen; while they were near a shed which always had spare engines in steam, the most sensible thing would be to attach an extra locomotive and double-head the train. But the stationmaster said he hadn't received permission and he didn't think that it was within his responsibility. The only thing he could think of was to provide them with five or six wooden shovels to clear the rails should the need arise. Pecqueux took the shovels and **232** stowed them in a corner of the tender.

As expected, *La Lison* crossed the plateau without too much difficulty and maintained a good speed. But she was beginning to tire. Every minute Jacques had to stretch out his foot to open the firebox door so that his fireman could add more coal; each time he did so, the comet's tail flashed across the night above the dark outline of the train, with whiteness all around, enclosing it like a shroud. It was a quarter to eight, and it was beginning to get light, although, in the great swirls of snow that filled the sky from one end of the horizon to the other, the dawn was hardly noticeable. It was a murky half-light in which nothing could yet be seen, making things even more difficult for the two men, whose eyes, despite their goggles, were streaming as they peered into the distance. Jacques kept one hand on the reversing wheel and the other on the whistle, sounding it almost continuously to warn of their approach and sending a wail of distress across the empty wastes of this desert of snow.

They passed through Bolbec and Yvetot without incident. At Motteville, Jacques again summoned the assistant
stationmaster, but he was unable to give him any precise
information on conditions up the line. So far, no train had
arrived; they had merely been informed by telegraph that
the stopping train from Paris was being held at Rouen as
a precaution. *La Lison* set off once more, lumbering slowly
down the gentle three-league descent to Barentin. By now
it was daylight. But the light was very pale, a livid glow that
seemed to emanate from the snow itself. The snow continued to fall more thickly, as if dawn were descending from
above, cloudy and shivering, strewing the heavens' waste
across the surface of the earth. As it grew lighter, the wind
rose sharply, driving the snowflakes towards them like
bullets. The fireman had to keep taking his shovel to
remove the snow at the back of the tender, between the two
water-tanks. The countryside on both sides of the train 233
appeared so unrecognizable that the two men felt they were
travelling through a dream world; the broad, open fields,
the lush meadows surrounded by green hedges, the little
orchards planted with apple trees were now but a sea of
white with small waves rippling across its surface, a vast,
empty expanse, cold and frozen, in which everything
seemed to dissolve into whiteness. The engine driver stood
on the footplate, his face lashed by the gusts of wind, his
hand on the reversing wheel. He was beginning to feel the
cold that bit into him mercilessly.

When they eventually reached Barentin, Monsieur Bes-
sière, the stationmaster, came up to the engine and told
Jacques that heavy falls of snow had been reported at La
Croix-de-Maufras.

'You might be able to get through,' he said, 'but it will
be difficult.'

Jacques lost his temper.

'God Almighty!' he yelled. 'What did I tell them at

Beuzeville? They could easily have put another engine on! We're going to be in trouble, I'm telling you!'

The guard had left his van; he too was getting annoyed. He was frozen stiff from sitting in his observation cabin; he said he couldn't tell a signal from a telegraph post. They might just as well have been travelling blind in all this snow!

'Anyway,' said Monsieur Bessière, 'you've been warned.'

The passengers were beginning to wonder why there was such a long delay in this silent, snow-bound station; there was nothing happening on the platform, no carriage doors opening and closing. People started to lower their windows and look out. There was a very large woman with two charming, fair-haired young girls, her daughters no doubt, all three unmistakably English, and a little further down the train a pretty young woman with dark hair, with a man rather older than her who was pulling her back into the compartment. There were two men, one older and one younger, leaning out of the windows, talking to each other from one compartment to the next. But as Jacques looked down the line of carriages, he saw only one person – Séverine. She too was leaning from her carriage, looking along the train towards him, obviously very concerned. Dear Séverine! How worried she must be! His heart ached to think of her there, so near yet so far, and in such danger. He would have given anything to have arrived in Paris and to have brought her there safe and sound.

'Come on,' said the stationmaster, 'you'd better get going. There's no point in making everyone nervous.'

He gave the all clear. The guard, who had climbed back into his van, blew his whistle, and once again *La Lison* was on her way.

Jacques immediately sensed that the condition of the line had changed. They were no longer on the plateau, with the train crossing an endless carpet of thick snow like a ship ploughing its way through the sea, leaving a wake behind it; they were now entering a more rugged country of hills and valleys that rose and fell continuously all the way to Malaunay. Here the snow had not settled evenly. In some places the track was clear, but in others the line was blocked by huge drifts. The wind had blown the snow away from the embankments but had driven it into the cuttings. A continual succession of hazards confronted them, stretches of clear track which were suddenly cut off by huge walls of snow. It was now broad daylight, and under its covering of snow the wild countryside with its steep hills and narrow gorges took on the desolate appearance of an ocean frozen solid in the middle of a storm.

Never had Jacques felt the cold cut through him like this. His face was pricked by thousands of icy needles, and he felt as if it were covered in blood. He had lost all sensation in his hands; they were stiff with cold and, to his dismay, **235** so numb that he could no longer feel the reversing wheel that he was holding. When he reached up to sound the whistle, his arm hung heavily from his shoulder like the arm of a dead man. His stomach heaved; he could not tell whether his legs were continuing to support him or not as he was flung violently backwards and forwards by the continual lurching of the engine. He was overcome with fatigue, and the cold was beginning to affect his brain; he had the frightening sensation of not knowing whether he was really there or not, whether this was him driving the engine, for he was operating the reversing wheel automatically and simply gazing at the falling pressure gauge as if he were in a trance. All the old stories about drivers having hallucinations kept going through his head. Was that a fallen tree across the track in front of him? Was there a red flag waving from the top of that bush? Were those not detonators he could hear repeatedly going off above the noise of the wheels? He could no longer tell; he kept telling himself he should stop but he simply lacked the will-power to do so. This agony of mind lasted several minutes. He suddenly caught sight of Pecqueux, who had once again fallen asleep over the toolbox, worn out by the cold like himself. It made him so angry that for a moment he felt almost warm again.

'You useless bastard!' he screamed.

Jacques was normally very tolerant of his companion's drunken habits, but he started kicking him to wake him up and didn't desist until he was on his feet. Pecqueux, still in a daze, merely grunted and picked up his shovel.

'All right, all right,' he said, 'I'm seeing to it!'

When he had mended the fire, the pressure rose again, and in the nick of time, for *La Lison* had just entered a cutting where there was more than a metre of snow to get through. Jacques was trying to get the maximum effort from her and she was shaking all over. For a moment she appeared to lose strength and seemed about to grind to a halt, like a ship caught on a sandbank. What was adding to her burden was the heavy layer of snow that had gradually accumulated on the carriage roofs. The dark line of carriages was being drawn along through the snow, with a white blanket stretched over them, and where the snow had melted and run down the sides of *La Lison*'s boiler it looked as though she wore a black cloak trimmed with ermine. Once again, despite the great weight she was pulling, she managed to free herself and get through. Round a wide bend, high on an embankment, the train could still be seen, like a piece of dark ribbon, steadily making its way through this fairytale world of dazzling whiteness.

Further ahead, however, lay more cuttings. Jacques and Pecqeuex had felt *La Lison* beginning to struggle. They steeled themselves against the cold, standing at their post, determined to brave things out to the bitter end. Once again the engine began to lose speed. She had run between two banks of snow. Slowly but surely she came to a halt. It seemed as if she were stuck in glue, with all her wheels seized up, held fast and gasping for breath. She had stopped moving. It was all over. The snow held her powerless in its grip.

'That's it!' cursed Jacques. 'We've had it!'

He stood at the controls, his hand on the reversing wheel, trying every device he knew to see if the obstruction would give way. *La Lison* coughed and choked in vain; eventually Jacques closed the regulator and swore out loud. He was furious.

The principal guard leaned out of the door of his van and, seeing Pecqueux on the footplate, called out, 'That's that! We're stuck!'

He jumped down into the snow, which came up to his knees, and walked up to the engine. The three men discussed the situation.

'The only thing we can do,' Jacques said finally, 'is to try and dig her out. Fortunately we've got some shovels. Get the other guard. Between the four of us we should be able to free the wheels.'

They called to the other guard at the back of the train, who had already got down from his van. He struggled through the snow towards them, sometimes sinking right into it. The passengers were beginning to get worried. The train had stopped in the middle of nowhere, with empty wastes of snow all around them. They could hear loud voices, discussing what was to be done, and they saw the guard staggering along beside the train. They started to lower their windows. People were shouting and asking questions in an ever-increasing chorus of confusion.

'Where are we? Why have we stopped? What's wrong? Has there been an accident?'

The guard felt he needed to offer some reassurance. As he walked along the train, the podgy, red face of the

Englishwoman appeared at one of the carriage windows, flanked by those of her two charming daughters.

'I trust we're in no danger, monsieur,' she said, with a pronounced accent.

'Not at all, madame,' he replied. 'A bit of snow, that's all. We shall be on our way again shortly.'

The window was pulled up again amidst the girls' happy chatter, that melodious symphony of English syllables that trip so lightly from the lips of children. The two girls were laughing; they found the whole thing highly amusing.

Further along the train the elderly gentleman was beckoning him, with his pretty, dark-haired young wife peering timidly through the window behind him.

'This is outrageous!' he was saying. 'Why wasn't something done about it? I've travelled all the way from London and I have important business to attend to in Paris this **238** morning. I warn you that I shall hold the Company responsible for any delay!'

'Monsieur, we shall be off again in a few minutes,' was all the guard could find to say.

The cold was terrible, and the snow was blowing into the carriages. The heads disappeared and the windows were drawn up. But inside the closed carriages, the disturbance continued; it was clear from the buzz of voices that people were uneasy. Only two windows remained open; leaning out of them, three compartments apart, two passengers were talking to each other, an American of about forty and a young man from Le Havre, both of them very interested in the snow-clearing operation.

'In America, monsieur,' said the American, 'everyone gets out and helps with the shovelling.'

'Oh, this is nothing,' replied the other. 'I was caught in the snow twice last year. My job takes me to Paris every week.'

'Mine takes me there about every three weeks.'

'What, from New York?'

'Yes, monsieur, from New York.'[5]

Jacques was supervising the snow clearing. He caught sight of Séverine looking out of a window in the first carriage. She always travelled in the first carriage in order to be nearer to him. He pleaded to her with his eyes; she understood what he was trying to say and withdrew into the compartment to escape the icy blast that stung her face. The thought of Séverine made Jacques redouble his efforts. Then he noticed that the barrier of snow that had caused them to stop had nothing to do with the wheels, which cut through even the deepest drifts. It was the ash-pan situated between the wheels that had caused the snow to build up, pushing it forward so that it became compacted in great blocks beneath the locomotive. Jacques had an idea.

'We must remove the ash-pan,' he said.

At first the guard objected. Jacques was under his orders, and he was reluctant to allow him to tamper with the locomotive. Eventually he allowed himself to be persuaded.

'All right,' he said, 'but on your head be it!'

It was a dreadful job. Jacques and Pecqueux were forced to lie on their backs in melting snow underneath the engine. It took them nearly half an hour. Fortunately there were some spare spanners in the toolbox. Eventually, having several times been nearly crushed and scorched, they succeeded in removing the ash-pan. But they still had to pull it from beneath the engine. They could barely lift it, and it became trapped between the wheels and the cylinders. However, with four of them tugging at it, they managed to drag it clear of the track and placed it at the side of the cutting.[6]

'Right! Let's finish clearing the snow!' said the guard.

For nearly an hour the train had been at a standstill, and the passengers were becoming increasingly distressed.

239

Carriage windows kept being opened and voices demanded why the train wasn't moving. People were beginning to panic; there were shouts and tears and a feeling of mounting hysteria.

'No, we've cleared enough,' Jacques insisted. 'Get back in and leave it to me.'

Jacques and Pecqueux had climbed back on to the footplate. As soon as the two guards had returned to their vans, Jacques opened the cylinder taps. The deafening jet of hot steam quickly melted the remaining blocks of snow that were still stuck between the rails. He put the engine into reverse and moved the train slowly backwards for about three hundred metres in order to get a good run. He built up a huge fire, raising pressure to beyond the permitted level, and launched *La Lison* with all her weight, and the full weight of the whole train behind her, into the wall of snow which blocked their way. She hit the snow with a sickening thud, like a woodcutter striking his axe against a tree. Her sturdy cast-iron frame shuddered. Still she could not get through. She came to a stop, with steam gushing from everywhere, shaking from the impact. Jacques had to repeat the operation twice, drawing the train back and then running it into the wall of snow to try to clear a passage. Each time, *La Lison* braced herself and valiantly charged forward, snorting like an angry giant. Eventually she seemed to recover her breath, flexed her steel muscles for one last effort and finally managed to force her way through. The train followed slowly behind her through the opening between the two walls of snow. She was free!

'See,' muttered Pecqueux. 'She's not so bad, after all!'

Jacques couldn't see a thing. He took off his goggles to wipe them. His heart was beating fast, and he no longer felt the cold. Then he remembered that there was another deep cutting ahead, about three hundred metres from La

Croix-de-Maufras. The wind would be blowing directly into it, and the snow would be very deep. He had a sudden premonition that this was the reef on which they were destined to founder. He leaned out. In the distance, round one last bend, appeared the cutting, a straight line like a long trench, completely blocked with snow. It was broad daylight. The snow continued to fall. Everything shone white as far as the eye could see.

La Lison proceeded steadily on her way, encountering no further obstacles. As a precaution, Jacques had left the lights burning at both the front and the rear of the train. The white headlamp at the base of the chimney outshone the light of day like the glaring eye of a Cyclops. *La Lison* was nearing the cutting, her eye wide open and staring ahead. Suddenly she seemed to be breathing in little short gasps, like an unwilling horse. She began to shake violently and lurch from side to side. It was only the firm hand of her driver that kept her moving forward. He kicked open the firebox door for the fireman to see to the fire, and now, in place of the comet's tail that had blazed out into the night, a wreath of thick, black smoke darkened the pale, wintry sky.

Still *La Lison* advanced. She was about to enter the cutting. On either side the snow was piled high, and the line ahead had completely disappeared from view. It was like a pool of still water in a stream, with the snow filling it to the very top. In she went, running forward another fifty metres or so, puffing and panting for all she was worth, but getting gradually slower and slower. The snow that she was pushing in front of her formed a barrier that built up and towered above her like an angry wave threatening to engulf her. For a moment it appeared that it was too much for her; that she was beaten. Then, summoning all her strength for one final effort, she broke free and advanced a further thirty metres. But she could do no more. It had been her last, dying gesture. The snow fell back around her in great mounds, burying her wheels, stealing inside her until every moving part was held fast in a grip of ice. She could move no further. Out there in the bitter cold, her life was ebbing away. She stopped breathing. She lay still. She was dead.

'There!' said Jacques. 'That's as far as we're going! I knew this would happen!'

His instinct was to reverse the locomotive and try again. But this time *La Lison* didn't move. She would go neither backwards nor forwards. She was shut in on all sides, stuck to the ground, inert, lifeless. Behind her, the train too seemed dead, buried up to its doors in the deep layer of snow. And still the snow continued to fall, in long, swirling gusts, even heavier than before. It was like being caught in quicksand, with the engine and carriages slowly sinking from view, already half buried, amidst the icy silence of this vast, snowbound waste. Nothing moved. The snow continued to weave its shroud.

'Shall we try again?' shouted the guard, leaning out of his van.

'We're buggered!' was Pecqueux's only comment.

This time, the situation had become critical. The guard at the rear of the train ran back to lay detonators on the track to protect them from behind. The driver, in desperation, sounded short, repeated blasts on the whistle, a breathless, plaintive cry of distress that rose in the morning air. But it was deadened by the falling snow; the sound didn't carry. It would probably not even reach Barentin. What was to be done? There were only four of them. They couldn't possibly clear such an amount of snow on their own. It needed a whole team of men. They would have to go and get help. To make matters worse, the passengers were once again beginning to panic.

A carriage door opened, and the pretty, dark-haired lady

jumped down from the train, terrified, thinking there had been an accident. Her husband, the businessman, who was considerably older than her, jumped down after her.

'I shall write to the minister!' he shouted. 'This is disgraceful!'

Carriage windows were being lowered angrily, and from inside the train came the sounds of women crying and men losing their temper. The two little English girls were the only ones who seemed to be enjoying themselves, peering through the window and smiling serenely. As the principal guard attempted to calm everyone down, the younger of the two girls, speaking in French with a slight English accent, asked him, 'Is this the end of the journey, monsieur?'

Several men had got down from the train, despite the deep snow which came up to their waists. The American once more found himself next to the young man from Le **243** Havre, both of them having walked up to the engine to see what was happening. They stood there, shaking their heads.

'It's going to take four or five hours to dig her out of that lot.'

'Four or five hours at least! And it'll need about twenty men!'

Jacques had persuaded the principal guard to send the rear guard on to Barentin to ask for help. Neither he nor Pecqueux could leave the locomotive.

The guard set off and was soon out of sight at the far end of the cutting. He had a walk of four kilometres in front of him and probably wouldn't be back for another two hours. In despair, Jacques jumped down from the footplate and ran towards the first carriage, where he had seen Séverine lowering her window.

'Don't be frightened,' he said quietly. 'You've nothing to fear.'

'I'm not afraid,' she replied. 'But I was worried about you.'

Like him, she didn't raise her voice, lest anyone should hear her. But it was such a joy to speak together that they both felt heartened and smiled at each other. As Jacques turned to go back to the engine, who should he see coming along the top of the cutting but Flore and Misard, followed by two other men whom he didn't at first recognize. They had heard his distress signal, and Misard, who was off duty at the time, had come to help, accompanied by his two friends, with whom he happened to be having a glass of white wine, the quarryman Cabuche, who was prevented from working by the snow, and the signalman Ozil, who had walked through the tunnel from Malaunay to pay his respects to Flore. Despite her show of indifference towards him, he still had his heart set on her. Flore, being the big strapping girl she was, with the strength and courage of any man, had come along too, out of curiosity. For both her and her father this was quite an event; it wasn't every day that a train stopped outside their front door. They had been living there for five years and had watched the trains go thundering by, in fair weather and in foul, every hour of the day and night. They seemed to rush past them like a gush of wind; not one of them had even slowed down. They watched them fly into the distance and disappear without knowing a thing about them. The whole world passed in front of their house, a crowd of living souls whisked by at high speed, and all they ever saw of them were faces, glimpsed in a flash; sometimes faces they would never see again, sometimes faces they might recognize because they always appeared on a particular day, but all faces without names. And here, in the snow, was a train unloading its passengers at their very door! The natural order had been turned upside down. They looked at all these unknown people who found themselves stranded on the railway line, gazing at them open-eyed, like savages gathering on some far-flung shore to witness a group of shipwrecked Europeans. Through the open doors they could see women wrapped in furs, and there were men walking beside the train in heavy overcoats. The sight of such wealth and luxury, cast adrift on this sea of ice, made them stand and stare in amazement.

Flore did, however, recognize Séverine. She always looked out for Jacques's train whenever it went by and for some weeks she had noticed the presence of this woman on the Friday-morning express, particularly because she looked out of the window as she approached the level-crossing, to catch a glimpse of her property at La Croix-de-Maufras. Flore's eyes darkened as she saw her and Jacques whispering to each other.

'Why, Madame Roubaud!' exclaimed Misard, also recognizing her and immediately assuming his obsequious manner. 'What a terrible thing to happen! You can't stay out here. You must come down to our house.'

Jacques shook hands with the crossing-keeper and advised Séverine to accept his invitation.

'He's right,' he said. 'We might be here for hours. You could die of cold.'

But Séverine appeared reluctant. She was well wrapped up, she said. And she didn't like the idea of walking three hundred metres through the snow. Flore came up to her, looked her straight in the face and said, 'Come on, madame, I'll carry you.'

And even before she had time to say yes, Séverine found herself being lifted off her feet by two strong, muscular arms and carried away like a child. Flore put her down on the other side of the track, where the snow had been trodden underfoot and she wouldn't sink in. Some of the passengers began to laugh in amazement. What a girl! If we had a dozen like her, we'd clear the snow in a couple of hours.

Meanwhile, the offer of shelter in the gatekeeper's cottage, where there would be a fire and perhaps some bread and wine, had passed along the train. Once people realized they were in no immediate danger, the panic began to subside. Even so, the situation was decidedly unpleasant. The foot-warmers were getting cold, it was nine o'clock, and unless help arrived soon, people would be getting hungry and thirsty. They could be stuck there for ages; they might even have to spend the night there. The passengers were divided about what to do. There were those who simply abandoned hope and wouldn't leave the train, shutting themselves inside, wrapping themselves in their rugs and stretching out on the seats as if they were waiting to die. Others preferred to risk a trek through the snow in the hope of finding somewhere better, determined at all costs to avoid the awful prospect of freezing to death in a 246 broken-down train. These latter constituted quite a sizeable group: the elderly businessman and his young wife, the Englishwoman with her two daughters, the young man from Le Havre, the American and a dozen others, all of them ready to set off into the snow.

Jacques tried to persuade Séverine to go with Flore, assuring her that he would come and tell her how things were progressing, the minute he could get away. Flore was eyeing them disapprovingly. Jacques made an effort to be polite and friendly towards her.

'Flore,' he said, 'would you take these ladies and gentlemen with you? Misard and the others can stay with me. We'll make a start and do what we can until help arrives.'

Cabuche, Ozil and Misard had in fact immediately taken shovels and had gone to join Pecqueux and the principal guard, who were already digging away the snow. The little team worked hard to free the engine, removing the snow from under the wheels and flinging it on to the bank.

They worked in silence; all that could be heard was the determined sound of shovelling amidst the eerie silence of this world of snow. As the little group of passengers walked away, they took one last look at the train, standing there all forlorn, a thin black line beneath the heavy layer of snow that pressed down upon it. All the doors had been closed and the windows pulled up. The snow still fell; silently, inexorably, the train was slowly but surely being buried.

Flore had again offered to carry Séverine in her arms, but she had declined the offer, determined to go on foot like the others. The three-hundred-metre walk to the cottage was not easy, especially in the cutting, where they sank in up to their waists. On two occasions they had to go and rescue the fat Englishwoman, who had become half buried. Her two daughters continued to find the whole thing hilarious; they were thoroughly enjoying themselves. **247** The young wife of the elderly gentleman slipped and was helped up by the young man from Le Havre, while her husband ranted on to the American about the dreadful state of things in France. Once they were through the cutting the going became easier. But they were now walking along an embankment. They advanced in single file, battered by the wind and taking care not to fall over the edge; with all the snow that had fallen, they couldn't tell where it was, which made progress very dangerous. But eventually they arrived at the cottage. Flore took the passengers into the kitchen. She couldn't provide chairs for everybody because there were at least twenty people crammed into the room. Fortunately, the room was fairly large. Her solution was to go and fetch some planks and set up a couple of benches, using the chairs she had. She threw some wood on to the fire and shrugged her shoulders, as if to say she couldn't be expected to do anything more. All this time, she hadn't spoken a word. She now stood looking round at everyone, with her big green eyes and her blonde hair, like some wild, Nordic savage. There were only two faces she recognized, having noticed them frequently through the carriage windows over the last few months: the American and the young man from Le Havre. She studied them carefully, as one might examine a flying insect when settled, which could not be examined on the wing. They seemed strange; having seen nothing of them but their faces, she hadn't imagined them to be quite like this. As for everyone else, they seemed to be of a different race, people from another planet who had dropped out of the sky, walking into her kitchen and bringing with them styles of dress, ways of behaviour and topics of conversation that she would never have expected to find there. The Englishwoman was telling the businessman's young wife that she was on her way to join her eldest son in India, where he had an important position in the civil service, while the young wife joked about her bad luck on the very first occasion she had chosen to accompany her husband to London, where he went twice a year. They all dreaded the prospect of being cut off in such an out-of-the-way place; they would have to eat and sleep here. How on earth would they manage? Flore stood listening to them, without moving. She caught Séverine's eye as she sat on a chair in front of the fire and motioned her towards the adjoining room.

'Mother,' she said as she went in, 'here's Madame Roubaud. Would you like to speak to her?'

Phasie lay on her bed; her face was a sickly yellow, and her legs were badly swollen. She was so ill that she hadn't left her bed for a fortnight. She spent all day long in this dingy room, nearly suffocated by the heat from an iron stove, dwelling continually on the fear that obsessed her, and with nothing to distract her but the shaking of the house every time a train thundered past.

'Ah, Madame Roubaud,' she murmured. 'Yes, of course.'

Flore told her about the accident, and all the people she had brought to the house, who were through there in the kitchen. But Phasie showed no interest.

'Good! Good!' she kept repeating, in the same weary voice.

Then she suddenly remembered something and raised her head for a moment.

'Flore,' she said, 'if madame would like to go and look at her house, you know that the keys are hanging next to the cupboard.'

Séverine shook her head. The thought of going back to La Croix-de-Maufras in all this snow and in such gloomy weather made her shudder. No, there was nothing she especially wanted to see. She would rather stay here and wait in the warm.

'Do sit down, madame,' said Flore. 'It's much better here **249** than in the kitchen. We shall never have enough bread for all these people. But if you're hungry, I'm sure I'll be able to find some for you.'

She had brought up a chair and was doing her best to be pleasant, making an obvious effort to curb her usual rough manner of dealing with people. But she couldn't take her eyes off Séverine, as if she were trying to read her mind and resolve a question that had been puzzling her for some time. This show of politeness was dictated by a need to get close to her, to stare at her and touch her in order to discover an answer.

Séverine thanked her and sat by the stove, preferring to be left there alone with a sick woman and hoping that Jacques would soon come to find her. Two hours went by. Eventually the heat from the stove made her fall asleep. Suddenly, Flore, who had had to keep answering demands from the kitchen, opened the door and called out gruffly, 'Come through; she's in here.'

It was Jacques. He had come with good news. The man who had been sent to Barentin had just returned with a team of helpers – thirty soldiers who had been stationed at likely trouble spots in case of emergency. They were all hard at work with picks and shovels. But it was going to take a long time. They probably wouldn't be leaving before nightfall.

'You'll be all right here,' he said. 'Just be patient! You won't let Madame Roubaud starve, will you, Aunt Phasie?'

On seeing her big boy, as she called him, Phasie had, with great difficulty, sat up in her bed. She looked at him and listened to his voice, suddenly brought back to life and happy again. Jacques came up to her bed.

'Of course I won't,' she declared. 'Oh, my boy! My big boy! You're here! It was you who was stuck in the snow! And that silly girl never told me!'

250   She turned towards her daughter and spoke to her sternly: 'At least try and be polite. Go and see to those ladies and gentlemen. Look after them. Make sure they don't all go complaining to the management that we're a lot of peasants.'

Flore had stood watching Jacques and Séverine. For a moment she hesitated, wondering whether to disobey her mother and stay where she was. But she decided she would discover nothing by remaining; they wouldn't give themselves away in her mother's presence. She went out saying nothing, without taking her eyes off them.

'What's the matter, Aunt Phasie?' said Jacques, clearly worried. 'Aren't you able to get out of bed? Do you feel really ill?'

She pulled him towards her and made him sit on the edge of the bed. She appeared to have forgotten all about Séverine, who had tactfully moved further away. Speaking in almost a whisper, she told him all her worries.

'Yes,' she said, 'it's serious. It's a miracle I'm still alive.

I almost died, but I'm a bit better now. I think I'll pull through again this time.'

Jacques looked at her, horrified to see how she had declined. There was nothing left of the fine, healthy woman he had known before.

'Poor Aunt Phasie!' he said. 'Are you still getting those cramps and dizzy spells?'

She squeezed his hand tight and lowered her voice further: 'I caught him at it! I'd given up trying to find out what he was putting the poison in. I never drank or ate anything he touched. But it made no difference. Every night it still felt as if my tummy was on fire. Well, he was putting it in the salt. One night I saw him doing it. I put salt on everything, and a lot too, to make sure it's healthy to eat!'

Jacques had felt that his own malady was cured from the moment he had become Séverine's lover, and since then he had often thought about this tale of slow, deliberate 251 poisoning as one thinks of a nightmare; he couldn't believe it was real. He gently squeezed the poor woman's hands in his, trying to calm her down.

'Do you really think he's been trying to poison you?' he said. 'You have to be really sure before you start saying things like that. It's been going on too long. It's more likely to be some illness the doctors don't recognize.'

'An illness!' she exclaimed scornfully. 'Yes, it's an illness I've caught off him! As for the doctors, you're right. Two of them came to see me and they couldn't understand it. They couldn't even agree between themselves. I never want to see a doctor here again. Can you believe it? He was sticking it in the salt! I swear I saw him doing it! He's after my thousand francs. The thousand francs Dad left me. He thinks that once he's got rid of me, he'll find where I've hidden them. But he won't! They're somewhere where nobody will ever find them. Never! I can die in peace. No one will ever get my thousand francs!'

'But Aunt Phasie, if I were you and I was as certain as that, I'd call the police.'

She was horrified at this suggestion.

'Oh, no!' she said. 'I'm not having the police here! It's got nothing to do with them. This is a matter between him and me. I know he wants to get rid of me, and I don't want to be got rid of, as you can imagine! So I'll just have to look after myself, won't I? I'll have to be a bit more careful! Putting it in the salt! Who'd have thought it? A little runt like him! A little squirt you could fit in your pocket, getting the better of a big, strong woman like me! Once he's got his teeth into you there's no stopping him!'

She shuddered and gasped for breath before continuing.

'Never mind,' she said, 'it's not going to work this time. I'm getting better. I'll be back on my feet in a fortnight. And he'll have to be really clever to catch me out again. I'm curious to see what he gets up to. If he finds some other way of poisoning me, it'll be because he's cleverer than me. If that happens, too bad! I'm done for! I don't want anyone getting involved. It's between him and me!'

Jacques thought it must be the illness that was putting such dark thoughts into her head and he tried to make a joke of it. But all of a sudden she began to shake under the bedclothes.

'Here he is!' she whispered. 'I can sense when he's coming.'

Sure enough, a second or two later, in walked Misard. Phasie had turned deathly pale. She was terrified, just as a colossus instinctively fears the tiny insect that pricks its flesh. Despite her determination to outwit Misard single-handed, she had developed a growing fear of him that she was not prepared to admit to. Misard on the other hand, who the minute he opened the door had clearly spotted Jacques and Phasie talking together, now appeared not even to have noticed them; he stood there with a vacant expression on his face, mincing his words and grovelling abjectly in front of Séverine.

'I thought that madame might perhaps wish to take this opportunity of inspecting her property. I am at your service, madame. If madame would like me to accompany her . . .'

Séverine once again declined. But his voice whined on and on.

'I imagine madame was surprised about the fruit . . . It really wasn't worth the cost of sending it; it was all rotten . . . And then there was a gale that did so much damage . . . It is such a pity that madame cannot sell her house! There was one gentleman, but he wanted repairs carried out. Of course I am entirely at madame's disposal; she may count on me to act in her best interests.'

He insisted on serving her some bread and pears – pears **253** from his own garden, he said, which weren't rotten. She accepted.

As he walked through the kitchen, Misard had told the other passengers that work on clearing the line was progressing but that it would still take another four or five hours. The clock had just chimed midday. Everyone groaned, for they were all getting very hungry. Flore told them that she didn't have enough bread to feed everyone but that she did have some wine. She had just come from the cellar with ten litre-bottles, which she placed on the table in a row. Then, of course, there weren't enough glasses, so people had to share – the Englishwoman and her two daughters, the elderly gentleman and his young wife. The young wife had acquired a new admirer in the person of the young man from Le Havre, who was waiting on her hand and foot and showing her the utmost solicitude and consideration. He went away and came back with some apples and a loaf of bread, which he had found in the woodshed. Flore was annoyed, saying that the bread was for her sick mother. But the young man had already cut it and was sharing it out among the ladies, beginning with the young wife, who smiled at him, obviously feeling highly honoured. Her husband had still not calmed down and was taking no notice of his wife, extolling the commercial achievements of New York to the American. Never had the two young English girls bitten into apples with such relish. Their mother was very tired and half asleep. Two women sat on the floor in front of the fire, exhausted by the long wait. A few of the men went outside for a smoke to help pass the time and came back in, frozen stiff and shivering. Everyone was becoming more and more disgruntled; they were still hungry and tired and they were growing restless and impatient. The scene in the kitchen resembled a party of survivors from a shipwreck, people from the modern world who had had the misfortune to be marooned on a desert island.

As Misard kept walking in and out of the room, leaving the door open behind him, Aunt Phasie was able to see everything from her sickbed. These were the people that she too had seen flashing past the window for almost a year, as she dragged herself backwards and forwards between her bed and her chair. It was only rarely now that she could get outside; her days and nights were spent alone, stuck in this room, looking out of the window, with no other company than the trains that came speeding past. She had always complained about living in such an outlandish place, where no one ever came to see her, and now a whole crowd of people had suddenly dropped out of the blue! To think that there in her own kitchen, amongst all those people rushing madly about their business, not one of them suspected a thing, not one of them knew about the poison being put in her salt! She couldn't get over it. It was so ingenious! She wondered how God could allow anyone to perform such a crafty trick without it being spotted. Enough people went past their front door, thousands and thousands of them, but they were all in such a rush. Not one of them could have imagined that, here in this little house, someone was calmly and quietly killing her. Aunt Phasie looked at them one by one, all these people who had dropped from the skies, and reflected that when you were so busy it wasn't surprising if you walked into some untoward situation without noticing it.

'Are you coming back to the train?' Misard asked Jacques.

'Yes,' said Jacques, 'I'll follow you.'

Misard went out, shutting the door behind him. Phasie held Jacques back and whispered into his ear: 'If I peg it, you watch his face when he can't find the money! It makes me laugh to think about it. So I shall die happy!'

'But then, Aunt Phasie, no one would find it. Aren't you 255 going to leave it to your daughter?'

'Leave it to Flore! So that he can take it off her! I should think not! I'm not even leaving it to you, dear, because you're a bit soft too. He'd find a way of getting his hands on it. I'm leaving it to nobody ... except the earth! And when I die I'll have it all to myself!'

She was now very weak. Jacques laid her back on the bed and calmed her down, giving her a kiss and promising to come and see her again soon. She appeared to drop off to sleep. Jacques walked over to Séverine, who was still sitting beside the stove. He smiled at her and raised a finger to warn her not to make a noise. He came up behind her. Without a sound, she threw her head back, offering him her lips. He leaned over her, quietly put his mouth to hers and kissed her passionately. As their lips came together, they closed their eyes. When they opened them again, they were horrified to see Flore, who had walked in through the door, standing in front of them, staring at them.

'Has madame finished with the bread?' she asked bluntly.

Séverine was annoyed and confused.

'Yes. Thank you. Yes,' she muttered vaguely.

Jacques glared at Flore angrily, not knowing quite what to do. His lips moved as if he were about to say something. Then with a furious wave of his hand he stormed out of the room, slamming the door behind him.

Flore remained standing where she was, tall and proud like an Amazon, her thick blonde hair falling in long tresses about her face. So her suspicions about this lady whom she saw in Jacques's train every Friday were right. She had been looking for some explanation all the time they had been there, and now she had it; everything had become clear. The man she loved would never love her. He had chosen this other woman, this thin slip of a girl sitting in front of her! Why had she refused herself that night when he had tried to take her by force? She now regretted it so bitterly she could have wept. To her simple way of thinking, it would be her he would be kissing now, if she had given herself to him before this other woman. But what chance did she have now of being alone with him, of flinging her arms round his neck and crying, 'Take me, I was stupid, I didn't know!' She could do nothing about it; she felt herself growing angrier and angrier towards the frail little creature that sat there in front of her, muttering with embarrassment. She could have taken her in her big, brawny arms and crushed her to death like a tiny bird. Why didn't she? Was it because she didn't have the courage? She swore that one day she would be avenged. She knew things about her rival that could have landed her in prison. But they had let her go free, like all the other whores who have sold themselves to old men with money and influence. She was consumed with jealousy and could hardly contain her anger. She snatched away the rest of the bread and the remaining pears with neither a please nor a thank you.

'If madame has finished with these, I'll take them in to the others.'

It struck three, and then four. Time dragged on and on. Everyone was overcome with weariness and they were getting more and more frustrated. It was now beginning to grow dark again, and a general gloom settled over the snow-covered landscape. The men, who went out every ten minutes or so to see how the work was progressing, came back saying that the engine still seemed to be stuck in the snow. Even the two English girls were crying from tiredness. In a corner of the room, the pretty dark-haired woman had fallen asleep on the shoulder of the young man from Le Havre. Her husband hadn't even noticed; things had reached such a pass that social conventions were forgotten. The room was getting colder, and people were **257** shivering. Yet it never occurred to anyone to put more wood on the fire. It eventually became so cold that the American left, saying that he would be better off lying on a seat in one of the carriages. Everybody else was beginning to feel the same – they should have stayed on the train; that way at least they wouldn't have been worried sick, not knowing what was going on. They had to restrain the Englishwoman, who said she was going back to sleep in the train as well. The room was getting darker and darker. Someone placed a candle on a corner of the table to give a little light, but it just seemed to make everyone even more depressed. The situation appeared hopeless.

Outside, however, the snow-clearing was almost finished. The team of soldiers who had freed the locomotive were sweeping the track clean ahead, while Jacques and Pecqueux once more took up their positions on the footplate.

Jacques observed that it had finally stopped snowing

and began to feel more confident. Ozil the signalman had told him that on the Malaunay side of the tunnel the snow had not fallen so heavily. Jacques asked him about it again.

'When you walked through the tunnel,' he said, 'did you have any difficulty getting in or out of it?'

'No,' said Ozil, 'I told you. You'll get through, don't worry.'

Cabuche, who, with his enormous strength, had set to and done the work of ten men, was about to walk away. He had always been a shy, timid sort of man, and his latest brush with the law had made him even more so. Jacques called to him.

'Cabuche!' he said. 'Do us a favour. Could you pass us our shovels? They're there, on the bank. We might need them again if we have any more trouble.'

258   The quarryman handed him the shovels. Jacques shook his hand warmly to thank him for his help and to assure him that he still had the greatest respect for him.

'You're a good man!' he said. 'One of the best!'

Cabuche was so touched by this mark of friendship that he had to fight back his tears.

'Thank you,' he said simply.

Misard nodded his agreement, pursing his lips in a thin smile. He had accused Cabuche before the examining magistrate but had since made up his differences with him. For some time he had been walking around doing nothing, with his hands in his pockets, looking shiftily all around the train as if he were waiting to see if he might pick up a bit of lost property from underneath it.

At last, the principal guard and Jacques decided that they should try to get the train restarted. But Pecqueux, who had jumped down on to the track, called out to his driver.

'Look,' he said, 'one of the cylinders has taken a knock.'

Jacques came down to look, crouching beside the cylinder. He had already examined the engine carefully and had noticed that the cylinder was damaged. While clearing the track, they had discovered that some wooden sleepers, which had been left on the side of the cutting by a gang of platelayers, had slipped down the bank in all the snow and bad weather, and had fallen on to the rails. This must have been partly why the train had come to a stop, for the engine was lodged against them. They could see a long scratch on the cylinder casing, and the piston rod seemed slightly out of line. But there didn't seem to be anything else wrong, and initially the driver had not been too concerned. However, there was perhaps more serious internal damage; nothing is more delicate than the complex arrangement of a locomotive's valve gear, the very heart and soul of the engine. Jacques climbed back on to the footplate, blew the whistle and opened the regulator to **259** see if everything was working properly. *La Lison* took a long time to respond, like someone injured in a fall who is unsteady on their feet. Eventually, with much coughing and hissing, she moved forwards. Slowly and sluggishly her wheels began to turn. She was going to be all right. She would make it. She would get there. But Jacques was shaking his head. He knew her inside out, and now, as he placed his hands on the controls, he sensed that there was something odd, something different. She seemed to have suddenly aged, as if she were succumbing to some fatal illness. It must have been something she had caught in the snow, something that had found its way into her, a chill, like one of those healthy young women who die of pneumonia after coming home from a dance one night in the freezing rain.

Pecqueux opened the cylinder taps, and Jacques gave one more blast on the whistle. The two guards had got back into the train. Misard, Ozil and Cabuche climbed on to the step of the leading van. The train slowly emerged from the cutting, between the two lines of soldiers who, armed with their shovels, formed a guard of honour on each side of the track. They stopped outside the crossing-keeper's house in order to pick up the passengers.

Flore was standing outside. Ozil and Cabuche jumped down and went to stand next to her, while Misard tried to ingratiate himself with the passengers, wishing them well as they came out of his house and gratefully accepting the silver coins they placed in his hand. At last they had been rescued. But it had been a long wait. Everyone was shaking from cold, hunger and exhaustion. The Englishwoman had to carry her two daughters, who were both half asleep. The young man from Le Havre climbed into the same compartment as the pretty, dark-haired woman, who was very weary, so that he could be of assistance to her husband. Looking at all these people splashing around in the mud and trampled snow, it seemed more like a routed army that was boarding the train, pushing and shoving, desperate to find a place, and not in the least bothered about getting themselves dirty. For a brief moment, Aunt Phasie's face appeared at one of the bedroom windows. Her curiosity had got the better of her, and she had dragged herself from her bed to see what was going on. She stood there, pitifully thin, her great sunken eyes peering at this crowd of strangers, these birds of passage from a world that never stood still, these people she would never see again, blown to her door and whisked away as if by a gale.

Séverine was the last to leave the house. She turned and smiled at Jacques, who leaned out of the engine to see that she reached her compartment safely. Flore had been watching out for them and once again turned pale when she saw the quiet look of affection that passed between them. She suddenly walked away and went to stand beside Ozil. Up until then she had wanted nothing to do with him, but now, it seemed, in her contempt for Séverine, she needed the presence of a man.

The principal guard signalled to the driver, and *La Lison* replied with a mournful screech on her whistle. This time, Jacques had no intention of stopping until they got to Rouen. It was six o'clock; night had fallen and the white landscape was now shrouded in darkness. A last ghostly flicker of light drifted over the snow, revealing the desolation wrought by the storm. And there, dimly visible in the gathering gloom, stood the house at La Croix-de-Maufras, at an angle to the railway line, looking even more dilapidated than ever, black against the snow, with its 'For Sale' board nailed to the closed shutters.

8

The train didn't reach Paris until ten forty that night. They had stopped at Rouen for twenty minutes to allow the passengers to get something to eat. Séverine had immediately telegraphed her husband to let him know that she would not be getting back to Le Havre until the following evening. A whole night with Jacques! The first they had ever spent together in a room of their own, free to do as they chose without fear of being disturbed!

As the train was leaving Mantes, Pecqueux had had an idea. Madame Victoire had been in hospital for a week, having fallen and seriously twisted her ankle. He knew
262 another little place in Paris where he could spend the night, as he put it jokingly, so, if she wanted to, Madame Roubaud could stay in his own room. It would be much better than a room in a hotel; she could stay until the following evening and come and go as she pleased. Jacques immediately saw the practical advantages of the idea, especially as he hadn't known where to take Séverine. She came up to the locomotive as the crowd of passengers was finally leaving the platform, and Jacques advised her to accept the proposal, offering her the key which Pecqueux had already given him. She hesitated and seemed confused. She was clearly embarrassed by the cheeky smirk on Pecqueux's face; he must have known everything.

'No,' she said, 'I have a cousin in Paris. I can sleep on her floor.'

'It'll be much better at my place,' said Pecqueux, teasing her. 'There's a lovely soft bed, big enough for four!'

Jacques had such a pleading look in his eye that she took

the key. He leaned towards her and whispered, 'Wait for me.'

Séverine only needed to go a little way along the Rue d'Amsterdam and turn into the impasse, but it was so slippery underfoot that she had to walk very carefully. Fortunately the door on to the street was still open, and she was able to go up the stairs without being seen by the concierge, who was engrossed in a game of dominoes with a friend from next door. She reached the fourth floor[1] and let herself in, closing the door behind her very quietly so that none of the neighbours could guess she was there. As she crossed the third-floor landing she had distinctly heard sounds of singing and laughter coming from the Dauvergnes' apartment; no doubt the two sisters were having one of their little weekly get-togethers, when they invited their friends round to play music. Séverine closed the door and stood in the darkness, with the sounds of youthful merriment coming up through the floor from below. At first she couldn't see a thing; suddenly, in the pitch black, the cuckoo clock began to strike eleven. It made her jump. She recognized the sound of the chimes, deep and resonant.[2] As her eyes grew accustomed to the dark, she made out the shape of the two windows, two pale squares casting their light on the ceiling with the reflection from the snow. Having got her bearings, she felt on the sideboard for the matches. She remembered having seen them there before. It was not so easy to find a candle, but eventually she came across an old stub at the bottom of a drawer. She lit it, and the room filled with light. She glanced nervously around her as if to make sure there was no one else in the room. Everything was just as it was before – the round table at which she and her husband had eaten lunch, the bed with the red quilt draped across it where he had struck her to the ground. It was all there; nothing in the room had changed since her visit ten months earlier.

263

Séverine slowly removed her hat. She was about to take off her coat when she began to shiver. The room was freezing cold. Beside the stove there was a little box with some coal and firewood in it. She decided that before undressing further she would light the fire. She was glad to have something to do; it made her feel less uneasy. These preparations for a night of love and the thought that soon they would be lying warm in each other's arms made her heart quicken with a sense of joy and excitement. They had dreamed for so long of a night such as this, without ever daring to hope that their dream might some day come true. As the stove began to roar she set about making other things ready; she arranged the chairs as she wanted them, looked out some clean sheets, and remade the bed, which was not easy as the bed was indeed very large. Her only disappointment was that she could find nothing in the sideboard to eat or drink. Presumably, if Pecqueux had had to fend for himself for the last three days, he had even eaten the crumbs from the floor! All she had found to light the room was a burned-out stub of candle! She consoled herself with the thought that once they were in bed it wouldn't matter if it was dark. All this activity had made her feel very hot. She stood in the middle of the room, looking round it to make sure that everything was ready.

She was beginning to wonder why Jacques had not yet arrived when the sound of an engine whistle drew her towards one of the windows. It was the 11.20 through train to Le Havre, which was just leaving. Down below, the station approaches and the cutting leading out to the Batignolles tunnel were covered in a vast carpet of snow, with the railway lines fanning out across it like the dark branches of a tree. The engines and carriages standing on the sidings appeared as white lumps, as if they were curled up asleep beneath an ermine blanket. Between the spotless white covering of snow on the glass roof of the two great train sheds and the lace-trimmed girders of the Pont de l'Europe, the houses directly opposite in the Rue de Rome stood out, despite the fact that it was dark, as dirty yellow smears in a vast expanse of white. The train for Le Havre came out of the station, silhouetted darkly against the snow, creeping slowly forward, the light from its headlamp cutting through the night. She watched it disappear under the bridge, its three tail lamps casting a blood-red stain on the snow behind it. She turned back into the room. A shiver ran through her. Was she really alone? She thought she had felt someone breathe on her neck, a hand touching her clumsily through her clothes. She looked around the room a second time, wide-eyed. There was no one.

What was Jacques up to? Why was he taking so long? Another ten minutes went by. Then she heard a faint scratching sound, like fingernails scraping wood. Her heart missed a beat. Suddenly realizing what it was, she **265** ran to open the door. It was Jacques, with a cake and a bottle of Malaga.[3]

Shaking with laughter, she threw her arms impulsively round his neck.

'You angel!' she said. 'You remembered to bring some food!'

Jacques hurriedly warned her not to talk so loud.

'Sh! Sh!' he said.

She lowered her voice, thinking that the concierge might have followed him up the stairs. No, he had been lucky. Just as he was about to ring, the door had opened for a lady and her daughter, just leaving the Dauvergnes' no doubt. So he had been able to slip upstairs without anyone noticing.[4] However, one of the doors across the landing had been left ajar, and he had seen the lady from the newspaper kiosk finishing some washing in a bowl.

'We mustn't make any noise,' he said. 'We'll have to talk quietly.'

Her answer was to take him in her arms, hug him closely and silently cover his face with kisses. She loved it when things were all mysterious and she had to speak in low whispers.

'Don't worry!' she said. 'We'll be as quiet as two little mice!'

She laid the table as silently as she could – two plates, two glasses, two knives – pausing to stop herself laughing when she put something down too quickly and made a noise.

Jacques sat happily watching her.

'I thought you might be hungry,' he whispered.

'I'm starving,' she said. 'The food at Rouen was awful!'

'Shall I go and see if I can find us a chicken?' he suggested.

'No,' she answered, 'you might not be able to get back in! The cake will be plenty.'

They sat down, side by side; they were almost sitting on the same chair. They shared the cake between them, huddling close to each other as they ate it. Séverine said she had never felt so thirsty and drank two glasses of Malaga, one after the other, which quickly brought the colour to her cheeks. Behind them, the stove was glowing red; they could feel its warmth. He began to kiss her neck, passionately. She placed her hand on his lips.

'Sh!' she whispered. 'They will hear us.'

She gestured to him to listen. Once more from below came the sound of people dancing, accompanied by someone playing the piano. The Dauvergne sisters were obviously having a party. They heard the newspaper woman from the room next door emptying her bowl of soapy water down the sink on the landing. She went back and closed her door. Downstairs, the dancing stopped for a moment. Outside beneath the window, the sounds were muffled by the snow; all that could be heard was the faint rumble of a departing train and the half-hearted toot-toot of its whistle, like someone crying.

'A train for Auteuil,' he murmured. 'Ten to twelve.'

Then he whispered gently into her ear: 'Darling, shall we go to bed?'

She didn't answer him. She had been feeling blissfully happy, when suddenly the past had overtaken her. She found herself reliving the hours she had spent there with her husband. The cake she had just shared with Jacques seemed a continuation of that lunch with Roubaud, eaten at the same table, with the same sounds coming up from the apartment below. Everything in the room awakened the past; memories flooded over her. Never had she felt such a burning need to tell her lover everything, to surrender herself to him completely. It was an almost physical need, inseparable from her sexual desire. It seemed to her that she would belong to him more fully and that she 267 would receive the greatest joy from being his if she could whisper her confession into his ear as she lay in his arms. Everything was coming back to her. Her husband was there in the room. She looked round, thinking she had just seen his hand, with its short, hairy fingers reaching over her shoulder for the knife.

'Shall we go to bed, darling?' Jacques repeated.

She shuddered as she felt his lips fasten upon hers, as though once again he wished to keep the confession sealed within her. Without a word she stood up, quickly undressed and slipped between the sheets, leaving her petticoats strewn across the floor. Jacques left the table as it was; it could be cleared in the morning. The candle was almost finished and was already beginning to go out. He too undressed and got into the bed. Their bodies came together in a sudden embrace, a frenzy of possession that left them breathless and gasping for air. In the deathly silence of the room, as the music continued downstairs, there was no exclamation, not a sound, nothing but a thrill of abandonment, a wave of ecstasy, which made them almost faint.

Séverine was no longer the sweet, passive, blue-eyed woman that Jacques had first known. She seemed to have grown more passionate with every day that passed. Her hair fell thick and dark about her face. Gradually, in his arms, he had felt her waking from the long night of virginal frigidity which the senile indecencies of Grandmorin and the intemperate demands of her husband had merely succeeded in prolonging. As a lover, she had hitherto simply complied. Now, she was alive; she gave herself fully and was in turn deeply grateful for the pleasure she received. She had come to adore and even venerate the man who had shown her she was capable of love. It was because she felt so intensely happy to lie with him freely at last, to put her arms around him and hold him to her breast, that she had been able to remain silent, with not so much as a sigh.

They opened their eyes again. Jacques was the first to speak.

'Look,' he said with surprise, 'the candle's gone out!'

Séverine turned over, as if to say she couldn't care less. Then, stifling a laugh, she whispered:

'Did I behave myself?'

'Yes,' he answered. 'No one could have heard us. We were as quiet as mice!'

They lay back again, and she at once took him in her arms, pulling herself close to him and resting her nose on his neck. She sighed with pleasure.

'Isn't this wonderful!' she said.

They fell silent. The room was completely dark; they could just make out the two pale squares where the windows were. On the ceiling, the stove cast a circle of light the colour of blood. They lay looking up at it, wide-eyed. The music had stopped. They heard the sound of doors being closed. The whole house fell into a deep, peaceful sleep. Down below, the train from Caen came clattering over the turntables, but the sound hardly reached them; it seemed to come from a long way away.

As she lay holding Jacques in her arms, Séverine's desire returned, and with it the urge to confess her crime. It had been on her mind for weeks! The circle of light on the ceiling grew larger; it seemed to be spreading outwards like a bloodstain. As she gazed at it, shapes began to appear before her eyes; things around the bed began to speak, telling the whole story out loud. As her flesh responded to his touch, she felt the words rising to her lips. How good it would be to have nothing more to hide, to be merged with him completely!

'Darling,' she said, 'there is something I must tell you . . .'

Jacques, who had also been staring fixedly at the red **269** patch of light on the ceiling, knew what she was about to say. He could feel her delicate body lying against his. He had sensed the gathering wave within her that was about to break, the guilty secret, the awful truth which both of them thought of but could never speak about. Until now he had persuaded her to say nothing; he was afraid it might bring back his old malady, or that talk of murder would alter their feelings for each other. But this time, lying there so deliciously relaxed in this warm bed with her arms wrapped gently around him, he lacked the energy even to lean over her and silence her with a kiss. The moment had come, he thought. She was about to tell him everything. Having anxiously waited for her to begin, it came as a relief when she seemed to become embarrassed, to hesitate and change her mind.

'Darling,' she said, 'there is something I must tell you . . . My husband suspects I am sleeping with you.'

At the last minute, what had sprung to her lips,

involuntarily, was not the confession, but the memory of the night before at Le Havre.

'Do you think so?' murmured Jacques, incredulously. 'He seems very friendly to me. He shook hands with me only this morning.'

'I tell you, he knows everything,' she said. 'He will be picturing us, this very minute, in bed, in each other's arms, making love! I know he will!'

She fell silent, holding him tighter, in an embrace in which passion was tinged with bitterness. She lay there thinking. Suddenly she shuddered.

'I hate him!' she said. 'I hate him!'

Jacques was surprised. He had nothing against Roubaud. He found him very easy to get on with.

'Why do you hate him?' he asked. 'He doesn't bother us.'

She didn't answer, simply repeating: 'I hate him. I hate 270 even feeling him near me. I can't bear it. If only I could get away from him! If only I could always be with you!'

Jacques was moved by this passionate outburst. He drew her still closer and held her tight, feeling her whole body against his, from her feet to her shoulders. She was his entirely. Once again as she lay enfolded in his arms, and scarcely without removing her lips from his neck, she began to whisper: 'Darling, there is something you should know . . .'

This was the confession. It was inevitable; sooner or later it had to come. This time he realized that nothing in the world would prevent it, for it rose from within her like an uncontrollable desire to be taken and possessed. Not a sound could be heard in the house. Even the newspaper woman must have been fast asleep. Outside, Paris lay covered in snow. There was no sound of wheels; everything was buried and draped in silence. With the departure of the last train for Le Havre, which had left at twenty past twelve, the station seemed to have closed down. The stove had stopped roaring, and the fire had burned through to its last embers, which made the circle of red light on the ceiling even brighter. It stared down at them like a startled eye. The room was so hot that it felt as if a heavy, suffocating fog had descended on to the bed where the couple lay blissfully entwined.

'Darling, there is something you should know . . .'

He answered her. What else could he do?

'Yes,' he said, 'I know.'

'No,' she answered, 'you might have guessed something, but you don't know what happened.'

'I know he did it to get the legacy,' he said.

She turned over and gave a nervous little laugh.

'Oh, that!' she muttered.

Then, very quietly, so quietly that a fly on the window-pane would have made more noise, she began to tell him of the years she had spent as a child at Doinville. She was tempted to lie to him and not tell him about her relationship with Grandmorin, but decided that she should be totally frank and found it a relief, almost a pleasure, to tell him all about it. The confession had begun, whispered softly into his ear, unstoppable.

'Can you imagine it?' she said. 'It was here, in this room, last February, when there was all that trouble with the Sub-Prefect . . . we'd had lunch. It was lovely . . . just like us eating now, at that table, there . . . He knew nothing, of course . . . Why should I tell him all about it? Then all of a sudden, just because of a ring, an old present, something of no importance . . . I don't know how it happened . . . Suddenly he knew everything . . . Darling, you can't imagine what he did to me . . .'

She was shaking. He felt her hands on his naked flesh, clutching him.

'He punched me and knocked me to the floor . . . He dragged me round the room by my hair . . . He lifted his

271

foot and threatened to kick me in the face . . . I shall never forget it as long as I live . . . And then he started to hit me again . . . Oh my God . . . If I told you all the questions he asked me . . . what he forced me to tell him! I'm being honest with you, Jacques. I don't have to tell you all this, but I want you to know. I couldn't bear to repeat half of what he forced me to tell him . . . it was disgusting! But he would have killed me; I know he would! I suppose he loved me . . . It must have been awful for him to suddenly find out about it like that. Perhaps I should have told him before we got married . . . it would have been more honest. But it was in the past, it was forgotten . . . can you understand? I've never seen anyone so insanely jealous. He was like an animal . . . Jacques darling, will you stop loving me now you know all this?'

272   Jacques had not moved. He lay there thinking, absolutely still, with Séverine's arms around him, encircling his neck and his waist like the coils of a snake. He was amazed; he had never suspected anything like this. Everything seemed to have become more complicated. The legacy had been a much simpler way of explaining things! But he preferred it like this. The knowledge that they had not killed merely for money dispelled a vague feeling of contempt he had sometimes felt towards her, even when she was in his arms.

'Why should I stop loving you?' he said. 'What you did in the past doesn't bother me; it's none of my business. You're married to Roubaud; for all I know, you might have been married to somebody else too.'

There was a silence. They hugged each other so tightly they could hardly breathe. He felt her hard, swollen breasts against his body.

'So you were Grandmorin's mistress. What a strange thought!'

She drew herself across him and lifted her mouth to his, kissing him and murmuring: 'You're the only one I love.

I've never loved anyone but you. If only you knew. With them, I didn't even know what love meant. But you, darling . . . you make me so happy!'

He felt her hands upon him and was inflamed with desire. She was offering herself to him, wanting him and drawing him passionately towards her. He longed to take her, yet he held her away from him at arms' length.

'Not now,' he said. 'Later! Tell me about Grandmorin.'

Her whole body shook, and, in a barely audible whisper, she confessed.

'Yes,' she said, 'we killed him.'

As the memory came back to her, her shudder of desire became a shudder of death.[5] At the moment of supreme ecstasy her agony was about to begin again. Her head slowly began to swim. She pressed her face to her lover's neck and continued in the same low whisper: 'He made me write to the President, telling him to leave Paris on the same train as us, but to keep out of sight until it reached Rouen . . . I sat in a corner seat, shaking with fright, horrified at the thought of the awful thing we were about to do . . . Opposite me there was a woman dressed in black. She said nothing. She terrified me. I couldn't see her properly but I imagined she could read our thoughts and that she knew exactly what we were planning to do . . . It took two hours to get from Paris to Rouen. I didn't say a word. I didn't move. I kept my eyes closed, pretending to be asleep. I could feel Roubaud sitting next to me. He didn't move either. What was so terrible was that I knew the awful things he was turning over in his mind, but I couldn't tell exactly what he had decided to do . . . Ah, what a journey! All those things going round and round in my head, the engine whistling, the constant drumming of the wheels, and the train lurching from side to side!'

Jacques had buried his mouth in her thick, sweet-scented hair. He kept kissing it with long, distracted kisses.

'But if you weren't in the same compartment, how did you manage to kill him?' he asked.

'Wait!' she said. 'I'm coming to that. My husband had worked out a plan, and it succeeded. But it was more by luck than judgement. There was a ten-minute stop at Rouen. We got out on to the platform and he made me walk down to the President's coupé, as if we were stretching our legs. When we reached it we saw Grandmorin standing at the carriage window. My husband pretended to be surprised, as if he had no idea he was on the train. There were crowds of people on the platform, all pushing and shoving to try and get into the second-class carriages; there was some big event in Le Havre the day after. As they started shutting the doors, the President asked us to join him in his carriage. I didn't know what to say; I muttered something about our suitcase. But he wouldn't take no for an answer. He said he was sure no one would steal it and that we could go back to our own compartment when we got to Barentin; that was where he was getting off. For a moment my husband seemed worried and thought of running back to fetch it. But just then the guard blew his whistle. Roubaud decided to leave the suitcase, pushed me into the coupé, climbed in behind me and closed the door and the window. How it was that nobody saw us I still can't understand. There were people dashing about everywhere; the railway staff could hardly cope. Anyway, there wasn't a single witness prepared to say they saw anything. The train slowly started to leave the station.'

For a moment or two Séverine remained silent, reliving the scene in her mind. She was by now so relaxed in his arms that she was unaware of an involuntary twitch in her left leg which at intervals caused it to rub against one of his knees.

'Ah, that first moment in the coupé when I realized the train had started to move! My mind was in a whirl. All I could think of was the suitcase. How were we going to get it back? If we left it where it was it would give us away. We were going to commit a murder. The whole thing seemed crazy, impossible, like something a child might dream of in a nightmare. We must be mad to go ahead with it. We would be arrested in the morning and convicted. I tried to reassure myself that my husband wouldn't go through with it; that it wouldn't happen, that it couldn't happen. But no! I could tell from the way he was talking to the President that his mind was made up, that nothing would deter him. Yet he seemed perfectly calm, chatting away happily as he always did. It must have been the steady, clear look in his eyes every time he turned towards me that told me he was absolutely determined to do it. He was going to kill him, another kilometre further on, two perhaps, wherever it was he had decided it would happen. Where it would be I didn't know. But it was going to happen. You could tell **275** from the way he kept calmly looking at Grandmorin, the man who in a few minutes' time would no longer be alive. I said nothing. I was all churned up inside; I tried to hide it from them by forcing myself to smile every time they looked at me. Why did it never occur to me to try and stop it happening? It was only later, when I tried to understand what I'd done, that I realized I should have shouted to someone through the window or pulled the communication cord.[6] But at the time it was as if I was paralysed; I felt totally incapable. I dare say I thought my husband was in the right, and if I am to be honest, darling, I must tell you that despite everything he'd done to me I was completely on his side against Grandmorin because, well, they'd both had me, hadn't they, but Roubaud was young . . . when Grandmorin put his hands all over you, it was . . . ugh! Anyway, who knows? Sometimes you do things that you'd never think you were capable of. When I think that I couldn't even kill a chicken! It was awful! It was like a dark storm raging inside me; a terrifying darkness . . .'

To Jacques, the frail little creature that lay so small and slender in his arms had become a mystery, an impenetrable abyss; a darkness, as she had put it. No matter how tightly he held her to him, he could not enter her soul. This tale of murder, whispered into his ear as they lay in each other's arms, excited him.

'Tell me,' he said, 'did you help to kill him?'

'I was sitting in one of the window seats,' she continued without answering him. 'My husband was sitting between me and the President, who was in the other window seat. They were talking about the coming elections . . . From time to time I noticed my husband lean forward and look outside to see where we were; he seemed to be getting impatient. Every time he looked outside, I looked outside as well; so I knew how far we had come too. It wasn't very dark, and you could see the shape of the trees rushing past the window. All the time you could hear the carriage wheels squealing on the railway line; it wasn't the usual sound, it was a terrible clamour of hysterical, whining voices, like the pitiful howling of animals being slaughtered. The train ran on, faster and faster . . . Suddenly we saw some lights through the window, and the noise of the train grew louder as it went through a station. It was Maromme, already two and a half leagues from Rouen. The next station was Malaunay, and then Barentin. Where was it going to happen? Was he going to wait until the last minute? I had lost all sense of time and distance; I had abandoned myself like a falling stone, plummeting through the echoing darkness. Then suddenly, as we went through Malaunay, it came to me; he was going to do it in the tunnel, a kilometre further on . . . I turned towards my husband, and our eyes met. Yes, it would be in the tunnel, in another two minutes . . . The train ran on. We passed the junction for Dieppe; I noticed the signalman standing beside his cabin. The railway runs through a series of hills at that point on the line, and I had a clear impression that there were men standing on the top of them with their hands raised in the air shouting curses at us. Then the engine gave a long whistle . . . the train was about to enter the tunnel. Its walls closed in around us. The noise was deafening! A great clanging of iron, like hammers striking an anvil! I didn't know what was happening. To me it sounded like thunder.'

She was shaking all over. She paused. Then, in a different voice, almost jokingly, she said, 'Isn't it silly? I feel chilled to the bone, and yet it's so lovely and warm in bed with you. I feel so happy! Anyway, I don't have to worry about it any more; the inquiry has been shelved. The government bigwigs want to keep it quiet as much as we do, I know they do. So I'm not bothered.'

She laughed out loud and added: 'Heavens above, Jacques! You gave us a real fright, and no mistake! Tell me, I've always wondered about it . . . what exactly did you see?'

'What I told the judge,' he said. 'No more than that! One man slitting another man's throat. But you were so nice to me I began to doubt my own mind. At one point I thought I recognized your husband . . . but it was only later that I became absolutely certain . . .'

She interrupted him, with a little laugh.

'I know,' she said. 'It was in the square in Paris, when you held my hand and said you loved me and I told you we might be seen. Do you remember? It was the first time we were on our own together in Paris . . . How strange! I told you it wasn't us, and all the time I knew perfectly well that you knew it was! It was almost as if I had told you everything. I've thought about it so often, darling. I think that was when I first fell in love with you.'

They hugged each other so tightly that they seemed to

melt into each other. Séverine continued: 'The train ran on through the tunnel . . . It's a very long tunnel; it takes three minutes to get through. It seemed to me that we were in it for an hour . . . The President had stopped talking because of the awful noise made by the train. My husband must have lost his nerve at the last minute, because he still made no move. The carriage lamp was swaying backwards and forwards, and all I could see was that his ears were going red . . . Was he going to wait until we were out of the tunnel? For me it had now become so inevitable, so certain that I wanted only one thing: I wanted the awful suspense to be over, I wanted it to be over and done with. Why didn't he kill him, since that was what he had to do? I would have taken the knife and done it myself, I was so terrified and worked up . . . He looked at me and must have read my thoughts. Suddenly he threw himself at the President, who had turned towards the window, and grabbed him by the shoulders. The President didn't know what was happening. He instinctively shook himself free and reached out to pull the communication cord, which was just above his head. He got his hand to it, but Roubaud pulled him back and flung him on to the seat, with such force that he was bent double. His mouth was wide open, screaming in terror and amazement, but his cries were drowned by the noise of the train. I could hear my husband's voice, hissing with rage and shouting at him repeatedly: "You swine! You swine! You swine!" Suddenly the noise stopped; we were out of the tunnel and in the open countryside with dark trees rushing past the window . . . I had remained where I was, rigid, pressing myself against the upholstery, trying to keep as far away as possible. How long did the struggle last? Probably no more than a few seconds, but it seemed to me that it would never end, that all the passengers in the train were listening to the shouts and that the trees were watching us. My husband had his knife open but he couldn't get near the President. Grandmorin kept kicking him away, and the movement of the train made him lose his balance; he almost fell over. The train was travelling very fast; I heard it whistle as it approached the level-crossing at La Croix-de-Maufras ... That was when I threw myself over his legs to stop him struggling. I can't remember now how I did it; I just fell on him like a bundle, pinning his legs down with all my weight so that he couldn't move them. I couldn't see a thing, but I felt it happen; the knife being thrust into his throat, the body writhing in agony, and his three dying gasps, like a broken clock unwinding. I can still feel that final shudder in my bones!'

Jacques was eager to know all the details. He wanted to stop and question her. But Séverine preferred to get her story over and done with.

'Wait,' she said. 'As I stood up again, the train was running past La Croix-de-Maufras. I distinctly saw the front of the house, all closed up, and then the crossing-keeper's hut. In another four kilometres, five minutes at the most, we would be at Barentin ... The body was slumped on the seat; the blood was running down into a thick pool on the floor. My husband just stood there, dazed, swaying from side to side with the movement of the train, staring at the body and wiping the knife with his handkerchief. This must have lasted a minute, without either of us giving a thought to how we were going to get out of such a dangerous situation. If we stayed in the compartment with the dead body, we were bound to be discovered when the train stopped at Barentin ... Roubaud had put the knife back in his pocket. Suddenly he seemed to wake up. I saw him going through Grandmorin's pockets and taking his watch, his money and whatever he could find. He opened the carriage door and tried to push the body out on to the track. He didn't want to lift it in his arms in case he got blood on his clothes. He was shouting, "Help me! Help me push!" I could hardly do a thing; my whole body felt numb. "For God's sake, come and help me!" The body was half out of the door, with the head nearly touching the carriage footboard, but the legs were caught up underneath it, and it wouldn't go through. The train continued on its way. Eventually, after pushing for all we were worth, it tilted forwards and disappeared under the wheels. "That's the end of him, the swine!" Roubaud said. Then he picked up the travelling rug and threw that out too. Then there were just the two of us, and a great big pool of blood on the seat. We stood looking at it; we didn't dare go near it. The door was still wide open, banging in the wind. I didn't understand what was happening at first; I was too shocked, too upset. I saw my husband climb out of the train and disappear from sight. Then he reappeared. He shouted, "Come on, quick! Follow me! It's our only chance!" I still didn't move. He was losing his temper.

'"Come on, for God's sake!" he said. "Our compartment's empty. We can go back there." Our compartment empty! How did he know? Had he been to have a look? What about the woman in black? The one who said nothing and hid herself in the corner! How could he be sure she wasn't still there? He said, "If you don't come, I'll bloody well chuck you out like Grandmorin!" He got back in, grabbed hold of me and started pushing me towards the door like someone gone mad. I found myself outside on the footboard, clinging with both hands to the brass handrail.[7] He got out behind me, making sure that the door was shut. "Go on! Go on!" he shouted. But I was too frightened to move. The train was travelling at full speed; the wind was blowing in my face like a hurricane. My hair came undone; my hands were so stiff I thought I was going to let go of the handrail. "Go on, for God's sake!" He kept pushing me forward; I had to walk along the footboard, passing one hand over the other, clinging to the side of the carriage with my skirts flapping about in the wind and getting caught round my legs. You could already see the lights of Barentin station in the distance, round a bend. The engine started to whistle. "Go on, for God's sake!" The noise was terrible! Everything was shaking around me. I felt as if I'd been caught in a violent storm, like a wisp of straw blown about in the wind that was going to be smashed against a wall. The countryside was flying past behind me; the trees seemed to be galloping after me like wild horses, twisting and turning, each crying out as we flew past. When I got to the end of the carriage I had to step across to reach the footboard on the next one and catch hold of the other handrail. I couldn't do it; I didn't have the courage and I didn't have the strength. "Go on, for God's sake!" He was right behind me, pushing me. I shut my eyes and moved forward. I don't know how I did **281** it; it was pure instinct, like an animal digging its claws in to stop itself falling. How nobody saw us I don't know. We walked along three carriages, including a second-class one absolutely full of passengers. I remember seeing rows of heads through the carriage windows; I think I would recognize them if I ever saw them again: a fat man with red sideburns, and especially two young girls leaning forward and laughing. "Go on, for God's sake! Go on, for God's sake!" I can't remember anything more; the lights of Barentin were getting nearer, the engine was blowing its whistle. The last thing I was conscious of was being pulled and dragged along by my hair. My husband must have grabbed hold of me, leaned over my shoulders to open the carriage door and thrown me into the compartment. When the train stopped I was sitting in the corner, gasping for breath, barely conscious. I couldn't move. I heard my husband exchange a few words with the Barentin station-master. The minute the train started again he fell on to the seat, exhausted. We didn't say another word all the way to Le Havre . . . I hate him! I hate him! It was terrible what he put me through! I love you, darling. You make me feel so happy!'

With the telling of her long tale, Séverine's desire had slowly mounted, and this cry to Jacques was the sign that in the midst of these awful memories she now longed for her joy to be made complete. Jacques, like her, was burning with desire but he held her back. Her tale had disturbed him.

'Wait!' he said. 'Wait a moment! You said you were lying flat across his legs and you felt him die.'

There were things he had to know. He felt a wave of burning curiosity run through him. His mind was invaded by a sea of red. The murder fascinated him.

'Tell me about the knife. Did you feel it go in?'

'Yes. I felt a thud.'

'Just a thud? Didn't you feel his neck being slit open?'

'No, it was just a blow.'

'Did he have a convulsion?'

'Yes, he had three. They ran from one end of his body to the other, very slowly. I felt them run right down to his feet.'

'Did they make him go stiff?'

'Yes. The first one was very strong. The other two were weaker.'

'And then he died. How did you feel when you felt him die like that, with his throat slit?'

'How did I feel? I don't know.'

'What do you mean, you don't know? Come on, tell me. I want to know. Tell me honestly, how did you feel? Were you upset?'

'No, I wasn't upset.'

'Did it give you pleasure?'

'Pleasure! Ah, no, certainly not!'

'What then, love? I beg you! Tell me what it was like . . . If only you knew . . . Tell me what it feels like.'

'How can you describe a thing like that, for heaven's sake? It's awful; you're just carried away . . . completely carried away! I lived more in that minute than in all my previous life put together!'

Jacques clenched his teeth, muttered something incoherent and took her. Séverine took him also. They possessed each other, finding love in the midst of death, and the same agonizing pleasure as beasts that tear each other apart as they mate. All that could be heard was the heavy sound of their breathing. The circle of red light had gone from the ceiling. The stove went out, and, with the wintry conditions outside, the room began to grow cold. Not a sound rose from the street as Paris lay muffled in snow. There were a few snores from the newspaper seller's room next door. Then the house sank into a dark, fathom- **283** less sleep.

All this time, Séverine had been lying in Jacques's arms. He suddenly felt her give in to sleep as if she had been struck down. The journey, the long wait at the Misards and a night of passion had finally taken their toll. She murmured a childlike goodnight and immediately fell fast asleep, breathing peacefully. The cuckoo clock had just struck three.

For nearly another hour Jacques lay with Séverine across his left arm, which gradually sent it to sleep. But his eyes would not remain closed; unseen fingers seemed to keep opening them again in the dark. By now he couldn't see a thing in the room; it was pitch black. The stove, the furniture, even the walls – everything had disappeared. He turned his head to look for the two pale window squares, outlined on the wall, faint and dreamlike. Although he was exhausted, his mind would not rest; thoughts came teeming into his head – the same thoughts, returning again and again. Every time he succeeded in putting them from him and was about to fall asleep, the vision returned to haunt him, a succession of images, the same as before, each time more disturbing. The scene that presented itself with such mechanical regularity, as he stared open-eyed into the darkness, was the murder, in all its details. It kept coming back, identical, invading his mind, tormenting him. The knife entered the throat with a thud, the body had three long convulsions, its life drained away in a stream of warm blood, a red stream; he imagined he could feel it running over his hands. Twenty times, thirty times, the knife went in, the body jerked. The images grew bigger and bigger, they seemed to suffocate him, spill over him and banish the night. He longed to kill with a knife, to satisfy his old desire, to know what it feels like and to savour that moment in which one lives more than in a whole lifetime.

He became more and more breathless. Perhaps it was simply the weight of Séverine on his arm that was preventing him from sleeping. He gently freed himself from her and, without waking her, placed her beside him. Immediately he felt more at ease and began to breathe more freely, thinking that at last he was about to drop off to sleep. But once again those unseen fingers opened his eyelids; in the darkness he saw the murder re-enacted, in all its gory detail. The knife went in; the body jerked. Streaks of blood stained the night; the wound in the throat gaped wide open, like an axe mark in a tree. He gave up the struggle and lay on his back; the nightmare must run its course. He could hear the wheels of his mind turning. His brain groaned in its effort to make sense of the thoughts that assailed him. They came from far back, from his childhood. He had thought he was cured. For months, ever since he had first possessed Séverine, there had been no sign of his old craving; and now, after listening to this tale of murder, whispered into his ear as she lay naked against him, their bodies intertwined, it had returned, more intense than ever. He moved away from her so that she was not touching him; the least contact with her flesh sent a fire running through him. He felt a terrible burning along his back, as if the mattress he lay on had become a bed of coals. There was a pricking sensation in his neck, like red-hot needles. He tried putting his hands outside the bedclothes, but they quickly became frozen and made him shiver. His hands frightened him; he drew them back under the bedclothes and clasped them together across his stomach, finally sliding them under his buttocks to pin them down, as if he were afraid they might do something awful, something he had no wish to do but did all the same.

Every time the cuckoo clock struck the hour, Jacques counted. Four o'clock, five o'clock, six o'clock. He longed for day to come; he hoped that the dawn might chase this nightmare away. Again he turned towards the windows, peering at the glass for the first sign of daylight. But all he could see was the pale reflection of the snow. At a quarter to five he had heard the train arrive from Le Havre. It was only forty minutes late; the line was obviously clear again. It was not until after seven that he saw the windows begin to whiten, and a pale milky glimmer slowly filtered into the room. At last the light returned; a strange half-light in which the furniture seemed to be floating. The stove reappeared, then the cupboard and the sideboard. He could still not close his eyes; in fact they ached from trying to see in the dark. Suddenly, even before it was completely light and before he could actually see it, he sensed, on the table beside him, the presence of the knife he had used to cut the cake the night before. And now, this knife was all he could see, a little knife with a pointed blade. As it grew lighter, all the light coming in through the two windows was reflected in that one small blade. He was so frightened of his hands that he thrust them further beneath him; he could feel them growing restless, defying him, asserting their will. Were these hands his own? He must have inherited them from someone else. They must have been passed down by some remote ancestor from the days when men strangled wild beasts in the forest!

In order not to see the knife, Jacques turned over towards Séverine. She was sleeping peacefully, utterly exhausted, breathing like a child. Her thick, black hair was undone and fell down over her shoulders like a dark pillow. Between the strands of hair, under her chin, he saw her throat, delicate, milky white with just a trace of pink. He looked at her as though she were a stranger. Yet he adored her; he carried her image with him wherever he went and never stopped desiring her, even when he was driving his train. So much so that one day he had woken up as if from a dream to find himself driving at full speed through a station with the signals at red. He could not take his eyes away from her white throat; he was seized with a sudden, irresistible fascination. He was still fully aware of what was happening and to his horror he felt himself being compelled to take the knife from the table and plunge it to the hilt into this woman's flesh. He heard the thud of the blade as it went in; he saw the body jerk three times and then go stiff as the blood flowed from the wound. He tried desperately to put the nightmare from his mind, but with every second that passed his resolve was weakening, as if it were being drowned by this one obsession and driven towards that distant shore where one accepts defeat and surrenders to instinct. Everything became a blur; his hands had defiantly overcome his attempt to hide them and had freed themselves. He realized only too well that he was no longer in control of them and that if he continued to gaze at Séverine they would have their way and kill her. With one final effort he threw himself out of the bed and fell rolling on the floor like someone who was drunk. He picked himself up, but his feet got caught in the clothes that Séverine had left lying there, and he nearly fell down again. He lurched about, desperately looking for his own clothes. His one thought was to get dressed, take the knife and go and kill some other woman out in the street. The urge was too strong to resist; he had to kill someone. But he couldn't find his trousers; he had them in his hand three times before realizing what they were. He had great difficulty trying to put his shoes on. Although it was now broad daylight, the room seemed to be filled with a red mist, like dawn on a cold, foggy morning, when everything appears hazy. He was shaking uncontrollably. He had finally managed to get dressed. He had taken the knife and hidden it up his sleeve, determined to go out and kill the first woman he met in the street, when he heard a movement from the bed and a long drawn-out sigh. He **287** stood by the table, rooted to the spot, his face turning white.

Séverine was waking up.

'What is it, darling? Do you have to go so soon?'

He didn't answer her or look at her, hoping she would go back to sleep.

'Where are you going to, darling?'

'I won't be long,' he said. 'I've got to go to the station. Go back to sleep.'

She was still very drowsy and had closed her eyes again.

'I'm so tired,' she murmured. 'So tired. Come and kiss me before you go, darling.'

Jacques did not move. He knew that he only had to turn round with the knife in his hand and take one look at her lying naked in bed, with her hair undone, so delicate, so pretty, and the willpower that restrained him would collapse. His hand would rise of its own accord and plunge the knife into her throat.

'Kiss me, darling . . .'

Her voice faded to a whisper; she murmured that she loved him and fell quietly back to sleep. In desperation, he opened the door and fled.

It was eight o'clock when Jacques found himself outside in the Rue d'Amsterdam. The snow had not yet been cleared away; the footsteps of the few people that were about could scarcely be heard. He immediately spotted an old woman, but she disappeared round a corner into the Rue de Londres. He didn't follow her. He almost bumped into two men as he walked down towards the Place du Havre, clutching the knife, with the blade hidden up his sleeve. A girl of about fourteen emerged from a house on the other side of the street, and he crossed over towards her, only to see her disappear into a baker's shop next door. He was too impatient to wait for her to come out and continued his search further on down the street. From the minute he had left the room with the knife in his hand he had become a different person, another being, a creature he had often felt stirring within him, a strange visitor from the distant past, consumed by an inborn desire to kill. It had killed before and it wanted to kill again. Everything around him appeared to Jacques as if in a dream; he had only one thought in his mind. He must kill. His normal day-to-day life no longer existed; he moved through the streets like a sleepwalker, with no recollection of the past and no sense of the future, driven by this one overriding obsession. He had become an automaton. He was no longer himself. Two women brushed past him as they came up from behind. He quickened his step and had just caught them up when they stopped to talk to a man. The three of them stood laughing and chatting. Once again he had been thwarted. Another woman walked past, and he followed her. She was dark-skinned and looked ill. She wore a thin shawl and was obviously very poor; she walked slowly, on her way to some thankless, underpaid job, no doubt; she was certainly in no rush to get there. She looked desperately sad. Jacques had chosen his victim and walked after her. He was in no hurry. He was looking for a place where it would be easy to attack her. She must have noticed that she was being followed because she turned and looked at him, with a look of unspeakable sadness, amazed that anyone should want anything from her. He followed her along the Rue du Havre. Twice she turned to look at him, making him hold back as he was taking his knife out to stab her. She had such a pathetic, pleading look in her eyes. He decided he would wait until she stepped off the pavement a little further on. That was where he would strike. Then suddenly he turned round and began to follow another woman, who was walking in the opposite direction. There was no reason why; it was not something he chose to do. She simply happened to be walking past at the time.

He followed her back towards the station. She walked quickly, with little, short steps, her shoes tapping on the pavement; she was extremely pretty, twenty years old at the most, very shapely, with blonde hair and beautiful bright eyes that seemed to have a permanent smile in them. She didn't even notice that someone was following her. She must have been in a hurry because she ran up the steps from the Cour du Havre into the main hall, dashed over to the booking office for the circle line and hurriedly ordered a first-class ticket to Auteuil. Jacques did likewise and followed her through the waiting rooms and out on to the platform to her compartment. He got in and sat beside her. The train left at once.

'I've got plenty of time,' he thought. 'I'll kill her in the tunnel.'

Sitting opposite them, however, was an old lady, the only other passenger in the compartment. She recognized the young woman.

'Why, fancy seeing you!' she exclaimed. 'Where are you off to so early?'

The young woman raised her hands in a gesture of mock despair.

'You can't do anything without running into someone, can you?' she said with a laugh. 'I hope you won't give me away . . . It's my husband's birthday tomorrow. I waited for him to leave for the office and caught the first train I could. I'm going to Auteuil. There's a market garden there where he saw an orchid that he really wanted . . . I'm going to buy it for him as a surprise.'

The old lady nodded approvingly.

'And how's the little baby?' she asked.

'She's a joy! I weaned her last week. You should see her eat her soup! In fact we're all very well. It's scandalous!'

She laughed again, more loudly, showing her white teeth
290 between her blood-red lips. Jacques was sitting on her right, holding the knife hidden against his leg. He was in just the right position to stab her, he thought to himself. All he had to do was raise his arm and turn towards her; it would be perfect. But as the train ran into the Batignolles tunnel he thought of her bonnet-strings. They're tied under her chin, he thought. They'll get in the way. I want to be certain.

The two women chatted happily away to each other.

'I can see you're very happy.'

'Happy! I've never felt happier! It's like a dream come true! Two years ago I was nothing. Do you remember? It was so dull living with my aunt, and I didn't have a penny to my name. When he came to see me my heart would be all of a flutter. I was so in love with him. He was so handsome and so rich . . . And now he's mine! He's my husband! And we've got our little baby! I can't believe it!'

Jacques was carefully inspecting the way her bonnet-strings were tied. He saw that beneath the knot she wore a large gold medallion on a black neckband. He worked out what he was going to do.

'I'll grab her by the neck with my left hand and turn her head round so that the medallion's not in the way,' he thought to himself. 'Then I can get at her throat.'

The train was constantly stopping and starting. They had passed through two short tunnels, at Courcelles and at Neuilly. Any minute now! It would not take more than a second!

'Did you go to the seaside this summer?' the old lady asked.

'Yes, we spent six weeks in Brittany, miles from any-where. It was heaven! Then during September we stayed at my father-in-law's in Poitou; he owns a lot of woodland down there.'

'And aren't you going to the Midi for winter?'

'Yes, we'll be at Cannes from the fifteenth . . . The house is already booked. It's got a really lovely garden facing the sea. We've sent someone on ahead to get things ready . . . It's not that we don't like the cold, but it's so nice to be in the sun . . . We shall be back in March. Next year we're going to stay in Paris. In a couple of years' time, when baby's grown up, we'll do some travelling. I don't know, life seems one long holiday!'[8]

She seemed to be brimming over with happiness, so happy in fact that she turned towards Jacques, a man she had never met, and smiled at him. As she did so, the bow on her bonnet-strings shifted, the medallion slipped to one side, and he saw her neck, rosy pink, with a little hollow at its base that formed a patch of golden shadow.

Jacques's fingers tightened on the handle of the knife; he had made his decision.

'That's where I'll do it,' he thought to himself. 'In the tunnel, just before Passy! We're nearly there!'

But when the train stopped at Trocadéro, a railway

employee who knew him got into the compartment and started telling him about an engine driver and his fireman who had been convicted of stealing coal. Everything started to become confused; later, Jacques was never able to piece together exactly what happened. The woman sitting next to him had carried on laughing, radiating such happiness that it worked its way into him and calmed him down. Perhaps he had stayed on the train with the two women until it reached Auteuil, but he couldn't recall them getting off. He ended up finding himself walking along the Seine, but how he got there he didn't know. What he did remember very clearly was standing on the bank of the river and throwing away the knife, which he had kept tucked inside his sleeve. After that he could remember nothing. His mind was a blank; he was totally empty. The creature that had taken hold of him was no more; it had

292 gone when he threw away the knife. He must have carried on walking for hours, following streets, crossing squares, going wherever his legs took him. People and houses slipped past him like ghosts. He must have gone somewhere to eat; he recalled a room crowded with people, and white plates on the tables. He also retained a vivid image of a red poster in an empty shop window. After that, all he was aware of was a black abyss, a void, in which there was neither time nor space, and where, for centuries perhaps, he had lain unconscious.

When he came to, Jacques found himself back in his little room in the Rue Cardinet, slumped across his bed, fully dressed. He had found his way there by instinct, like an exhausted dog dragging itself back to its kennel. He could not remember climbing the stairs or going to sleep. When he woke up, it came as a shock to suddenly find himself in possession of his senses again, as if emerging from a coma. Had he slept for three hours or three days? Then it all came back to him; he had spent the night with

Séverine, she had told him about the murder, and he had rushed out like a beast of prey in search of blood. He had taken leave of his senses but was now beginning to come back to himself. He was horrified to think of the things he had done and to know that he had been powerless to prevent them. He suddenly remembered that Séverine was still waiting for him. He leaped to his feet and looked at his watch; it was already four o'clock. His mind felt empty, and he was now perfectly calm, as if his blood had been drained from him. He hurried back to the Impasse d'Amsterdam.

Séverine had slept soundly until midday. When she woke up she was surprised to find that Jacques was no longer there. She relit the stove, finally got dressed and at about two o'clock, dying of starvation, decided to go down and have something to eat in a nearby restaurant. When Jacques arrived she had just got back from doing some shopping.

'Darling,' she said, 'I was so worried!'

She flung her arms round his neck and looked him in the eyes.

'Where on earth have you been?'

He was exhausted and felt cold to the touch. He calmly reassured her that there was nothing wrong.

'I had to do some work on the engine,' he said. 'I couldn't get out of it. Sometimes they expect you to work all the hours God sends!'

She spoke quietly; there was a pleading, apologetic note in her voice.

'Do you know what I thought?' she said. 'It was awful! I couldn't bear it! . . . I thought that, after what I told you, perhaps you didn't want me any more . . . And I thought that you'd left me and that you'd never come back . . . ever!'

She could no longer hold back her tears. She clung to him desperately, weeping on his shoulder.

293

'Oh my darling!' she said. 'If only you knew how much I need someone to love me! Love me! Be kind to me! Only your love can make me forget! Now that I've told you all my troubles, promise you will never leave me! I beg you!'

Jacques was overcome by this heartfelt plea. He felt himself gradually beginning to soften.

'No,' he murmured, 'I won't leave you. I love you. Never fear!'

It was too much for him, and he wept. He thought of the evil thing that once more possessed him; it was inescapable, he would never be cured. All that lay ahead of him was an endless night of shame and despair.

'Love me too!' he said. 'Be kind to me! Love me with all your heart! I need your love as much as you need mine.'

She started. What did he mean?

'Darling,' she said, 'if you have troubles, you must tell me about them.'

'No,' he said, 'not troubles. They're things that don't exist. I get depressed, and it makes me feel very unhappy. I can't talk about it.'

They drowned their sadness in an embrace. There would be no end to their suffering; what had happened could be neither forgotten nor forgiven. They wept in each other's arms; they were victims of the blind forces of life – unending strife and death.

'Come on,' said Jacques as he released her, 'it's time we thought of leaving . . . Tonight you'll be in Le Havre.'

A dark look came into Séverine's eyes. She gazed into the distance, saying nothing.

'If only I were free!' she murmured. 'If only I didn't have my husband! It would be so much easier to forget!'

Jacques raised his hands in a gesture of frustration and, as if thinking aloud, said, 'But we can't kill him, can we!'

Séverine stared at him. Jacques gave a start, amazed at what he had just said; the thought had never entered his head until that moment. But if he wished to kill someone, why not kill Roubaud, the man who stood in their way? As he was leaving her to go back to the engine sheds, she once more took him in her arms and covered him with kisses.

'Oh, my darling!' she said. 'Love me for ever! I'll love you more and more . . . We shall be happy, you'll see!'

9

For the next few days back in Le Havre, Jacques and Séverine were extremely careful. They were worried. If Roubaud knew what was going on between them, he would probably be keeping an eye on them, looking for an opportunity to catch them out, so that he could wreak some terrible revenge. They remembered the jealous rages he had before and the sheer brutality of this man who had worked in the shunting yards and who let fly with his fists at the least suspicion. He had become taciturn and lethargic and he had a permanently worried look in his eyes. They were convinced he was planning some nasty trick, setting a trap 296 so that he could discover their secret. So for the next month they were constantly on the alert and only ever saw each other when they had made absolutely sure it was safe.

But Roubaud was spending less and less time at home. Perhaps he only went away in order to come back unexpectedly and catch them in each other's arms. But this never happened. On the contrary, he stayed away longer and longer, to the point that he was hardly ever there, disappearing the minute he was free and returning just in time to begin his shift. When he was on duty during the day, he would come back at ten o'clock, eat his breakfast in five minutes and then not reappear until half past eleven. When his colleague came down to take over at five o'clock, he would rush off straight away and sometimes be out all night. It was as much as he did to come back for a few hours' sleep. When he was working at night, it was the same. He finished work at five in the morning, but must have gone somewhere else to eat and sleep, because he didn't come back home till five in the evening. Despite this chaotic regime, he had continued to turn up punctually for work, like a model employee, always on time, even though he was sometimes so exhausted he could hardly stand on his feet. None the less, he had gone about his business and performed his duties conscientiously. Recently, however, there had been a few lapses. Twice already, the other assistant stationmaster, Moulin, had had to wait an hour for him to arrive, and one morning, decent fellow that he was, hearing that he hadn't reappeared after breakfast, he had even come down and stood in for him, so that he wouldn't get into trouble. Roubaud's job was beginning to suffer the effects of the dissipated life he was leading. During the day, he was no longer the energetic man he used to be, personally inspecting every train that arrived or departed, noting everything down in his report to the stationmaster, making sure everyone was working hard and working hard himself. At night he just fell fast **297** asleep in his armchair in his office. Even when he was awake he appeared to be half asleep, wandering up and down the platform with his hands behind his back, giving orders in a monotone and totally unconcerned whether anyone carried them out or not. If he managed to get things done, it was by sheer force of habit, although on one occasion his negligence led to a collision, when a passenger train was accidentally run into a siding. His colleagues merely joked about it, saying he shouldn't spend so much time womanizing!

The truth was that Roubaud was now virtually living in the little back room upstairs at the Café du Commerce. It had gradually become a veritable gambling den. People said there were women there every night; in fact there was only ever one woman there, the mistress of a retired sea captain, who was at least forty years old, an incurable gambler herself, and totally sexless. The only appetite Roubaud satisfied when he visited the Café du Commerce was his

melancholy passion for cards. It had started shortly after
the murder, through a chance game of piquet; since then
it had grown into an irresistible habit, providing release
from all his cares and complete oblivion. It had taken such
a hold on him that his desire for women, which had previously been insatiable, was now totally dead. It held him
completely in its grip, providing the only distraction that
afforded him any pleasure. His need to forget came not
from any feelings of remorse over the murder, but from
the break-up of his marriage; his life had been ruined, and
this was his one consolation, a form of happy self-
indulgence which numbed his senses and which he could
enjoy alone. His passion had now taken over his whole life
and it was destroying him. Alcohol could not have provided him with such pleasure and freedom from care or
made the time go by more swiftly. He had even stopped
298 caring about life itself, yet he had the impression he was
living life to the full. It was as though he were somewhere
else, cut off; none of the things that used to irritate him so
intensely now seemed to affect him at all. Apart from feeling tired as a result of his late nights, he was really quite
well; he was even putting on weight, growing rather fat
and flabby in fact. His eyes had lost their sparkle and
seemed always to be half asleep. When he did come home,
he just lounged around and showed absolutely no interest
in anything.

On the night that Roubaud had come back to take the
three one-hundred-franc coins from under the floor, it was
in order to pay Monsieur Cauche, the safety officer, after
a succession of losses. Monsieur Cauche was an experienced card player and he knew how to keep his head, which
made him a formidable opponent. He said he only played
for the fun of it; he was a retired soldier, and his position
as magistrate required him to keep up a respectable appearance. He had never married and spent most of his time at

the café as a regular customer, which didn't prevent him from frequently playing cards all evening and pocketing everybody else's money. People said he was so lackadaisical about his job that he had been told he might be asked to resign. But nothing had come of it, and there was so little work for him to do that it seemed pointless to ask him to work harder. So he simply put in an appearance on the platform for a few minutes, where everyone said hello to him.

Three weeks later, Roubaud owed Monsieur Cauche almost four hundred francs more. He had told him that his wife's legacy had left them very well off, adding jokingly that it was his wife, however, who held the purse-strings, which was why he was a bit slow in paying off his debts. One morning, when he was at home on his own, having been harassed by Monsieur Cauche, he once again lifted the floorboard and removed a thousand-franc note from its hiding place. He was shaking all over; he hadn't **299** felt like that when he removed the gold coins. He had probably thought then that he was merely borrowing a bit of loose change. With the thousand-franc note, however, he knew it was theft. A shiver ran through him at the thought of this tainted money that he had sworn he would never touch. He used to say that he would rather die of starvation; and here he was, helping himself. How had it happened? The murder had slowly eaten away at his conscience, day by day, little by little, until he no longer had the will to resist. As he put his hand down into the hole, he thought he felt something wet, something soft and disgusting. It made him feel sick. He quickly replaced the floorboard, telling himself that he would cut his hand off rather than take it up again. His wife hadn't seen him; he breathed a sigh of relief and drank a large glass of water to steady his nerves. His heart was beating with excitement; he could pay off his debt and he had all this money to wager!¹

But when it came to changing the note, Roubaud's anxiety quickly returned. Before, he had been prepared to brave things out; he might even have given himself up had he not foolishly involved his wife in the murder. Now, however, the mere thought of the police brought him out into a cold sweat. He knew that the police didn't have the numbers of the missing banknotes and that, in any case, the inquiry had been shelved and filed away indefinitely, yet the minute he went anywhere intending to ask for change, he was overcome with panic. For five days he kept the note on him, moving it from one pocket to another, feeling to see that it was still there and even taking it to bed with him. He devised various complicated strategies, each of which ran into some unforeseen difficulty. At first he had thought of the station; perhaps someone in the accounts department could change it for him. He decided it was too 300 risky. He then thought of going to buy something on the other side of town, not wearing his stationmaster's cap. But they would think there was something odd about using such a large note to pay for something worth next to nothing. In the end he decided the simplest thing would be to use the note at the tobacconist's on the Cours Napoléon; he went there every day, they knew he had inherited some money, and it would come as no surprise to the woman behind the counter. He went up to the door, but his nerve failed him. He walked down towards the Vauban dock trying to screw up his courage. Half an hour later he came back, still undecided. That evening at the Café du Commerce, Monsieur Cauche was there. On a sudden impulse, Roubaud took the note from his pocket and asked the proprietress if she could change it for him. She didn't have enough change and sent one of the waiters with it to the tobacconist's. They joked about it, saying it seemed brand new, even though it was ten years old! The safety officer took it, turned it over in his hand and pronounced that it must have been kept hidden away somewhere, which launched the retired sea captain's mistress into an interminable tale of some vast fortune that had been hidden and eventually found again under the top of a chest of drawers!

The weeks went by. With so much money at his disposal, Roubaud's passion for gambling knew no bounds. It wasn't that he wagered large sums of money, but he was constantly dogged by the worst luck imaginable. Little losses every day soon added up to large amounts. By the end of the month he had nothing left and was once again heavily in debt. He didn't dare carry on playing, which made him feel quite ill. He tried hard to overcome the temptation but he almost ended up having to take to his bed. The knowledge that there were another nine banknotes lying beneath the dining-room floor went round and round in his head all day long; he could see them through the floor- **301** boards and felt them burning the soles of his feet. To think that, if he had wanted to, he could have taken another one! But he had vowed not to; he would sooner put his hand into the fire than go feeling under the floor again! Then, one evening when Séverine had gone to sleep early, he lifted the floorboard, furious with himself for giving in and feeling so miserable that his eyes filled with tears. Why resist? Why suffer? It was pointless; he now knew that he would take the banknotes, one by one, until there were none left.

The next morning, Séverine happened to notice a new scratch in one of the pieces at the edge of the parquet. She bent down and saw that it had been lifted. Clearly her husband was still helping himself to the money. She suddenly felt very angry, which surprised her, as normally money matters didn't bother her. More to the point, she had thought that she too would rather starve than lay hands on money that was tainted. But surely this money belonged to her as much as to him! Why should he make use of it secretly, without even telling her about it? All day long she was tormented by the desire to know for certain whether the money had been taken; she would have lifted the floorboard herself to see, but the thought of feeling around down there on her own sent a shiver down her spine. Perhaps the dead man's ghost would rise from beneath the floor! The thought terrified her; it was childish, she knew, but she couldn't bear to stay in the room. She picked up her work and shut herself in her bedroom.

That evening, as the two of them sat silently eating the remains of a stew, it again annoyed her to see his eyes continually wandering towards the corner of the parquet floor where the money was hidden.

'You've taken some more, haven't you?' she said suddenly.

He looked up in surprise.

'Taken some more what?' he replied.

'Oh, don't come the innocent, you know very well what I mean . . . I won't have you taking that money, do you hear! It's no more yours than mine! It makes me feel ill to know you're stealing it.'

Roubaud did his best to avoid arguments. The only time they were together was the bare minimum that being married to each other imposed; they spent whole days without exchanging a word, coming and going like two strangers, totally indifferent to each other and leading their own separate lives. He simply shrugged his shoulders and said nothing.

But Séverine was angry and wanted to settle this hidden money business once and for all; it had worried her since the day of the murder.

'I insist on an answer,' she shouted. 'I defy you to say you haven't touched it!'

'What's it got to do with you?' he answered.

302

'What it's got to do with me is that it turns my stomach! It frightens me! Today I couldn't stay in the room. Every time you move that floorboard I have awful dreams, night after night. We never talk about it. So keep away from it! I don't want to have to think about it!'

He looked at her with big, staring eyes, struggling to find an answer.

'What's it got to do with you if I take some of his money? I'm not forcing you to put your hands on it. It's for me. What I do with it is my business.'

She raised her hand to slap him, but managed to stop herself. It was unbearable. She looked at him in despair; he disgusted her.

'I don't understand you,' she said. 'You used to be an honest man . . . You wouldn't have stolen a penny from anyone . . . I could have forgiven you for what you did; you weren't in your right mind. You made me lose my head **303** too . . . But this money! . . . This awful money! You said you wanted nothing to do with it and now you're stealing it, bit by bit, just for your own amusement! What's happened to you? How could you sink so low?'

What she said seemed to bring him momentarily to his senses; he was suddenly amazed to realize he had been reduced to stealing money. He could no longer remember how he had managed to lower himself to this or piece together the bits of his life that the murder had undone. He couldn't understand how this new life, this new person, had come to exist, with his marriage in ruins and his wife estranged from him and despising him. But it was too late; what was done could not be undone. He waved his hands in the air as if to dispel these unpleasant thoughts from his mind.

'When it's no fun at home,' he muttered, 'you go and get your pleasures somewhere else. As you don't love me any more . . .'

'No, I certainly don't love you . . .'

He looked at her and thumped the table with his fist; he was purple with rage.

'Right! You can mind your own damned business then!' he shouted. 'Do I stop you enjoying yourself? Do I tell you what you should or shouldn't do? I don't know why I put up with you! Any decent-minded bloke would kick you out of the house! Perhaps then I wouldn't steal!'

She went white. It had often occurred to her that when a jealous husband is so tormented within himself that he turns a blind eye to his wife having a lover, it must indicate some mental gangrene, taking over everything, clouding his judgement and destroying his mind. But she was not going to give in to him; it was not she who was to blame. She was choking with rage.

'I forbid you to touch that money!' she screamed.

304 He had finished eating. He slowly folded his serviette and got up from the table.

'All right then,' he sneered, 'we'll share it.'

He was already on his knees, about to lift the floorboard. She rushed forward and placed her foot on it.

'No! No!' she cried. 'You know I'd rather die. Don't open it! I can't bear to look!'

That evening, Séverine had arranged to meet Jacques behind the goods station. When she got back home, after midnight, the thought of the argument earlier that evening came back to her. She went into her bedroom and turned the key twice. Roubaud was on night duty, so she needn't worry that he might come back home to sleep, as he sometimes did. She lay in bed with the cover wrapped round her and the lamp dimmed. Yet she could not sleep. Why had she refused to share the money? The idea of using it no longer seemed so outrageous. After all, she had accepted the legacy of La Croix-de-Maufras. Why not take the money as well? A shudder ran through her. No! Never!

The fact that it was money didn't bother her; what she couldn't bring herself to lay her hands on without fear of burning her fingers was money that had been stolen from a corpse, the ill-gotten gains of a murder. On the other hand, she reasoned with herself, beginning to think more calmly, if she did take it, it wouldn't be in order to spend it, it would be to hide it somewhere else, to bury it in a place known only to her, where it would lie hidden for ever. If she did it now, she would still have saved half of it from the hands of her husband. It would prevent him from taking it all for himself, and he would no longer be able to gamble money that belonged to her. The clock struck three. She bitterly regretted not having agreed to share the money. Gradually an idea began to take shape in her mind, slowly at first and still not very clear. She must get out of bed. She must lift the floorboard. Her husband must not take any more of the money. But the very thought made **305** her feel so cold that she didn't think she could do it. Yet if she took the money now and kept it herself, Roubaud wouldn't be able to stop her. It slowly dawned on her that this was her only chance. Her determination gathered strength, rising from deep within her subconscious self, overcoming her resistance, compelling her to act whether she wished it or not. She suddenly leaped out of bed, turned up the wick of the lamp and went into the dining room.

She was no longer shaking. Her fears had left her. She went about her task with the cool, unhurried precision of a sleepwalker. She fetched the poker that he used for lifting the floorboard. It was difficult to see into the hole, so she brought the lamp closer. She leaned forward. The hole was empty! She remained rooted to the spot, horror-stricken, unable to move. When she had gone to meet her lover, Roubaud had evidently returned, intent, as she had been, on taking the money and keeping it himself. The banknotes had all gone; not one was left. She knelt on the floor. Down in the hole she saw a glint of gold between the dusty joists; the watch and chain was all he had left behind. She remained for a moment, white with rage, stiff, half-naked, muttering repeatedly to herself: 'Thief! Thief! Thief!'

She thrust her hand angrily into the hole and seized the watch, disturbing a big black spider, which ran off over the plaster. She replaced the floorboard with her heel and went back to bed, putting the lamp on the bedside table. When she was warm again, she looked at the watch, which she still held clutched in her hand. She turned it over and examined it carefully. She recognized Grandmorin's two intertwined initials, engraved on the case. She opened it and read the figures 2516 – the maker's number. It was a very precious watch, and the police knew its number; it would be dangerous to keep it. But she was so furious that

306 it was the only thing she had managed to retrieve that this didn't bother her. She even felt she would stop having nightmares now that this corpse had gone from under the floor. At last she would be able to walk about freely in her own house, without feeling frightened. She slipped the watch under her pillow, put out the lamp and fell asleep.

The following day being his day off, Jacques had arranged to wait until Roubaud had gone down to the Café du Commerce as usual and then join her for dinner. They did this occasionally, when they felt it was safe. Séverine told him about the money, shaking as she spoke. She explained how she had found the hiding place empty. She still felt very bitter towards her husband.

'Thief! Thief! Thief!' she kept saying.

She went to fetch the watch, and insisted on giving it to him, despite his obvious reluctance to take it.

'Please, darling,' she said, 'no one will ever know you've got it. If I keep it here, he'll take it from me again. I'd rather he flayed me alive! He's had more than his fair share! I never wanted anything to do with the money. I couldn't bear to touch it! I wouldn't have spent a single penny of it. Why should he have it all for himself? I hate him!'

She was in tears, imploring him, begging him. Eventually Jacques took the watch and put it in his waistcoat pocket.

An hour went by. Séverine still sat on his lap, half-dressed, leaning against his shoulder, with her arm draped lazily around his neck. Suddenly, Roubaud walked into the room; he had a key. Séverine leaped to her feet. But it was too late; he had seen them. He stood by the door, apparently unable to move. Jacques remained seated, not knowing what to do. Without even bothering to attempt an explanation, Séverine walked up to him and screamed furiously: 'Thief! Thief! Thief!'

For a moment Roubaud did nothing. Then, with a shrug of his shoulders, which was how he dismissed most things these days, he went over to the bedroom to look for his report-book, which he had forgotten to take with him. Séverine ran into the room after him, shouting: 'You've stolen the money! Go on, deny it if you can! You've taken it, haven't you! All of it! Thief! Thief! Thief!'

Roubaud walked across the room without a word. When he reached the door, he turned round, fixing her in a sullen gaze.

'Go to hell!' he muttered.

He went out, not even bothering to shut the door behind him. He didn't appear to have noticed Jacques sitting there; he didn't even mention him.

After a long silence, Séverine turned towards Jacques. 'I don't believe it!' she said.

Jacques had not spoken, but he now stood up.

'He's finished!' he declared.

They agreed. At first they were amazed that, having killed one lover, he should put up with another. Then they found themselves despising him; how could a husband be so complacent? When a man reached that stage, he was in a mess; he would end up in the gutter.

From that day on, Séverine and Jacques were free to do as they wanted; they no longer needed to bother about Roubaud. Their main worry now, however, was Madame Lebleu, the nosy woman next door; she was convinced something was going on. When he came to see Séverine, Jacques crept along the corridor as quietly as possible. But to no avail; every time, he saw the door opposite being inched open and an eye watching him through the crack. It was becoming intolerable; he hardly dared come any more. When he did come, Madame Lebleu always knew he was there and would be outside with her ear glued to the door; they couldn't kiss or even hold a proper conversation. Séverine was so exasperated by this new intrusion into her love life that she once more began to press to have the Lebleus' apartment transferred to her. Traditionally the apartment had always been assigned to the assistant stationmaster. It was no longer the splendid view that attracted her, with the windows looking out on to the station forecourt and the Ingouville hills; her only reason for wanting it, although she kept this to herself, was that the apartment had a back door opening on to the tradesman's entrance. Jacques would be able to come and go as he pleased, and Madame Lebleu would be none the wiser. They would at last be free!

It was to prove far from easy, however. This dispute had been the subject of heated debate before; everyone on the corridor knew about it. But things had now come to a head. Madame Lebleu, feeling herself threatened, made no secret of her objections. It would kill her if she was shut up in a dingy room at the back, with only the station roof to look at; it would be like living in a prison cell! How could she be expected to live in a pokey little hole like that, when she was used to a nice, bright room with a fine view, where she could watch all the passengers coming and going? Her legs were so bad she couldn't get out for a walk; she'd just have to sit looking at a lead roof! They might as well just kill her and have done with it! But no matter how upset she got, in the end she had to admit she was only living there as the result of a favour; the previous assistant stationmaster, Roubaud's predecessor, had let them have it because he was a bachelor and lived on his own. Her husband had even written a letter undertaking to return it if the new assistant stationmaster wanted it. The letter could no longer be found, and Madame Lebleu denied that it had ever existed. The more untenable her position seemed to be, the more violent and aggressive she became. At one point she tried to get Madame Moulin, the other assistant stationmaster's wife, on her side by involving her in the quarrel; Madame Moulin, she claimed, had seen **309** Madame Roubaud kissing men on the stairs. Moulin had got very angry. His wife was a quiet, retiring person, whom you hardly ever saw. She had been reduced to tears; she swore she had seen nothing and had said no such thing. For a week the arguments raged from one end of the corridor to the other. Madame Lebleu's mistake, which was eventually to lead to her downfall, was to annoy Mademoiselle Guichon, the office secretary, by constantly prying into her affairs. Madame Lebleu was convinced that Mademoiselle Guichon spent every evening with the stationmaster. It had become an obsession; she had a pathological desire to catch her out, exacerbated by the fact that she had been spying on her for two years and had discovered absolutely nothing, not a whisper. Yet she was sure they were sleeping together; it drove her mad. It made Mademoiselle Guichon very angry that she could neither leave nor return to her apartment without being watched, and she had asked that Madame Lebleu be moved to the other side of the corridor. That way there would be an apartment between them, they wouldn't be living opposite each other, and she would no longer have to walk past her door every day. It was becoming obvious that Monsieur Dabadie, the stationmaster, who hitherto had not wanted to get involved in all this arguing, was now beginning to lose sympathy with Monsieur and Madame Lebleu, which did not augur well.

The situation was made worse by other personal animosities. Philomène now supplied Séverine with new-laid eggs, and every time she saw Madame Lebleu in the corridor, she made a point of being rude to her. As Madame Lebleu deliberately left her door open to annoy everybody, whenever Philomène walked past there were always unpleasant exchanges between them. The friendship between Séverine and Philomène had reached the stage where they were sharing each other's secrets; Philomène was bringing messages from Jacques to his mistress when he couldn't risk coming himself. She would come with her eggs, tell her when her meetings with Jacques had to be rearranged, explain how he'd had to be careful the night before and how they'd spent an hour together at her place. Sometimes when Jacques couldn't come, he was quite happy to while away the time at the Sauvagnats, chatting with the shed foreman. He used to go there with his fireman, Pecqueux; it was as if he needed to distract himself and was frightened of spending an evening alone. Even when Pecqueux went off drinking in the sailors' bars, he would call on Philomène, give her a message to take to Séverine and then sit down and stay for hours. Gradually Philomène became drawn into his love affair. She grew quite fond of him; all her previous lovers had treated her roughly. Jacques had delicate hands; he seemed so very sad, but he was always polite and gentle towards her. These were delights she had never sampled. With Pecqueux, it was like being married; he was always getting drunk and he gave her more cuffs than cuddles. But when she carried some little endearment from Jacques to Séverine, she herself tasted the sweet flavour of forbidden fruit. One day she confided in him, complaining about Pecqueux. She didn't trust him; he seemed a genial sort of chap, but when he got drunk he could be really nasty. Jacques noticed that she was looking after herself better; she was still very thin and rather unkempt, but not unattractive, with lovely soulful eyes. She was drinking less and keeping the house tidier. One evening her brother heard her talking with a man and came in, his hand raised ready to strike her, but when he saw who it was he simply offered them a bottle of cider. Philomène always made Jacques very welcome, and he seemed to enjoy his visits there; he was able to forget his worries. Philomène became a very close friend of Séverine and went round telling everyone that Madame Lebleu was an old cow!

One night she met the two lovers behind her little garden and accompanied them in the dark to the tool-shed where they used to hide.

'You're too kind to her,' Philomène said to Séverine. 'The apartment belongs to you. If it was me, I'd drag her out by her hair! I don't know why you put up with her.'

But Jacques didn't want to make a fuss.

'Monsieur Dabadie's seeing to it,' he said. 'It's best to wait till it's sorted out officially.'

'Before the end of the month I'll be sleeping in her bedroom,' declared Séverine, 'and we'll be able to see each other whenever we want.'

In the dark, Philomène sensed Séverine gently squeezing Jacques's arm at the thought of their being together. She left them and went back to her house. She had only walked a few paces when she stopped, turned round and hid herself in the shadows. It moved her to know that they were together. She felt no jealousy; she simply wished she could love and be loved like them.

With every day that went by, Jacques was becoming more and more depressed. On two occasions when he could have seen Séverine he had invented excuses not to. The fact that he sometimes stayed so long at the Sauvagnats was also in order to avoid seeing her. He still loved her; indeed the longer his love remained unfulfilled, the stronger it grew. But now, whenever she took him in her arms, he felt his fearful malady returning. His head began to spin, and he would quickly draw away from her, frozen with terror; he felt as if he were no longer himself and that the beast was about to seize him in its jaws. He had tried to exhaust himself by driving the long-distance trains, asking to work overtime and standing on a lurching footplate for twelve hours at a stretch in the teeth of the gale.

312 The other drivers all grumbled about what a hard job it was; they said it would finish a man off in twenty years. Jacques wished he could be finished off straight away. He couldn't do enough to tire himself out; he was only happy when he was being swept along on *La Lison*, with nothing else to think about, staring ahead on the lookout for signals. At the end of a journey he would collapse on to his bed before he had even had time to wash himself. But the minute he woke up, his obsession returned to torment him. Once more he tried to devote himself to *La Lison*, spending hours cleaning her and making Pecqueux polish the metalwork until it shone like silver. Inspectors who travelled on the footplate with him always congratulated him. But Jacques shook his head; he knew there was something wrong. Ever since they had been caught in the snow, *La Lison* had not been the sturdy, reliable engine she used to be. The pistons and valve gear had been repaired, but she had lost something of her soul, that mysterious perfection of balance and timing which certain locomotives acquire,

as if by magic, when they are first assembled. It distressed him; her poor performance led to bitter complaints and unreasonable requests to his superiors for pointless repairs and impractical improvements. They were all refused. Jacques became more and more despondent, convinced that there was something seriously wrong with *La Lison* and that she would never run properly again. His feelings towards her had changed. Why bother to look after her? Whatever he loved he destroyed! He now loved her with a fierce, desperate passion that neither anguish nor weariness could assuage.

Séverine had noticed the change in him. It saddened her; she thought he must be upset because of her, because of what she had told him. When he shuddered in her arms and suddenly turned away from her kiss, she thought it must be that he remembered the murder and that she horrified him. She hadn't dared mention it again and regretted ever having spoken of it. It amazed her to think how she had come to confess to him as they lay together in a strange bed, burning with passion. She could no longer remember how urgent then was her need to confide; she was simply happy to have him with her, knowing that he shared her secret. She certainly loved him and desired him more than ever, now that he knew everything. Her passion was insatiable. She was at last a woman roused; she wished to be taken and embraced, to love, not as a mother, but as a lover. Jacques meant everything to her, and she spoke no more than the truth when she told him how she longed to melt into him, for it was her cherished dream that he might take her and keep her as a part of his own body. She remained the quiet, gentle woman she had always been. Her only pleasure came from Jacques; she wished she could have curled up like a cat and slept on his lap from morning till night. The only feeling she now had about the murder was astonishment that she had ever been involved in it; she also seemed to have remained pure and undefiled, despite the foul treatment she had received during her youth. But it was all a long time ago; she could smile about it now. She wouldn't even have felt angry towards her husband, had he not stood in her way. But the more her love for Jacques grew and the more she needed him, the more she despised Roubaud. Now that Jacques knew about the murder and had forgiven her, he was her master; she would do his bidding and he could dispose of her as he wished. She had asked him to give her a photograph of himself;[2] she took it to bed with her and went to sleep with her lips pressed against the picture, feeling sad to see him so unhappy, yet unable to work out exactly what was wrong.

Meanwhile they continued to meet outside until they could move into Séverine's newly acquired apartment, where they would be able see each other whenever they wished. Winter was drawing to a close. That February, the weather was very mild; they walked for hours on end round the station yards and precincts. Jacques never wanted to stop; he always preferred to be on the move. But when Séverine clung to his shoulder and compelled him to sit down and make love to her, he always insisted that it was somewhere dark, terrified that if he caught even a glimpse of her naked flesh he would strike her down dead. As long as he could not see her he might be able to resist. In Paris, where she still accompanied him every Friday, he always made sure the curtains were pulled to, telling her that making love in broad daylight spoiled his pleasure. She now made this weekly trip without bothering to give her husband any explanation. As for the neighbours, she used the old excuse of having treatment for her knee, and also told them that she went to visit her foster-mother, Madame Victoire, whose convalescence in hospital was taking longer than expected. For both of them the outing always provided a welcome change. On this occasion Jacques was particularly interested in seeing how the engine performed, and Séverine was delighted to see him in better spirits. The journey, for her, was always a pleasure, although by now she was getting to know every little hill and clump of trees along the way. From Le Havre to Motteville the line ran through meadows and flat fields, surrounded by hedges and planted with apple trees. Then, as far as Rouen, the country became more hilly and deserted. After Rouen the railway followed the Seine, crossing it at Sotteville, Oissel and Pont-de-l'Arche. The river then broadened out across the open plain, now and then rejoining the railway at various points along the line. After Gaillon the line ran alongside the river, which flowed more slowly to its left, between low banks lined with poplar and willow. The railway followed the foot of the hillside, leaving the river at Bonnières, only to rejoin it at Rosny, at the other end of the Rolleboise tunnel. The river kept company with the train for the whole journey; the line crossed it three more times before reaching Paris. The journey continued: Mantes with its church tower among the trees, Triel with its white chalk-pits, Poissy, where the line cut right through the centre of the town, the two green walls of the forest of Saint-Germain, the slopes of Colombes abloom with lilac, and finally the outskirts of the capital and a glimpse of Paris as the train crossed the Pont d'Asnières, with the Arc de Triomphe in the distance rising above rows of shabby houses and bristling factory chimneys.[3] The train plunged into the Batignolles tunnel, ran into the noisy station, and the passengers all got off. Jacques and Séverine then had the whole day to themselves, free to do as they wished. The return journey was made in the dark. Séverine would close her eyes and relive the pleasures of the day. But whether it was morning or night, every time they passed La Croix-de-Maufras, she glanced quickly out of the window, making sure she couldn't be seen, for she knew that Flore would be standing beside the level-crossing, with her flag in its holster, watching the train with blazing eyes.

Ever since Flore had seen them kissing, on the day of the blizzard, Jacques had warned Séverine to be wary of her. He now knew the fierce, naive passion she had harboured for him since her youth, and he sensed she was jealous, smarting like a jilted lover, seething with unbridled, murderous resentment. What was more, he suspected she knew things. He remembered her mentioning the President having an affair with a young girl that nobody knew about, and that he had married her off. If she knew that, she must surely have guessed who killed him; she probably intended to speak or write to someone, to take her revenge by denouncing her. But days and weeks went by, and nothing happened; the only time he ever saw her was at her position beside the railway line, standing stiffly to attention, holding her flag. As soon as she spotted the train approaching in the distance, Jacques felt her eyes burning into him. She could see him despite the smoke; her eyes seemed to latch on to him and follow him, as the train sped past with a deafening roar. She inspected the carriages as they went by, from the first to the last, peering into them, looking, searching. And every time, she saw her sitting there, the woman who had stolen the man she loved and whom she now knew travelled on the train every Friday. She was always leaning forwards, as if there were something she must see; it was the merest inclination of the head, but enough for Flore to spot her. The glances of the two women crossed like swords, and the train had gone, carrying with it her only chance of happiness. Flore was left standing at her post, feeling angry and frustrated. Every time the train went past, she seemed to Jacques to grow taller. It worried him that she had done nothing, and he wondered what scheme was being hatched in the mind of this dark, menacing figure as it stood motionless beside the railway line whenever he passed.

There was also another railway employee who bothered them – Henri Dauvergne, the guard. He had been assigned to the Friday express, and his politeness towards Séverine was becoming embarrassing. He had realized she was having an affair with the train driver and told himself that his turn would perhaps come later. Roubaud would make jokes about it if he was on morning duty when the train left Le Havre. The reasons for Dauvergne's behaviour were patently obvious; he would reserve a whole compartment just for her, help her into the train and check the foot-warmer. Once even, Roubaud was chatting quietly with Jacques, when he winked in the direction of Dauvergne, who was engaged in his usual little game, as if to ask Jacques how he managed to put up with it. Whenever they 317 argued, Roubaud would baldly accuse his wife of sleeping with both of them. For a while Séverine imagined that Jacques thought so too, and that that was what was making him unhappy. One day she burst into tears, protesting her innocence and telling him to kill her if ever she was unfaithful to him. Jacques had turned very pale and had made a joke about it, kissing her and telling her that he knew she had done nothing wrong and that he hoped he would never kill anyone.

During the first few evenings in March the weather was dreadful, and they weren't able to meet. The trips to Paris and their few hours of freedom there no longer satisfied Séverine. She felt a growing need to have Jacques to herself, all to herself, to live together with him day and night, and never leave him. Her loathing for her husband increased; his mere presence made her feel sick with nervous irritation. It was becoming unbearable. This gentle woman, previously so loving and compliant, now lost her temper the minute she had anything to do with her husband and flew into a rage if he made the least attempt to prevent her doing what she wanted. Her clear blue eyes seemed to take on the dark colouring of her hair. She became totally intractable, accusing him of wrecking her life and making it impossible for them to continue living together. It was all because of him. If their marriage was in ruins and she had taken a lover, it was his fault. His sluggish apathy, his indifference when she got angry, the way he slouched around, apparently content with life, and growing repulsively fat and flabby, was more than she could bear. She had to get away from him, make a break, find a new life somewhere else! This was all she could think of. If only she could make a fresh start, put the past behind her, and begin her life again as it was before all these dreadful things happened. If only she could be fif-318 teen again, and love and be loved, and live as she had dreamed of living then! She spent a week dreaming of how she might escape. She would leave with Jacques. They would hide somewhere in Belgium and find a house to live in like any other hard-working young couple. But even before she had spoken to Jacques about it, she immediately foresaw all sorts of complications: their situation would be most irregular, they could never feel settled, and above all, she would be leaving everything she possessed in the hands of her husband – all her money and La Croix-de-Maufras. They had each made wills leaving everything to the surviving spouse. Besides, she was in his power, since in law the wife was considered the dependant of her husband. She would rather stay where she was and die than leave and lose a single penny. One day Roubaud came back looking very shaken; he said he'd just crossed the line in front of an oncoming locomotive and the buffer had caught him on the elbow. It occurred to her that if he had died she would be free. She gazed at him open-eyed. Why could he not die? He no longer loved her and he was in everybody's way!

From that day, Séverine's dream changed. Roubaud had died in an accident, and she was leaving with Jacques for America. They were married, they had sold La Croix-de-Maufras and they were now rich. All their fears were behind them. They were leaving France to start a new life together, hand in hand. In America, all those things she wanted to forget would no longer exist; she would be able to believe she was starting life all over again. She had made mistakes in the past, but would now set out to do only what brought her happiness. Jacques would easily find a job, and she could find something to do herself. They would make money and no doubt have children. It would be a new life of prosperity and good fortune. As soon as she was on her own, lying in bed in the morning or doing her needlework during the day, she would dream her 319 dream, changing it, embellishing it, constantly adding to its delights and finally imagining herself happier and better off than anyone in the world. Previously she had ventured out very little, but now she loved to go and watch the liners as they sailed away over the sea. She would walk down to the jetty, lean against the wall and watch the smoke from the ships until it merged with the clouds on the horizon. She became two separate persons, imagining herself standing on the deck with Jacques, already far away from France, on her way to the paradise of her dreams.

One evening towards the middle of March, Jacques, having risked coming to visit her in her apartment, informed her that he had just brought one of his old friends at the Technical College down from Paris in the train. He was leaving for New York to promote a new invention – a machine for making buttons. He needed a partner, a trained mechanic; he'd offered to take Jacques with him. It was a fine opportunity; all it needed was about thirty thousand francs investing in it, and he'd probably make millions. Jacques told her all this simply by way of conversation. Naturally he'd said no, although he admitted it was very tempting; it's hard to turn down the chance of a fortune when one comes along.

Séverine stood listening to him, with a faraway look in her eyes; it seemed like her dream, about to come true.

'Ah!' she murmured. 'We could leave tomorrow . . .'

Jacques looked up in surprise.

'What do you mean, "We could leave tomorrow"?' he asked.

'We could leave tomorrow,' she said, 'if he were dead.'

She didn't mention Roubaud by name, but it was clear from the look she gave whom she had in mind. Jacques knew what she was thinking and raised his hands in the air, as much as to say that, unfortunately, he wasn't dead.

320 'We could leave,' she continued, speaking slowly and seriously. 'We'd be so happy in America! I could get the thirty thousand francs by selling La Croix-de-Maufras, and there'd be enough left over to buy a house for ourselves. You'd do really well for yourself. I'd make us a nice cosy home where we could love each other to our hearts' content. It would be good. It would be so good!' Then she added in a whisper: 'Far away from these horrible memories! Each day would be a new beginning!'

Jacques felt a wave of delight run through him; their hands met and remained instinctively clasped together. Neither of them spoke; they were both lost in their dream. Séverine was the first to break the silence.

'I think you should go and see your friend again before he leaves,' she said. 'You could ask him not to take a partner until he's spoken to you.'

Again Jacques was amazed.

'What would be the point of that?' he asked.

'You never know,' she said. 'The other day, when the

train hit him . . . one second later and I'd have been a free woman! You're alive one minute and dead the next!'

She looked steadily into his eyes.

'If only he were dead!' she said again.

'You're not asking me to kill him, are you?' he said, trying to make a joke of it.

She assured him three times that she wasn't, but each time her eyes betrayed her. They were the eyes of a woman in love, a woman at the unforgiving mercy of her own passion. Roubaud had killed someone else, so why shouldn't he be killed himself? The thought came to her suddenly, as if it were the logical solution, the natural conclusion. Kill him and go and live somewhere else! What could be simpler? Once he was dead, it would all be over. She could start her life again. No sooner had the thought occurred to her than she could see no other possible alternative. In an instant she had made up her mind; there could be no **321** turning back. Yet she still sat gently shaking her head, denying it, lacking the courage to admit to her murderous thoughts.

Jacques stood, leaning against the sideboard, still trying to make light of what she had said. But he had seen the knife, which had been left lying there.

'If you want me to kill him,' he said, 'you'd better give me the knife. I've already got the watch! I'll have quite a little collection!'

He pretended to laugh.

'Take the knife,' she said in all seriousness.

Jacques put the knife into his pocket, trying to keep up the pretence, and kissed her.

'I'll wish you goodnight, then,' he said. 'I'll go and see my friend straight away and tell him to wait. Meet me round the back of the Sauvagnats on Saturday if it's not raining, all right? Don't worry, we're not going to kill anyone. I'm only joking.'

Late as it was, Jacques walked down to the harbour and found the hotel where his friend who was leaving the next day had said he would be staying. He told him that he might be coming into some money and that he should be able to give him a definite answer in a fortnight. As he made his way back along the dark streets towards the station, he paused to think about what he had just done. It surprised him. If he imagined himself married to Séverine and using her money, did it mean he had already resolved to kill Roubaud? Surely not! He had decided nothing; it was simply a wise precaution, in case he did decide. But the thought of Séverine came back to him, squeezing his hand in hers, her eyes looking into his and saying yes, when with her mouth she denied it. She obviously wanted him to kill Roubaud. His mind was in turmoil. What was he to do?

322 He went back to his room in the Rue François-Mazeline and lay on his bed, with Pecqueux snoring in the other bed beside him. He could not sleep; the thought of murdering Roubaud kept turning over in his mind. He pictured how the deed might be done, trying to imagine how everything would eventually work out. He went over it again and again, weighing the pros and cons; in the end, when he considered it coolly and dispassionately, everything seemed to suggest it was the right thing to do. Roubaud was the one obstacle standing in the way of his happiness. Once Roubaud was out of the way, he could marry Séverine, whom he adored. He would no longer have to see her secretly; she would be his, his alone, for ever. There was also the money to consider – a small fortune. He could give up his exhausting job and become the owner of a company; his friends said that mechanics in America were paid big money. He saw his new existence unfolding like a dream – he had a wife who was passionately in love with him, he would be earning millions in next to no time, life was full of opportunities, and there was no limit to what he might achieve. It was everything he could wish for. And to make this dream come true, all he had to do was get rid of one man – like the plant or the animal that stood in the way and that had to be crushed underfoot. Roubaud was no use to anybody; he had grown fat and sluggish. Whatever energy he once had was now consumed by his mindless addiction to gambling. Why spare him? Nothing, absolutely nothing, argued in his favour. He stood condemned. However you looked at it, it was in everyone's best interest that he should die. To delay would be both foolish and cowardly.

Jacques had been lying on his stomach because his back felt hot. Suddenly he turned over. A thought had entered his head, previously only vaguely perceived but now so sharp that it felt like the point of a knife inside his skull. He had wanted to kill since he was a child and had suffered **323** agonies as a result of this grim obsession. So why not kill Roubaud? Perhaps he might once and for all slake his thirst for murder on this one chosen victim. He would not only be doing something useful, he would also be cured. Cured! God, if only he could be free of this desire to kill, if only he could possess Séverine without that fearful awakening of the primitive male bent on slaughter! He broke out into a sweat; he saw himself with the knife in his hand, plunging it into Roubaud's throat as Roubaud had done to the President, and feeling the satisfaction and relief as the blood ran over his hands. He would kill him; he had decided. He would be cured, he would have the wife he adored and his future would be assured. If he had to kill, and someone had to be killed, he would kill Roubaud. He would at least know why he was doing it; it made sense logically and it was in his own best interests.

Having taken his decision and as it had just struck three, Jacques tried to sleep. He was about to drop off when a violent shock made him come to and sit up in his bed gasping for breath. Good God! What right had he to kill Roubaud? If a fly annoyed him he would squash it with his hand. Once he had nearly tripped over a cat and had kicked it from under his feet and broken its back; he hadn't meant to, it's true. But Roubaud was a man like himself. Jacques had to rethink all his arguments in order to persuade himself of his right to murder – the right of the strong to destroy the weak who get in their way.[4] It was he whom Roubaud's wife loved, and she wanted to be free to marry him and give him her inheritance. He was simply removing the obstacle that stood in their way. When two wolves meet in the forest in search of a mate, the stronger dispatches the weaker with a single snap of its jaws. In ancient times, when men lived in caves like the wolves, the most sought-after woman belonged to the member of the tribe who could win her by slaying his rivals. This was the law of life, and it had to be obeyed, whatever moral scruples had since been invented to keep men living together.[5] Gradually Jacques came to feel that his right to murder Roubaud was beyond question, and his resolve grew stronger; tomorrow he would choose the place and time, and plan how to do it. It would probably be best to stab him at night in the station when he was on his rounds, so that it would look as if he had been killed while trying to apprehend a gang of intruders. He knew a good spot behind the coal stacks, if Roubaud could be lured there. Although he had been trying to get to sleep, Jacques was now wide awake, rehearsing the scene in his mind, wondering where he would place himself, how he would strike the blow so that he would be killed outright. As he thought the whole thing through detail by detail, slowly but surely his reluctance to do the deed returned; an instinctive refusal swept through him. No, he couldn't do it! It was monstrous, impracticable, impossible! The civilized man in him revolted – everything he had been brought up to believe, the indelible print of all he had been so carefully taught. It was wrong to kill. He and generations before him had been weaned on this idea. The minute he sought reasons to justify it, the voice of his education and moral conscience rejected the idea of murder as something repulsive. He could understand someone killing because they had to, or because they had lost control. But to commit deliberate, premeditated murder, in order to get something he wanted . . . no, he could never do it!

It was almost daybreak when Jacques finally managed to get to sleep, but his sleep was so fitful that the agonizing debate continued to reverberate in his head. The next few days were the unhappiest of his life. He avoided seeing Séverine. He had sent a message telling her not to meet him on Saturday, for he was frightened what might happen if he looked into her eyes. On the Monday, however, he **325** had to see her, and as he feared, her big blue eyes, so gentle, so serious, filled him with anguish. She made no attempt to persuade him; not a word, not a gesture. But her eyes said it all, asking him, begging him. It was impossible to avoid their look of impatience and reproach. Every time he turned towards her, her eyes gazed into his, astonished that he should hesitate when his future happiness was at stake. When he left her, he kissed her, taking her suddenly in his arms to assure her that his mind was made up. And so it was . . . until he reached the bottom of the stairs, when all his doubts returned. When he saw her again two days later, he was pale and confused; he had an uneasy, furtive look in his eye, like a coward, loath to do what he knows he should. She burst into tears, weeping on his shoulder. She said nothing, but it was clear that she was terribly unhappy. Jacques was distraught and filled with self-loathing. He had to decide, once and for all.

'I'll see you on Thursday, in the usual place,' she whispered.

'Yes,' he answered, 'I'll be waiting for you.'

Thursday came. It was a very dark night – overcast, with not a star in the sky, and a fog coming in from the sea, deadening all sound. As usual, Jacques was the first to arrive and waited behind the Sauvagnats' house, looking out for Séverine. But it was so dark and she approached so softly that he didn't see her coming. He was startled by her touch. He took her in his arms, but she could feel that he was trembling.

'Did I frighten you?' she whispered.

'No,' he answered, 'I was expecting you. Let's walk this way; we won't be seen.'

They wandered out across the railway yard, holding each other gently by the waist. On this side of the engine shed, there were very few gas lamps, and in certain dark corners there were none at all. They could see the station lights glittering in the distance, like sparks from a fire.

They walked on without speaking. Séverine rested her head on his shoulder, looking up from time to time to kiss him on the chin. Jacques responded by inclining his head towards hers and kissing her on the forehead just below her hair. They heard the distant church bells solemnly strike one o'clock. They did not speak, for in their close embrace they could divine each other's thoughts. They were thinking of Roubaud. He had become an obsession; whenever they were together now, they thought of nothing else. Why waste words going over it again and again when what was needed was action? As she raised herself towards him to receive his kiss, she felt the knife in his trouser pocket. Had he decided?

Her lips parted, and, as if speaking her thoughts aloud, she said in a barely audible whisper, 'He came back from the station earlier on. I had no idea why. Then I saw him take his revolver. He'd forgotten it. He'll be going to look for prowlers, I know he will.'

They walked a little further. After a while, Jacques broke the silence.

'Some intruders got in here last night and stole some lead. He'll be coming to check. I know he will.'

A shiver ran down her spine. Neither of them spoke. They walked on slowly. She began to wonder, was it really the knife she had felt in his pocket? She kissed him twice, pressing herself against him to see if she could feel the knife again, but she could not be certain. She kissed him a third time and placed her hand on his pocket. Yes, it was the knife. Jacques understood and drew her towards him, burying her head in his chest and whispering in her ear, 'We'll wait for him to come. You will be free.'

The murder had been decided. They walked on, but their feet no longer seemed to touch the ground; it was as if they 327 were being borne along by some force beyond themselves. Their senses had suddenly become more acute, their sense of touch especially. It hurt them to hold hands. The least touch of their lips felt like the sharp scratch of a fingernail. Their ears were filled with sounds which earlier they had hardly heard – the distant hissing and clanking of locomotives, bumps and bangs, and footsteps walking past in the dark. They could see things in the night, black shapes, as if a cloud had been lifted from their eyes. A bat flew past, and they were able to follow it as it turned and darted in the sky. They stopped beside one of the coal stacks, motionless, straining their eyes and ears, every muscle of their bodies tense and alert. They spoke in whispers.

'Did you hear that?' she said. 'It was a cry for help.'

'No,' he said, 'it's a carriage being shunted.'

'On our left! There's someone there. I can hear footsteps.'

'No, it's the rats in the coal.'

The minutes went by. Suddenly she squeezed his arm.

'It's him!' she whispered.

'Where? I can't see.'

'He's just walked round the goods shed. He's coming towards us. Look! That's his shadow on the wall.'

'Are you sure it's him? Is he on his own?'

'Yes, he's on his own.'

The moment had come. She threw herself into his arms and pressed her burning lips to his in a long, passionate kiss. She wanted to give herself to him with all her heart. How she loved him! How she detested Roubaud! If she had dared, she would have killed him twenty times and saved him the horror of it. But she couldn't bring herself to do it. She didn't have the strength. It needed the firm hand of a man. And now, in this one enduring kiss, she wished to breathe her resolution into him and to promise him that
328 she was his, totally, to have as his own, body and soul. A train whistled in the distance, sending its mournful cry across the night. From somewhere far away came the regular, insistent thud of a giant steam-hammer. The fog from the sea drifted across the sky like an army in disarray. Tattered wisps of cloud obscured the lights from the station. When at last she removed her lips from his, she no longer belonged to herself; she felt she had given herself entirely to him.

He took out the knife and snapped it open. No sooner had he done so than he swore under his breath.

'Damn it!' he said. 'He's gone the other way. We can't do it.'

The shadow on the wall had come within fifty paces of them, had turned to the left and was now walking away with the steady, unhurried gait of the night watchman quietly doing his rounds.

Séverine gave Jacques a push.

'Go on!' she said.

The two of them moved forward, Jacques in front and Séverine behind him. They followed their prey, taking care to make no noise. At one point, as Roubaud went round the corner of the repair shops, they lost sight of him. They cut across a siding and spotted him again, twenty paces in front of them. They hid against every wall they came to, so that he wouldn't see them. One false step would have given them away.

'We're not going to catch him,' Jacques muttered. 'If he gets to the signal box, we've lost him.'

Séverine kept whispering encouragement.

'Come on!' she said. 'Come on!'

Although he was out in the dark, in a huge empty railway yard at the dead of night, Jacques's mind was made up as firmly as if he were quietly lying in wait in a corner of some secluded alleyway. He moved forward quickly but cautiously. His heart was beating fast; he kept telling himself that this murder was perfectly justified, that it was a sensible and legitimate act that had been carefully thought through and properly decided. He was simply exercising a right – the right to live in fact, since Roubaud's death was a prerequisite for his own survival. All he had to do was stab him with the knife and his happiness was assured.

'We're not going to catch him, we're not going to catch him,' he repeated furiously, as he saw the shadow move towards the signal box. 'We've had it. He's going to get away.'

Suddenly, Séverine placed her hand on his arm and held him close. She was trembling.

'Look!' she said. 'He's coming back!'

Roubaud had turned to the right and was coming towards them. If he had any inkling that there had been somebody behind him waiting to pounce on him, it didn't seem to affect him; he continued calmly on his way, carefully making sure that all was in order, and in no hurry to leave until his inspection was complete.

Jacques and Séverine remained standing where they were, without moving. As chance would have it, they had stopped near the edge of one of the coal stacks. They leaned against it, pressing their backs to the wall of coal, as if trying to melt into it and lose themselves in its inky blackness. They hardly dared breathe.

Jacques watched Roubaud as he came towards them. He was now no more than thirty metres away, and every step brought him nearer, like the steady, inexorable pendulum of fate. Another twenty steps, another ten steps, and Roubaud would be in front of him; he would raise his arm thus and plant the knife in his neck, twisting it backwards and forwards to silence his screams. The seconds seemed unending; his head was teeming with so many thoughts
330 that he had lost all sense of time. One by one, his reasons for murdering Roubaud passed through his mind yet again. He saw the murder clearly; he understood both its cause and its consequences. Roubaud was now only five steps away. Jacques's resolve was stretched to breaking point, but he held firm. He had made up his mind to kill and he knew why he was going to do it.

Roubaud was within two steps of him. One step more and . . . Suddenly Jacques's courage abandoned him; his determination collapsed. He couldn't do it. How could he kill a defenceless man? Reasoning alone could never impel someone to murder; something more was needed – the killer instinct, the will to seize the prey, the hunger, the passion maybe, to tear it limb from limb. Conscience was probably no more than a vague assortment of ideas instilled by the slow workings of a centuries-old tradition of justice. Even so, he knew he didn't have the right to kill, and no matter how hard he tried to convince himself, he felt that it was not a right he could assume.

Roubaud walked past, quite undisturbed. His elbow brushed against them as they stood pressing themselves to the stack of coal. If either of them had as much as breathed, Roubaud would have spotted them, but they stood there like corpses. Jacques did not raise his arm and he did not plant the knife in Roubaud's neck. Nothing disturbed the stillness of the night; nothing moved. Roubaud was already ten steps away from them, and they remained motionless, pressed against the coal stack, not daring to breath, terrified of the man who, alone and defenceless, had just calmly walked past them.

Jacques let out a sob of pent-up rage and humiliation. 'I can't do it! I can't do it!' he cried.

He wanted to take Séverine in his arms, to lean against her, to be forgiven and comforted. But without a word she moved aside. He stretched out his hands towards her, only to feel her skirt slip through his fingers as she silently ran **331** away. He started to run after her but quickly realized that it was pointless. To see her rush off like that was more than he could bear. Was it his weakness that had made her so angry? Did she despise him? He had decided it was better not to follow her, but now that he found himself alone in this vast, deserted railway yard, with the yellow lights of the gas lamps scattered across it like tears, he was seized with despair. He rushed back to his room to bury his head in his pillow and erase all the misery of his life from his mind.

About ten days later, towards the end of March, the Roubauds finally won their battle against the Lebleus. The management approved their request. It had had the full support of Monsieur Dabadie, especially as the missing letter from Lebleu, promising to vacate the apartment should it be required by the new assistant stationmaster, had been discovered by Mademoiselle Guichon while looking through the station's files for some old bills.

Madame Lebleu, in her frustration, made a great song and
dance about having to move; the Roubauds were obviously
doing their best to ensure her early demise, so she might
as well move out straight away and have done with it. For
three whole days, while the epoch-making move took
place, the corridor was the scene of feverish activity. Even
little Madame Moulin, normally so shy and unobtrusive,
and hardly ever seen, got herself involved by carrying
Séverine's work-table across to her new apartment. But
it was Philomène who was mainly to blame for the ill feeling that was caused. She was there on the first day,
bundling things together, moving furniture about, and
marching into the apartment at the front even before the
tenants had left. It was Philomène who eventually showed
Madame Lebleu the door, with the furniture from both
apartments still lying jumbled together in the middle of
332 the corridor. Philomène had come to show such an interest
in Jacques and everything he did that Pecqueux had begun
to grow suspicious. One day when he was in one of his
drunken, bullying moods, he had taunted her and asked
her if she was sleeping with Jacques, warning her that if
he ever caught them together they would both live to regret
it. This merely succeeded in increasing her attachment to
Jacques all the more. She acted as their self-appointed
housemaid, looking after both him and his mistress, in
the hope that by serving the two of them she might have
something of him for herself. When she had moved out
the last chair, the doors were slammed shut. She then
noticed that Madame Lebleu had left a stool behind. She
opened the door again and flung it across the corridor.
And that was that.

Slowly life returned to its old routine. Madame Lebleu
sat glued to her armchair by her rheumatism, bored to
death, her eyes full of tears because all she could see out
of her window was the zinc cladding of the station roof,

which shut out the sky. Séverine meanwhile sat at one of the windows at the front, working at her never-ending bed-cover, and looking down at the lively activity of the station forecourt. People and carriages were continually coming and going, the big trees along the pavements were already beginning to turn green with the early spring, and in the distance she could see the wooded slopes of the Ingouville hills, dotted with white summer houses. She was surprised to discover what little pleasure it gave her to finally have her dream come true, to find herself in the apartment she had so jealously coveted, so light and airy and sunny. Madame Simon, her cleaner, was always grumbling and getting annoyed because things weren't in their usual place, and this made Séverine herself sometimes wish she had never left the 'grotty little hovel next door', as she put it, where at least the dirt didn't show as much. As for Roubaud, he simply let things take their course; he didn't even seem to notice that he now lived in a different apartment. He often went to the wrong door and only discovered his mistake when his new key wouldn't fit the lock. He hardly ever came home now, and his general decline continued. He did show brief signs of a recovery when his political sympathies were rekindled. His ideas had always been rather vague and somewhat lukewarm; but he hadn't forgotten his argument with the Sub-Prefect, which had nearly cost him his job. The government had been badly shaken by the general elections[6] and was going through a terrible crisis. Roubaud was cock-a-hoop and went round telling everyone that Napoleon's lot wouldn't be in charge for much longer. His revolutionary comments were overheard by Mademoiselle Guichon, who informed Monsieur Dabadie. Monsieur Dabadie gave Roubaud a friendly warning, and this sufficed to calm him down. Now that the squabbles over accommodation had been settled and people on the corridor were being more friendly towards each other, with Madame Lebleu pining away from distress, why stir things up again over the government and its difficulties? Roubaud simply raised his hands, as much as to say that he couldn't care less about politics, or anything else for that matter. He grew fatter by the day, but it didn't seem to bother him. He plodded about his business and turned his back on the world.

Jacques and Séverine were now free to meet as they wished, but their relationship had become more strained. Nothing stood in the way of their happiness; he could come and see her whenever he liked, using the back staircase so that no one would notice him. The apartment was theirs; he could have slept there if he'd had the effrontery to do so. What caused them to feel so ill at ease with each other and created an insuperable barrier between them was the thought of his failure to accomplish the one thing they both wanted, the thing they had agreed upon and which remained undone. Jacques chided himself for his timidity. Each time he came to see Séverine she was more depressed; she had grown sick of this futile waiting. They no longer attempted to kiss; there was no more to be gained from only half belonging to each other. The happiness they sought lay elsewhere – in another world across the sea, where they could marry and lead a new life.

One evening Jacques found Séverine in tears. When she saw him at the door she wept more bitterly and put her head on his shoulder. She had sometimes cried like this before, but he had always managed to take her in his arms and comfort her. Now, however, the closer he held her to him, the more he felt her succumb to a mounting despair. He was distraught. After a while he took her head in his hands, put his face close to hers and, looking into her tear-filled eyes, he pledged himself to do her will. He knew that the reason for her despair was that she was a woman whose sweet, gentle nature prevented her from doing the deed herself.

'Forgive me,' he said. 'Wait a little longer. I swear that I will do it. Soon. As soon as I can.'

She fastened her lips on his as if to seal his oath. They came together in a profound kiss, uniting their two bodies as one.

Aunt Phasie had suffered a final seizure and had died at nine o'clock on the Thursday evening. Misard had been waiting at her bedside and had tried to close her eyes, but they remained obstinately open. Her neck had stiffened, with her head tilted slightly over one shoulder as if she were looking round the room, and her lips were drawn back in what appeared to be a sardonic grin. On the corner of a table near her bed there burned a single candle. The trains that had been rushing past the house since nine o'clock, totally unaware of the dead woman who was lying there not yet even cold, made the body momentarily shake **336** in the flickering light of the candle as they went by.

In order to get Flore out of the way, Misard had immediately sent her to Doinville to report the death. She wouldn't be back before eleven; he had two hours in front of him. First of all, he calmly cut himself a piece of bread; his stomach felt empty because he hadn't eaten, Aunt Phasie having taken an unconscionably long time to die. He ate standing up, walking backwards and forwards, putting things in their place. Now and then he would be seized by a fit of coughing that bent him double. He was half-dead himself, as thin as a bone, with no strength left in him and the colour gone from his hair. It looked as though his final victory would be very short-lived. But it didn't worry him. He had destroyed her. She had been a fine, handsome, healthy woman, and he'd eaten her life away, as woodworm eats away oak! There she lay – on her back, finished, reduced to nothing! And he was still alive! A thought suddenly occurred to him; he knelt down and took a pan from under the bed containing some bran-water that had been prepared as an enema. Ever since she had begun to suspect he was trying to kill her, Misard had been putting the rat poison into her enemas rather than mixing it with the salt.[1] This was something that had never occurred to her; she should have had more sense. She had taken the poison without knowing it, and this time it had finished her off. Having emptied the pan outside, he came back and mopped down the bedroom floor to remove the stains. Why had she been so stubborn? She had thought she could outwit him! Well, serve her right! When husband and wife are secretly trying to see each other into the grave, you need to keep your eyes open. He chuckled to himself. It amused him to think of her unknowingly imbibing poison through her bottom while being so careful to watch what went into her mouth. Just then an express went by, shaking the house like a rushing wind. Although this was a regular occurrence, Misard jumped and turned towards the window. Ah, yes, he thought, the never-ending stream! All those people! They came from far and wide, all in such a hurry to get wherever it was they were going, and all of them either oblivious or indifferent to anything they trampled underfoot on their way. In the deep silence that settled on the house after the train had gone by, Misard caught sight of the dead woman's eyes, staring at him, wide open. Their fixed gaze seemed to be watching his every movement, and the corners of her mouth were turned up in a mocking sneer.

Misard, who normally never let things bother him, suddenly found himself feeling annoyed. He could hear her saying to him, 'Go on, start looking!' One thing was certain; she hadn't taken her money with her, and now that she was dead, he would eventually find it. She should have given it to him and not made such a fuss about it; it would have saved him a lot of trouble. The eyes followed him everywhere. 'Go on,' she was saying, 'start looking!' He had never dared search the bedroom while she had been

alive. He glanced round it. He would try the cupboard
first. He took the keys from under her pillow, rummaged
through the shelves of linen, emptied the two drawers
and even took them out to see if there was a hiding place
behind them. There was nothing! Next he turned his attention to the bedside table. He removed the marble top and
turned it over. Again, nothing! He looked behind the mirror above the mantelpiece, a little mirror bought at a fair
and fixed to the wall by two nails. He poked behind it with
a flat ruler, but only succeeded in dislodging an accumula-
tion of black fluff. 'Go on, keep looking!' In order to avoid
the staring eyes that he felt were watching him, he got
down on his hands and knees and went round the room
tapping the floor with his knuckles, listening for a hollow
sound that might indicate a space beneath. Several tiles
were loose, and he pulled them up. Nothing! Still nothing!
338 When he got back to his feet, the eyes were still staring at
him; he turned round and tried to stare back into the
unblinking gaze of the corpse. The corners of her lips had
now retracted further, emphasizing her horrible grin. He
felt sure she was mocking him. 'Go on,' she was saying,
'keep looking!' By now he had worked himself up into a
frenzy. He went up to her; a vague suspicion had entered
his mind. What he was contemplating was nothing short
of sacrilege and made him turn even paler than he already
was. How could he be sure she had not taken her money
with her? Perhaps she had! Shamelessly, he drew back the
sheets, undressed her and inspected the bends of her arms
and legs. She had told him to keep looking, so he looked.
He felt underneath her, behind her neck and the small of
her back. He pulled off the bedclothes and thrust his arm
full length inside the straw mattress. He found nothing.
'Keep looking! Keep looking!' The head had fallen back
on to the pillow, which lay where he had left it, and continued to stare at him derisively.

Misard was shaking with anger. As he was trying to rearrange the bed, in walked Flore, having completed her errand in Doinville.

'It's arranged for the day after tomorrow,' she said. 'Saturday, at eleven.'

She was referring to the funeral. A single glance was enough to tell her what Misard had been spending his energy on while she'd been away. She raised her hands in a gesture of indifference and contempt.

'Why don't you just give up?' she said. 'You'll never find it.'

Misard imagined that she too was defying him. He went up to her.

'She's given it to you, hasn't she?' he muttered between clenched teeth. 'You know where it is, don't you?'

Flore merely shrugged her shoulders. The idea that her mother could have given her thousand francs to someone else, even to her, her own daughter, was laughable.

'Given it to me!' she said. 'You must be joking! She's got rid of it, that's for sure. It's out there somewhere, buried in the ground. You'll just have to keep looking for it.'

With a broad sweep of her hand she indicated the house, the garden with its well, the railway line and the open countryside beyond. The money was out there, buried in a hole, somewhere where no one would ever find it. Misard was beside himself. Once again he began frantically moving furniture about and tapping on the walls, not in the least bothered that Flore was still in the room. She went over to the window.

'How lovely it is outside!' she whispered. 'Such a beautiful night! I walked fast. With all those stars shining, it's as light as day! What a fine day it will be tomorrow when the sun comes up!'

For a moment she remained standing at the window, looking out at the tranquil countryside, softened by the first warm days of April. Her walk had reopened the wound in her heart and had left her feeling pensive and sad. But when she heard Misard walk out of the room and start moving furniture about in other parts of the house, she went over to the bed and sat looking at her mother. The candle was still burning on the bedside table with a long, steady flame. A train went by, shaking the house.

Flore had decided she would stay beside her mother through the night. She began to ponder. The sight of the dead woman took her mind off an idea that had haunted her for some time, an idea she had been turning over and over in her head beneath the starry skies, in the stillness of the night, all the way back from Doinville. There was something that puzzled her, and for a while it stopped her thinking about her own troubles: why hadn't she felt more upset at the death of her mother? Why, even now, wasn't she weeping? It was true that she had never spoken much to her; she was a law unto herself, and preferred to be out on her own, roaming the countryside the minute she was off duty. Even so she had been genuinely fond of her. During her final illness she had come and sat beside her a score of times, begging her to call a doctor. She was sure that Misard was up to no good and hoped that a doctor might frighten him off. But all she ever got from her sick mother was an angry 'no', as if she prided herself on accepting help from no one in her battle against her husband, a battle she was certain of winning whatever the outcome, since she was going to take her money with her. And so Flore had not insisted; she was too absorbed in her own troubles. She spent most of her time pacing furiously about the countryside in an attempt to forget her sorrows. It must have been this that stopped her weeping for her mother; when the heart is already heavy-laden, it has no room for further grief. Her mother had gone. She looked at her as she lay on the bed, pale and lifeless. Try as she might, she could not make herself feel any sadder. What was the point of calling the police and accusing Misard, since her world was about to collapse? Her eyes remained fixed on the body, but she no longer saw it. Slowly, inescapably, she was drawn back into the private realm of her own thoughts, and the idea which had planted itself in her brain took hold of her once again. All she felt was the violent rattle of the trains, marking the hours as they hurtled past.

In the distance she heard the rumble of an approaching stopping train from Paris. When the engine's headlamp eventually passed in front of the window, the room was lit up as if by a flash of lightning or a sudden burst of flame.

'Eighteen minutes past one,' she thought. 'Another seven hours! They will pass here at sixteen minutes past eight, tomorrow morning.'

For the past few months, waiting for this particular train once a week had become an obsession. She knew that the Friday-morning express was always driven by Jacques and that it would also be carrying Séverine, on her weekly trip to Paris. She was consumed with jealousy; all week long she waited for the moment the train went by, when she could look out for them and see them, and picture them in Paris, happy in each other's arms. How she hated seeing the train fly past, wishing she could cling on to the last carriage and be carried away to Paris herself! It seemed to her as if the wheels of the train were cutting her heart to pieces. She felt so hurt that one night she had hidden herself in her room to write to the police. If she could get this woman arrested, her troubles would be at an end. She had once seen Séverine at La Croix-de-Maufras and knew that she had been one of Grandmorin's mistresses. All she had to do was inform the authorities, and Séverine would be brought to trial. When she attempted to put pen to paper, however, the words wouldn't come. She wondered whether the police would even listen to her. These high-up people were all in it together. She might well end up being put in prison herself, as had happened to Cabuche. No! If she sought revenge, she would do it on her own; she needed help from no one. Flore thought of revenge not as it was usually understood – hurting someone in order to remedy the hurt done to oneself – but as a final solution, a cataclysm, in which all was destroyed as if by lightning. She was a proud girl, physically stronger and more handsome than her rival, and was convinced that she had as much right to be loved as her. On her solitary excursions into the wild countryside near by, her long blonde hair flying freely in the wind, she wished she could take hold of her and settle the dispute like two maiden warriors, face to face in the depths of a forest. She had never been taken by a man. She was a match for any of them. She was indomitable. Victory would always be hers.

342   The idea had suddenly occurred to her the week before; it had struck her like a bolt from the blue. In order to stop them going past her house every week, in order to stop them going to Paris together, she must kill them. It was not something she had thought out; it was simply a crude, instinctive urge to get rid of them. When she had a thorn stuck in her finger she pulled it out; she would have cut her finger off if she'd had to. She must kill them. She must kill them the next time they went past. She must wreck the train, drag a beam of wood across the track, lift one of the rails, smash everything to pieces, destroy it. Jacques would be driving the locomotive; he couldn't get off it. He would be crushed. His mistress always travelled in the leading carriage in order to be close to him; so she wouldn't escape either. As for everyone else, the never-ending stream of passengers, she didn't even give them a thought. They meant nothing to her; she didn't know them. This train crash, and the sacrifice of so many lives, had become a waking obsession. Only a catastrophe on this scale,

involving so much loss of life and human suffering, could possibly ease the enormous ache in her heart and assuage the tears she had shed.

On the Friday morning, however, her resolve had weakened; she was unable to decide where and how she was going to lift a rail. That evening, after she had finished duty for the day, another idea occurred to her. She walked through the tunnel and out to the Dieppe junction. She often came this way. The tunnel was a good half-league long, a vaulted passageway, completely straight. It excited her to see the trains coming towards her with their blinding headlamps; she was nearly run over every time. It must have been the sense of danger that attracted her, a need to do something reckless. This evening, however, having managed to avoid being seen by the night watchman, she had walked half-way through the tunnel, keeping to the left so that she could be sure that any train coming towards her would pass on her right, when she foolishly turned round to watch the tail-lights of a train for Le Havre. As she set off again, she had tripped, which forced her to turn round on herself a second time, with the result that she could no longer tell in which direction the red lights had been travelling. Her head was still spinning from the noise of the wheels. Bold as she was, she dared not move; she was so frightened that her hands went cold and her hair stood on end. She realized that, when another train went past, she wouldn't know whether it was an up train or a down train; she might throw herself to the right or to the left and could be cut to pieces. She tried desperately to hold on to her reason, to remember, to think it through. But she was suddenly overcome with panic and ran forward blindly, frantically, into the darkness before her. She must not allow herself to be killed until she had killed the two she most hated. Her feet stumbled over the rails; she kept slipping and falling to the ground as she tried to run faster and faster. She felt as if she were going mad; the tunnel walls seemed to be closing in around her, the vaulted roof re-echoed with imaginary noises, fearful cries and horrible groans. She kept looking behind her, thinking she could feel the hot steam from a locomotive on her neck. Twice she was convinced she had made a mistake; she was running in the wrong direction and would be killed. She turned and ran the other way. She ran on and on. In front of her in the distance appeared a star, a shining eye, which was growing bigger and bigger. She steeled herself against the temptation to turn yet again and run the other way. The eye had grown to an incandescent ball, a savage mouth of flame. Without knowing what she was doing, she had leaped blindly to her left. The train thundered past, and a great gust of wind blew around her. Five minutes later she walked out of the Malaunay end of the tunnel, safe and **344** sound.[2]

It was nine o'clock. The express from Paris would be there in a few minutes. She walked steadily on towards the junction for Dieppe two hundred metres ahead, look-ing carefully along the track for something that might serve her purpose. It so happened that the line to Dieppe was being repaired. Her friend Ozil had just changed the points for a ballast train[3] to run on to the branch line, and it was waiting there. In a sudden flash of inspiration, she hit upon an idea. All she had to do was prevent the signal-man from changing the points back to the Le Havre line, so that the express would crash into the ballast train. Ever since Ozil had tried to take Flore by force and she had nearly cracked his skull open with a stick, she had remained quite fond of him and liked to turn up on him unexpect-edly, scampering through the tunnel like a goat running down from its mountain. Ozil was an ex-soldier, very thin and rather taciturn; he was completely dedicated to his job and so far had an impeccable record, keeping watch day and night. But there was something about Flore that attracted him. Her ways were strange, she had the strength of a man and had once given him a thrashing; yet she only had to lift her little finger and he would come running. Even though he was fourteen years older than her, he still desired her and had sworn he would have her; since force had not succeeded, he had decided he would bide his time and be nice to her. When she came up to his cabin in the dark and called to him to come outside, he left what he was doing and joined her straight away. She led him off towards the fields, trying to distract him with a long, involved account of how her mother was very ill and how she would leave La Croix-de-Maufras if she died. All the time, she was listening to the sound of the express in the distance, as it left Malaunay and sped towards them. When she thought the train had reached the junction, she turned to watch. What she had not taken into account was the new **345** interlocking warning system. As the express ran on to the Dieppe branch line, it automatically set the signal at red,[4] and the driver had been able to bring it to a halt a few metres short of the ballast train. Ozil let out a cry as if he had woken up to find his house falling down on top of him and ran back to his cabin. Flore stood in the dark, stiff and motionless, watching as the express was reversed back on to the main line. Two days later, the signalman had called to say goodbye to her. He was being transferred. He still had no idea that Flore had planned a train crash. He asked her to come and see him again once her mother had died. Ah well, she thought, her plan hadn't worked. She would have to think of something else.

Suddenly, as she recalled this incident, the dreamy mist that floated before her eyes lifted and there in front of her, in the yellow light of the candle flame, she once again saw the dead woman. Her mother was no more. Should she leave and marry Ozil? He wanted her and might make her happy. But her whole being rejected the idea. If she was such a coward that she allowed Jacques and Séverine to go on living, and went on living herself, she would sooner become a tramp or hire herself out as a servant than belong to a man she didn't love. She heard a strange noise and turned to listen. It was Misard breaking up the earthen floor of the kitchen with a mattock. He was so desperate to get his hands on the hidden treasure that he would have torn the whole house apart. Flore had no desire to continue living with Misard either. What was she to do? There was a sudden rush of wind, the walls of the house shook, and the glow from the firebox of a passing train moved across the dead woman's white face, making her staring eyes and the sneering grin on her lips turn blood-red. It was the last stopping train from Paris, making its slow, laborious progress towards Le Havre.

346   Flore turned to gaze at the stars twinkling in the stillness of the spring night.

'Ten minutes past three! In another five hours it will be their train going past.'

The thought pained her. She must do something to stop them. Seeing them every week on their way to make love was more than she could bear. She couldn't stand it. Now that she knew she would never have Jacques to herself, she would rather he no longer existed; she would rather that nothing existed any more. This gloomy bedroom, where she sat watching over her mother, filled her with a sense of loss, and a growing longing that everything might be swept clean away. As there was no longer anyone in the world who loved her, everyone else might as well end their days along with her mother. More people were going to die – many more. They would all be taken in one fell swoop. But what was she to do? Her sister was dead, her mother was dead, and her love was at an end. She was alone. Whether she stayed or left, she would always be alone, whereas they would have each other. No! She would put an end to everything. Even now, sitting in that dismal room, she was in the presence of death. Death would lie in wait beside the railway line, ready for the moment of retribution!

Having finally taken her decision, she began to consider how she could put her plan into action. She came back to the idea of removing a section of the track. It seemed the most practical solution; it was certain to work and would be easy to do. She simply needed to knock the keys out of the rail-chairs with a hammer and pull the rail off the sleepers. She had the tools, and in such a deserted spot no one would see her. The best place would be at the far end of the cutting, towards Barentin, where the line was on a curve and crossed a valley on an embankment, seven or eight metres high. The train would come off the rails and crash down the side of the embankment. But the timing was crucial and would not be easy. The express from Le Havre came past on the up line at sixteen minutes past eight. The only train before that was a stopping train at seven fifty-five. This gave her twenty minutes to do what she had to, which was ample. Between the trains that were timetabled, however, they often sent out an unscheduled goods train, especially when the goods depot was busy. If that happened, her efforts would all have been in vain. How could she make sure that it was the express that crashed? For a long time she sat weighing up the possibilities. Outside it was still dark. She had not trimmed the candle; the wick had become charred and burned with a long, sooty flame.

Misard returned just as a goods train from Rouen was approaching. He had been searching through the woodpile, and his hands were filthy. He was out of breath, and furious at having found nothing. In his impotent frenzy he once more started looking under the furniture, in the chimney, everywhere. The goods train came slowly clanking past; it seemed as if it would never end. The wheels let out a series of heavy thuds as the train rolled by, each one sending a jolt through the house that shook the dead woman as she lay on her bed. As Misard stretched out his arm to take a little picture from the wall, he once again met the staring eyes, watching him. The grinning lips moved.

He went pale and shivered with a mixture of fear and anger.

'I know what you're saying!' he muttered. '"Keep looking!" You'll see! I'll find it, damn you! Even if I have to take the house apart stone by stone and dig up the whole neighbourhood!'

The goods train had finally gone past and was rumbling slowly away into the night. The dead woman had stopped moving but continued to look at her husband; a look of such scorn and triumph that he once again walked from the room, without closing the door behind him.

Misard had interrupted Flore in the middle of her reflections. She stood up and closed the door. She didn't want him coming back again and disturbing her mother. Suddenly, to her own amazement, she heard herself saying: 'Ten minutes before will be enough.'

It would only take ten minutes to lift the rail. If no other train had been signalled ten minutes before the express was due, she could go ahead. Once she had taken her decision and knew what she was going to do, her anxiety left her and she became quite calm.

Day dawned at about five o'clock, fresh and perfectly clear. Although it was still quite chilly, she pulled the window wide open. The sweet morning air streamed into the gloomy bedroom, blowing away the candle smoke and the sickly smell of death. The sun was still below the horizon, behind a clump of trees on top of a hill. Suddenly it rose into the sky, in a splash of crimson, spilling down the hillside and flooding the sunken lanes and by-ways, as the earth rejoiced at the yearly return of spring. She had known it the night before; it was going to be a fine morning, a morning bursting with youth and radiant health, a morning that makes one feel glad to be alive. How good it would be to be out there, free to go where she wished, walking along untrodden pathways, wandering over hill and dale. She turned from the window and came back to the middle of the room. She noticed with surprise that the candle was almost out, flickering in the broad light of day, like a pale tear. The dead woman now seemed to be looking out at the railway line as the trains went by, without noticing the pallid glow from the candle beside her.

Flore only worked during daylight hours, so she didn't leave the bedroom until twelve minutes past six, for the stopping train to Paris. At six o'clock Misard had also gone to relieve his colleague, who had been on night duty. When Flore heard him sound his horn, she came and took up her position in front of the gate, holding her flag. She watched the train as it went by.

'Another two hours!' she said to herself.

Her mother had no further need of anyone, and the thought of going back into the bedroom sickened her. It was all over; she had kissed her mother goodbye and could now dispose of her own life and of everyone else's. Usually between trains she would wander off on her own, but this morning something seemed to be holding her back. She remained at her position near the gate, sitting on a bench, a simple plank beside the line. The sun was rising over the distant horizon, shedding its golden warmth into the pure air like a shower of rain. She did not move, content to sit there, bathed in the sun's gentle radiance, with the open countryside all around her, quivering with the approach of spring. For a while she watched Misard in his wooden hut on the other side of the line; he was visibly agitated, and quite unlike his usual sleepy self. He kept darting in and out of his hut, fiddling with the controls on his receiver and continually looking towards the house as if his mind were still there, looking for the money. But she soon forgot about him, and after a while she was no longer aware that he was there. She was waiting for something, concentrating, silent and tense, her eyes fixed on the railway line in the distance, towards Barentin. Out of that shimmering haze of sunlight would appear the vision that her wild eyes so eagerly anticipated.

The minutes went by. Flore did not move. Eventually, at seven fifty-five, when Misard sounded two blasts on his horn for the stopping train from Le Havre on the up line, she got to her feet, closed the gate and stood in front of it, holding her flag. The train went by, shaking the ground beneath it, and quickly vanished into the distance; she heard it plunge into the tunnel, and the noise suddenly stopped. She didn't return to her bench but remained standing where she was, once more starting to count the minutes. If, in ten minutes' time, no goods train had been signalled, she would run down through the cutting and take up a rail. She remained very calm, feeling only a certain tightness in her chest, as if the enormity of what she was about to do bore down upon her. But the thought that Jacques and Séverine were coming nearer and nearer and that, unless she stopped them, they would once again rush past her towards their lovers' tryst strengthened her resolve as the moment approached. Her mind was made up; there would be no turning back. The decision was beyond recall. Like the wolf lashing out with its claws, she was blind and deaf to persuasion. All she saw, in her selfish desire for revenge, were two mutilated bodies. The other passengers didn't enter her head – the nameless crowd of travellers that had been passing her window every day for years. She didn't know them. There would be deaths and there would be bloodshed. Perhaps the sun would hide its face in shame. Its warmth and brightness had begun to irritate her.

Two minutes more, one minute more, and she would be on her way. As she turned to go, she heard the sound of a wagon trundling down the road from Brécourt. It's someone from the quarry, she thought. They'll want to get across. I'll have to open the gate and stop for a chat. I'll be stuck here. I'll miss my chance. Without giving it a further thought, she turned and ran, leaving her post unattended. The driver and his wagon would have to fend for themselves. But she heard the crack of a whip in the still morning air and a voice cheerfully calling her name. It was Cabuche. She stopped in her tracks, in front of the gate.

'What's up?' said Cabuche. 'Having a nap in the sunshine, were you? Hurry up! I want to get across before the express comes!'

Flore felt everything collapsing around her. Her plan was ruined. Jacques and Séverine would be in each other's arms again. She could do nothing to stop them. She slowly opened the gate. It was old and falling apart and squeaked on its rusty iron hinges. She was desperately trying to think of something, some object that she could throw across the rails. She would have lain across the line herself, had she thought her bones were hard enough to make the engine jump the track. Suddenly she caught sight of the wagon, a heavy, low-slung cart laden with two blocks of stone, attached to five strong horses that were having considerable difficulty in pulling it. The stones were just what she needed – two massive lumps of rock, big enough to block the whole line. Her eyes lit up; she had a sudden, mad desire to seize hold of them and place them on the crossing. The gate was wide open and the five horses stood blowing

clouds of steam from their nostrils, waiting to move
forward.

'What's the matter with you this morning?' called Cabuche. 'You're in a funny mood.'

'My mother died last night,' she told him, when at last
she could bring herself to speak.

Cabuche felt really sorry for her.

'My poor Flore!' he said, putting his whip down and
taking her hands in his. 'You said you'd been expecting it
for some time. But that doesn't make it any easier, does it?
If she's in the house I'd like to see her. We could have been
friends if it hadn't been for what happened to Louisette.'

He slowly accompanied her towards the house. As he
reached the door he turned to look at his horses. She
quickly reassured him.

'Don't worry,' she said. 'They're not going to move. The
352 express is still a long way off.'

She was lying to him. Above the gentle whisperings of
the countryside, her practised ear had heard the train leaving Barentin. In another five minutes it would be there,
leaving the cutting, a hundred metres from the level crossing. As Cabuche stood in her mother's bedroom, deep in
thought and moved to tears as he remembered Louisette,
Flore remained outside by the window, listening to the
steady bark of the engine's exhaust as the train drew nearer
and nearer. Suddenly, she thought of Misard; he must have
seen her and he would try to stop her. She turned to look.
It was as if something had struck her in the chest; he was
not at his post! She found him at the back of the house,
digging up the earth round the well. Not for a minute could
he give up his crazy search. He must have suddenly decided
that that was where the money was. He was completely
absorbed in his labours, totally unaware of anything else,
digging and digging for all he was worth. Flore needed no
further encouragement. Things were falling into place of

their own accord. One of the horses started to neigh as the train approached the far end of the cutting, hissing and wheezing like someone running towards them in a hurry.

'I'll see to them,' said Flore. 'Leave it to me.'

She ran over to them, took the leading horse by the bit and pulled it forward with all the strength she could muster. The horses took the strain. The wagon with its enormous load rocked from side to side but remained where it was. Flore pulled on the harness herself, as if she were an extra horse. The wagon moved forward over the crossing. It was half-way across when the express emerged from the cutting one hundred metres away. In order to stop the wagon and prevent it from clearing the track, Flore seized hold of the harness and, with a superhuman effort that made her limbs crack, she held the horses back. She was an exceptionally strong woman; her feats of strength were legendary – stopping a wagon as it ran down 353 an incline, pushing a cart from in front of an oncoming train. And now there she was, single-handed, holding back five horses with a grip of iron, as they reared and snorted in terror.

It all happened in less than ten seconds. But it seemed an eternity. The two great stones seemed to block out the horizon. The locomotive came gliding out of the beautiful, golden sunrise, moving smoothly forward at great speed, its gleaming brass and polished steel glinting in the sun. The crash was now inevitable; nothing on earth could prevent it. The moment seemed to last for ever.

Misard had run back to his position as fast as he could. He was screaming and waving his hands in the air, in a desperate attempt to warn the train and get it to stop. Cabuche had heard the wheels of the train hammering on the track and the horses neighing with fright and he too rushed out of the house, shouting at the top of his voice to get the animals to move forward. But Flore, who had by now jumped clear, held him back, which saved his life. Cabuche imagined that she hadn't been able to control the horses, and that it was they who had dragged her forward on to the line. He thought that he was to blame and sobbed uncontrollably, choking with fear and desperation. Flore, however, remained motionless, standing upright, staring, her eyes ablaze, watching intently. Just as the front of the locomotive was about to hit the blocks of stone, when it was perhaps only a metre away, in one split second she clearly saw Jacques, with his hand on the reversing wheel. He turned round, and their eyes met in a look that seemed to Flore never-ending.

That morning Jacques had greeted Séverine with a smile as she came down to the platform at Le Havre to catch the express, which she did every week. Why let his troubles ruin his whole life? Why not enjoy the good days, when he had the chance? Perhaps everything would come right in the end. He was determined to enjoy today at least and had been thinking of how they might spend their time together; perhaps he could take her to lunch in a restaurant. So when she had pulled a long face because there wasn't a first-class carriage at the front of the train and she would have to sit further back, away from him, he had tried to cheer her up by giving her a bright smile. They would still arrive together in Paris and could make up for being separated when they got there. He was in such good spirits, in fact, that, as he leaned out to watch her get into a compartment at the far end of the train, he even had a dig at Henri Dauvergne, the principal guard, who he knew had his eye on her. The previous week, Jacques had had the impression that Dauvergne was being more forward than usual and that Séverine, in need of some distraction that might take her mind off the wretched situation she found herself in, had begun to encourage him. Roubaud had already said that something like this would happen – that she would end up sleeping with Dauvergne, not because she was attracted to him but because she fancied doing something different. Jacques asked Dauvergne who he'd been blowing kisses to the night before from behind one of the elm trees in the station forecourt. Pecqueux, who was shovelling coal on to the fire and getting *La Lison* ready to leave, roared with laughter.

From Le Havre to Barentin the express had travelled at its usual speed, with no undue incident. It was Henri who first spotted the wagon across the line from his lookout post in the guard's van as the train came out of the cutting. The guard's van, at the front of the train, was full of luggage, for the train was carrying a shipload of passengers who had disembarked from a liner the night before. The guard was standing at his desk in what little space was left, sorting out his paperwork, surrounded by piles of trunks and suitcases that swayed backwards and forwards with the motion of the train. His little bottle of ink, suspended from a nail, swung constantly to and fro. Every time the train stopped and luggage was unloaded, the guard had to spend four or five minutes filling in forms. Two passengers had just got off at Barentin; he had finished putting his papers in order and had climbed up to sit at his lookout, glancing quickly along the line in both directions as he always did. When he wasn't otherwise engaged, he always sat in his glass observation box, keeping an eye on the line ahead. He couldn't see the driver because he was hidden from view by the tender, but because of his elevated position he could often see further ahead and spot things more quickly than the driver could. The train was still rounding the bend in the cutting when he saw the obstruction in front of them. It came as such a shock that at first he couldn't believe his eyes and sat there motionless, petrified. A few valuable seconds were lost; the train was already out of the cutting and there were loud cries coming from the footplate when he finally managed to pull the cord of the alarm bell that dangled in front of him.

Jacques at that crucial moment was in a world of his own, standing with his hand on the reversing wheel, gazing into space and dreaming of vague, faraway things. He had even for a moment stopped thinking about Séverine. He was brought to his senses by the frantic ringing of the bell and a loud scream from Pecqueux just behind him. Pecqueux had raised the damper in the ash-box because he didn't think the fire was drawing properly and had leaned out to check the speed. It was then that he had seen what lay ahead. And now Jacques saw too. He saw everything and knew what was about to happen. He went deathly pale. The wagon lay across the track. The train was hurtling towards it. There was going to be a terrible crash. He saw it clearly and sharply. He could even make out the grain on the two blocks of stone. Already in his bones he could feel the shock of the collision. It could not be avoided. He frantically turned the reversing wheel, shut off steam and applied the brakes.[5] He put the engine into reverse and leaned out of the cab, tugging desperately at the whistle in the frenzied and forlorn hope that the warning might be heard and the fearsome obstacle removed. The whistle gave out a long, agonized wail of distress that rent the air. But *La Lison* was not responding; she simply ran on ahead, hardly slowing down at all. She was no longer the willing creature she once had been. Since the blizzard, she hadn't steamed as well and was not as quick off the mark; she had become temperamental and crotchety, like a woman who had caught a cold on her chest and had suddenly aged. She let out steam and shuddered as Jacques applied the brake. But there was no stopping her; she was carried forward under the powerful impetus of her own weight. Pecqueux, in sheer terror, leaped from the footplate. Jacques stood stiffly at the controls, his right hand on the reversing wheel and the other, without him realizing it, still pulling at the whistle, waiting for the worst. *La Lison*, in a cloud of steam and smoke, her whistle still screaming wildly, crashed into the wagon with the full weight of the thirteen carriages she drew behind her.[6]

Twenty metres away, standing beside the track, transfixed with horror, Misard and Cabuche, their arms in the air, and Flore, her eyes starting from her head, watched the catastrophe unfold. They saw the train being flung upwards, seven carriages piling on top of each other and then, with a sickening crash, falling back into a twisted mass of wreckage. The three leading carriages were reduced to nothing. Four others lay in a tangled heap of torn-off roofs, broken wheels, carriage doors, couplings, buffers and pieces of broken glass. They had heard the locomotive crash into the stones, a dull crunching sound **357** followed by a scream of agony. *La Lison* was completely crushed and had been thrown to the left on top of the wagon. The stones had been split apart and filled the air with a cloud of splinters as if they had been blasted from a quarry. Of the five horses, four had been knocked off their feet, dragged along the ground and killed outright. The rest of the train, a further six carriages, was still intact and had come to a stop without even leaving the rails.

People began to shout. There were calls for help, which tailed off into inarticulate cries of pain.

'Help me! Save me! Oh God, I'm dying! Help! Help!'

There was a confusion of sounds and it was impossible to see. *La Lison* had fallen over on to her back, with her underside to the air. Steam came gushing from open valves and broken pipes with a fierce hiss, like the dying gasps of an angry giant. Dense clouds of white vapour swirled across the ground. Burning coal spilled from the firebox, like blood pouring from her belly, filling the air with a pall of black smoke. The force of the impact had buried her chimney in the ground; the chassis was broken where it had taken the shock, and both side frames were bent. She lay with her wheels in the air, like a monstrous steed that has been gored by some savage beast, displaying her twisted coupling-rods, her broken cylinders, and her shattered piston rods and valve gear to the sky, like a hideous gaping wound through which her life ebbed away with groans of anger and despair. Beside her lay the horse that had not been killed; its two front legs had been ripped off and, like her, its innards were spilling out through an open gash in its belly. It was straining its head forward, straight and rigid, in a hideous contortion of pain; they could see it gasping and screaming pitifully, but above the terrible noise that came from the dying locomotive, no sound reached their ears.

358 Strangled cries filled the air, but they went unheard and were carried away on the breeze.

'Help me! Kill me! I can't stand the pain! Kill me! Please kill me!'

Amid the deafening noise and blinding smoke, the doors of the undamaged carriages had begun to open, and crowds of passengers were leaping in panic from the train. They fell in a heap on to the railway line, got to their feet and started kicking and punching each other in order to disentangle themselves. As soon as they felt solid ground beneath their feet and saw open countryside in front of them, they made off as fast as their legs would carry them, leaping over the hedge and running across the fields, intent on one thing only – to get out of danger, to get as far away as possible. Women and men alike ran screaming into the woods.

Séverine, having been trodden underfoot, her hair undone and her dress torn to shreds, eventually managed to free herself. Without a thought for her own safety she ran along the train towards the hissing locomotive. Suddenly she came face to face with Pecqueux.

'Jacques! Jacques!' she cried. 'Is he safe?'

The fireman had miraculously come to no harm; he hadn't even sprained an ankle. He too was running towards the engine, feeling sick at the thought of his driver lying beneath the wreckage. The two men had worked on the footplate together for so long, driving their train through storm and tempest! And now their locomotive, their poor locomotive, the much-loved lady in their *ménage à trois*, lay on her back, a complete wreck, breathing her last!

'I jumped off,' he stammered. 'I don't know anything! Come on, we must get there quick!'

As they ran forward they bumped into Flore. She had seen them coming. She was standing in the same place as before, astonished at what she had accomplished. This massacre was of her making! She had done it! And she had **359** done it well! Her only feeling was of a need fulfilled. She felt no remorse for the suffering she had caused; it didn't affect her. But when she recognized Séverine, her eyes opened wide, and an expression of intense pain darkened her face. How could it be that this woman was still alive when Jacques was certainly dead? She had murdered her love. She had driven a knife into her own heart. In her torment she suddenly realized the enormity of her crime. She had done this! She had killed Jacques! She had killed all these people! She let out a great scream and ran madly up and down, wringing her hands.

'Jacques! Oh, Jacques!' she cried. 'He's under there! I saw him! He was thrown backwards! Jacques! Jacques!'

The noise from the engine had begun to subside. All that came from her now was a pathetic, dying wheeze that grew steadily weaker and above which could be heard the cries of the injured, getting louder and louder. Thick smoke still blew everywhere, and the huge pile of wreckage from which these cries of pain and terror issued seemed to be cloaked in an immovable layer of black dust that the sun could not penetrate. What were they to do? Where should they start? How could they get to all these people in distress?

Flore continued to cry out for Jacques.

'I tell you he looked at me,' she shouted. 'He was thrown over there, under the tender. Quick! Come and help me!'

Cabuche and Misard had been offering assistance to Henri, the guard, who had also jumped out at the last minute. He had dislocated his foot. They sat him down on the ground against the hedge, where he watched the rescue operations in stunned silence, apparently unhurt.

'Cabuche! Come over here!' yelled Flore. 'Jacques is under here, I tell you!'

Cabuche didn't hear. He had run off to see to some of the other injured passengers and came back carrying a young woman, both of her legs hanging limp, broken at the thigh.

Séverine had heard Flore calling to Cabuche and ran over to join her.

'Jacques! Jacques!' she cried. 'Where is he? Let me help you!'

'Come on then!' yelled Flore. 'He's over here.'

The two women joined hands and started tugging at a broken wheel. Séverine's dainty fingers were of little use, but Flore simply grabbed hold of things and pulled them aside.

'Careful!' shouted Pecqueux, who had come to join them.

He had put out his hand to prevent Séverine from treading on an arm, torn off at the shoulder and still wearing a blue sleeve. She recoiled in horror. She didn't recognize the sleeve, and there was no knowing who the arm belonged to; it had just rolled there. No doubt the body would be found somewhere else. It made her feel so shaky that she could hardly move; she stood there weeping and watching the others struggling with the wreckage. She couldn't even bring herself to pick up bits of broken glass lest she cut her hands.

The rescue work and the search for bodies became even more desperate and fraught with danger when the fire from the engine began to spread to other pieces of wood. In order to contain the blaze it was necessary to shovel earth on to the flames. Someone ran to Barentin to ask for help, and a telegraph message was sent to Rouen. Meanwhile, everyone bravely set about helping to clear the wreckage. Many of those who had run away had come back, apologizing for having been so scared. Work progressed slowly and cautiously. Every piece of wreckage had to be removed with great care; if it all collapsed, the unfortunate people trapped underneath would be killed. Some **361** of the injured were buried up to their chest, unable to move as if held in a vice, screaming. The rescuers spent a quarter of an hour trying to free one of them. He was as white as a sheet but didn't complain; he said he wasn't in pain and that he was all right. When they got him out, he had lost both legs; he died immediately. He had been so frightened that he didn't realize he had been so terribly mutilated and he hadn't felt a thing. An entire family was rescued from a second-class carriage which had caught fire; the father and mother had both injured their knees, and the grandmother had broken her arm. They too felt no pain, but were weeping and calling out to their daughter, who had disappeared in the crash, a little girl hardly three years old with beautiful blonde hair. They found her underneath a shorn-off carriage roof, safe and sound, laughing, and apparently quite happy. They found another girl, however, covered in blood, and with both her hands crushed. They moved her to one side while someone went to look for her parents; and there she waited all alone. No one knew her name; she was so distraught that she couldn't speak, and froze in sheer terror the moment anyone went near her. The carriage doors couldn't be opened because the locks had been jammed by the shock of the collision; they had to get in through the broken windows. Within a very short time, four bodies had been placed in a row at the side of the track. Ten or so injured passengers lay on the ground beside them, waiting for help, but there was no doctor to dress their injuries, and no one to treat them. The work of clearing the wreckage had hardly begun. They found a new victim under every piece of debris they lifted, but the seething mound of severed limbs and mangled bodies seemed to get no smaller.

'I tell you Jacques is under here!' Flore kept repeating. She seemed to derive some comfort from this obstinate, mindless cry, as if it allowed her to vent her despair.

'Listen! He's calling!'

The tender was pinned beneath the carriages, which had piled on top of each other and collapsed on to it. Now that the engine was making less noise, they could hear a man screaming at the top of his voice from inside the wreckage. As they picked their way towards him, the screaming grew louder and louder; he sounded in such terrible pain that the rescuers could not bear to hear him and started weeping and shouting themselves. When they eventually reached him and freed his legs to lift him out, the screaming stopped. He was dead.

'That's not him,' shouted Flore. 'He's underneath, further down!'

With a remarkable display of strength, she lifted wheels and flung them out of the way, tore the cladding from the carriage roofs, smashed open doors and removed lengths of coupling. When she came across a body or someone who was injured, she called to one of the others to come and take them away, not wishing to abandon her frantic search for even a second.

Cabuche, Pecqueux and Misard worked behind her. Séverine, weary from standing on her feet doing nothing, had sat down on a broken carriage-seat. Misard, having recovered his usual implacable indifference to all around him, avoided the more tiring work and spent most of his time carrying away bodies. Like Flore, he examined each corpse as if hoping to recognize someone from the thousands and thousands of faces that for the last ten years had flowed past their window, coming and going in a flash, leaving behind them only the uniform impression of a nameless crowd. But no! It was still the same anonymous stream of people, always on the move. Death had come to them, cruelly and unexpectedly, but death was as faceless as the frantic pace of life, which had borne them past their window, rushing madly towards some unknown future. They could attach no name, no piece of information to the horror-struck faces of these wretched individuals, who had been brought down in full flight, trampled underfoot and crushed, like soldiers whose bodies fill holes in the ground before the charge of an advancing army. There was one person whom Flore thought she recognized, a man she had spoken to on the day the train was caught in the blizzard, an American. His face was quite familiar, but she didn't know his name or anything about him or his family. Misard carried him away, along with the other bodies that had met their end there. No one knew where they came from and no one knew where they were bound.

In the first-class compartment of an overturned carriage another harrowing spectacle met their eyes. They found a young couple, newly-weds no doubt. They had been thrown together awkwardly; the woman had fallen on top of her husband and was unable to move to take her weight

off him. He was being suffocated and was about to expire.
The woman, whose mouth was free, was calling desperately for someone to help them quickly, heartbroken and
horrified at the thought that she was killing him. When
they succeeded in getting them out, the woman died immediately; there was a large hole in her side, made by one of
the buffers. The man regained consciousness and knelt
beside her, wailing inconsolably. The woman still had tears
in her eyes.

The dead now numbered twelve, and there were more
than thirty injured. They had at last managed to free the
tender. From time to time Flore stopped to thrust her head
down between the splintered wood and twisted metal,
frantically looking for some sign of the driver. Suddenly
she shouted out, 'I can see him! He's down there! That's
his arm with the blue woollen sleeve! He's not moving!
He's not breathing!'

She stood up, swearing like a man: 'For Christ's sake,
hurry up! Get him out of there!'

With her bare hands she tried to tear away the flooring
of a carriage that was jammed between other pieces of
wreckage. She ran back to the house and fetched the axe
they used for splitting logs. Brandishing it like a woodcutter felling oak trees, she cut through the floorboards with
a furious rain of blows. Everyone stood out of the way and
let her get on with it, shouting to her to be careful. But the
only person she could think about was Jacques, lying down
there beneath a tangle of wheels and axles. She did not
hear their warning; she was completely carried away, fear-
less and unstoppable. She cut away the carriage floor and,
with blow after blow, forced aside the obstacles that barred
her way. Her fair hair flew about her face, her blouse was
torn open, and her arms were bare. She was like an awe-
some reaper, furiously scything her way through the havoc
she herself had wrought. One final blow landed on an axle

and split the axe-head in two. The others came over to help her as she moved aside the wheels that had been protecting Jacques and had undoubtedly saved him from being crushed to death. She lifted him up and carried him away in her arms.

'Jacques! Jacques!' she cried. 'He's breathing! He's alive! Thank God! He's alive! I saw him fall! I knew he was down there!'

Séverine ran after her, overcome with emotion. Together they laid him on the ground beside Henri, who was still totally stupefied, unable to comprehend where he was or what was going on around him. Pecqueux came over to them and stood looking at his driver; it was awful to see him in such a terrible condition. The two women kneeled down beside him, one on his left and the other on his right, supporting his head and peering anxiously at his face for the least movement.

Jacques eventually opened his eyes. He looked vaguely at each of them in turn, without seeming to recognize them. They meant nothing to him. Then, a few metres away, he caught sight of the dying locomotive. He was startled. He gazed at her steadily, his eyes flickering as the emotion welled up inside him. He recognized *La Lison* only too well. Everything came back to him – the two stones across the track, the terrible impact, the shudder that ran through the two of them. He might recover, but she would surely die. He couldn't blame her for being slow to respond; she hadn't been herself since they were caught in the blizzard. If she was no longer quite as agile, it wasn't her fault; old age came to everyone, tiring the limbs and stiffening the joints. Seeing her lying there mortally wounded and about to expire, he was overcome with grief and willingly forgave her. She had only a few more minutes to live. She was already growing cold. The coal from her firebox fell to the ground as ash. The steam that had gushed so fiercely from her open flanks now leaked from her sides with a pathetic, whimpering sound, like a child crying. She lay on her back in a pool of black sludge, her gleaming metal-work spattered with dirt and grease; it was like the tragic end of a magnificent horse, accidentally knocked down in the street. For a while, as she lay there with her belly ripped open, they had watched the final throes of her stricken body – the pistons still beating like twin hearts, steam pulsing through her cylinders like blood in the veins. But now the piston rods gave only a spasmodic jerk, like two arms twitching involuntarily, in a last defiant assertion of life. Her soul was ebbing away, along with the power that had kept her alive – the store of living breath, which even now continued to seep from her. The mighty creature grew calmer, sank gradually into a gentle sleep and fell silent. She was dead. The twisted heap of iron, steel and brass, which was all that remained of the fallen giant, its body broken in two, its limbs torn apart, lying bruised and battered in the full glare of the sun, took on the pitiful appearance of an enormous human corpse, of a life that had been lived and then violently snatched away.

Realizing that *La Lison* was no more, Jacques closed his eyes, wishing that he might die too. He felt so weak that he thought the last dying whisper of the locomotive had carried him off with her. Tears ran slowly down his cheeks. Pecqueux stood there motionless with a lump in his throat; this was more than he could bear. Their faithful companion had died, and his driver wished to follow her. The marriage of man and machine which had united the three of them was, it seemed, now at an end. Never again would they climb aboard *La Lison* and travel for league upon league, without exchanging a sign or a word, relying solely on the tacit understanding that existed between them. *La Lison*'s days were over; her power and elegance, her gleaming beauty had gone for ever! Although perfectly sober, Pecqueux burst into violent sobs that shook his great frame uncontrollably.

Séverine and Flore too were dismayed to see Jacques lose consciousness again. Flore ran to the cottage and came back with some camphorated spirit, which she rubbed on to his chest, not knowing what else to do. Despite their concern for Jacques, however, they were even more disturbed by the interminable sufferings of the one surviving horse, which had had its two front legs torn off. It lay near them, producing a continuous, almost human whinny of pain, so loud and expressing such unspeakable agony that two of the injured passengers, following its example, began screaming themselves, like animals. Never was there a death-cry like it – an unforgettable, deep-throated complaint that made the blood run cold. Its torment became unbearable. Voices rang out, horrified and 367 enraged, begging someone to put the wretched horse out of its misery; now that the engine was silent, the animal's endless cry of distress rose into the air like a last, doleful lament for the disaster that had occurred. Pecqueux, still sobbing, picked up the broken axe and felled the horse with a single crushing blow to its skull. Silence descended over the scene of carnage.

After a two-hour wait, help finally arrived. The force of the collision had thrown the carriages to the left, so that the down line could be cleared in only a few hours. A three-coach train had arrived from Rouen, drawn by a requisitioned pilot engine,[7] bringing the Prefect's chief assistant, the Public Prosecutor and a number of engineers and doctors employed by the Company, all looking very serious and businesslike. Monsieur Bessière, the Barentin stationmaster, was already there with a gang of men, attempting to clear the debris. For a remote country spot that was normally so silent and deserted, it was an extraordinary scene of panic and confusion. The passengers who had escaped uninjured had still not recovered from their shock and were in a state of great agitation. Some, terrified at the thought of having to get back into the train, had gone in search of other means of transport. Others, realizing that there wasn't even a wheelbarrow to be found in this place, began to worry about where they were going to get something to eat or find somewhere to sleep. They all wanted to get to a telegraph office, and several set off on foot towards Barentin, with messages ready prepared. While the officials and the Company staff began their inquiries, the doctors quickly set about tending the injured. Many had fainted and lay in pools of blood. Feeble moans were heard as the doctors used their forceps and needles. Altogether there were fifteen dead and thirty-two seriously injured. The dead had been laid out in a row alongside the hedge, face-upwards, waiting to be identified. They had been left to the Public Prosecutor's assistant to deal with, a pink-faced, fair-haired little man, who was busily going through their pockets looking for any papers, cards or letters that might allow him to label them with a name and address. A circle of curious bystanders had formed around him; although there wasn't a house anywhere near by, people had turned up from somewhere or other, to stand and gape – thirty or so men, women and children, who merely got in the way and did nothing to help. Now that the black dust and the cloud of steam and smoke had cleared, the brilliant April sunshine beamed down on the scene of carnage, shedding its soft, entrancing light on the dead and dying, on *La Lison*, lying on her back, dismembered, and on the mountainous heap of wreckage that the gang of workmen were attempting to clear, like so many ants trying to repair an anthill that had been kicked apart by an inadvertent passer-by.

Jacques was still unconscious. Séverine stopped one of

the doctors as he walked past and insisted that he look at
him. The doctor examined him, but could find no obvious
sign of injury. He feared there might be internal damage,
however, because there were traces of blood on his lips.
Unable to be more precise, he advised them to take him
away and put him to bed as soon as possible, taking care
not to jolt him.

As the doctor's hands were feeling him, Jacques had
once again opened his eyes. He gave a little cry of pain.
Although still confused, he recognized Séverine and murmured, 'Take me away! Take me away!'

Flore leaned forward. Turning his head, he recognized
her too. A look of fear came into his eyes, like a frightened
child. He recoiled from her in horror and turned again
towards Séverine.

'Take me away! Take me away, my darling! Quick!'

Séverine spoke tenderly, lovingly, as if Flore were no
longer there, as if she were on her own with him.

'Darling,' she said, 'shall I take you to La Croix-de-
Maufras? Would you like that? We would be in our own
home.'

Jacques accepted. He was still shaking and kept gazing
at Flore.

'Anywhere you like,' he said. 'But be quick!'

Flore stood motionless. Jacques's look of fear and loathing had made her turn pale. Despite the slaughter of so
many unknown, innocent people she had not managed to
kill either of them. Séverine had escaped without a scratch
and Jacques too would probably now recover. All she had
done was to draw them closer, to bring them together, the
two of them alone, in this isolated house. She pictured
them living there – Jacques getting over his injuries and
regaining his strength, while his mistress saw to his every
need, rewarded for her trouble by his constant love and
affection, the two of them undisturbed and free to live out

the honeymoon which this disaster had unexpectedly bestowed upon them. She looked at the dead, whom she had killed to no purpose, and her blood ran cold.

As she surveyed the carnage, she caught sight of Misard and Cabuche, who were being questioned by a group of men – the police no doubt. At the centre of the group stood the Public Prosecutor and the Prefect's chief assistant; they were trying to establish how the quarryman's wagon had come to be stuck half-way across the line. Misard was unable to tell them, although he swore that he had not left his post. He claimed that he'd had his back turned while attending to his instruments, and that he knew absolutely nothing. Cabuche was still in a daze and gave them a long, involved story about how he shouldn't have left the horses unattended, but that he'd wanted to pay his respects to the deceased, and how the horses had moved off on their own and Flore hadn't been able to stop them. He kept getting confused and starting all over again; no one could understand what he was trying to say.

Flore had a sudden, instinctive urge to get away. Her heart was beating fast. She wanted to be free and on her own, free to think and do as she pleased. She had never needed anyone to tell her what she should or should not do. Why wait around now to be pestered with questions, and maybe arrested? She knew that, apart from the crime she had committed, she had neglected her duty and would be held responsible. But while Jacques was still there, she could not tear herself away.

Séverine had asked Pecqueux several times to fetch them a stretcher. Eventually he found one, and came back with a friend to help carry Jacques away. The doctor had persuaded Séverine to look after Henri as well; he seemed to be suffering from concussion and was very confused. Pecqueux promised to come back for him after he had taken Jacques.

As Séverine leaned forward to unbutton Jacques's collar, which was too tight, she kissed his eyelids in front of everyone, encouraging him to be brave as he was being carried away.

'Have no fear!' she said. 'We are going to be happy.'

He smiled at her and returned her kiss. For Flore, this was the end of any hope she might still have had; it tore her away from Jacques for ever. She felt as if she too had been mortally wounded and that her blood was draining from her in great waves. As soon as Jacques had been taken away, she turned and ran. As she passed in front of the cottage, she caught sight through the window of the room where her mother lay dead, with the candle still burning next to the body, a pale glow against the broad light of day. The dead woman had been left there on her own since the accident first happened, her head half turned, her eyes wide open, her lips twisted into a fixed grin, as if she had been watching all these unknown people meet their violent end. 371

Flore ran on. When she reached the bend in the Doinville road she turned to her left and plunged into the undergrowth. She knew this countryside like the back of her hand; if the police were sent on her tail she could defy anyone to catch her. She stopped running and walked more slowly, making for a hiding place she often came to when she was feeling out of sorts – a little cavity hewn out of the rock above the railway tunnel. She looked up at the sky and saw from the sun's position that it was midday. Once inside the hole, she stretched herself out on the bare rock, lying motionless, her hands clasped behind her head, thinking. An awful feeling of emptiness came over her – a sensation of being already dead, which gradually numbed her whole body. It had nothing to do with regret at having pointlessly killed so many people; regret and disgust were feelings she had to forcibly remind herself of. What she realized, however, and now knew for certain, was that Jacques had seen her restraining the horses. She could tell by the way he had shrunk away from her; she filled him with horror and revulsion, as if he had been looking into the eye of a hideous monster. He would never forget. She had failed to take his life and she must now make sure she did not fail when it came to taking her own. She must kill herself, and very soon. All her hopes were gone. As she lay there thinking it through and becoming calmer in her mind, she realized that there was absolutely no alternative. The only thing that stopped her jumping to her feet and looking for some implement, with which she might dispatch herself there and then, was a feeling of exhaustion, a feeling of utter fatigue. And yet, as she succumbed to the invincible drowsiness that began to take hold of her, there rose from deep within her a love of life, a need to be happy, a final dream, now that she had left Jacques and Séverine free to be happy together, of finding happiness herself. Why not wait until nightfall and seek help from Ozil? He loved her and would protect her. Her mind began to drift and become filled with pleasant fantasies; she fell into a deep, dreamless sleep.

372

When she woke up, night had fallen, and it was completely dark. Not realizing where she was, she felt around her. As she touched the bare rock on which she lay, she suddenly remembered. It came to her like a bolt of lightning. There was no escaping it; she knew that she must die. For a moment her resolve had weakened and she had been tempted to think that life was still possible; but all such thoughts had vanished along with her fatigue. Death was the only answer. She could not live with so much blood on her hands, her heart torn from her, abhorred by the one man she had wanted and who now belonged to another. While she still had the strength to do it, she must die.

Flore stood up and climbed out of the hole in the rock. She had no hesitation; she knew instinctively where she must go. Once more she looked up at the sky; the stars told her it was almost nine o'clock. As she came towards the railway a train sped past on the down line. She seemed pleased. Her plan was going to work. The down line had obviously been cleared; the other must still be blocked, as there didn't yet seem to be any trains passing in that direction. She followed a hedge. All around, the countryside lay silent and deserted. There was no hurry; there wouldn't be another train until the express from Paris, which wasn't due until nine twenty-five. She continued to follow the hedge, walking slowly and calmly through the darkness, as if out on one of her habitual solitary excursions. Before reaching the tunnel, however, she climbed over the hedge and, still walking at the same leisurely pace, proceeded along the railway line itself, towards the oncoming express. She had to be careful to avoid being seen by the watchman, as when she used to visit Ozil at the other end 373 of the tunnel. Once inside the tunnel, she continued walking forwards, further and further into the darkness. It was not the same as the week before; she was no longer frightened of turning round and losing her sense of direction, there was not the usual feeling of crazy excitement pounding inside her head, the feeling of being deafened, with the tunnel closing in around her, and of losing all sense of time and place. But this no longer mattered to her. She didn't ask why she was doing this. She wasn't thinking at all. She had but one resolve. She must keep walking, walking ahead, until the train came, and then, when she saw its headlamp shining in the darkness, she must continue walking, straight towards it.

What surprised her, however, was that she seemed to have been walking for hours. How long in coming was the death she craved! For a moment, the thought that it might never come, that she might continue to walk on and on, endlessly, began to disturb her. Her feet were aching.

Would she be obliged to rest, and wait for death to come to her as she lay across the rails? No, it would be unworthy! She must keep walking to the very end. She must walk to her death like the proud, unconquered woman she was! Far away in the distance, she saw the headlamp of the express, like a single, tiny star, twinkling in the darkness of the sky. Her strength returned, and she continued forward. The train had not yet reached the tunnel. There was no sound of it coming; there was simply a tiny, bright light, gradually getting bigger. She drew herself up to her full height, like a graceful statue, and advanced steadily, with long firm strides, as if to greet a friend as she came towards her.[8] The train had entered the tunnel; the noise was coming nearer, shaking the ground like an approaching hurricane. The star was now a huge eye, growing bigger and bigger and seeming to leap from its dark socket. For some unexplained reason, perhaps simply so that she should take nothing with her when she died, she emptied her pockets, and without pausing in her heroic progress, placed her belongings beside the track – a handkerchief, a bunch of keys, a piece of string and two knives. She took the headscarf from round her neck, unfastened her blouse and let it hang from her shoulders. The eye had become a fiery blaze, like the open mouth of a furnace belching out flames; she could feel the monster's hot, steaming breath, and the sound of thunder grew louder and louder. She continued to walk forwards, her eyes fixed on the approaching conflagration, drawn towards it like a moth attracted by a candle in the dark. At the final, terrible moment of impact, the final embrace, she stood straight and tall, as if in a last gesture of defiance and revolt she wished to seize hold of this colossus and strike it to the ground. Her head struck the headlamp and it went out.

It was more than an hour later when they came to retrieve the body. The driver had seen the tall, pale figure walking towards the train, like a strange, frightening apparition illuminated by the shaft of brilliant light from the headlamp. When the lamp had suddenly gone out, the train was plunged into total darkness as it roared through the tunnel. The driver had shuddered as he sensed death passing by. As the train left the tunnel he had tried to shout to the watchman, but it was only when it reached Barentin that he was able to report that someone had been run over. He was certain that it was a woman. Pieces of matted hair and flesh were still stuck to the broken glass of the head-lamp. When the search party found the body, they were amazed at how white it was, as white as marble. It was lying across the up line, where it had been flung by the force of the impact. The head was a terrible mess, but the rest of the body was without a mark. It was half naked and remarkably beautiful – strong and unblemished. The men quietly covered the body. They had recognized her. She 375 must have killed herself in desperation, to escape the awful responsibility she carried on her shoulders.

By midnight, Flore's body lay beside her mother's in the cottage. They had put a mattress on the floor and had lit a new candle between them. Phasie's head was still turned sideways, and her mouth was still twisted in a horrible grin. Her big, staring eyes now seemed to be looking at her daughter. In the empty silence could be heard the sound of someone breathing heavily; it was Misard, back at his endless task, looking for the hidden money. Now that the service had been restored in both directions, the trains went by at their appointed times – unstoppable, all-powerful, unknowing machines, indifferent to the disasters and crimes that had just occurred. What did it matter that a few nameless people had come to an end beneath their wheels? The dead had been carried away, and the blood had been cleaned up. People were on the move again – towards a bright, new future!

11

It was the large bedroom at La Croix-de-Maufras, hung with red damask, and with two tall windows looking out on to the railway line a few metres away. From the old four-poster bed facing them you could see the trains go by. For years nothing had been removed from the room; the furniture stood just where it always had done.

Séverine had had Jacques brought up to this room, injured and still unconscious. Henri Dauvergne had been taken to another, smaller bedroom downstairs. Séverine moved into a room close to Jacques's, just across the landing. It took only an hour or two to settle in and make themselves reasonably comfortable; the house had been kept fully appointed, and there was even fresh linen in the cupboards. Having sent a telegram to Roubaud telling him not to expect her because she would probably be there several days looking after some of the injured, who had been brought to the house, Séverine tied an apron over her dress and set about her nurse's duties.

By the following day the doctor was feeling more confident about Jacques and expected to have him back on his feet within a week. It was quite miraculous; he had only a few minor internal injuries. Even so, he insisted that he needed careful looking after and that he must be kept absolutely still. So when Jacques opened his eyes, Séverine, who had been sitting at his bedside like a child, begged him to be good and do exactly as she told him. He was still very weak and simply nodded. His mind, however, was perfectly clear, and he recognized the bedroom from Séverine's description of it on the night she had confessed to him – the red room, in which, at the tender age of sixteen and a half, she had been subjected to Grandmorin's unwholesome desires. He was lying in Grandmorin's bed. Those were the windows through which, without even having to raise his head, Grandmorin had watched the trains rush past, shaking the house to its foundations. This house that he was now inside was the house he had so often noticed when he drove past it on his train. He could picture it clearly, standing at an angle to the line, silent and abandoned, its shutters closed, and since it had been put up for sale, looking even more forlorn and neglected, with a huge board outside it adding to the unkempt appearance of the garden, which was overgrown with brambles. He remembered the horrible feeling of sadness that came over him every time he saw it, and the sense of unease it filled him with, as if it had been placed there deliberately, to bring misfortune upon him. Now, as he lay in this room feeling so weak, he thought he understood. It must mean that he **377** had been brought here to die.

As soon as she saw that he was able to understand her, Séverine had done her best to reassure him. As she pulled up the bedclothes, she whispered into his ear:

'Don't worry, darling. I've emptied your pockets and hidden the watch.'

He looked at her, his eyes wide open, trying to remember.

'The watch? . . . Ah yes, the watch.'

'They might have looked through your belongings, so I've hidden it with some things of mine. There's nothing to fear.'

He thanked her with a squeeze of the hand. As he turned his head, he caught sight of the knife on the table, which she had also found in one of his pockets. There had been no need to hide that; it was just a knife, like any other.

By the next day, Jacques was already stronger, and beginning to think that perhaps after all he wasn't going to die there. He was overjoyed when he recognized Cabuche, standing near his bed, tidying things up and clumping round the room on his big, heavy feet. Ever since the accident, Cabuche hadn't left Séverine's side. He felt he had to do something to help. He gave up working at the quarry and came every morning to help Séverine with the heavy jobs around the house. He was like a faithful dog; he doted on her. She was a tough woman, even if she was only a 'little-un', as he put it. She did so much for others that she deserved to have someone do something for her. Jacques and Séverine got used to him being there. They talked happily together and even exchanged kisses, while Cabuche did his best to avoid disturbing them and tried to make himself as small as possible.

Jacques, however, was surprised that Séverine was away from him so often. The first day, on the doctor's instructions, she hadn't told him that Henri was downstairs, realizing that the thought that they were completely alone would have a calming effect on him.

'Are we alone?' he asked.

'Yes, darling, absolutely alone . . . relax and go to sleep.'

But she kept constantly disappearing. The next day he heard the sound of footsteps downstairs, and people whispering. The day after that, there were sounds of subdued laughter and hilarity, and the bright, animated voices of two girls talking incessantly.

'Who's that downstairs?' he asked. 'We're not alone, are we?'

'Well, no, we aren't, darling. There's another injured man downstairs, just underneath your room. I had to bring him here as well.'

'Who is it?'

'It's Henri. You know, the guard.'

'Henri . . . Oh yes!'

'His sisters have come to see him. It's them you can hear.

They laugh at anything. Henri is much better, so they're going back tonight. Their father can't do without them. Henri needs to stay for another two or three days until he's completely well. Can you believe it? He jumped off the train and he didn't break a single bone. The only thing wrong was that his mind had gone a complete blank. But he's more like himself again now.'

Jacques said nothing, fixing his eyes steadily upon her.

'You do understand, don't you?' she added. 'If he weren't here, people would start talking about us. So long as I'm not on my own with you, my husband has no cause for complaint. It gives me a good excuse for staying here. Do you understand?'

'Yes,' said Jacques, 'that's fine.'

He lay listening to the laughter of Henri's two sisters until the evening. He remembered hearing it in Paris, from the floor below, in the room where Séverine had lain in 379 his arms and confessed to him. Eventually quiet returned, and all he could hear was the sound of Séverine's footsteps as she tripped backwards and forwards between him and her other patient downstairs. The door downstairs would close, and there would be complete silence. Twice, feeling particularly thirsty, he had to bang on the floor with the leg of a chair to summon her upstairs. She came into his room all smiles, fussing over him and explaining that she couldn't come to him sooner because she had to keep putting cold compresses on Henri's forehead.

By the fourth day, Jacques was able to get out of bed and spend a couple of hours in an armchair by the window. By leaning forward a little, he could see the narrow garden, cut in two by the railway line, enclosed by a low wall and overgrown with pale-flowered rose bushes. He remembered the night he had stood on tiptoe to look over the wall. He recalled the larger piece of ground at the back of the house, surrounded by only a hedge; he had walked through it and had come across Flore sitting outside the little ruined greenhouse, untangling some stolen twine with a pair of scissors. What a terrible night that had been; what torments he had suffered as a result of his murderous affliction! As he became able to remember things more clearly, he had been obsessed by an image of Flore – tall, athletic and majestic, her eyes ablaze and staring straight into his. At first he hadn't spoken about the accident, and no one spoke about it in his presence, for fear of upsetting him. But now, the details were all coming back to him. He tried to piece them together; he could think of nothing else. It absorbed him so completely that, as he sat at the window, his sole concern was to look for some clue, to observe those who had been involved in the tragedy. Why did he no longer see Flore standing at her post by the level-crossing, holding her flag? He did not dare ask; the question simply added to the unease inspired in him by this gloomy house, which seemed to be haunted by ghosts from the past.

380

One morning, however, as Cabuche was standing near him, helping Séverine, he made up his mind.

'Where's Flore?' he asked. 'Is she ill?'

The question took Cabuche by surprise. Séverine made a sign, but Cabuche, mistakenly thinking that she was telling him to answer, said, 'Poor Flore, she's dead!'

Jacques looked at them. He was shaking all over. They had to tell him the whole story. Between them they told him of Flore's suicide; how she had walked into the tunnel and thrown herself under a train. Her mother's funeral had been delayed until the evening so that her daughter could be buried at the same time; they had been laid to rest side by side in the little cemetery at Doinville, where they had joined the first victim of this sorry tale, Phasie's younger daughter, the poor, unfortunate Louisette, who had likewise met a violent end, having been beaten and dragged through the mud. Three pitiful women who had fallen by the wayside, crushed and discarded, like refuse blown away in the fearful blast of the passing trains!

'Dead! Oh God!' whispered Jacques. 'My poor Aunt Phasie, and Flore and Louisette!'

At the mention of Louisette, Cabuche, who was helping Séverine move the bed, raised his eyes instinctively towards her, pained by the sudden recollection of his former love; he was completely besotted by his new-found admiration for Séverine. Being the soft-hearted, simple soul he was, he doted on her like an obedient dog that fawns on its master the minute it is stroked. Séverine knew about his tragic love affair. She gave him a look of sympathy and understanding. Cabuche was deeply touched. As he passed the pillows to her, his hand accidentally brushed against hers. He gasped, and stammered something in reply to Jacques. Jacques had asked him whether 381 Flore had been accused of causing the accident.

'Oh, no,' he mumbled. 'They said she was responsible for it, but . . .'

Speaking slowly and hesitantly he told him what he knew. He hadn't seen anything himself. He had been inside the house when the horses moved forward and pulled the wagon across the line. He could never forgive himself. The police officers had given him a severe talking to. Horses should not be left unattended. If he'd stayed with them this terrible accident would never have happened. The inquiry had arrived at the conclusion that it was a case of simple negligence on Flore's part, and as she had already inflicted such a terrible punishment on herself, no further action was needed. Nor did they propose to dismiss Misard, who in his usual grovelling, obsequious way had got himself out of difficulties by blaming Flore. She only ever did her job as it suited her. This wasn't the first time he'd had to leave his post to close the crossing gate. The Railway Company, moreover, could only certify that on that particular morning Misard had performed his duties meticulously and they authorized him, until such time as he chose to remarry, to share his house with an old woman living near by by the name of Ducloux, who would act as the new gate-keeper. Madame Ducloux had at one time worked as a barmaid and now lived off the immoral earnings she had amassed previously.

Cabuche left the room. Jacques motioned to Séverine to remain behind. He was very pale.

'You know, don't you,' he said, 'that it was Flore who pulled the horses forward and blocked the line with the stones?'

It was Séverine's turn to go pale.

'Darling, what are you saying? You've got a temperature. You must get back to bed.'

382 'It's not just a bad dream,' he said. 'I saw her, do you understand? As plainly as I see you. She had her hand on the horses, holding them back and preventing the wagon from crossing.'

Séverine's legs gave way and she sank on to a chair in front of him.

'Oh, my God,' she said. 'It's terrifying! It's monstrous! I shall never be able to sleep again.'

'It's perfectly clear,' Jacques went on. 'She tried to kill us ... both of us ... along with everyone else. She had wanted me for years and she was jealous. What's more, she was crazy. Her head was full of mad ideas. All those people! Killed just like that! In one huge bloodbath! What a monster!'

His eyes were wide open, and a nervous twitch played on his lips. He fell silent, and they continued to look at each other. A whole minute went by. Then, tearing himself away from the fearful visions that were forming in their minds, he continued in a whisper, 'If she's dead, then it's her ghost that comes to haunt me! Ever since I regained consciousness, she seems always to be there. This morning I thought she was standing by the bed. I turned round to look . . . She is dead and we are alive. Let us hope that she won't take her revenge!'

Séverine shuddered.

'Stop it! Stop it!' she cried. 'You'll drive me mad!'

She went out. Jacques heard her going downstairs to tend to Henri. He remained by the window, once again absorbed in the scene below – the railway line, the gate-keeper's cottage with its large well, the little wooden section box, where Misard, for all the world as if he were asleep, performed his endless, repetitive tasks. Jacques sat contemplating these things for hours on end, as if he were pondering a problem he could not solve, yet on whose solution his life depended.

He could not take his eyes off Misard – such a pathetic, **383** inoffensive, washed-out-looking character, continually racked by a nasty little cough, a man who had poisoned his wife and reduced a fine healthy woman to nothing, like a voracious insect that is driven by only one impulse! For years he must have thought of nothing else, day and night, every minute of the twelve interminable hours he was on duty. Each time the telegraph sounded to announce a train he would blow his horn; then, once the train had passed and he had closed the line behind it, he would press one button to offer it to the next section and another button to free the line to the section it had just left. These were simple mechanical operations that had become an integral part of his dreary vegetable existence, a kind of bodily reflex. He was uneducated and obtuse; he never read anything, but simply sat waiting for the bells to ring, with his arms dangling at his sides and his eyes gazing vacantly into space. He spent nearly all his time sitting in his cabin, with no other distraction than trying to make his lunch last as long as possible. He would then relapse into his stupor, his mind completely blank and not a thought in his head, overcome with insuperable drowsiness and sometimes dropping off to sleep with his eyes wide open. At night, in order to stop himself falling asleep, he would get up and totter about like someone who had had too much to drink. For months on end, the battle with his wife, the silent contest over which of them would have the hidden one thousand francs after the death of the other, must have been the sole preoccupation of this lonely man's empty mind. When he went out to sound his horn or change the signals, performing the unvaried routine that ensured the safety of so many lives, he was thinking about poison. As he sat in his hut, waiting, with his arms hanging limp and his eyes heavy with sleep, the same thoughts ran through his head. He thought of nothing else; he would kill her, he would look for the money and it would be his.

384

Jacques was surprised to see that Misard seemed no different. So it was possible to kill, without any fuss, and continue one's life as before. Indeed, after his initial bout of frantic searching for the money, Misard had slipped back into his old apathetic ways, keeping himself to himself, like someone who didn't want to be disturbed. In the end, he had done away with his wife to no purpose; she was the winner and he was the loser. He turned the house upside down and still found nothing, not a single centime. Only his eyes revealed his constant preoccupation – worried, prying eyes that peered at you from an ashen face. He continually saw the dead woman's large, staring eyes and hideous grin and heard her voice telling him to 'Keep looking!' He looked and looked; he could not give his mind a moment's rest. He racked his brains ceaselessly, trying to guess where the money might be buried, thinking of possible hiding places, eliminating those he had already tried and getting so excited when he thought of a new one that he would immediately drop whatever he was doing and run to see. But all to no avail! It became unbearable, an agonizing retribution, a kind of cerebral insomnia that kept his addled brain alert and thinking, in spite of himself, as the obsession ticked steadily away inside his head. When he sounded his horn, once for down trains and twice for up trains, he was searching. When he answered the bells in his cabin and pushed the buttons on his control panel to block or clear the line, he was still searching. He never stopped searching, searching desperately, all day long as he sat at his desk doing nothing, and all through the night, hardly able to stay awake, alone in the darkness and silence of the countryside, like an exile banished to the far ends of the earth. Old Madame Ducloux, who for the time being was looking after the level-crossing and who was very keen to find herself a husband, looked after him most solicitously and was very worried that he never seemed to close his eyes.

One night, Jacques, who by now was able to take a few steps around his bedroom, had got up and walked over to the window, when he saw a lamp moving in and out of the Misards' cottage. It must have been Misard looking for the money! The following night, as he was looking out of the window again, he saw a tall dark shape standing in the road, under the window of the room next to his, in which Séverine slept. To his amazement he saw that it was Cabuche. He didn't know why, but instead of feeling annoyed it made him feel sad and rather sorry for him. Poor Cabuche! A clumsy great fellow like him, stuck out there in the dark like a tame watchdog! Séverine was such a small girl, and, objectively speaking, not exactly pretty, yet with her jet-black hair and her periwinkle blue eyes, she obviously possessed the sort of charm that could captivate even a great oaf like Cabuche and make him stand at her door all night long, like a frightened little boy. He recalled his eagerness to do jobs for her, the slavish looks he gave her when he offered to help her. There was no doubt about it, Cabuche was in love with her and desired her. The next day he watched him carefully and saw him surreptitiously pick up a hairpin that had fallen from her chignon while she had been making the bed. He hid it in his hand so as not to have to give it back to her. Jacques thought of all the agonies he had suffered as a result of his own sexual desires and how his troubles and fears were coming back as his health returned.

Another two days went by. The week was nearly over, and, as the doctor had predicted, the injured were ready to go back to work. One morning, Jacques was standing at the window when he saw a brand-new locomotive go past with his fireman, Pecqueux, waving to him from the footplate as if he were telling him to come and join him.

386 But he was in no hurry to get back to his job. He preferred to stay where he was and wait for things to take their course. On the same day he once again heard peals of fresh, young laughter from downstairs, sounds of girlish merriment that echoed through the dismal house like the noise of a school at playtime. He knew it was the two young Dauvergne girls but he didn't speak about it to Séverine. Séverine, in fact, was out of the room for most of the day and didn't seem able to stay with him for more than five minutes. Then in the evening, the house once again became as silent as the grave. She sat in his room looking rather pale and serious. Jacques looked hard at her and asked, 'Has Henri gone? Have his sisters taken him home?'

'Yes,' she answered tersely.

'So are we alone at last? Just you and me?'

'Yes,' she said, 'just you and me. Tomorrow we must part. I shall go back to Le Havre. We can't stay camping out in this wilderness for ever.'

Jacques continued to look at her, smiling awkwardly.

'You're sorry he's left, aren't you?' he said suddenly.

The question took her by surprise, and she started to deny it, but he stopped her.

'I'm not trying to pick a quarrel with you,' he said. 'You can see I'm not jealous. You once told me to kill you if you were unfaithful, didn't you? Well, I don't think I look like a lover who is thinking of killing his mistress . . . but you hardly moved from that room downstairs. I couldn't have you to myself for a minute. It reminded me of what your husband once told me. He said that one of these days you would sleep with Dauvergne. Not for pleasure, but just to do something different.'

'Something different, something different,' she repeated slowly.

She had stopped trying to protest her innocence; she suddenly felt impelled to be completely honest with him. **387**

'All right,' she said, 'it's true. You and I don't need to hide anything from each other; we share too many secrets already . . . Dauvergne has been after me for months. He knew that we were lovers, and thought it would make no difference to me if I was his lover too. When I was with him downstairs, he spoke about it again and said he was head over heels in love with me. He seemed so grateful to me for looking after him and he was so tender and affectionate that, yes, for a moment I thought I might fall in love with him too, do something different, something better, something quiet and gentle . . . not exactly pleasure perhaps, but something that would have calmed me . . .'

She broke off, and paused for a moment before continuing.

'You and I have no future,' she said. 'We can go no further. We're stuck. All our dreams of sailing away and being rich and happy in America, that wonderful future which depended on you . . . it's all gone, because you couldn't do it . . . I'm not blaming you, Jacques . . . perhaps it's just as well it never happened . . . but you must understand that there's nothing more I can hope for from you. Tomorrow will be no different from yesterday . . . there will be the same problems, the same anxieties.'

Jacques let her talk, only speaking when he saw that she had finished.

'Is that why you slept with him?' he asked.

She had moved across the bedroom, but came back towards him.

'I didn't sleep with him,' she said, with a shrug of her shoulders. 'I don't have to try and convince you because I know you will believe me; there's no point in our lying to each other. No, I couldn't bring myself to do it . . . any more than you could bring yourself to kill Roubaud. Does it surprise you that a woman can't give herself to a man, even when she decides that, all things considered, it would be in her interest to do so? I didn't really give it too much thought. It has never cost me anything to be nice . . . to give pleasure, I mean . . . to my husband, or to you when I saw how much you loved me. But this time I couldn't do it. I didn't even let him kiss me on the lips, I promise you. He just kissed my hands. He'll be waiting for me in Paris; he seemed so disappointed that I didn't want to leave him thinking he had no hope.'

Jacques believed her. She was right; he could tell she wasn't lying. But his anxiety was beginning to return. He felt the terrifying curse of his desire stirring within him as he thought of himself alone with her in that isolated house, with the flame of their passion rekindled. He wished he could get away.

'But there's someone else as well,' he exclaimed. 'There's Cabuche!'

She turned towards him.

'Ah! You've noticed,' she said. 'You've noticed that

too. Yes, it's true. There's Cabuche. What's the matter with all these men! Cabuche hasn't said a word to me, but I've seen him wringing his hands together when we kiss. When I sit close to you and take your hand, he runs away and cries. He steals my belongings . . . gloves, handkerchiefs . . . they keep disappearing. He carries them off to his hovel, as trophies . . . Surely you don't imagine I could give myself to an overgrown brute like him; I'd be terrified. Anyway, he hasn't said a thing . . . big chaps like him are sometimes very shy; they might be desperately in love, but they don't demand a thing. You could leave me alone with him for a month, and he wouldn't as much as touch me . . . any more than he did Louisette; of that I am now quite certain.'

At this reminder of the past their eyes met, and they looked at each other in silence, remembering all that had happened between them – their meeting at the examining **389** magistrate's office in Rouen, their first magical trip to Paris, their secret lovers' meetings in Le Havre, and all that had occurred since, both the good and the bad. She drew close to him, so close that he could feel the warmth of her breath.

'No,' she said, 'I couldn't give myself to Henri, and I certainly couldn't give myself to Cabuche. I couldn't give myself to anyone . . . And do you know why? I'll tell you, because now I know, and I know I'm right. It's because you have taken me . . . taken all of me. What other word is there? You have taken me, like something you seize in both hands and carry away and use every minute of the day, a possession. Before you, I hadn't belonged to anyone. But now I'm yours, and I'll be yours for ever . . . even if you don't want me to be, and even if I don't want to be either . . . I don't know how to explain it. It was simply the way we met. Other men frightened me . . . disgusted me. But with you it has been wonderful, a blessing from heaven . . . Jacques, you are the only one I love. I can never love anyone but you!'

She put out her arms to draw him towards her and was about to lay her head on his shoulder and offer her lips to his. But he took hold of her hands and held her away from him, panic-stricken and terrified, as he felt the old familiar tremor run through his body and the blood pulsing through his brain. He heard the same ringing in his ears, the same pounding and clamouring in his head as when he had his terrible attacks as a youth. For some time already, he had been unable to make love to Séverine in broad daylight or even by the light of a candle for fear that the mere sight of her might drive him mad. But now there was a lamp beside the bed, shining brightly on both of them, and the reason he was shaking and becoming so agitated was no doubt because he had glimpsed the white curve of her breasts, 390 through the unfastened top of her dressing-gown.

Séverine continued to entreat him, with ever-increasing passion.

'What does it matter if we have no future together? Even if I don't expect you to change my life and I know that tomorrow will bring us the same problems and torments as before, I don't care. I want nothing more than to live out my life and to share my suffering with you. We'll go back to Le Havre. Things can carry on as they like. If only I can be with you for an hour from time to time, like this . . . I haven't slept for three nights. I've been lying in my room across the landing, longing to come and join you. But you've been so ill and you seemed so unhappy that I didn't dare . . . Let me stay with you tonight. It will be lovely, I promise you. I'll curl up small so as not to disturb you. It's the last night we shall be here . . . in this house, away from everything. Listen! Not a sound! Nothing! No one will come. We're on our own . . . completely on our own. No one would know if we died in each other's arms.'

Jacques, aroused by her caresses and his furious desire to possess her, having no weapon, stretched out his hands to strangle her, when Séverine, from force of habit, turned and put out the lamp. He took her in his arms and carried her to the bed. It was one of their most passionate nights of love . . . a night like no other . . . the only time they had ever been truly as one, lost in each other. Their pleasure left them exhausted and so drained of strength that they lost all feeling in their bodies. They lay tight in each other's arms, but they did not sleep. As on the night Séverine had confessed her secret to him in Madame Victoire's room in Paris, Jacques listened without speaking as she whispered softly into his ear. Perhaps that night, before putting out the lamp, she had sensed death brush past her. Until that day, she had lain in her lover's arms quite happily, oblivious to the ever-present threat of being murdered. But a little shiver of death had run through her; a fear she could not explain made her press herself against him, seeking protection. As she lay beside him, breathing gently, it was as if she were surrendering her soul to him.

'Oh, my darling, if only you had been able to do it, how happy we would have been in America! I'm not asking you again to do something you cannot do. But it was such a beautiful dream! Just a moment ago I felt frightened. I don't know why. I feel as if something is threatening me. It's childish, I know. I keep looking behind me, as if there were someone there, about to strike me down . . . You're the only one who can look after me, darling. My happiness depends on you. You are my only reason for living.'

Without answering, he held her closer, expressing in his embrace what he could not say in words – all his unspoken feelings, his genuine desire to be good to her, the deep love she had always inspired in him. Yet earlier that evening he had wanted to kill her. If she had not turned to put out the light, he would certainly have strangled her. He would never be cured. His attacks were dictated by circumstance; he would never know or even begin to understand what caused them. Why had it happened that evening, when he had discovered how faithful she was to him, how open and trusting? Was it that the more she loved him, the more he sought to imprison her in the dark confines of his male egoism, even if it meant destroying her? He wanted to possess her, dead, like a handful of dust!

'Darling, tell me, why am I frightened? Am I in danger?'

'No, no, don't worry; you're in no danger.'

'Sometimes I start shaking all over. All the time there's something lurking behind me. I can't see it, but I know it's there . . . Why am I frightened?'

'There, there, don't be frightened . . . I love you and I'll never let anyone hurt you . . . See! How good it is when **392** we're together like this!'

There was a long, blissful silence.

'Oh, my darling,' she continued in a soft, gentle whisper, 'if only there could be night after night like this, night after night when we were together, the two of us, as one . . . We could sell this house and take the money and sail away to America. We could meet up with your friend; he's still waiting for you . . . Not a day goes by when I don't go to bed dreaming of our life over there . . . Every night would be like tonight. You would make love to me, and I would be yours; we would fall asleep in each other's arms . . . But you can't do it, I know. When I talk about it, it's not because I'm trying to hurt you; it's just that I can't stop myself thinking about it.'

There and then, Jacques decided. It was a decision he had taken many times before. If he was to avoid killing Séverine, he must kill Roubaud. This time, as before, he felt absolutely determined to go through with it; he would not be deterred.

'No, I couldn't bring myself to do it,' he murmured. 'But I will do it. I've promised you.'

Séverine made a half-hearted attempt to dissuade him.

'Please don't make promises,' she said. 'It only makes us feel bad afterwards, if you can't go through with it . . . Besides, it's horrible. You mustn't do it. You really mustn't.'

'But it must be done,' he said. 'You know it must. And it's because it must be done that I shall find the strength to do it . . . I've been wanting to talk to you about it, and now we can; we're alone, we're not going to be disturbed, and we can be perfectly honest with each other.'

Séverine had begun to resign herself. She let out a sigh. Her chest heaved, and her heart beat so fast that he could feel it against his own.

'Oh my God!' she muttered. 'When I thought it would never happen, I wanted it to happen . . . Now you say you mean to do it, I want to die.' 393

They sat in silence: Jacques's new-found resolve had left them lost for words. They could feel the desolate emptiness of the wild countryside around them. They were both very hot; they lay with their limbs entwined, their moist bodies melting into each other.

His hand wandered over her, and he kissed her on the neck, beneath her chin.

'We could get him to come here,' whispered Séverine. 'I could invent some excuse and send for him. I don't know what, but we could think of something . . . you could be waiting for him. You could hide somewhere . . . it would be easy . . . you wouldn't be disturbed. That's what we must do. What do you think?'

He let her talk; his lips moved from her neck to her breast.

'Yes, yes,' was all he could reply.

Séverine was deep in thought, working out the details

of her plan. As it took shape in her head, she considered it and thought of ways it might be improved.

'But we would still have to be careful, my darling,' she said. 'We can't afford to do anything stupid. If we were to get ourselves arrested the next day, I'd rather stay as we are . . . I read somewhere, I can't remember where, in a novel probably, that the best thing to do is make it look like suicide. He's been acting very strangely of late; he's been so miserable and down in the dumps. It wouldn't surprise anyone if they suddenly found out he'd come here and killed himself . . . But we'd have to find a way of arranging things so that people would be convinced it was suicide . . . wouldn't we?'

'Yes, I suppose so,' he murmured.

She wondered how it could be done. She gasped for breath as he lifted her towards him to cover her breast with kisses.

'We must make sure we leave no trace,' she said. 'Listen! If you slit his throat with this knife, we could simply lift him up and carry him on to the railway line. We could put his neck across one of the rails, do you see, so that the first train to come along would cut his head off. Then they could look for evidence as much as they liked. They wouldn't find a wound. They wouldn't find anything. Because his head would be completely crushed! What about that?'

'Yes,' he said, 'it's very good.'

They were becoming more and more excited. Séverine was almost laughing, very pleased with herself at having had such a bright idea. Jacques drew her towards him in a strong embrace, but she resisted him.

'Not now,' she said. 'Wait a bit . . . When I think about it, it's still not quite right. If you stay here with me, suicide will look suspicious. You must leave. You must leave tomorrow, do you understand, openly, in front of Misard and Cabuche, so that your departure is witnessed. You must catch a train at Barentin and find some excuse for getting off at Rouen. Then, as soon as it gets dark, you must come back here. I'll let you in by the back door. It's only four leagues away; you can be back in less than three hours . . . This time we've thought of everything! If you're willing, we can do it.'

'Yes,' he said, 'I'm willing. We will do it.'

Jacques lay there thinking. He had stopped kissing her. There was a long silence. They both remained motionless in each other's arms, lost in contemplation of the deed that was to be perpetrated. It had been decided; their minds were made up. Gradually they became aware of their two bodies, locked together in an ever-tightening embrace. Séverine loosened her arms and drew away from him.

'What excuse can we use to get him here?' she said. 'Whatever we tell him, the earliest train he can catch is at eight o'clock, when he comes off duty, and he won't be here before ten, which is even better . . . I know! We can say it's about the buyer for the house. Misard spoke to me about him; he's supposed to be coming to have a look at it the day after tomorrow, in the morning! I'll send my husband a telegram first thing in the morning, telling him his presence is essential. He'll be here tomorrow night. You can leave in the afternoon and be back before he arrives. It will be dark, with no moon . . . nothing can go wrong. It's all working out perfectly.'

'Yes, perfectly,' said Jacques.

They embraced each other and made love, fainting in ecstasy. When they finally went to sleep, still in each other's arms, a vast silence descended on the house. It was still not daylight, but the first signs of dawn were beginning to whiten the shadows that had hidden them from each other like a dark mantle. Jacques slept until ten o'clock, in a deep, dreamless sleep. When he opened his eyes, he found

395

himself alone. Séverine had gone to her room across the
landing to get dressed. A shaft of bright sunlight fell
through the window, giving an incandescent glow to the
red hangings around the bed and the red wall coverings.
The whole room seemed to be aflame. The house was shaking with the noise of a passing train. It must have been the
train that had woken him up. He was dazzled by the sunlight and the blaze of red all around him. Then he
remembered. It had been decided. That night, when this
blinding sun had disappeared, he would kill.

The day passed as the two of them had planned. Before
breakfast, Séverine asked Misard to go to Doinville with
the telegram for her husband. At about three o'clock, as
Cabuche was there and could see what he was doing,
Jacques made very obvious preparations for leaving. Cabuche even accompanied him as he left to catch the 4.14 train
396 at Barentin, partly because he had nothing else to do, and
partly because he vaguely felt he had something in common with him, Jacques being the lover of the woman he
so much desired himself. Jacques arrived at Rouen at
twenty to five. He got off the train and booked into an inn
near the station, run by a woman who came from his own
home town. He told her that in the morning he intended
to call in on some friends before going back to Paris to
start work again. He was very tired, however; he was still
recovering from his injuries and he'd overtaxed himself.
At six o'clock he went to his room to sleep. He had chosen
a room on the ground floor, which had a window opening
on to a quiet back street. Ten minutes later he was on his
way back to La Croix-de-Maufras, having climbed out of the
window without being seen, and carefully leaving the shut-
ter open so that he could get back in again unperceived.

It wasn't until a quarter past nine that Jacques found
himself back outside the lonely house, standing empty and

forlorn, at an angle to the railway line. It was very dark; the front of the house was completely closed up and not a single light was visible. Once again he felt the pang of anxiety, the feeling of awful sadness that seemed to herald the fateful calamity which awaited him there. As arranged with Séverine, he threw three pebbles against the shutters of the red room. He then walked round to the back of the house, where eventually a door quietly opened. He closed it behind him and groped his way up the stairs, following the light footsteps that went before him. At the top of the stairs he stopped in amazement; by the light of a large lamp standing on the corner of a table, he saw that the bed was unmade, Séverine's clothes were thrown over a chair and Séverine herself was in her nightdress, her legs bare, ready for bed, with her thick hair tied up over her head, exposing her neck.

'Why have you gone to bed?' he asked.

'It's better this way,' she answered. 'I'm sure it is. I had an idea. You see, when he arrives and I go down to let him in dressed like this, he'll be less suspicious. I'll tell him I had a migraine. Misard already thinks I'm not feeling well. Then, when they find him on the railway line, I'll be able to say I never left this room.'[1]

But Jacques was shaking.

'No,' he shouted angrily, 'get dressed. You've got to be ready to help me. You can't stay like that.'

She was surprised at his reaction.

'Why not, darling?' she said, beginning to smile. 'You don't need to worry. I'm not cold, I promise you . . . Feel me . . . See how warm I am!'

She moved towards him, invitingly, placing her bare arms around him. Her nightdress had slipped down over one shoulder, revealing her round breasts. Jacques drew away from her. He was becoming increasingly agitated.

'Don't be angry,' she pleaded. 'I'll cuddle up in bed, and then you won't be frightened I'll catch cold.'

Once she was back in bed with the sheet pulled up round her chin, Jacques seemed to grow a little calmer. Séverine talked happily about the various plans that had been running through her head.

'As soon as he knocks, I go down and open the door. At first I thought I could just leave him to come up here, where you would be waiting for him. But if we had to get him back downstairs, it would be more difficult. Besides, there's a parquet floor in this room, whereas the hall downstairs has tiles, which would make it easier to clean if there are splashes of blood . . . While I was getting undressed, just before you arrived, I remembered a novel in which a murderer takes his clothes off in order to kill someone. You wash yourself afterwards, and there isn't a stain on your clothes . . . It makes sense, don't you see . . . Why don't you take your clothes off? Why don't we both get undressed?'

He looked at her, terrified. But she looked as sweet and innocent as a little girl. She was simply concerned that everything went according to plan and that it was a success. She had been thinking about it carefully. But Jacques was horrified at the thought of them both naked and splashed with blood. Once more he felt the stirrings of his fearful malady.

'No!' he protested. 'It's barbaric! You'll be suggesting we eat his heart next! How you must hate him!'

Séverine's face suddenly darkened. Jacques's outburst had transported her from her carefully planned preparations to the horror of the deed. Her eyes filled with tears.

'I've had too much to put up with these last few months,' she wept. 'How can I have any love for him? I've said it a hundred times: I'd do anything rather than stay with him another week. But you're right. It's awful that it should come to this. It shows how desperately we both want to be happy . . . Anyway, we'll go downstairs in the dark. You stand behind the door. When I've opened it and he's inside, you do as you choose . . . My only part in this is to help you, so that you don't have to do everything yourself. This is the best I can think of.'

Jacques had stopped in front of the table, his attention drawn to the knife, the weapon that Roubaud himself had already used to kill Grandmorin, and which Séverine had obviously put there for him to use now. It was open and the blade gleamed in the light of the lamp. He picked it up and examined it. Séverine looked at it too, saying nothing. Now that he was actually holding it, there was no point in mentioning it to him. Only when he replaced it on the table did she speak.

'Darling,' she said, 'I'm not forcing you to do it. If you can't face it, you still have time to go.'

Jacques clenched his fist angrily.

'Do you think I'm a coward?' he exclaimed. 'This time it will be done. I've given my word!'

Just then the house was shaken by the noise of a train thundering past, so close that it seemed to be passing through the room itself.

'That's Roubaud's train,' he said. 'The semi-fast for Paris. He will have got off at Barentin. He'll be here in half an hour.'

Neither of them spoke. There was a long silence. They thought of Roubaud, out there in the night, coming along the path towards them. Jacques began to walk mechanically backwards and forwards across the bedroom, as if he were counting Roubaud's steps, each one bringing him closer and closer. One more, and then another, and when he took the last one, he would be lying in wait behind the hall door, and the minute he walked in he would plunge the knife into his neck. Séverine lay in bed on her back,

the sheet still pulled up round her chin, watching him walk
up and down[2] with big, staring eyes, her mind lulled by
the rhythm of his steps, which came to her as an echo of
the steps that were approaching from outside. One more
and then another, getting relentlessly nearer! Nothing
would stop them now. When they reached the house, she
would jump out of bed and go downstairs in the dark in
her bare feet to open the door. 'Is that you, dear? Come in.
I was in bed.' But he wouldn't have time to answer. He
would fall to the ground in the dark, with his throat slit.

Another train went by on the down line, the stopping
train which passed La Croix-de-Maufras five minutes after
the semi-fast. Jacques stopped in surprise. Only five minutes! Half an hour was going to be a long time to wait! He
must keep moving. He started pacing up and down the
room again. He was beginning to have doubts about himself. He was getting anxious, like one of those men whose
nerves affect their virility. Would he be able to do it? He
knew what was happening because it had happened ten or
more times before. It always started off with him being
convinced he could do it and determined to kill. He would
then experience a tightening in his chest, his hands and
feet would go cold, and his strength would suddenly fail
him completely – his muscles would simply refuse to do
what he wanted them to do. He tried to strengthen his
resolve, as he had so often done before, by reminding himself of what he stood to gain by getting rid of Roubaud – the
fortune awaiting him in America, being together with the
woman he loved. The trouble was that when, a moment
before, he had found Séverine half naked, he had thought
he could no longer go through with it; the minute he sensed
a return of his old affliction, he was no longer his own
master. For a moment, the temptation had been almost
too strong; Séverine was offering herself to him, and the
knife lay open on the table. But he had not succumbed. He

braced himself for the final effort. He could do it. He paced backwards and forwards from the door to the window, each time passing close to the bed, which he avoided looking at. The wait continued.

Séverine lay in the bed, where, the night before, in total darkness, they had made love so passionately. She did not move; her head rested motionless on the pillow, her eyes following him backwards and forwards. She too felt anxious, afraid that tonight, as before, his courage might fail him. She simply wanted to have done with it and start afresh. Her only concern was to be loved and to surrender herself to the man who loved her. She had given herself entirely to the man who had won her heart; towards her husband, whom she had never wanted, she felt nothing. He was being got rid of because he stood in their way; it was perfectly natural. It was only when she dwelled upon it that she felt at all moved by the awfulness of the crime **401** they were about to commit; the minute she stopped thinking about blood and the horrible practicalities of the murder, she became quite calm again, as sweet and docile as a child. Well as she thought she knew him, there was something about Jacques's appearance that puzzled her. He had the same round, good-looking face, the same curly hair, dark moustache and brown eyes with the little flecks of gold in them, but his jaw was pushed forward in a savage grimace that made him appear almost deformed.[3] As he came towards her, he had looked at her, but as if he were doing his best not to, and a red mist seemed to dull his eyes. He jumped back, his whole body recoiling from her. Why was he trying to avoid her? Was he beginning to lose his nerve again? For some time now, totally unaware that her life was in danger whenever she was with him, Séverine had attributed the inexplicable, instinctive fear she felt in his presence to the possibility that their relationship might shortly come to an end. She suddenly realized that if Jacques could not now bring himself to kill Roubaud, he would run away, never to return. She determined that this time he would kill him, and that if need be she would somehow give him the strength to do it. Another train passed by outside, an endless goods train, with a long string of wagons, invading the deep silence of the room with its interminable clatter. Séverine raised herself on her elbow, waiting for the noise to fade into the distance and disappear into the stillness of the night.

'Another quarter of an hour!' said Jacques. 'He'll be past the Bécourt wood by now. He's half-way. I can't stand this waiting!'

As he turned to walk back towards the window, he found Séverine standing beside the bed in her nightdress.

'Why don't we go downstairs with the lamp?' she suggested. 'You could decide where you're going to stand. I'll show you how I'm going to open the door and you can see what you need to do.'

Jacques backed away from her, trembling.

'No! Not the lamp!' he exclaimed.

'We can easily hide it afterwards,' she said. 'We need to know what we're doing.'

'No, no!' he stammered. 'Get back into bed.'

She took no notice, advancing towards him with the invincible, triumphant smile of the woman who knows she is irresistible. Once he was in her arms, he would yield to her nakedness and do as she wished. She continued to talk to him, coaxing him, trying to allay his fear.

'What is it, darling?' she said. 'Anyone would think you are frightened of me. The minute I come near you, you try to avoid me. If only you knew how much I need you at this moment. I want to know that you are there, that we are together, now and for ever. Do you understand?'

She had driven him back against the table. He could retreat from her no further. He had never seen her like this, with her nightdress unfastened and her hair tied up over her head, utterly naked, her neck laid bare and her breasts exposed. He was gasping for breath, fighting to control himself, reeling from the rush of blood to his head as his murderous desire rose within him. He remembered that the knife lay on the table behind him. He could almost feel it; all he had to do was stretch out his hand.

With a supreme effort he managed once again to stammer, 'Please, I beg you, get back into bed.'

Séverine was convinced that his shaking was due to uncontrollable desire. It made her feel almost proud. Why should she obey him? That night she wanted to be loved, loved beyond measure, loved to distraction. She pressed herself against him, softly, invitingly.

'Darling,' she whispered. 'Kiss me. Kiss me as you've never kissed me before. Show me how much you love me. It will give us courage. We shall need all the courage we have. **403** Our love must be a love that has no equal, a love greater than any love on earth, if we are to do what we have to do . . . Kiss me. Give me your heart. Give me your soul.'

It was as if he were being strangled. He couldn't breathe. There were voices screaming inside his skull, deafening him. Burning pains pierced his head, starting behind his ears and spreading to his arms and legs. He felt as if he were being chased from his own body, trampled underfoot by the unnamed creature, the beast within that now possessed him. Her nakedness made his senses reel; he would not be able to control his hands. She pressed her breasts against him and offered him her neck, so white and delicate, so irresistibly tempting. The sharp, warm scent of her body overcame him, sending him into a wild paroxysm of desire. He felt as if he were swaying endlessly backwards and forwards. He could no longer resist; his will had been torn from him, obliterated.

'Kiss me, darling,' she pleaded, 'while we still have

time ... He'll be here in a moment. If he has walked quickly, he could knock at the door any second now. If you won't come with me downstairs, remember ... I will open the door. You stand behind it. Don't hesitate. Do it straight away. Straight away, so that it's over and done with ... I love you so much! We're going to be so happy! Roubaud is a wicked man. He's been cruel to me. He's the only thing that stands in the way of our happiness ... Kiss me, darling. Kiss me violently. Kiss me as if you were eating me. Kiss me so there's nothing left of me that is not yours!'

Without turning round, Jacques felt behind him with his right hand and took hold of the knife. For a moment he remained where he was, with the knife clasped in his hand. Was this the return of his desire to avenge ancient wrongs that were lost in the mists of time, the accumulated bitterness that had been passed down from man to man since the first infidelity in some primeval cave? He stared at Séverine, wild-eyed. He had but one desire, to fling her dead over his shoulder like a trophy won in combat. The fearful door that guarded the dark abyss of sexual desire lay open. If she loved him she must die. To possess her fully he must kill her.

'Kiss me, kiss me ...' she insisted.

She threw back her head, offering herself to him, gently imploring him, exposing her bare neck above the voluptuous curve of her breasts. At the sight of her white flesh, Jacques, like a fire suddenly bursting into flame, raised the knife to stab her. Séverine saw the glint of the blade and flung herself backwards, with a look of utter astonishment and terror on her face.

'Jacques, Jacques!' she screamed. 'My God! Why me? Why? Why?'

Jacques made no answer. He clenched his teeth and walked towards her. There was a brief struggle and he pulled her back to the bed. She shrank away from him, terrified, defenceless, her nightdress torn open.

'Oh God! Why?'

He brought down the knife and the question froze on her lips. As he struck her, he had twisted the knife, as if his hand were asserting its own devilish will. It was identical to the way in which Roubaud had stabbed Grandmorin – in exactly the same place and with the same ferocity. Whether she cried out he never knew. Just at that moment the Paris express went by, so fast and with such a commotion that it made the floorboards shake. Séverine lay dead, as if struck down by the passing hurricane.

Jacques stood looking at her, stretched out at his feet beside the bed. The sound of the train vanished in the distance. Still he looked at her, in the empty silence of the red room. Séverine lay on the floor, surrounded by the red **405** wall coverings and the red curtains, bleeding profusely, a red stream running down between her breasts, spreading across her stomach to one of her thighs and dripping in thick blobs on to the floor. Her nightdress, torn apart, was soaked in blood. He would never have thought that she could bleed so much. What caused him to stand staring at her, mesmerized, was the look of unspeakable terror imprinted on the dead face of this once pretty, charming, inoffensive woman. Her black hair, tied up over her head, seemed like some ghastly head-dress, sombre as the night. Her periwinkle-blue eyes, staring at him wide open, questioned him, bewildered, terrified, uncomprehending. Why, why had he killed her? She had been taken away and destroyed, as murder took its inevitable course, an unsuspecting victim whom life had dragged through the mud and drawn into crime, never understanding why it had happened, and despite everything, tender-hearted and innocent to the end.

Jacques stood in amazement. His head rang with the cry of some savage beast, the squealing of a wild boar, the roaring of a lion. As he grew calmer, he realized it was the sound of his own breathing. At last! At last he had done it! He had killed! Yes, this was his doing! A sense of unbridled joy, an extraordinary feeling of elation bore him aloft. He savoured the long-awaited fulfilment of his desire. He felt a curious sort of pride, an enhanced sense of his male superiority. He had killed this woman, and he now possessed her as he had so long desired to possess her, totally and utterly, even to the point of destroying her. She was now no more and would never belong to anyone else. He suddenly had a vivid recollection of the other victim of murder, of Grandmorin's body, which he had seen on that dreadful night only five hundred metres from where he stood now. The delicate body that lay at his feet, 406 its white skin streaked with red, had like Grandmorin been reduced by the single thrust of a knife from a living creature to a tattered shred, a broken puppet, a limp rag. This was what murder was. He had murdered, and his victim lay on the floor. Like Grandmorin, she had fallen over, but on to her back, her legs spread apart, her left arm folded under her body and her right arm twisted and almost wrenched from her shoulder. It was on that night, when the sight of the murdered man had turned his irresistible itch to kill into an all-consuming desire, making his heart beat with excitement, that he had sworn he would one day find the courage to do this thing himself. He must not be a coward. He must follow his instinct. He must take a knife and kill. Without his realizing it, this idea had taken root and gradually grown inside his head. During the last year not a single hour had passed without it bringing him closer to the inevitable; even when he was holding Séverine in his arms and she was kissing him, the deadly process had continued. And now the two murders linked hands; the one was simply the logical outcome of the other.

As he gazed blankly at the dead woman, Jacques was awakened from his musings by a tremendous banging and clattering that sounded through the house and made the floor shake. Was someone breaking the doors open? Had they come to arrest him? He looked out of the window. Outside, nothing stirred. All was quiet. Ah yes, he thought, another train! He suddenly remembered the man who was about to knock on the door downstairs, the man he had been going to kill. He had forgotten all about him. Although he had no regrets, he was already beginning to think that he had acted foolishly. What had happened? The woman he loved, and who passionately loved him, lay dead on the floor, with her throat slit, whilst her husband, the man who had stood in the way of his happiness, was still alive and walking towards him, step by step, out there **407** in the dark. During the last few months, what had spared Roubaud was the sense of right and wrong that Jacques had acquired from his upbringing, a sense of the value of human life that had been gradually passed down from generation to generation. But that night, he had hardly been able to wait for Roubaud to arrive. Then, disregarding all he stood to gain, he had been carried away by an inherited streak of violence, by the same killer instinct that in the primeval forests drove one animal to slay another. There was nothing rational about killing. One was driven to kill by some physical, nervous impulse, a remnant of the primitive struggle for survival, a desire to live and celebrate one's superior strength. Having gratified his desire, Jacques felt exhausted. He was frightened and tried to understand what had happened; but his gratification left him with only a sense of amazement and deep bitterness that what had been done could not be undone. The sight of his pathetic victim, still staring at him with a look of terror and incomprehension in her eyes, was becoming unbearable. He was about to look away, when he suddenly had the impression that there was another white figure standing at the foot of the bed. Was it the dead woman's ghost? He looked again and saw that it was Flore. She had come back to him once before, when he was delirious after the accident. This must have been her moment of triumph, her moment of revenge! He froze in terror. What was he doing, waiting here in this room? He had killed. He was sated, replete, intoxicated with the fearful sweetness of his crime. He fled, tripping over the knife which had been left on the floor and, almost tumbling down the stairs in his haste, ran to the big door at the front of the house, as if the back door would be too small for him. He flung it open, rushed out into the inky blackness and vanished like a madman into the night. He did not stop to look behind

408 him. The sinister house, set at an angle to the railway line, stood with its door wide open, stark and silent as the grave.

That night, as on previous nights, Cabuche had walked through the hedge into the garden and had been waiting beneath Séverine's window. He knew that she was expecting Roubaud and wasn't surprised to see a light shining through a gap in one of the shutters. What did surprise him and root him to the spot, however, was the sight of a man rushing down the steps at the front of the house and making off into the fields like some crazed animal. He had disappeared before he had time to set off after him. Cabuche was worried. He stood before the open door, peering into the dark entrance hall, wondering what he should do. What was going on? Should he go in? The dead silence and the complete stillness of the house, even though there was still a light in the room upstairs, made him feel increasingly uneasy.

He finally decided he must go in and groped his way up the stairs. He stopped outside the bedroom door, which also had been left open. From where he stood, he thought he could see a pile of underclothes lying on the floor in a pool of light cast by the lamp. Séverine must have got undressed. He called softly. Suddenly he was frightened; his heart was beating wildly. Then he saw the blood. He immediately knew what had happened. He leaped forward. A terrible, heart-broken cry came from his mouth. Oh God! It was Séverine! Murdered! Flung in pitiful nakedness to the floor! He thought she might still be breathing. He was filled with such despair, such an agony of shame, to see her dying naked in front of him, that he threw his arms around her in a respectful embrace, raised her from the floor and laid her on the bed, drawing up the sheet in order to cover her. As he had lifted her in his arms, in the one and only demonstration of love that he was ever able to offer her, he had got blood on his hands and chest. He was covered in her blood. At the same moment he **409** saw that Roubaud and Misard had entered the room. They too, finding the doors of the house wide open, had decided to climb the stairs. Roubaud was late because he had stopped to talk to the crossing-keeper, and Misard had accompanied him to the house while continuing their conversation. They looked at Cabuche in disbelief. His hands were dripping with blood, like a butcher's.

'Just like Grandmorin,' Misard finally commented, after examining the wound.

Roubaud nodded, without saying anything. He could not take his eyes from Séverine, from the mask of sheer terror which congealed her face, from the black hair tied up over her head, and the blue eyes, staring wildly, beseeching . . . 'Why?'

12

Three months later, on a warm night in June, Jacques was driving the Le Havre express, which had left Paris at six thirty. His new locomotive, number 608, was fresh from the works. Jacques had been entrusted with running her in – with her 'initiation', as he put it. Although he was getting to know the locomotive, she didn't handle easily; she was awkward and temperamental, like a young horse that has to be broken in before it will accept the harness. He swore at her frequently; he really missed *La Lison*. He had to watch her very carefully; he could hardly take his hand off the reversing wheel. That night, however, the sky was so beautifully calm that Jacques felt more able to relax and give the locomotive its head. He breathed in the sweet night air. He had never felt better. He felt no remorse; he even seemed relieved and quite at peace with himself.

Although he didn't usually talk when driving the engine, he was teasing Pecqueux, who had been allowed to stay with him as his fireman.

'What's up with you?' he was saying. 'How come you're so wide awake? Have you given up drinking?'

It was true, Pecqueux seemed for once to be perfectly sober, and not at all his usual jovial self.

'You have to be wide awake,' he answered gruffly, 'if you want to see what's going on around you!'

Jacques looked at him uneasily, as if there were something on his conscience. The week before, he had enjoyed the favours of Pecqueux's mistress, the redoubtable Philomène, who had been pestering him for some time, like a scrawny cat on heat. He had taken her, not for sexual gratification, but to find out whether, having satisfied his desire to kill, he was finally cured. Could he make love to Philomène without wanting to slit her throat? He had made love to her twice already, and there had been no sign of his old malady, not a flicker, nothing. Without him realizing it, his present good humour and happy, relaxed manner must have been due to the pleasure of discovering that he was now no different from other men.

Pecqueux had opened the firebox door to put on more coal, but Jacques stopped him.

'Leave it,' he said. 'We don't want to overdo it. She's running well.'

Pecqueux started to mutter and swear.

'Running well, is she? Call this running well! She's a load of rubbish! She's bloody useless! When I think what we got out of *La Lison*! She did what you asked her to do! All this lousy thing's worth is a kick up the arse!'

Jacques didn't want to lose his temper, so he said nothing. But he knew that the old *ménage à trois* was a thing of the past. With the death of *La Lison*, the close, working partnership between him, his colleague and the locomotive had gone for good. They argued over the least little thing – a nut that was too tight, a shovelful of coal not put on properly. He would have to tread carefully where Philomène was concerned; he didn't want it to come to open war between him and his fireman, when the two of them had to work together in such a confined space. Until now, Pecqueux had been devoted to Jacques, like a faithful dog, and would have done anything for him, grateful for being left to his own devices, allowed to have the occasional nap and finish the leftovers in Jacques's lunch box. The two of them had lived together like brothers, resolutely facing the constant dangers of their job and understanding each other without the need for words. If they could no longer get on together, life was going to be hell, having to work side by side so closely, at daggers drawn. Only the week before, the Company had had to separate the driver and fireman of the Cherbourg express, because of a quarrel over a woman, the driver having physically attacked the fireman for not following instructions. They had come to blows, and there had been a fight, on the footplate itself, in complete disregard of the trainload of passengers they were carrying behind them.

Twice Pecqueux opened the firebox door and threw on more coal, deliberately trying to antagonize his driver. Jacques pretended not to notice, keeping his eye on the controls, each time carefully putting the injector on to reduce the pressure. The air was so soft, the night was warm and there was a lovely fresh breeze as the train sped along! When the train reached Le Havre at five past eleven, the two men cleaned down the locomotive, apparently the best of friends as always.

412   Just as they were leaving the engine shed and setting off for the Rue François-Mazeline to get some sleep, a voice called them: 'Hey, you two, what's the rush? Why don't you come in for a minute?'

It was Philomène; she must have been looking out for Jacques from the door of her brother's house. She seemed put out when she saw that he was with Pecqueux; she only decided to call them because she wanted to speak to her new lover, even if it meant doing so in front of her old one.

'Sod off!' snarled Pecqueux. 'You're a bloody nuisance. We need to get some sleep.'

'Charming!' Philomène retorted merrily. 'What about you, Monsieur Jacques? You'll come and have a little drink, won't you?'

Jacques, thinking it best to err on the side of caution, was about to refuse when Pecqueux suddenly accepted the invitation, realizing that it would give him a chance to observe the two of them together and find out what was going on between them. They went into the kitchen and sat down at the table, on which she placed some glasses and a bottle of brandy.

'We must try to keep our voices down,' she whispered. 'My brother's asleep upstairs and he doesn't like me having people in.'

She poured them a drink.

'By the way,' she continued, 'did you know old Mother Lebleu kicked the bucket this morning? I always said it would kill her if she was put into one of those rooms at the back. It's like living in a prison. She stuck it for four months, going on and on about how all she could see out of her window was a zinc roof … What finished her off, when she couldn't get out of her chair any more, was not being able to spy on Mademoiselle Guichon and Monsieur Dabadie. I'm sure of it. It was all she ever did. She was absolutely furious she never managed to catch them out. It killed her.'

Philomène paused to swallow her brandy.

'They must be sleeping together,' she said with a laugh. 'But they're too clever. You'll never catch that pair napping … I think Madame Moulin saw them together one evening, but she's not likely to say anything, she's too stupid. Besides, her husband's an assistant stationmaster and . . .'

She paused.

'Hey!' she continued excitedly. 'It's the Roubaud trial next week, in Rouen!'

So far, Jacques and Pecqueux had listened to her without saying a word. Pecqueux couldn't help but notice how talkative she was; she never had much to say when she was with him. He couldn't stop looking at her, gradually becoming more and more jealous as he saw how animated she was in the presence of Jacques.

'Yes,' said Jacques calmly, 'I've had the summons.'

Philomène moved herself closer, happily allowing her elbow to rest against him.

'Me too,' she said. 'They've called me as a witness …

Ah, Monsieur Jacques! They asked me all sorts of questions about you! They wanted to know the exact truth about you and poor Madame Roubaud. What I said to the judge was: "Monsieur, he adored her. He couldn't possibly have hurt her!" I'd seen you both together, you understand, and I could tell them all about it.'

'Oh,' said Jacques with a shrug of the shoulders, 'I wasn't worried. I was able to tell them what I was doing every hour of the day. The Company kept me on because they knew I'd done absolutely nothing wrong.'

They sat in silence, slowly sipping their brandy.

'It makes you cringe,' said Philomène. 'That beast they arrested, that Cabuche, covered in her blood! Some men must be mad! Why kill a woman just because he fancies her! What good's she going to be to him when she's dead? Anyway, I'll never forget it, as long as I live, that day when Monsieur Cauche came and arrested Roubaud too. He was on the platform. I was there. It was only a week afterwards. He'd started back at work the day after his wife's funeral and he seemed quite normal. Then Monsieur Cauche came and tapped him on the shoulder and told him he had orders to take him to prison. Can you imagine it! They'd been inseparable. They'd played cards together, night after night! Still, there you are! If you're a policeman you'd send your own mother and father to the guillotine! That's your job! Monsieur Cauche couldn't care less! I saw him again the other day, shuffling the cards in the Café du Commerce and never giving his friend a thought!'

Pecqueux clenched his teeth and banged his fist on the table.

'God Almighty! His wife was running rings round him! If I was in Roubaud's shoes ... Look, you were the one sleeping with her, someone else murders her, and it's Roubaud who gets sent for trial! It makes me mad!'

'Listen, you idiot,' said Philomène, 'Roubaud is accused

of persuading Cabuche to get rid of his wife for him. It was something to do with money. It seems they found President Grandmorin's watch at Cabuche's place – you remember . . . the one who was killed on the train eighteen months ago. They say the two murders are connected; it's a long story, and all very complicated. I couldn't begin to explain it, but it was in the paper – two whole columns of it!'

Jacques's mind was on something else; he didn't seem to be listening.

'What's the point of getting worked up about it?' he muttered. 'What's it got to do with us? If the law doesn't know what it's doing, there's not much we can do to help.'

He suddenly turned pale and sat looking into space.

'The only one I feel sorry for is that poor woman,' he said. 'That poor woman!'

'Well, I've got a woman,' Pecqueux exclaimed angrily, 'and if anyone started messing with her, I'd strangle the pair of them. They could cut my head off – I couldn't care less!'

There was another silence. Philomène shrugged her shoulders dismissively and refilled the glasses. Deep down, Pecqueux disgusted her. She glanced at him out of the corner of her eye. He wasn't looking after himself; he was dirty, and his clothes were in tatters. Since breaking her leg, Madame Victoire had been unable to get about; she had had to give up her job at the lavatories and had been admitted to a home. She was no longer there to mollycoddle him, to slip him the odd silver coin and mend his clothes, in case his other woman, the one in Le Havre, accused her of neglecting 'their man'. She pulled a face. Jacques looked clean and smart and so much more attractive.

'Is it your Paris woman you'd strangle?' she gibed. 'Who'd want to run off with her?'

'Never you mind!' he muttered.

Philomène raised her glass, taunting him: 'Here's to you! You can bring me your dirty washing. I'll get it washed and mended. You're a disgrace . . . to both of us. Cheers, Monsieur Jacques!'

Jacques shuddered, as if he were emerging from a dream. Since the murder, he had felt absolutely no remorse and had experienced a sense of relief and physical well-being, but now and then the thought of Séverine moved his gentle nature to the point of tears. Trying to hide his emotion, he raised his glass and suddenly blurted out: 'Did you know there's going to be a war?'

'Surely not!' exclaimed Philomène. 'Who against?'

'Against the Prussians, of course . . . just because some prince of theirs wants to be King of Spain!¹ That's all they talked about yesterday in the Assembly.'

'That'll be fun!' Philomène grumbled. 'As if they haven't caused us enough trouble already, with their elections and plebiscites and riots in Paris² . . . If there's going to be fighting, will all the men get called up?'

'Oh, we'll be all right,' said Jacques. 'They'll need to keep the railways running . . . but it's going to make life difficult. There'll be soldiers and provisions to be transported . . . Anyway, if it happens, we'll just have to do our duty.'

Whereupon he stood up, realizing that she had slipped one of her legs under his. Pecqueux noticed it too; he went red in the face and clenched his fist.

'Come on,' said Jacques, 'it's time for bed.'

'Yes,' Pecqueux muttered, 'it certainly is.'

He had grabbed Philomène by the arm and was squeezing it so hard that she felt it would break. Stifling a cry of pain, she whispered into Jacques's ear, as Pecqueux knocked back his brandy, 'Be careful. When he's had a drink he can get really rough.'

Just then they heard heavy footsteps coming down the stairs.

'It's my brother,' said Philomène in a panic. 'Quick, you'll have to go!'

They hadn't walked twenty paces from the house when they heard the sound of blows, followed by screams. Philomène was being given a beating, like a little girl who'd been caught stealing jam from the cupboard. Jacques stopped and wanted to go back to help her, but Pecqueux restrained him.

'It's none of your business,' he said. 'The bitch! She deserves all she gets!'

Jacques and Pecqueux reached the Rue François-Mazeline and went to bed without exchanging a word. The room was so tiny that their two beds almost touched; they remained awake for a long time, their eyes open, listening to the sound of each other's breathing.

The hearings in the Roubaud case were due to begin on the Monday, in Rouen. For Denizet, the examining magistrate, the investigation had been a signal triumph; people in legal circles could not speak highly enough of the way he had brought such a complicated and involved case to so successful a conclusion. It was a masterpiece of astute analysis, they said, a superb, logical reconstruction of the truth; in short, a triumph of creative imagination.

The first thing that Denizet did when he arrived on the scene of the crime at La Croix-de-Maufras, a few hours after Séverine's murder, was to have Cabuche arrested. Everything clearly pointed to him being the murderer – the fact that he was covered in blood, and the damning evidence of Roubaud and Misard, who described how they had found him in the room with the body, alone and distraught. When questioned and asked to explain why and how he came to be there, Cabuche had mumbled some tale that Denizet simply dismissed with a shrug of his shoulders, so naive and predictable did it seem. It was just the sort of story he had been expecting; he had heard it so many times before – the fictitious murderer, the invented criminal, whom the real criminal claimed to have heard running off into the night.

If this mysterious person was still running, he would be well away by now, wouldn't he! When asked what he was doing outside the house at such a late hour, Cabuche became flustered and couldn't give a straight answer, eventually claiming that he was just out for a walk. It was childish. How could Denizet take this unknown intruder seriously – committing a murder and then running away, leaving all the doors of the house open, without touching a thing or helping himself to even a handkerchief? Where had he come from? Why had he killed her? From the very beginning of his inquiry, however, the judge had known about Jacques's affair with the victim and was concerned to establish his whereabouts on the day of the murder. But, in addition to Cabuche's own testimony that he had accompanied Jacques to Barentin, to catch the 4.14 train, the hotel proprietor in Rouen was quite adamant that her guest had gone to bed straight after his evening meal and had not left his room until the next morning, at about seven o'clock. Surely a lover does not murder the woman he loves for no reason at all, when there has never been the slightest disagreement between them. It would be absurd! It was unthinkable! There was only one possible murderer, the obvious murderer – the man they had arrested, the man found in the room with his hands covered in blood and the knife lying on the floor at his feet, the inhuman beast who was trying to spin him a ridiculous fairy story.

Having come to this conclusion, however, although convinced he was right, and even though his instinct, which, he said, he always relied on more than actual proof, told him that Cabuche was indeed the murderer, Monsieur Denizet encountered a minor difficulty. An initial search of Cabuche's hovel in the Bécourt woods had revealed nothing. It had proved impossible to establish theft as a motive, and he needed to find some other reason for the murder. Then, quite by chance, during the course of one of his interviews, Misard had put him on the track. Misard said that one night he had seen Cabuche climbing over a wall to watch Madame Roubaud through the window as she was going to bed. When Jacques was questioned about Cabuche, he simply stated what he knew: Cabuche secretly adored her, he followed her everywhere, he always wanted to be near her and he would do anything for her. To Denizet, it seemed obvious; Cabuche had been driven by pure animal instinct. Everything fell into place perfectly. He had let himself in through the front door – he may even have had a key – he had left the door open in his unseemly haste, and there had been a struggle, after which he had murdered her and finally raped her, interrupted only by the arrival of her husband. One final question remained in his mind; it was odd that Cabuche, knowing Roubaud might arrive at any minute, should choose precisely the moment when he could be caught. But when he thought about it, this simply made the crime appear worse and convinced him that Cabuche was guilty; it suggested that he had acted out of sheer carnal desire and was afraid that, if he didn't seize the opportunity when Séverine was still alone in an empty house, he would never have another chance, as she was due to leave the next day. Monsieur Denizet's mind was made up; there could be no other explanation.

Cabuche was questioned again and again, gradually becoming ensnared in the skilful web of Denizet's investigation, completely unaware of the traps that were being set for him to fall into. He stuck to his original story. He was walking along the road, enjoying the cool night air, when someone brushed past him, running off into the dark so fast that he couldn't even say which way he went. He had been worried and when he went to look at the house he noticed that the front door had been left wide open. He had eventually decided to go upstairs and had found the woman, dead but still warm, looking at him with her eyes wide open. He had put her on the bed, thinking she was still alive, and had covered himself in blood. That was all he knew. He repeated it over and over again, never changing a single detail, as if he were simply rehearsing a predetermined story. When they tried to get him to say anything different, he became frightened and fell silent, like a man of low intelligence who didn't understand what he was being asked. The first time Monsieur Denizet asked him whether he had been in love with the victim, he blushed violently, like a young boy being told off the first time he had kissed a girl. Cabuche denied it; he had never allowed himself to think of sleeping with her, as if it were something dreadful and unspeakable, yet at the same time something delicate and mysterious, something hidden away at the bottom of his heart, which he could reveal to no one. No, he hadn't been in love with her, and he hadn't wanted to sleep with her. He refused to say anything; to talk of such things now she was dead seemed to him to be a sacrilege. But his persistent denial of something that several witnesses had testified to also went against him. Naturally, according to the prosecution, he had a vested interest in concealing the insane attraction he felt towards the unfortunate woman he was to kill in order to satisfy his desire. When the examining magistrate, putting all the evidence together, attempted to force an admission from him by directly accusing him of murder and rape, Cabuche flew into a blind rage, protesting his innocence. How could he have killed her to have sex with her? He worshipped her like a saint! The police had to be called in to restrain him; he was saying he'd kill the whole damned lot of them. Cabuche, concluded Monsieur Denizet, was the most dangerous sort of villain – a devious character, but one who was betrayed by his own violent temper, which in the end plainly attested to the crimes he was attempting to deny.

It was at this point in the investigation, with Cabuche

losing his temper every time he was accused of murder and shouting that it was the other man, the unknown person who had run away, that Monsieur Denizet made an important discovery, which transformed the whole affair and put an entirely new complexion on things. Monsieur Denizet had always claimed to have a nose for the truth. Some instinct prompted him to conduct another search of Cabuche's hovel. Behind one of the beams he found a little hiding place containing a woman's handkerchiefs and gloves, and underneath them a gold watch, which to his great delight he recognized immediately. It was President Grandmorin's watch, the one he had spent so much time trying to track down before, a large watch engraved with two initials intertwined and, on the inside of the case, the maker's number, 2516. This discovery came as a sudden revelation; everything became clear. The two crimes were connected. He was amazed at the way it all fitted together so logically. But **421** the consequences were going to be very far-reaching. First, before mentioning the watch, he questioned Cabuche about the gloves and the handkerchiefs. For a moment Cabuche was on the point of confessing everything – yes he adored her, yes he desired her, he even kissed the dresses she had worn, picked up and stole things she dropped – laces from her stays, grips, hairpins. Then he was suddenly overcome with shame and embarrassment and would say no more. Monsieur Denizet, deciding that this was the moment, produced the watch and showed it to him. Cabuche looked at it aghast. He remembered it clearly; he had discovered it tied inside a handkerchief, which he had stolen from beneath Séverine's pillow and taken home with him as one of his trophies. He had left it in his house while he racked his brains to think of a way of returning it. But what was the point of saying that? He would then have to admit to all the other things he had taken – bits of clothing and underwear with the scent of her perfume on them. He felt so ashamed of himself. They didn't believe anything of what he said already. He could no longer understand it himself; everything was confused in his mind. It was all too complicated for him; it was becoming a nightmare. He no longer flew into a rage whenever they accused him of murder but stood there looking bewildered, answering that he did not know to every question he was asked. He did not know about the gloves and the handkerchiefs. He did not know about the watch. The whole thing was beginning to irritate him. Why didn't they stop pestering him and take him off to be guillotined?

The following day, Monsieur Denizet had Roubaud arrested. Feeling that he now had the upper hand, he had issued the warrant in a moment of inspiration, thoroughly confident in his own perspicacity and before having any definite proof against him. Although there was still much 422 that remained unexplained, he sensed that Roubaud was the vital link and even the instigator in this double murder. His suspicions met with immediate success when he discovered the deed of gift leaving their estate to the survivor, signed by Roubaud and Séverine in the presence of Maitre Colin, a solicitor in Le Havre, a week after they had taken possession of La Croix-de-Maufras. From that moment, Denizet was able to reconstruct the whole story, with such powerful arguments and telling evidence that his case against him was unassailable; the truth itself would have appeared less convincing, more far-fetched and even fantastical by comparison. Roubaud was a coward who on two occasions, frightened to commit murder himself, had enlisted the service of his bestial accomplice, Cabuche. The first time, eager to get his hands on President Grandmorin's legacy, knowing what was in his will and also knowing that Cabuche bore a grudge against him, Roubaud had slipped the knife into his hand and pushed him into the coupé while the train was standing in the station at Rouen. Having shared the ten thousand francs between them, the two would probably never have seen each other again, had not one murder led to another. It was here that Monsieur Denizet displayed the profound understanding of criminal mentality for which he was so much admired; he had continued to keep his eye on Cabuche, he now revealed, because he was convinced that, statistically, the first murder would be followed by a second. In effect it needed only eighteen months: the Roubauds' marriage had broken up, Roubaud had squandered his five thousand francs in gambling, and his wife had been driven to take a lover to amuse herself. No doubt she had refused to sell La Croix-de-Maufras lest her husband dissipate that money too; they were continually arguing, and she might have been threatening to hand him over to the police. At all events, a number of witnesses had testified to the complete breakdown of their marriage, and it was this that had eventually led to the second murder. The bestial Cabuche had made his second appearance. Roubaud, lurking somewhere in the shadows, had once again thrust the knife into his hand, to ensure that ownership of the accursed house which had already cost one life should finally be his. Such was the truth, the blinding truth, to which all the evidence pointed: the watch found in the quarry man's hut, and especially the two bodies killed in exactly the same way, stabbed in the throat by the same person with the same weapon – the knife that had been recovered from the bedroom. On this last point the prosecution expressed some uncertainty; the President's wound appeared to have been made by a smaller and sharper implement.

At first Roubaud simply answered yes or no in the sleepy, lethargic drawl which had by now become his customary manner of speech. He didn't appear surprised that he had been arrested; as his personality slowly disintegrated, he had become indifferent to everything. In order to get him to talk, a warder was assigned permanently to his cell. Roubaud played cards with him all day long and was perfectly happy. He remained convinced that Cabuche was guilty; only he could have committed the murder. When asked about Jacques, he shrugged his shoulders and laughed, as much as to say that he knew all about the relationship between his wife and the engine driver. When, however, after his initial questions, Monsieur Denizet began to expound his theory of the murder and started to press him and accuse him directly of being an accomplice, in an attempt to extract a confession from him at the shock of having been found out, Roubaud had become more cautious. What tale was this, he thought? They were saying that it wasn't him but Cabuche who had killed Grandmorin, just as he had killed Séverine, yet on both occasions he was the truly guilty party because Cabuche had been acting in his interest and on his behalf. He was amazed at this involved rigmarole and became very wary; they must be setting him a trap, lying to him in order to get him to admit that one of these murders – the first murder – had been committed by him. The minute he was arrested, Roubaud had assumed it was because the earlier case had been reopened. When confronted with Cabuche, he swore that he did not know him. But, when he then insisted he had discovered him covered in blood and about to rape his victim, Cabuche flew into a rage, and there followed a violent and confused scene which complicated matters even further. Three days went by, during which the magistrate questioned them both repeatedly, convinced that the two accomplices had agreed to put on this display of hostility towards each other in order to confuse him. Roubaud, utterly exhausted, had decided he would answer no more questions, when suddenly, in a moment of exasperation, and wanting to have the whole thing settled – a vague compulsion that had been troubling him for months – he blurted out the truth, the whole truth and nothing but the truth.

That day Monsieur Denizet had conducted his inquiries with consummate skill, sitting at his desk, lowering his heavy eyelids and pursing his expressive lips in a display of great sagacity. For a whole hour he had tried every learned ploy he knew against Roubaud. Roubaud was overweight and looked flabby, sallow and unhealthy, but Denizet suspected that, beneath his unprepossessing exterior, he was really quite clever. He thought he had managed to track him down step by step, to hem him in and finally ensnare him, when Roubaud, like a man at the end of his tether, threw his hands in the air and exclaimed that he had had enough and that he would rather confess than go on being tormented like this. If they were determined to prove him guilty, he would rather be proved guilty of things that he had actually done. But as he told his story – his wife abused by Grandmorin when she was a young girl, his jealous rage when the sordid affair became known to him, how he had killed Grandmorin and why he had taken the ten thousand francs – the magistrate raised his eyelids sceptically, protruding his lips in a scornful expression of complete and utter disbelief. By the time Roubaud had finished speaking, there was a broad smile on Monsieur Denizet's face. This fellow was cleverer than he thought. To claim that he had committed the first murder and to represent it simply as a crime of passion, thus clearing himself of any premeditated theft and more importantly of any involvement in the murder of Séverine, was undoubtedly a bold move, which displayed intelligence and a sense of purpose beyond the ordinary. But his story didn't hold water.

'Come, come, Roubaud,' he said, 'please don't treat us like children ... Are you really asking us to believe that you were jealous and that you murdered in a fit of jealousy?'

'Most certainly,' Roubaud answered.

'If we are to accept your story, you married your wife without knowing anything about her relationship with the President . . . Is this likely? In your case everything would seem to suggest that, on the contrary, the arrangement had all been planned, discussed and agreed upon. You walk into marriage with a young girl who has been brought up like a lady. She receives a dowry. Her protector becomes yours as well. You are fully aware that she has been left a house in the country in his will. And you try to tell us that you knew nothing, absolutely nothing! Really! I put it to you that you knew everything. There is no other way that your marriage can be explained. What is more, your story is belied by one very obvious fact. You are not a jealous husband, and it is no use trying to claim that you are.'

'I am telling you the truth. I killed in a fit of jealous rage.'

426 'Please explain to me then how, having murdered the President because of some unspecified relationship in the past, for which, incidentally, you have no proof, you managed to turn a blind eye to the fact that your wife took a lover, this Jacques Lantier, an affair about which there can be no doubt whatever. A number of witnesses have mentioned it and you yourself have told me that you knew of it. And yet you left them free to see each other as they chose. Why?'

Roubaud sat slumped in his chair, gazing into the distance with a confused look in his eyes. He could find no explanation.

'I don't know,' he finally mumbled. 'I killed Grandmorin, but I didn't kill my wife.'

'Then stop trying to tell me that you were a jealous husband seeking revenge. I advise you not to repeat such fictions to the gentlemen of the jury; they would simply laugh at you. Believe me, you will have to change your tune. Only the truth can save you.'

But from then on, the more Roubaud insisted that he was indeed telling the truth, the more he was accused of lying. Everything seemed to turn against him; even the earlier statements he had made at the first inquiry, which should have corroborated his present account,[3] since he had then informed against Cabuche, were used on the contrary as evidence of a cunning plan that the two had hatched between them. Monsieur Denizet probed the psychology that lay behind the whole affair with true professional zeal. Never before, he said, had he delved deeper into human nature. It had been more a matter of divining the truth than of simply ascertaining the facts; he prided himself on being one of those judges who can read a criminal's mind, lead him where he wants and then demolish him with a single glance. Besides, there was now no shortage of evidence; the case was overwhelming. The inquiry had established a solid basis for prosecution; the truth shone forth with dazzling certainty, like light from the sun.

What further enhanced the merit of Monsieur Denizet's achievement was that, without anyone knowing a thing about it, he had carefully pieced things together and had brought the two cases together as one. Following the resounding success of the plebiscite, the country had been in a constant state of hysteria, displaying all those symptoms of frenzy that portend some great disaster. As the Empire drew to a close, society, politics and especially the press were infused with a sense of unease and nervous excitement, in which even occasions for celebration assumed an unhealthy, excessive character. So when, following the murder of a woman in an isolated house at La Croix-de-Maufras, it was learned that the examining magistrate at Rouen had by a stroke of genius reopened the inquiry into the Grandmorin affair and connected the two cases together, there was a veritable explosion of triumph in the official newspapers. There had still been occasional satirical references in the opposition press to the mysterious, mythical killer who had been invented by the police and given so much publicity in order to cover up the misdemeanours of certain highly placed individuals who had been compromised by the affair. These taunts could now be dealt with once and for all. The murderer and his accomplice were under arrest; President Grandmorin would emerge from the episode with his reputation untarnished. Once again there was fierce controversy; excitement grew day by day in both Rouen and Paris. The public, apart from being fascinated by a gruesome story of murder, was drawn to the case as if the future of the state itself depended on finally establishing the truth of the affair. For a whole week the press talked of nothing else.

Monsieur Denizet was summoned to Paris and presented himself at the private dwelling of the Secretary-General, Monsieur Camy-Lamotte, in the Rue du Rocher. He found him standing in his sparsely furnished study. He looked more drawn and tired than when he had last seen him; his star was on the wane and his scepticism was now coloured with regret, as if at this moment of great personal triumph he sensed the imminent collapse of the regime he had served. For the last two days he had been struggling to resolve a dilemma, still uncertain what use he should make of Séverine's letter, which he had kept and which would have completely undermined the case for the prosecution, confirming as it did Roubaud's account with a piece of incontrovertible evidence. No one knew it existed. He could destroy it. The day before, however, the Emperor had told him that on this occasion he demanded the law should take its course, without interference, even if the outcome should prove damaging to his government. It was a gesture of good faith, an intuition perhaps that, after the country had acclaimed him, a single miscarriage of justice could change the course of destiny. Although the

Secretary-General had no moral scruples of his own, having learned to resolve political issues in a purely mechanical way, these instructions troubled him, and he wondered whether his allegiance to the Emperor might entail disobeying him.

'Well,' exclaimed Monsieur Denizet, feeling very pleased with himself, 'my hunch was right! It was Cabuche who stabbed the President. There was some truth in the other line of inquiry, I agree, and personally I always felt there was something suspicious about Roubaud's evidence. Anyway, we've got both of them.'

Monsieur Camy-Lamotte looked at him steadily with his pale-coloured eyes.

'So all the facts in the dossier I received have been verified, and you are absolutely convinced?'

'Absolutely,' Monsieur Denizet assured him. 'There can be no doubt whatever ... It all fits together. I cannot remember a case in which, for all its apparent complications, the crime followed a more logical sequence and was easier to predict.'

'But Roubaud objects. He claims it was he who committed the first murder and tells some story about his wife being violated and him being driven by jealousy and killing in a fit of blind rage. The opposition newspapers are full of it.'

'The opposition newspapers will report any old gossip. But they don't really believe it. How can Roubaud be a jealous husband when he encouraged his wife to take a lover? Let him try telling that to the court! He just wants to stir up scandal, but he won't succeed. If he had some evidence ... but he hasn't. He talks of a letter, which he claims he made his wife write and which should have been found amongst the victim's papers. You went through those papers, monsieur, and you would have found it, wouldn't you?'

Monsieur Camy-Lamotte made no answer. It was true, the magistrate's findings would enable him to bury this scandal once and for all; no one would believe Roubaud, and the President's name would be cleared of all suspicion. The much-publicized rehabilitation of one of its most distinguished adherents could only be to the government's advantage. Besides, since Roubaud admitted he was guilty, it did not affect the principle of justice whether he was condemned on one charge or another. That left Cabuche. If he had had nothing to do with the first murder, he certainly appeared to be guilty of the second. Justice, after all, was nothing but a grand illusion! When the path to truth was so tangled and overgrown, the belief in justice was a snare. It was better to be safe than sorry, and do what he could to prop up this ailing remnant of Empire as it teetered on the brink of collapse.

430 'You didn't find this letter, did you, monsieur?' the magistrate repeated.

Once again Monsieur Camy-Lamotte raised his eyes and looked at him. The situation lay entirely in his hands, and, although he shared the Emperor's misgivings, he replied quite calmly, 'I found absolutely nothing.'

Then, smiling affably, he offered Monsieur Denizet his heartfelt congratulations. Only a slight quiver of his lips indicated the supreme irony of his words. Never had an investigation been conducted with such acumen. It had been decided officially that after the autumn recess he would be called to the bar in Paris. As he spoke he conducted him out into the hall.

'You alone were able to untangle this affair,' he continued. 'What you have achieved is truly remarkable ... Once the truth is allowed to speak for itself, nothing can stand in its way, neither personal ambition nor reasons of state ... Feel free to continue. Proceed with the case in the normal way, whatever the consequences.'

'I consider it no more than my duty,' replied Monsieur Denizet, bidding him farewell and leaving the house in a glow of satisfaction.

Left alone, the first thing Monsieur Camy-Lamotte did was to light a candle. He then opened the drawer in which he had filed Séverine's letter. The flame lengthened. He opened the letter, wanting to read again the two lines of handwriting. Immediately the thought of Séverine came back to him – the timid little criminal with periwinkle-blue eyes who had aroused such tender feelings in him all that time ago. Now she was dead, a tragic victim. Who could tell what secret she had taken with her? Truth, justice . . . it was all an illusion! For Monsieur Camy-Lamotte, all that remained of this charming young woman, whom he had never come to know, was the fleeting desire she had aroused in him on the day they met, a desire which would remain for ever unsatisfied. As he held the letter to the flame and it began to burn, a feeling of great sadness came over him, a sense of impending calamity. Why destroy this evidence and suffer a guilty conscience, if the Empire was destined to be swept away like the charred fragment of paper that fell from his fingers? 431

Monsieur Denizet completed his investigation in less than a week. The Western Railway Company was most cooperative, providing him with all the documents and statements he needed; it too was anxious to see the end of a distasteful affair, which had started with one of its employees, had spread to every corner of the company and had come close to unseating its board of directors. The diseased limb needed to be amputated as quickly as possible. Once again the station staff at Rouen filed through the magistrate's office – Monsieur Dabadie, Moulin and others – all providing damning evidence of Roubaud's lamentable conduct. They were followed by Monsieur Bessière, the stationmaster at Barentin, and by a number of

other employees at Rouen, whose statements were of crucial importance in connection with the first murder.
Finally Monsieur Denizet interviewed Monsieur Vandorpe, the stationmaster at Paris, Misard, the man at the
section post, and the principal guard, Henri Dauvergne.
Both Misard and Dauvergne confirmed that Roubaud had
shown little interest in married life. Henri, whom Séverine
had looked after at La Croix-de-Maufras, even alleged that
one night, while still recovering from the accident, he
thought he had heard Roubaud and Cabuche conspiring
together outside his window, which explained a great deal
and contradicted the assertion of the two accused that they
did not know each other. Amongst the staff of the Railway
Company there was a general feeling of anger and sorrow
for the unfortunate victims – the poor young woman
whose marital infidelity now seemed perfectly excusable,
432 and the distinguished old gentleman whose name was now
cleared of the ugly rumours that had been circulating
about him.

But the new investigation had also aroused the passions
of the Grandmorin family and, although they were quite
prepared to help Monsieur Denizet with his inquiries, they
made it more difficult for him to proceed with the charges
he had in mind. The Lachesnayes were cock-a-hoop; they
had always maintained that Roubaud was guilty and, being
the self-seeking, greedy pair they were, they resented the
bequest of La Croix-de-Maufras to Séverine. When the
case was reopened, they saw it as their opportunity to contest the will. The only way of having the legacy rescinded
was to disqualify Séverine on the grounds of animosity
towards Grandmorin, and so they partially subscribed to
Roubaud's version of events, claiming that his wife had
acted as an accomplice to the murder, helping Roubaud to
kill Grandmorin, not to avenge some imaginary wrong
done to her, but simply to rob him. Monsieur Denizet was

forced to take issue with them, and with Berthe in particular, who felt very bitter against Séverine, her former friend, accusing her of every wickedness imaginable. The magistrate defended her character, becoming quite heated and angry the minute he felt there was any threat to his own interpretation of events, to the masterpiece of logical construction, so perfectly assembled, as he himself proudly declared, that the slightest alteration would bring the whole thing tumbling down. At one point, there were heated exchanges between the Lachesnayes and Madame Bonnehon. Madame Bonnehon, who had previously had a high opinion of Roubaud, now had nothing good to say about him. But she still spoke up in favour of his wife, for whom she had a great affection. She had every sympathy for this charming young lady who had fallen in love, and she was overcome by the tragic story of her violent death. She clearly had a complete disregard for money. Her niece **433** should be ashamed of herself, raking up the question of the legacy again! If Séverine were guilty, it would mean that everything in Roubaud's confession was true, and once again the President's name would be dragged through the mud. If the truth had not been so ingeniously established by Monsieur Denizet's investigation, it would have been necessary to invent it in order to preserve the family's good name. She spoke with some bitterness of social circles in Rouen, where the affair was constantly on everyone's lips. Now that age was creeping up on her, and the opulent, classically sculpted beauty she had cultivated was beginning to fade, her reign amongst the elite had come to an end. Only the day before, at a reception given by Madame Leboucq, the wife of the Appeal Court judge, the tall, elegant, dark-haired lady who had usurped her position, all sorts of lurid tales were being whispered, including details of Louisette's misadventure, and any other piece of gossip that the public desire for vilification

could fabricate. It was at this point that Monsieur Denizet
intervened to inform her that Monsieur Leboucq would
be acting as an assessor[4] at the forthcoming Assizes. The
Lachesnayes looked worried and fell silent; they seemed
to have nothing more to say. Madame Bonnehon tried to
reassure them. She was sure that justice would be done;
the hearing would be presided over by her old friend Monsieur Desbazeilles, who these days, because of his
rheumatism, spent most of his time living in the past, and
the second assessor was to be Monsieur Chaumette, the
father of the young barrister she had taken under her wing.
So she was not worried, although as she mentioned the
name of Monsieur Chaumette, a wistful smile passed
across her lips as she thought of his son, who for some
time now was regularly to be seen at Madame Leboucq's,
where she herself had advised him to go so as not to hinder
434 his prospects.

When the celebrated trial finally began, its impact on
the general public was considerably lessened by rumours
of imminent war and by the general state of nervousness
that was affecting the whole of France. Even so, in Rouen
there were three days of feverish excitement, with crowds
jostling outside the doors and all the reserved seats taken
by fashionable ladies of the town.[5] Never, since being con-
verted into a court of law, had the old palace of the Dukes
of Normandy seen such an influx of people. It was towards
the end of June. The afternoons were warm and sunny.
The sunlight streamed through the ten stained-glass windows, illuminating the oak panels, the white stone crucifix
standing at the far end of the hall against a background of
red tapestry embroidered with Napoleonic bees,[6] and the
famous ceiling which dated from the time of Louis XII,
with its wooden compartments carved and picked out in
a soft-coloured antique gold. Even before the hearing
began, it was so hot that people could hardly breathe.

Some of the women were standing on tiptoe to look at the table of exhibits that would be used in the trial – Grandmorin's watch, Séverine's blood-stained nightdress and the knife used for both murders. A lawyer had come from Paris to act as Cabuche's defence and he too was the focus of much attention. The jury consisted of twelve citizens of Rouen, sitting in a row, dressed formally in black frock-coats and looking very stiff and serious. When the court entered there was such a disturbance in the public standing area that the presiding judge immediately had to threaten to clear the hall.

At last the hearing began, and the jury was sworn in. A fresh wave of excitement ran round the courtroom as the witnesses were summoned. At the names of Madame Bonnehon and Monsieur de Lachesnaye, all heads turned to look. But it was Jacques especially who caught the attention of the ladies; they could not take their eyes off him. 435 When the accused were brought in, each escorted by two police officers, everyone glued their eyes on them and began to exchange opinions. They found them frightening and uncouth, obvious criminals. Roubaud in his dark-coloured jacket and with his tie loosely knotted, like someone who was no longer concerned about his appearance, seemed surprisingly old; his face was bloated, and he looked bewildered. As for Cabuche, he was exactly as everyone had imagined he would be. He was dressed in a long blue smock and he looked every inch the murderer, with enormous fists and carnivorous jaws, not the sort of person you would want to meet on a dark night. When he was questioned, this unfavourable impression was quickly confirmed; some of his answers were greeted with gasps of disbelief. To every question from the presiding judge, he replied that he didn't know. He didn't know how the watch came to be in his house. He didn't know why he had let the real murderer get away. He stuck to his story about the strange man he claimed to have heard running off into the night. When questioned about his bestial passion for the unfortunate victim, he became incoherent and flew into such a violent rage that the two police officers had to hold him by the arms. It was all lies. He didn't love her. He hadn't desired her. It was indecent to even think of such a thing. She was a lady, whereas he had been to prison and lived like an animal! After a while he calmed down and resumed his sullen silence, only answering in monosyllables, apparently indifferent to the sentence that hung over his head. Similarly Roubaud stuck to what the prosecution referred to as his 'story', describing how and why he had killed Grandmorin and denying that he had had any part in the murder of his wife. He spoke in short, broken sentences that were almost unintelligible and kept having sudden lapses of memory. He had such a vague look in his eyes and his voice was so indistinct that it seemed at times as if he had forgotten what he wanted to say and was simply making things up. The judge persevered, pointing out to him the inconsistencies in his explanation. Eventually Roubaud shrugged his shoulders and refused to answer any more questions; what was the point of telling the truth when the court preferred to hear falsehoods? This display of wilful contempt for justice only made things worse for him. It was also noticed that the two accused remained completely uninterested in each other throughout the examination, a sure sign of some previous agreement between them, a cunning plan which they were determined to follow to the bitter end. They pretended not to know each other and even made accusations against each other in order to confuse the court. By the time the questioning was completed the verdict was a foregone conclusion, so skilfully had the judge conducted his examination, causing Roubaud and Cabuche to fall into every trap he had set them and making it appear that they had condemned themselves. On the same day, a few other minor witnesses were heard. By five o'clock the heat had become so insufferable that two ladies fainted.

The next day there was great excitement as further witnesses were called. Madame Bonnehon was a model of tact and refinement. Everyone listened with interest to the employees from the Railway Company, Monsieur Vandorpe, Monsieur Bessière, Monsieur Dabadie and especially Monsieur Cauche, who gave a long-winded account of how well he knew Roubaud, having frequently played cards with him at the Café du Commerce. Henri Dauvergne repeated his damning allegation that, although he was very drowsy and still feeling ill as a result of his accident, he was fairly certain he had heard the voices of the two accused whispering together outside his window. When asked about Séverine, he chose his words very carefully, giving them to understand that he had been in love 437 with her, but, knowing that she had promised herself to another man, he had felt duty bound to stand aside. When this other man, Jacques Lantier, was finally summoned, a buzz ran round the courtroom, people stood up to get a better look, and even the members of the jury seemed to become suddenly more attentive. Jacques had very calmly placed his hands on the rail of the witness-box, leaning forward in the same way as when he stood at the controls of his locomotive. Having to appear in court should have been deeply upsetting for him, but his mind remained perfectly clear and lucid, as if the whole affair had absolutely nothing to do with him. The evidence he was about to give came as from an outsider, a completely innocent party. Since the crime, he had not felt the slightest emotion. He hadn't given the murder a thought and had wiped it from his memory. His body felt perfectly relaxed, fit and healthy. As he stood at the rail of the witness-box he sensed neither remorse nor regret; his conscience was clear. He looked innocently at Roubaud and Cabuche. He knew that Roubaud was guilty. He gave him a quick nod, a little sign of acknowledgement, without stopping to think that everyone in the courtroom now knew about his affair with Roubaud's wife. He smiled at Cabuche, whom he knew to be innocent and whose place in the dock should have been assigned to him. He looked a rough customer, but really there was nothing wrong with him; he had seen how hard he worked and he had shaken hands with him. Jacques remained perfectly composed as he gave his evidence, answering the judge clearly and precisely. Having questioned him at length about his liaison with the victim, the judge asked him to describe how he had left La Croix-de-Maufras a few hours before the murder, taken a train at Barentin and spent the night in Rouen. Roubaud and Cabuche listened as he answered, and their reactions

438 appeared to confirm the truth of what he said. The three men looked at each other, and a feeling of unspeakable sadness passed between them. A deathly silence filled the hall. The members of the jury sensed that the moment was crucial, that the truth was at that minute passing unspoken before them. The judge asked Jacques what he thought of Cabuche's story of someone running away into the night. Jacques simply shook his head, as if he had no desire to make things worse for the man who stood accused. Then something happened which took everyone completely by surprise. Tears appeared in Jacques's eyes and began to run down his cheeks. He had suddenly had a vision of Séverine, as he had seen her once before, the image he had carried away with him as she lay dead on the floor, with her blue eyes staring, wide open, and her dark hair swept up above her head like some hideous garland of terror. He still loved her and was overcome with sorrow. He wept bitterly for her, apparently unaware of his crime, forgetting where he was and all the people who were watching

him. Some of the ladies were overcome by this display of emotion and were moved to tears; they found the spectacle of this broken-hearted lover altogether touching. The husband, they noticed, remained dry eyed. The judge asked the defence whether they had any further questions to put to the witness; they thanked him and declined. The two prisoners watched dumbfounded as Jacques went back to his seat amidst murmurs of sympathy.

The third day of the hearing was entirely taken up by the Public Prosecutor's indictment and by speeches from counsellors for the defence. The presiding judge began by giving his summing-up, taking care to appear completely impartial yet at the same time emphasizing the charges brought by the prosecution. Then it was the turn of the Public Prosecutor. He didn't appear to be at his best; normally he spoke with more conviction and less empty verbiage. People put it down to the heat; it really was **439** unbearable. On the other hand the lawyer from Paris who was representing Cabuche was most entertaining, though not at all convincing. Roubaud's defence was led by a distinguished member of the Rouen bar, who did the best he could with a very weak case. The Public Prosecutor was feeling tired and didn't even deign to respond. When the jury retired to consider its verdict, it was only six o'clock, and daylight still entered the hall through the ten stained-glass windows. A last ray of sunshine lit up the coats of arms of the towns of Normandy which adorned the mullions. A hum of voices rose to the ancient gilded ceiling, and people pressed themselves expectantly against the iron grill which separated the reserved seats from the standing public. When the jury returned and the court was reconvened a religious hush once again fell over the hall. The verdict made allowance for extenuating circumstances, and the two men were sentenced to hard labour for life. This was not at all what people had been expecting, and the announcement was greeted with noisy protests and catcalls, as if it were a theatre.

That evening the sentence was discussed endlessly all over Rouen. The general view was that it represented a slap in the face for Madame Bonnehon and the Lachesnayes. Nothing short of the death penalty, it seems, would have satisfied Grandmorin's family. There had obviously been pressure from some other quarter. The name of Madame Leboucq was being whispered; three or four of the jury were known to be close friends of hers. Her husband had no doubt performed his duties as assessor quite correctly, but people seemed to think that neither the second assessor, Monsieur Chaumette, nor even the presiding judge, Monsieur Desbazeilles, had been as fully in control of proceedings as they would have wished. Perhaps it was simply that the jury, in making allowance for extenuating circumstances, had had second thoughts, yielding to that awkward moment of doubt, when the melancholy truth had passed silently through the courtroom. None the less, the case was still seen as a triumph for the examining magistrate, Monsieur Denizet; nothing could detract from the masterly way he had handled the investigation, and the Grandmorin family lost much of the sympathy they still had when it was rumoured that Monsieur de Lachesnaye, in order to get his hands on La Croix-de-Maufras, had announced, contrary to legal advice, that despite the death of the legatee, he was going to instigate proceedings to have the bequest annulled, which, coming from a judge, was astonishing.

As he walked out of the courtroom, Jacques was greeted by Philomène, who had also been summoned as a witness. She wouldn't let him go, clinging on to him, trying to get him to spend the night with her in Rouen. He didn't have to start work again till the next day and he was quite willing to take her for a meal at the inn near the station, where he had supposedly slept on the night of the murder, but he was not going to sleep with her; he needed to be back in Paris the next day and was catching the night train at ten to one in the morning.

'Do you know what,' she said as she walked on his arm towards the hotel, 'I could have sworn I just saw someone we both know. It was Pecqueux, I'm sure. He was telling me the other day that he couldn't care less about the trial and that he wouldn't be seen dead in Rouen . . . When I turned round he ran off into the crowd . . . I only saw his back . . .'

Jacques interrupted her with a shrug of the shoulders.

'Pecqueux is in Paris,' he said, 'having a good time. He's enjoying himself while I'm off work.'

'Perhaps,' said Philomène, 'but you can't be too careful. He can be a real swine when he gets annoyed.'

She leaned against him, looking over her shoulder.

'Who's that following us?' she asked. 'Do you know him?'

'Yes,' said Jacques, 'stop worrying. He probably wants to ask me something.'

It was Misard, who had been following them at a distance ever since they had left the Rue des Juifs. He had given evidence too, although he had seemed half-asleep. He had hung around Jacques, trying to make up his mind to ask him something, some question that was clearly bothering him. When he saw them go into the inn, he followed them and ordered a glass of wine.

'Well, if it isn't Misard!' exclaimed Jacques. 'How are you getting on with your new wife?'

'Don't talk to me about her,' he grumbled. 'She's been leading me a real dance! I told you about it the last time we were here.'

Jacques found it highly amusing. Old Madame Ducloux, the one-time barmaid of easy virtue, whom Misard had taken on to look after the crossing, had watched him searching through the house and had quickly realized that he must be looking for money that his deceased wife had hidden away. In order to get him to marry her, she had hit upon the bright idea of letting him think, by way of veiled hints and knowing smirks, that she had found it. At first he had nearly strangled her, but then, realizing that, if he did away with her before getting his hands on the money, as he had done with his wife, the whereabouts of the thousand francs would remain a mystery, he had tried to be nice to her and show her he loved her. But she would have none of it; she wouldn't even let him touch her. When he married her he would have everything he wanted, she said – her and the money too. And so he had married her. But afterwards, she just laughed at him and said he was a fool if he believed everything people told him. The best of it was that, having found out about the money, she too became obsessed with it, and she started looking for it as frantically as him. Sooner or later that hidden money would be theirs. Now that there were two of them they were sure to find it! And so the search continued.

'Still no luck?' asked Jacques mischievously. 'I thought your missus was giving you a hand.'

Misard looked him in the eyes.

'You know where the money is,' he said. 'So why don't you tell me?'

This made Jacques angry.

'I know nothing at all,' he snapped. 'Aunt Phasie didn't give me anything. I hope you're not accusing me of stealing it!'

'I know she didn't give you anything,' Misard continued. 'But it's making me ill. If you know where it is, tell me.'

'You can bugger off!' retorted Jacques. 'Just you be careful I don't start talking . . . Why don't you try looking in the salt-box? It might be there!'

Misard went pale, continuing to look at Jacques with bloodshot eyes. He seemed to have a sudden flash of inspiration.

'The salt-box!' he exclaimed. 'You're right, there's a place under the drawer I haven't looked in!'

He quickly paid for his glass of wine and ran off to the station to see if he still had time to catch the 7.10. When he got back to his cottage, the endless search would continue.

Later that evening, when they had eaten and while they were waiting for the train at ten to one, Philomène persuaded Jacques to go for a walk with her. She led him through dark alleyways out into the neighbouring countryside. It was a sultry July night, very hot and with no moon. She leaned on his arm, breathing heavily. Twice, thinking she heard footsteps behind them, she had turned to look, but it was so dark she could see no one. Jacques was finding the oppressive weather very tiresome. Since **443** the murder he had been feeling calm, relaxed and in good health, but a little earlier, as he had been sitting at the dinner table, he had felt the return of a vague unease every time Philomène's hands had come in contact with him. It must have been due to tiredness, or perhaps it was the heavy weather that was affecting him. But now, as he walked along, holding her against him, he felt the terrible stirrings of his old desire, gathering strength and filling him with a sense of unspeakable dread. He had thought he was cured. He had proved it. He had made love to Philomène in order to convince himself and he had felt nothing. He became so agitated that he would have removed himself from her arms, fearing some dreadful recurrence of his malady, had not the surrounding darkness reassured him. Never, not even in the darkest days of his terrible affliction, would he have killed if he could not actually see his victim. But suddenly, as they were walking beside a grassy bank in a quiet lane, she pulled him to the ground and lay on her back in front of him. The monstrous urge returned. A wild frenzy took hold of him. He felt around in the grass for a weapon, a stone to smash her head open. He shook himself, got to his feet and fled in panic. Behind him he heard a man shouting and swearing, and the sounds of a violent struggle.

'You bitch! I waited to see what your game was, just to make sure!'

'It's not true. Let me go!'

'So it's not true, eh! He won't get away, you mark my words. I know who he is. I'll get even with him, you'll see. If you tell me it's not true again, I'll . . .'

Jacques vanished into the night, running not from Pecqueux, whom he had recognized, but from himself, wild with grief.

One murder had not been enough! He had killed Séverine, and it had not satisfied his thirst for blood! That morning he had thought he was cured. And now it was beginning again. First one, then another, and then another! He might gorge himself and gain a few weeks' respite, but his terrible hunger would return and would never be satisfied. He would kill woman after woman, and there would be no end to it. And now, he didn't even need to see his victim for his desire to be aroused; he only had to feel her, warm in his arms, and he would yield to his murderous lust, to the savage male instinct which demanded female blood. Life was at an end; all that lay before him was a night of darkness, an eternity of despair, from which there could be no escape.

A few days later Jacques was back at work. He avoided his comrades, keeping himself to himself, wrapped in his own thoughts. After several stormy sessions in the Chamber, war had been declared.[7] There had already been a skirmish at one of the frontier towns,[8] and it had apparently been successful. For a week, the mobilization of troops had been straining the resources of the railway companies to breaking point. Regular services were disrupted and there were long delays as a result of the great number of unscheduled trains. To make matters worse, the best drivers had been requisitioned in order to speed up the movement of troops. So it was that one evening at Le Havre, Jacques, instead of driving the express as usual, was put in charge of an enormous train of eighteen wagons packed full of soldiers.

That evening, Pecqueux had turned up for work very drunk. The day after he had followed Philomène and Jacques in Rouen, he had rejoined his driver on locomotive 608. He didn't speak about what had happened the night before, but he was in a very dark mood and hardly dared look him in the face. Jacques sensed that he had turned against him. He would do nothing he was asked; every time he gave him an order he simply responded with a grunt. In the end they had stopped talking to each other altogether. The locomotive footplate, the little, moving platform on which they had previously worked together as one, had now become the dangerous, confined stage of their disaffection. Their hatred had increased by the day, and they had reached the point where they could easily have come to blows within the few square feet of the cab, as the train sped on its way, lurching from side to side and threatening to throw them overboard. That evening, seeing Pecqueux so drunk, Jacques was wary. He knew that when his fireman was sober he had enough sense not to lose his temper; when he'd had too much to drink, however, he could go completely wild.

The train was due to leave at about six, but it was delayed, and it was already dark when the soldiers were herded like sheep into the cattle trucks. A few planks had been nailed together inside for them to sit on. They were piled in by the dozen, until the trucks could hold no more; they ended up sitting on each other's laps or standing so tightly squashed together that they couldn't move an arm. Another train awaited them in Paris to take them on to the Rhine the minute they arrived. They looked completely bewildered by the arrangements for their departure and half-dead with fatigue. However, they had all been issued with brandy and most of them had spent the day visiting the local bars. Warmed by the drink, the men laughed and made crude jokes as they waited, red-faced and uncomprehending, for the train to leave. As soon as the train began to move out of the station, they burst into song.

Jacques looked up at the sky; the stars were hidden by storm clouds. It was going to be a very dark night; there wasn't a breath of wind, and the air felt intensely hot. The breeze caused by the speed of the train, normally so cool and fresh, tonight felt warm and sticky. The only lights to be seen in the darkness ahead were the signal lamps, shining brightly in the night. Jacques increased the pressure as the train approached the steep gradient between Harfleur and Saint-Romain. Although he had been studying her for weeks, he still didn't feel confident driving locomotive number 608; she was still very new and she had a mind of her own. That night she seemed to be in a particularly awkward, capricious mood, producing sudden bursts of speed the minute she was given a few lumps of coal too many. Jacques kept his hand on the reversing wheel, watching the fire carefully and growing increasingly anxious at the behaviour of his fireman. The little lamp above the water-gauge cast a dim light over the footplate, tinged purple by the red glow from the firebox door. He couldn't see Pecqueux very well, but he had twice felt something brush against his legs as if a pair of hands were trying to grab hold of them. No doubt it was the drink making him clumsy. He could hear him above the noise of the train, snarling as he broke up the coal with great swings of his hammer and flailed around with his shovel. Every minute, he kept opening the firebox door and flinging excessive amounts of coal on to the grate.

'That's enough!' yelled Jacques.

Pecqueux pretended not to hear him and continued to throw on one shovelful after another. Jacques took hold of his arm. Pecqueux turned towards him threateningly. This was the quarrel he had been looking for as his drunken rage increased.

'Lay your hands off me, or I'll hit you! I like it when we go fast!'

The train was now travelling at full speed along the level section between Bolbec and Motteville. Apart from pausing to take on water, it was scheduled to run non-stop to Paris. The huge train, eighteen wagons crammed with their cargo of human livestock, raced through the darkened landscape, its wheels pounding continually on the track. As the train carried the men towards their grim fate, **447** they sang at the top of their voices, so loud that their singing drowned the clatter of the wheels.

Jacques shut the firebox door with his foot and put the injector on. He was still managing to restrain himself.

'The fire's too big,' he shouted. 'You're drunk. Get some sleep.'

Pecqueux immediately reopened the firebox door and frantically shovelled on more coal, as if he were determined to make the engine explode. This was open defiance; he was deliberately disobeying him, and in his blind fury completely disregarding the lives of the men in the train behind them. Jacques leaned forward to close the damper in order to lessen the draught to the fire. Suddenly Pecqueux grabbed hold of him, pushing him backwards, trying to topple him and throw him out on to the line.

'So that's your game, you swine!' Jacques shouted. 'You'd have said I'd fallen off, wouldn't you, you cunning bastard!'

Jacques had managed to catch hold of the side of the tender. The two men fell to the floor, and the struggle continued on the metal footplate as it lurched violently from side to side. They clenched their teeth and fought in silence, each trying to fling the other through the narrow opening in the side of the cab, which was protected by nothing more than a handrail. There was scarcely room to move, and the train rushed ahead at full speed. It ran through Barentin and plunged into the Malaunay tunnel, with the two men still locked together, on their backs in the coal, banging their heads against the water tank and trying to avoid the red-hot firebox door, which burned their legs every time they touched it.

At one point, Jacques thought that if he could get to his feet he would close the regulator and sound the whistle to call for help, so that someone could rescue him from this madman, driven crazy with drink and jealousy. But he was getting weaker and, being the smaller of the two, he knew he didn't have the strength to throw Pecqueux off him. He was beaten and could already feel the wind tugging at his hair as Pecqueux pushed him towards the edge of the footplate. With one last desperate effort he stretched out his hand, feeling for something to cling to. Pecqueux realized what he was trying to do, raised himself on to his knees and lifted Jacques up like a child.

'So you've had enough, have you! You stole my woman and you're going to get what you deserve!'

The train rushed on, thundering out of the tunnel and continuing its headlong progress through the dreary, deserted countryside. It swept through Malaunay like a whirlwind, so fast that the deputy stationmaster, who was standing on the platform, did not see the two men grappling with each other as it went hurtling past.

With a final lunge, Pecqueux pushed Jacques from the footplate. Jacques, feeling nothing behind him, clung

448

desperately to Pecqueux's neck, holding on to him so tightly that he dragged him out with him. There were two terrible screams, uttered simultaneously and quickly silenced. As they fell from the train, they were dragged beneath its wheels by the speed at which it was travelling. The two men, who had for so long lived together as brothers, were cut to pieces, locked together in their terrible embrace. The mangled bodies were later discovered, their heads and feet severed, still clasped together as if trying to strangle each other.

The locomotive, now completely out of control, continued on its precipitous course. At last she could have her own way and give reign to her youthful high spirits, like an untamed horse that has escaped from its trainer and gallops off across the open country. The boiler had plenty of water in it, and the coal that had been put on the fire was burning fiercely; for the next half-hour the pressure **449** continued to rise alarmingly, and the speed became frightening. The guard must have been overcome with tiredness and fallen asleep. The soldiers, piled together in the wagons, were becoming increasingly drunk; the crazy speed of the train seemed suddenly to lift their spirits, and they sang louder than ever. They shot through Maromme like a streak of lightning. The train no longer whistled as it approached signals or stations; it simply forged ahead like a dumb animal charging head down at some obstacle that barred its way. On and on it went, unstoppable, as if gradually driven to a frenzy by the harsh sound of its own breathing.

They were due to take on water at Rouen. Everyone watched with horror as the mad train rushed through the station, belching out smoke and sparks, with no driver or fireman, and its string of cattle trucks filled with soldiers, all singing patriotic songs at the top of their voices. The soldiers were off to war, and at that speed they would be out there on the Rhine sooner than they thought. People on the platform stood open-mouthed, waving their arms. Then suddenly everyone realized that if the train was out of control and had no driver, it would never get through the station at Sotteville. As at all stations with large goods depots, there were always shunting operations going on there, with wagons and engines blocking the lines. They rushed to the telegraph room to send a warning, just in time for a goods train to be backed off the main line and on to a siding. The runaway train could already be heard in the distance, roaring through the two tunnels outside Rouen and rushing madly towards them, like some powerful, irresistible force that could no longer be stopped. It swept through the station, avoiding obstacles to either side of it, and plunged into the night. Gradually its roar faded into the distance.

450   By now all the telegraph bells along the line were ringing, and hearts missed a beat as news came through of a ghost train that had been seen passing through Rouen and Sotteville at high speed. People shook with fear; there was an express on the line ahead, and there would surely be a collision. The train, like a wild boar running through a forest, continued on its headlong flight, heedless of signals at red and detonators. At Oissel it almost collided with a light engine. At Pont-de-l'Arche, people watched it go by in sheer terror; it showed no sign of slowing down. Once again it disappeared from view, on and on into the darkness of the night, whither no one knew.

What did it matter if a few people were killed as it went on its way? Was it not travelling towards the future? Why worry over a little spilled blood? The train ran on without a driver, on and on, like some mindless, unseeing beast, let loose on a field of carnage, with its burden of cannon-fodder, the soldiers, dead with fatigue, drunk and singing at the top of their voices.

Notes

Chapter 1

1. *Quartier de l'Europe*: A district in the 8th arrondissement of Paris, so called because the streets are named after major European cities. Many of them are mentioned in the novel. The station, which, curiously, is never named, is the Gare Saint-Lazare, the Paris terminus of the Compagnie des Chemins de Fer de l'Ouest, which operated trains to northern Brittany and Normandy.

2. *foot-warmer depot*: In the early days of rail travel (the action of the novel takes place between 1869 and 1870), carriages were not heated. For a small charge, the railway companies provided foot-warmers – flat, metal containers filled with hot water or, later, with a solution of soda acetate. Passengers were also advised to bring travelling rugs to protect themselves against the cold. It was not until the 1890s that carriages were regularly heated by hot water supplied from the locomotive.

3. *Pont de l'Europe*: A huge iron bridge, designed by Adolphe Jullien (1803–79), built (in 1867) over the railway lines at the mouth of the Gare Saint-Lazare. The bridge formed a meeting point for six streets and, viewed from above (as here), was indeed star-shaped. There are famous paintings of this bridge by Gustave Caillebotte (1848–94).

4. *a vivid splash of colour in the pale afternoon light*: The opening description of the station, with its emphasis on modern structures of glass and steel, the effect of hazy sunlight and the vivid red of the signal, calls to mind paintings of the Gare Saint-Lazare made in 1877 by Claude Monet (1840–1926). Zola had promoted the work of Impressionist painters and acknowledged that his own descriptive techniques owed much to them.

5. *cylinder taps*: An example of the sort of technical detail that Zola had researched and was determined to include in his novel. The cylinder taps, when opened, allowed steam to be passed at high pressure through the cylinders in order to expel water condensation and other chemical deposits which collected in them when the locomotive was stationary. The effect could be quite dramatic!

6. *the clatter of turntables*: In the early days of railway construction, turntables (or 'turnplates' as they were first called) were situated on the arrival tracks of mainline stations to enable wagons and carriages to be shunted around the station or into adjoining sidings. By the 1870s they had begun to disappear. In his preparatory notes for the description of the station, Zola records the distinctive sound made by the turntables as trains ran over them.

7. *six thousand francs*: Zola is determined to give his novel a sense of contemporary realism and he is specific about money throughout. The figures he mentions would have made the Dauvergnes a comfortably placed family, in receipt of two full-time salaries and housing and heating concessions too.

8. *Sub-Prefect*: Prefects and sub-prefects were responsible for the local administration of a *département*. They were appointed directly by the Emperor and wielded great authority. One of their most important functions was to control elections and ensure the return of government-nominated candidates (see note 13 below).

9. *and then it was back to the grind!*: This conversation between Roubaud and Henri Dauvergne exemplifies the way in which Zola handles spoken exchanges throughout the novel, with a mixture of direct speech, indirect speech and free indirect speech.

10. *Plassans*: Zola's fictional name for Aix-en-Provence, where he had spent most of his childhood and youth (1843–58). Plassans is the town in which the Rougon-Macquarts have their roots. Adélaïde Fouque, the ancestress of both branches of the family, is described in *La Fortune des Rougon* (chapter 2) as being born there in 1768. The town is referred to repeatedly throughout the novel cycle.

11. *President Grandmorin*: 'President' is a title designating a High Court judge, a title which Grandmorin retains, despite having officially retired, and which marks him out as a man of considerable means and influence.

12. *the Bon Marché*: A large department store in Paris, founded in 1852 by Aristide Boucicaut (1810–77). The life and intrigues of a Paris department store are portrayed in an earlier novel in the series, *Au Bonheur des Dames* (translated as *The Ladies' Delight* by Robin Buss, Penguin Classics, 2001).

13. *the forthcoming general elections*: These were not the sort of open, democratic elections that the present-day reader might be familiar with. Zola refers to elections to the lower house of the Legislative Assembly (L'Assemblée législative). The

Legislative Assembly was charged with converting national policy into law but it was given only limited powers. Laws were formulated by the upper house, which was appointed by the Emperor himself and which met in secret. Members of the lower house, which could ratify or reject but not initiate or amend legislation, were elected by male suffrage. These elections were carefully managed. Certain candidates were nominated by the government and designated as 'official' candidates. It was the responsibility of the prefects of the various *départements* of France (who were again appointed directly by the Emperor) to ensure that these 'official' candidates were elected. This was achieved by tight control of election publicity and propaganda, with the result that very few opposition candidates were elected to the Assembly during the whole period of the Second Empire. By 1869 opposition to such a 'closed' form of government had gained considerable momentum, and the government was threatened with the possibility of an election deafeat.

14. *local government councillor*: The local council (Conseil Général) was responsible for the administration of local regions within a *département*, in this instance Rouen and the surrounding district. It was an elected body but was answerable directly to the Prefect.

15. *which was twice as much as he was earning as an assistant station-master at Le Havre*: In other words Roubaud earns about 2,000 francs a year.

16. *what if it turned out he was your father?*: This is the third time that the possibility of Séverine being Grandmorin's daughter has been mentioned in this chapter. It appears to be a particular obsession of Roubaud's and is clearly a sensitive issue with Séverine. Zola leaves the suspicion unconfirmed, but by insisting on it he allows the possibility to take root in the reader's mind.

17. *the screws properly tightened*: The 'screw' reduced the slack in the coupling which linked the carriages together, improving the cohesion and stability of the train. Zola had evidently observed the operation carefully.

18. *coupé compartment*: An end compartment in a railway carriage with seating on one side only.

Chapter 2

1. *La Croix-de-Maufras*: A fictional name with a sinister ring to it (*mau* in French suggests 'evil').

2. *as silent and empty as the grave*: Zola had made a careful study of the topography of the region between Barentin and Malaunay. This and subsequent descriptions combine precisely recorded features of landscape with a desire to create a sombre setting for the dark happenings which occur here.

3. *Phasie*: A child's diminutive for Euphrasie. The name acts as a reminder of Jacques's childhood innocence.

4. *a Lantier*: Jacques comes as a late addition to the Rougon-Macquart genealogical tree, which Zola had originally devised in 1878. There is no mention of him in the earlier novels describing the fortunes of his parents and his two brothers (*La Fortune des Rougon*, *L'Assommoir*, *Germinal* and *L'Œuvre*).

5. *Paris-Orléans company*: The company was founded in 1838 and operated trains to southern Brittany and parts of central France.

6. *La Lison*: This is the locomotive mentioned in the previous chapter. It is explained later in the novel (chapter 5) that locomotives were named after towns served by the railway. Lison is a town in the Cotentin region of Normandy between Caen and Cherbourg.

7. *section box*: The 'block system' began to be introduced as early as the 1840s. It provided a means of maintaining a safe distance between trains which followed each other on the same track. A line was divided into 'sections', and a block telegraph circuit was set up for each section. A system of telegraphic bell codes was used to ensure that trains only passed from one section to another when the line was clear. Zola describes the procedure and the telegraphic equipment in comprehensive detail.

8. *she couldn't bring herself to repeat it*: The death of Louisette is mentioned several times throughout the novel. Exactly what happened is never made clear. It remains an unexplained mystery in the novel's catalogue of crime.

9. *hardy inner life*: Zola uses a horticultural term ('vivace' in French) to refer to the communities that are invaded by the mechanized progress of the railways. Horticultural imagery occurs throughout the novel (see below, chapter 6, note 1).

10. *he often thought he must have inherited this family flaw himself*: Jacques's mother, Gervaise Lantier (née Macquart), is abandoned by her husband, Auguste Lantier, soon after the family arrives in Paris. She is eventually driven to drink and dies destitute (*L'Assommoir*). Jacques's elder brother, Claude, becomes a painter, obsessed with radical new theories about art (*L'Œuvre*). His younger brother, Étienne, becomes a mine

worker and leads a miners' strike (*Germinal*). The influence of heredity is a recurring preoccupation throughout the cycle of Rougon-Macquart novels.

11. *in the dark recesses of some primeval cave*: This idea is derived from Zola's reading of Cesare Lombroso's (1835–1909) *L'Homme criminel* (*The Criminal Man*, original Italian title *L'Uomo delinquente*, 1876): 'The most barbaric crimes have a physiological, atavistic origin, deriving from animal instincts, which thanks to upbringing, social milieu or the fear of punishment may lie dormant, but which will suddenly flare up under the influence of illness, meteorites, or spermatic intoxication caused by a protracted period of sexual abstinence' (C. Lombroso, *L'Homme criminel. Criminel-né. Fou moral. Épileptique. Étude anthropologique et medico-légal*, translated by Régnier and Bournet (Paris: Alcan, 1887), p. 665).

12. *his fellow drivers, in the class-two and class-three grades*: These details are based on information which Zola obtained from Pol Lefèvre. Some employees were initially taken on as apprentice fitters or cleaners, for example, and trained as drivers by the railway company itself. Others (like Jacques) had received further education and technical training before joining the Company and could aspire to positions of greater responsibility. Although Jacques is one of the Company's top drivers and is well paid, it might have seemed odd to his colleagues that he was happy to remain as a driver.

13. *his train wasn't due to leave for Le Havre until seven twenty*: A minor discrepancy. Earlier Zola had given the time as seven twenty-six.

Chapter 3

1. *the station buildings were dull and dreary, with cracks everywhere*: The first railway line to Le Havre (from Rouen) was opened in 1843. Through trains from Paris to Le Havre began operating in 1847. It would appear that some of the station buildings described here date from the earliest years of Le Havre's railway history. The station was rebuilt in 1884. Zola visited it in 1889 and spoke to the stationmaster and to an employee of long standing, who were able to give him precise information about the station as it was in 1869. The dilapidated state of the buildings contrasts sharply with the impressive modernization of

the Gare Saint-Lazare. Eugène Flachat's huge train sheds at the Gare Saint-Lazare date from 1851.

2. *the safety officer*: Railway safety officers had been appointed as early as the 1840s, when the dangers of railway operation were becoming increasingly apparent. They were responsible for overseeing the safety of the travelling public and of employees. They were appointed, not by the railway company, but by the Ministry of Public Works (Ministère des Travaux Publics). They had a quasi-police title (*commissaire*) and were given powers of arrest. They wore a uniform. On his visit to Le Havre, Zola made a note of the safety officer's 'black cap with four silver braids'.

3. *piquet*: A card-game played by two persons with a pack of thirty-two cards, the low cards from the two to the six being excluded.

4. *a bloodstained fingerprint*: This is the closest the novel comes to any sort of forensic consideration. Given the novel's subject matter and Zola's declared interest in scientific methods, this appears surprising.

Chapter 4

1. *the examining magistrate*: The examining magistrate (*juge d'instruction*) was (and still is) responsible for a preliminary investigation into a crime. In current Anglo-American procedure, such an investigation would be carried out by the police. In France in the nineteenth century, investigation was passed on to the judiciary at an early stage of a criminal inquiry. The examining magistrate's investigation was conducted in private. If there was insufficient evidence, the case would be dismissed. If the examining magistrate felt that there was a case to be answered, it would be forwarded for trial by jury in an open court (*cour d'assises*).

2. *opposition newspapers*: From its inception in December 1852, the Second Empire had promoted 'official' government newspapers (such as *L'Opinion nationale*) and exercised rigorous censorship of the opposition press. The latter years of the regime, however, saw a more liberal attitude towards the press and the creation of a number of new opposition newspapers. According to James McMillan, 'in the run-up to the 1869 elections, some 150 newspapers were founded, 120 of them hostile to the regime. The most vituperative was *La Lanterne*' (James McMillan, *Napoleon III*, Longman, 1991, p. 125). The 'opposition' included a range of dissidents from Republicans on the

left to Orleanists on the right. Zola himself contributed frequently to the opposition press.

3. *two deputies who held official positions in the Emperor's personal entourage*: In March 1869, the Legislative Assembly challenged the right of two members of the Emperor's 'household' to sit as deputies in the lower chamber. The deputies concerned were Monsieur de Bourgoing, the Emperor's equerry, and Monsieur de Piennes, the Emperor's chamberlain. The debate raised important constitutional issues.

4. *the financial administration of the Prefect of the Seine*: The Prefect of the Seine was the famous Baron Georges-Eugène Haussmann (1809–91), who was responsible for the wholesale rebuilding of central Paris between 1853 and 1869. The issue in question was Haussmann's request for retrospective sanction of a loan from Le Crédit Foncier to the municipality of Paris amounting to about a quarter of the whole French budget. It was clearly felt that such arrangements should be subject to approval by a municipal council. At the time, no such council existed.

5. *the Tuileries Palace*: The palace of the Emperor, Napoleon III (1808–73).

6. *the Ministry of Justice*: In France, the judiciary was (and still is) conceived as an instrument of executive authority rather than an authority separate from government. It was overseen by the Ministry of Justice, whose officers were answerable directly to the Emperor. Monsieur Camy-Lamotte's position within the ministry is the equivalent of a permanent under-secretary.

7. *bring them face to face*: It was standard procedure for the examining magistrate to arrange a confrontation between a suspect and a witness in order to observe the suspect's reaction.

8. *Petit-Couronne*: A town on the river Seine, near Rouen. In the nineteenth century it was a small fishing village.

9. *they managed to get from their carriage to the President's . . . while the train was travelling at full speed*: In 1869, railway carriages did not have corridors; each compartment was self-contained. Zola assumes his readers will understand that in order to get from one carriage to another it would have been necessary to get outside the train and walk along the carriage footboard, jumping from one carriage to the next. Corridor trains were not introduced until the late 1880s. It is not surprising that Denizet finds such an operation difficult to believe.

10. *brain fever*: I.e. typhoid.

457

Chapter 5

1. *Séverine knew that he would be in at one o'clock*: How Séverine knew this is not explained. The audacity of this apparently casual visit to the private address of a high-placed government official would have appeared just as remarkable to readers of Zola's time as it does to the present-day reader. It serves to indicate the extent of the Roubauds' anxiety.

2. *their anxiety would be at an end*: Zola's novel has been interpreted as a 'riposte' to Dostoyevsky's *Crime and Punishment*, but this account of the criminal being driven by his own anxiety to confess his crime has a strong affinity with comments made by the investigator Porfiry in Dostoyevsky's novel. 'I make damn sure that every hour and every minute he knows, or at least suspects that I know everything . . . and that I'm keeping an eye on him night and day . . . and if he's conscious of the never-ending suspicion and terror in which I'm keeping him . . . he'll go off into a whirl, he'll come running of his own accord' (Dostoyevsky, *Crime and Punishment*, translated by David McDuff, Penguin Classics, 1991, p. 400).

3. *the police were so busy protecting politicians that they didn't have time to arrest murderers*: 'The elections of May–June 1869 unleashed pent-up political passions . . . In Paris the electoral campaign was accompanied by an upsurge in violence and threats to public order. Attendance at electoral meetings averaged 20,000 nightly, and rioting was commonplace' (McMillan, *Napoleon III*, p. 126).

4. *They were walking past the entrance to a little park*: The creation of parks and green space was an important part of Haussmann's rebuilding of Paris, and one which the Emperor himself took a particular interest in. 'In 1848 Paris had only 19 hectares of parks; by 1870 the total was 1,800' (Alistair Horne, *Seven Ages of Paris*, Macmillan, 2002, p. 270).

5. *the pain de gruau was exquisite, and to finish she treated herself to a plate of beignets soufflés*: 'Pain de gruau' was a speciality white bread made from finely milled flour of wheat. 'Beignets soufflés' might be described as small, light-textured doughnuts. They are served hot with confectioner's sugar and various flavourings. This menu is an indication that French culinary arts (and the culinary language to match) were well advanced in 1869.

6. *It was a broad-chested, long-limbed, powerful machine*: The analogy between steam locomotives and horses recurs throughout the novel. Zola seeks to 'animate' descriptions of locomotive technology by reference to something less technical and still perhaps, even in 1890, more familiar to his readers. The horses referred to are nearly always female ('fillies' or 'mares').

7. *sand boxes*: In difficult conditions, sand would be applied to the rails ahead of the driving wheels in order to improve adhesion, especially when a locomotive was moving a heavy train from stationary.

8. *warmly dressed in woollen trousers and smock*: The design of early steam locomotives took little account of the comfort or safety of the driving crew. The driver's footplate was usually protected by nothing more than a front weather-shield; the overhead roof and enclosed cab were a later luxury. Jacques and Pecqueux are thus exposed to the full force of the elements and also to sparks and cinders thrown out of the locomotive's chimney; hence the need for strong protective clothing, made out of heavy wool (or pilot cloth), and goggles.

9. *reversing wheel*: A hand-operated wheel used by the driver not only to reverse a locomotive but, as here, to control the admission of steam to the cylinders when the locomotive was moving forward. Once sufficient forward momentum was achieved, less tractive effort was needed, and the input of steam could be progressively reduced, a procedure referred to as 'cut-off'. This helped to economize on fuel consumption and to reduce wear and tear to the cylinders and valve gear.

10. *injector*: A mechanism invented in 1859 by the French engineer Henry Giffard, which enabled the water in the boiler to be replenished with the aid of steam pressure from the boiler itself. There was a critical point at which the mechanism functioned successfully; hence Jacques's attention to the pressure gauge.

Chapter 6

1. *She had put five or six pots of wallflowers and verbena in the valley of the station roof*: Séverine's roof garden is a striking example of the vein of horticultural imagery that runs through the novel. Zola's wife had an extensive knowledge of horticulture; her mother and sister-in-law were both florists.

2. *some strange city, lined with big, square palaces built of black marble*: In a novel which lays emphasis on realistic description, this

is a striking example of an 'unreal', almost futuristic representation of place.

3. *In spite of everything, she had remained virgin*: This is the third time in this chapter that Zola has referred to Séverine in these terms, insistently drawing the reader's attention to Séverine's purity and innocence of mind.

4. *sous*: The official unit of currency during the Second Empire was the franc, which was divided into one hundred centimes. In daily usage people referred (and still do) to an obsolete unit of currency, the *sou*, which was then worth five centimes. The extent of Roubaud's gambling debts becomes apparent later in the novel (see chapter 9, note 1).

5. *écarté*: A game of cards for two players, similar to piquet (see chapter 3, note 3). The players may discard (*écarter* in French; hence the name) any or all of the cards dealt and replace them from the pack.

Chapter 7

1. *the snowplough could easily clear a depth of one metre*: Snowploughs were not standard fittings on early French locomotives. Evidently a snowplough had been attached to *La Lison* before leaving the shed.

2. *detonators*: These were small explosive devices clipped to the track and activated by the wheels of the locomotive as they ran over them. They were used to warn engine drivers of any danger ahead.

3. *the damper*: A flap or door in the ash-pan underneath the fire grate, operated by means of a ratchet in the driver's cab and allowing the driver or fireman to control the amount of air entering the bottom of the firebox.

4. *ten atmospheres*: The 'atmosphere' is a measurement of pressure. 1 atmosphere is a notional measurement of air pressure at the earth's surface (14.7 lb on the square inch).

5. *Yes, monsieur, from New York*: In 1869, transatlantic crossings took over a week. Either the two men are talking at cross purposes or the American is exaggerating.

6. *and placed it at the side of the cutting*: Zola based this extraordinary exploit on an account of a similar occurrence described by Pol Lefèvre, which Lefèvre had witnessed, involving a train caught in the snow near Rouen in the winter of 1879–80.

Chapter 8

1. *she reached the fourth floor*: A minor discrepancy. At the beginning of the novel (chapter 1), Zola situates the room on the fifth floor.
2. *She recognized the sound of the chimes, deep and resonant*: The cuckoo clock is evidently one which both chimes and cuckoos. Wordsworth owned such a clock. The clock is one of several details used here which serve to reinforce the parallel between this scene and the opening scene of the novel.
3. *Malaga*: A white wine from the south of Spain.
4. *he had been able to slip upstairs without anyone noticing*: The concierge was often one of the first people to be questioned by the police in the event of any suspicious circumstance or criminal investigation. Séverine and Jacques's clandestine relationship and their concern to be unobserved reflect Zola's own experience at the time he was writing this novel. In 1888 he had begun a relationship with Jeanne Rozerot and had installed her in an apartment in the Rue Saint-Lazare, where he visited her secretly. Zola's wife, Alexandrine, knew nothing of the affair until 1891, by which time Jeanne had provided Zola with two children.
5. *her shudder of desire became a shudder of death*: This is a macabre variation on a very old literary conceit – sexual ecstasy as a form of death. Killing is given sexual connotations throughout the novel.
6. *communication cord*: Although it had become clear since the Poinsot murder in 1860 that the incidence of crime committed on trains was increasing, the Compagnie de l'Ouest did not in fact introduce any form of alarm system until 1882. The earliest communication system was a cord and bell arrangement, which enabled passengers to alert the guard if there was an emergency. When trains were fitted with continuous vacuum brakes (from 1890 onwards), the communication cord enabled passengers to apply the brakes themselves.
7. *I found myself outside on the footboard, clinging with both hands to the brass handrail*: Although Séverine and Roubaud perform this hazardous operation in only one direction, moving away from the coupé back to their own compartment, this is precisely the sort of scenario which Denizet had earlier dismissed as impossible (see chapter 4, note 9).

8. *life seems one long holiday*: It was the spread of railways that made areas such as Brittany and the Mediterranean more easily accessible to holidaymakers and accelerated the development of seaside resorts such as Cannes.

Chapter 9

1. *he could pay off his debt and he had all this money to wager*: Zola tells us above that Roubaud's gambling had begun 'shortly after the murder'. The murder took place in mid-February 1869, which at this point in the novel is still less than a year ago. If it is assumed that the money taken from under the floorboard is used to pay off Roubaud's gambling debts and that he had already paid money out of his own pocket, he appears to have so far lost something in the region of 1,000 francs and to be acquiring new debts as fast as he settles them. Zola had indicated earlier in the novel that Roubaud's annual salary was about 2,000 francs (see chapter 1, note 15).

2. *She had asked him to give her a photograph of himself*: Zola himself was a keen photographer.

3. *bristling factory chimneys*: Today Paris is not thought of as an industrial city, but during the Second Empire there was a considerable amount of industrial activity both in the suburbs and close to the city centre. Haussmann opposed the further development of heavy industry (including a proposal for a large railway works at Batignolles) in favour of the manufacture of luxury goods (see Jeanne Gaillard, *Paris la Ville*, Librairie Honoré Champion, 1976, pp. 55 ff.).

4. *the right of the strong to destroy the weak who get in their way*: It is here that Zola most clearly confronts the arguments of Raskolnikov in *Crime and Punishment*. Zola had toyed with the idea of giving his novel the title *The Right to Murder (Le Droit au meurtre)*. Raskolnikov had justified murder by reference to the concept of a 'superior being'. Jacques here attempts to justify murder by reference to the less rarefied concept of animal instinct.

5. *whatever moral scruples had since been invented to keep men living together*: In his 'discussion' of the rights and wrongs of murder, both here and elsewhere in the novel, Zola avoids specific mention of any religious imperative.

6. *The government had been badly shaken by the general elections*: 'In a poll of around eight million electors, government candidates won only 4.5 million votes, while opposition candidates

462

polled 3.5 million' (McMillan, *Napoleon III*, p. 126). This represented the most serious challenge to its authority that the Second Empire had ever faced.

Chapter 10

1. *Misard had been putting the rat poison into her enemas rather than mixing it with the salt*: This is the first confirmation that Misard had indeed been poisoning his wife. In June 1889, Zola had written for advice about poison to a doctor friend of his, Docteur Gouverné. Gouverné provided him with a detailed explanation of how various poisons worked, recommending white arsenic as the most appropriate to Zola's purposes in the novel, being a tasteless white powder used as an ingredient in rat poison and ideally suited to slow poisoning. Gouverné further explained that it was also used to treat farm animals and would therefore be easily available in a country district such as the one Zola had in mind.

2. *she walked out of the Malaunay end of the tunnel, safe and sound*: Zola based this episode on an official report on the dangers incurred by railway men working inside tunnels. The report emphasized the disorientating effect of the noise and the dark and recommended that all tunnels should be equipped with electric lighting. Zola himself had a mortal fear of tunnels and confined spaces. In the short story 'La Mort d'Olivier Bécaille' a train is immured inside a tunnel. In *Germinal* the miners are trapped below ground.

3. *ballast train*: Ballast was broken stone, used as a bed for the tracks.

4. *it automatically set the signal at red*: The system of 'interlocking signalling' had been described to Zola by Pol Lefèvre. It was a system which linked signals and points and was operated by the signalman. Zola appears to be confusing it with a system of 'automatic signalling', in which signal movements were controlled by the passage of trains. Automatic signalling did not come into general use until after the period referred to in the novel.

5. *applied the brakes*: Braking systems on early steam locomotives were notoriously inefficient.

6. *crashed into the wagon with the full weight of the thirteen carriages she drew behind her*: Zola based the account of this disaster on newspaper reports (in *Le Temps* and *Le Figaro*) of three actual

train crashes – at Charenton in September 1881, at Cabbé-Roquebrune (near Monte Carlo) in March 1886, and at Groenendael (Belgium) in February 1889. Although each of these accidents was dissimilar (and unlike the situation depicted in the novel), they provided Zola with details such as the fireman and guard jumping off the train, passengers running into the fields, the telescoping of the train on impact, the fire from the locomotive spreading to the rest of the train, examples of horrific injuries and the difficulty of obtaining assistance and medical help.

7. *pilot engine*: An engine used to assist another locomotive when, for example, a train had to climb a steep gradient.

8. *to greet a friend as she came towards her*: Zola is careful to make this 'friend' feminine ('*une amie*' in French). Flore remains fiercely independent of men to the end.

Chapter 11

1. *I'll be able to say I never left this room*: Séverine's reasoning here is difficult to follow.

2. *Séverine lay in bed on her back ... watching him walk up and down*: There is an echo here of the scene near the beginning of the novel in which Séverine lies on the bed while Roubaud paces the room, planning the murder of Grandmorin (chapter 1).

3. *his jaw was pushed forward in a savage grimace that made him appear almost deformed*: The pronounced jaw was, according to Lombroso, one of the bestial features that distinguished the criminal. Zola incorporates the detail into his initial description of Jacques (chapter 2). Here he imagines the feature becoming more pronounced as Jacques's murderous instinct takes hold of him.

Chapter 12

1. *just because some prince of theirs wants to be King of Spain*: In July, 1870, Prince Leopold of Hohenzollern-Sigmaringen (1835–1905) had been offered and had accepted the vacant throne of Spain. The deal had been arranged by Bismarck; Prince Leopold himself had little enthusiasm for the idea. In France, the prospect of a Prussian prince becoming King of Spain led to fears of encirclement by Prussia.

2. *elections and plebiscites and riots in Paris*: The elections of May 1869 had been fiercely contested and had led to civil disturbance. They resulted in a moral victory for the opposition (see chapter 9, note 6). The Emperor was forced to agree to opposition demands for a more liberal form of government. On 8 May 1870, a new constitution was voted on by plebiscite and overwhelmingly approved.

3. *which should have corroborated his present account*: It is not immediately obvious how Roubaud's evidence at the first inquiry should 'corroborate' the confession he has just made, since his earlier evidence had pointed in the direction of a murderer other than himself. It is clear, however, that Denizet is so confident he has solved the case that whatever evidence is put before him will simply confirm the conclusions he has already arrived at.

4. *assessor*: An assessor sits as adviser to a judge or magistrate and is often skilled in technical points of law.

5. *fashionable ladies of the town*: Roger Williams draws attention to the fact that audiences at trials during the Second Empire tended to be dominated by women, especially if the case involved details of a sordid or unseemly kind (Roger L. Williams, *Manners and Murders in the World of Louis-Napoleon*, University of Washington Press, 1975, p. 10).

6. *Napoleonic bees*: Bees were introduced as a heraldic device by Napoleon Bonaparte as a replacement for the royal fleur-de-lis.

7. *war had been declared*: France officially declared war on Prussia on 19 July 1870. Mobilization, however, had begun before this.

8. *a skirmish at one of the frontier towns*: The French army achieved an initial minor success at Saarbrücken (Lorraine) on 2 August 1870. This provides a terminal date for the events of the novel. The Franco-Prussian war is the subject of the penultimate novel in the Rougon-Macquart cycle, *La Débâcle*.